Sword in the Stars

Sword in the Stars

The Dark Sea Annals

LIVING
INK
BOOKS™
Writing Worth Reading™

WAYNE THOMAS BATSON

Sword in the Stars

Volume 1 in The Dark Sea Annals™ series

Copyright © 2010 by Wayne Thomas Batson

Published by Living Ink Books, an imprint of
AMG Publishers, Inc.
6815 Shallowford Rd.
Chattanooga, Tennessee 37421

ISBN 13: 978-0-89957-877-4
First Printing—October 2010

THE DARK SEA ANNALS is a trademark of AMG Publishers.

Cover designed by Daryle Beam at Bright Boy Design, Chattanooga, TN.

Interior design and typesetting by Reider Publishing Services, West Hollywood, California.

Edited and proofread by Jeff Gerke, Christy Graeber, and Rick Steele.

Printed in the United States of America
15 14 13 12 11 10 –DP– 7 6 5 4 3 2 1

To the One who rescues the wicked and the broken
and bears them to heights never imagined,
I bow my knee and offer my sword.

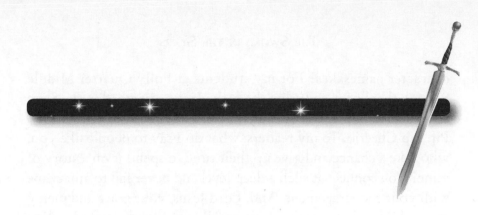

ACKNOWLEDGMENTS

Sword in the Stars—the whole Dark Sea Annals series—has been on my heart for many years. To finally have a chance to share it with readers is a such a weighty blessing that I may never be able to adequately thank those who have made it possible. To my wife, Mary Lu, you relentlessly gathered up every ball I dropped while trying to finish this book and so many others. Dinners made, laundry done, trips to the grocery store, a million home-work assignments--you did it all to spare me burden after burden. I know you didn't do it for credit. You simply put my needs and the needs of our family above your own. I love you. Oh, and I don't want to be around your place in heaven when you first open the door. You're going to be buried in crowns! To my parents who first breathed life into my imagination and who continue to support me and pray for me. Mom and Dad, I love you. Let every word I write be a feather in your cap! To my dear friends who pray for me, encourage me, hang with me, and understand when I can't hang at all: Doug, Chris, Dave, Heather, Chris, Dawn, Jeff, Leslie, Bill, Lisa, Todd, Dan, Warren, Don, Valerie, and many more who are geographically distant: I love you all very much. To the peeps in the Underground: Endurance and Victory! To all the Tribe Winners and Books-4-Life winners, did you find your character namesakes? For my students at Folly Quarter Middle School: thanks for enduring the early drafts of Sword in the Stars and for not killing me when you didn't get to read the ending. Pip Pip Cheerio. To my readers: what do I say to people like you, who take a chance and give up their time to spend it on a story of mine? You connect at such a deep level and never fail to amaze me with your encouragement. And, Lord Jesus, your grace and mercy are so deep and so vast that I cannot discern their boundaries. You loved me when I was an enemy. You are trustworthy even when I am worthless. And to think that you'd even go so far as to make my dreams come true just blows me away. The glory is yours.

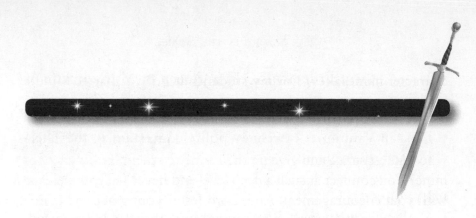

THE NINE RACES OF MYRIAD

HUMAN:
- Brayden Arum: the proprietor of the Hammer and Bow, Westmoor's most popular tavern.
- Warden Caddock of Chapparel: ruler of a council of coastal villages.
- Alastair Coldhollow: former assassin for Morlan's secret Wolfguard; now tenuously holding to the faith of the First One and searching for the prophesied Halfainin.
- Rhydic Cringeholt: King Morlan's chief astrologer.
- Daribel: Head Cook Mistress in Anglinore Castle; known for her truffles and her lightning quick spoon.
- Laeriss Fenstalker: feisty contestant in the Thel-Mizaret tournament.
- Binik Gelsh: Steward of Thel-Mizaret; collector, dealer of rare trinkets.
- Abbagael Rivynfleur: virtuous maiden from Edenmill; not-so-secret admirer of Alastair Coldhollow.
- Queen Fleut Silvalore: Regent (ruler) of the nation called Keening on the Naïthe.
- Aravel Stormgarden: bold-hearted High King Overlord of all of Myriad; brother of Morlan.

- Maren Stormgarden: wise High Queen of Myriad; wife of Aravel.
- Morlan Stormgarden: ruler of Vulmarrow; brother of Aravel.
- Duskan Vanimore: extremely polite contestant in the Thel-Mizaret tournament.

WAYFOLK:
- Cythraul Scarhaven: Morlan's bloodthirsty second in command.
- King Ealden Everbrand: strict ruler of the Prydian wayfolk.
- Yasmina Vanador: wife of Rhys Stonehand; becomes unlikely tutor of her husband's murderer.
- Queen Savron: willowy and lithe, beautiful and beloved ruler of the Vespal branch of the wayfolk.

WINDBORNE:
- King Drüst: winged Skylord of the Windborne; charged with monitoring the borders of the Gorrack Nation.

WILLOWFOLK:
- Sprye: curious and impulsive "Mistmaiden" of the fairy-like willowfolk.
- Alacritous Tracer: High Noble of the Kinship of Willow Dell, land of the willowfolk.

STONEHAND:
- King Vang: King of Tryllium, often called "Old Stone Hands" because he once knocked a panther unconscious with a single punch.
- Carraig Rendel: Alastair's favorite blacksmith; operates a smithy in Edenmill.

MARINAEN:
- Prince Navrill: ruling prince of the amphibious Marinaen people.

ELLADORIAN:
- Queen Briawynn: stunningly beautiful ruller of Ellador to the far south of Anglinore.
- Uncle Jak: Abbagael's hammer-wielding uncle; raised Abbagael after the death of her parents; only part-Elladorian.

GORRACK KIND:
- Diavolos eSkel: forward scremander of the Gorrack raiders, southern continent; one of many raiding parties.

THE SHEPHERDS:
- Jonasim Kindle: contestant in the Thel-Mizaret tournament; has latent Shepherd gift.
- Alfex Lastname: former Shepherd in Ellador, but, by Morlan's request, transferred to Vulmarrow.
- Mosteryn the Old: sage leader of the Shepherd Order; has the gift of storms and lightning.
- Sebastian Sternbough: High Shepherd of Anglinor, advisor to the First Lord and Lady of Myriad; gifted with control of plants.

CHAPTER 1

THE SWORD IN THE STARS

*When the moon is blood red
and the Sword is in the stars,
the Man of Ice will call Him,
the Hero from afar.*
From Canticles (XI.i)
Barde Smythe (r. 989 AS)

3 CELESANDUR 2212

Alastair Coldhollow tried to wipe the blood from his hands but failed. His gashed palm and torn knuckles had never had a chance to clot, not with all the struggling to pry off his mount's ruined horseshoes.

Steam hissed a few paces away as a burly man plunged a red hot shoe into a barrel of water next to his anvil. "Yuh want some 'elp wif that?" Carraig asked.

"Strong as you are, Carraig, I don't think even you can help me with this." Alastair gripped the horse's left hoof awkwardly between his legs and tried once more to pry free the shoe. The pliers snapped off the edge of the horseshoe, pinching Alastair's palm in the handle. He grunted and swore and slammed the bloody tool to the ground.

"Cut yer 'ands to ribbons that way, it will," Carraig said. He was a mass of muscle covered by mottled skin and prickly dark hair. His eyes shone brightly, though, reflecting red and orange from the forge. It was dusk, but the overcast sky darkened the province of Ardon as if it were night.

"I'll get it this time," Alastair said. Long, black, sweat-soaked hair whipped into his eyes as he bent over to fetch the pliers.

Carraig half-watched while he hammered a horseshoe three times. Satisfied with his work, he tossed the shoe in the water barrel. "I've never seen shoes so blasted, not even from a war 'orse. Yuh shouldna' waited so long t'change'm."

"Not much choice there," Alastair said, straining again with the pliers. "You know…very well…that I can't…just wander into any town I like. Not with so many nooses being held for me."

"Yeah, but what're the odds a'folk recognizin' yuh after all this time?"

"Rrrrr—ah!" The horseshoe popped off and clattered to the floor with a dead metallic thud. "I can't take that chance. Would you?"

The blacksmith shrugged. "Still searchin' fer that Hal… Halfin—"

"Halfainin." Alastair snorted in disgust.

"Right, Halfainin." Carraig pounded on a shoe. "Haven'a found 'em yet, then?"

Alastair hung his head and pinched the bridge of his nose. With a great, shuddering sigh, he whispered, "No."

"Meanin' yuh no disrespect, but never could figure that one out. Mighty warrior, right? S'posed to come and save the world, eh? Save it from what, I wonder? Seems t'me, Myriad's gone on pretty much the same fer ages of ages."

Alastair smeared more blood onto his breeches and sat up a little straighter. Weathered skin hung loosely on his oblong face, especially in the circles and folds under his glistening dark eyes. He was not old, as people in Myriad counted old. But he looked it. Knowledge of the world's troubles would be enough to do that to a man.

The Gorrack Nation threatened war from the north, and High King Aravel, once a mighty ruler, seemed reluctant to do anything about it. There were also rumors from the Hinterlands in the far west…rumors of legendary evils and fell deeds. And, of course, there was King Morlan in Vulmarrow—to this day he continued his eighteen year campaign, a desperate, secret quest to murder all followers of the First One. Things were definitely changing in Myriad…and not for the better.

But good for Carraig, thought Alastair. *Let him be blissfully ignorant of the cataclysmic war that is coming.* Alastair rubbed the criss-cross scar on his cheek below his right eye and then the longer, more pronounced scar that carved a pinkish furrow from his jawline to his chin. "I don't expect you to understand."

"Yer right. I don't understand yuh. But I respect yer passion… yer commitment." Carraig hacked and spat into the forge. "Heh, all I'm livin' fer is me next meal."

If you only knew, thought Alastair, staring at his bloodstained hands. *My passion is gone. I am committed to nothing. The only thing left for me now is a dark bottle.*

The bottle of Witchdrale had waited many winters in the loneliest corner of Alastair Coldhollow's dank basement. On a narrow shelf it stood, its dusty black glass shrouded in cobwebs, between the Books of Lore and the last of the king's gold. There the bottle rested, almost forgotten, like a skull in a charnel house. Alastair had sworn not to drink of that tempting, bitter fruit ever again. It was his way of purifying himself as he waited for the Promise to come true. *Ten years,* Alastair thought. The Promise had not come true. And the Witchdrale was calling.

Abruptly, he pushed aside the Books. *You've rescued me before*, Alastair thought. *But tonight...I do not want to be rescued.* He grasped the black bottle and charged up the stairs.

The Witchdrale felt heavy. It even made a weighty thud when he let the bottle slide from his hands to the small table by the window. Alastair lit a candle, sat down, and stared into the depths of the black glass.

At length, he roused himself. How much time had passed while he sat staring, he did not know. The candle seemed to have burned lower. Alastair found his hands on either side of the bottle, opening and closing absently. There were flecks of dried blood on the table. He realized he hadn't even washed his hands. *Just as well. A reminder of older stains, the innocent blood spilt by my sword.*

He clutched his head in his hands and wept. His mind was a melee of want: *Just open the bottle.* And hating to want: *Remember what happens to you. Remember what it does.*

But within his stormy thoughts, it seemed there was another voice. *Alastair, go back to the Books.* It was a deep, female voice—tender, concerned—not unlike his mother's. But she had been gone so many years. Alastair gripped his skull harder but the voice would not stop. *There is forgiveness in the Books. Mission. Hope. You are the Caller.*

Caller! Another voice spoke with a sneer, this one stern and commanding. *You have not called forth the Hero. You have not called anything since you left Morlan's service. In Vulmarrow you had mission and respect. In Vulmarrow, your talents were held in honor—rather than wasting away.*

Feared, the womanly voice returned. *As the icy fist of a bloodthirsty tyrant, you gained only fear—and visions that haunted you mercilessly, until you came to the Books. You are the Caller. Only you can bring the Halfainin to this dying world. Heed the Promise. When the moon is blood red and the Sword is in the stars, the Man of Ice will call Him, the Hero from afar.*

Ten winters wasted, waiting for one who will never come. It was the final word…Alastair's own thoughts. He snatched up the Witchdrale and went to the cupboard for a mug.

He froze in mid-stride, staring from the window into the night sky. The bottle fell from his hand and shattered. The full harvest moon had finally risen above the treetops of Ardon.

The moon was blood red.

Alastair stumbled over a chair, raced into his study, and delved into a dark cedar chest that hadn't been open in years. "Where is it?" he yelled, frantically searching. "Where is it?"

Finally from the depths of the wide chest he withdrew a proud broadsword, a weapon of infinitely better craftsmanship than the plain steel he'd been wearing on his recent journeys. The blade gleamed a cold blue, even in the dark.

Then up the spiral stairs and through the trapdoor Alastair flew until he stood out in the night air upon the naked stone turret he had built for this very occasion. That sturdy platform gave him a view of the sky like none other. Alastair wrung his hands on the sword's pommel and closed his eyes for a moment.

A shooting fear went through him. If the signs were there, everything would come together. The Halfainin would come. The Silence would end. The Convergence and its catastrophic war would be averted. *And at last,* thought Alastair, *I will be forgiven for the deeds of my past.*

But if the signs were not in the stars of the heavens, then what? Alastair did not know. He felt the sword's grip in his hands, and he had a terrible fleeting thought. *If the signs are not there, then perhaps I'll use this blade for something else.*

At last, he forced open his eyes and beheld the night sky. It was gloriously clear. There were so many stars, twinkling and blinking. Alastair knew them all. He had mapped them on his own, over the years. He had sketched their formations—the bull, the archer, the twins—and he knew where they should be at every season of the year. But never had the Sword been visible.

Until this night. "There!" He called aloud. "The nine stars of Elspeth Gawain are the haft. And there, Caedmon's Bow—three points for the hilt. And the blade…? Yes, oh, it is there! The Seven Lights of the First One have aligned at last!"

Alastair held his sword aloft, but inverted, and lined it up with the stars in the heavens. "The sword is in the stars, at last!" he cried, looking to the soft pink glow on the horizon. "And the Star Sword points to…why, that must be the mining city, Thel-Mizaret. So the Hero will come from the City of Jewels. And I, the Caller shall go with all speed to call Him forth!"

CHAPTER 2

THE BLACK STONE TABLE

Lyonette wept. The Table was gone.
The Eye of the north was now blind.
The Pureline betrayed by one of its own.
Sad questions linger behind.
From "The Ballad of Lyonette"
Aeld and Prys Valtaire, (w. 2114 AS)

3 CELESANDUR 2212 (THAT SAME NIGHT)

A thousand hammers fell, ringing like bells of judgment. An army of blacksmiths labored in the angry orange light and dragon-breath heat of their forges. And a formidable armory was born of fire.

There, in the northwest corner of the region of Fen, deep in the bowels of the Malerion Forest, the once-abandoned city of Vulmarrow teemed with more activity than it had seen even in the Elder Days. Training by the light of bonfires and torches, hosts of soldiers dueled, lunging and blocking, honing their warcraft. Stonewrights fortified the city's bulwarks and raised new walls.

And from the high turret, the only tower that pierced the forest canopy, a very curious eye peered through a crooked spyglass into the night sky. The man turned the glass sharply to the left, gasped, and turned away to scribble on a chart.

He went back to the spyglass and began to mutter, "'Folk-tales,' he says. 'Weak lore for the weak-minded.' Bah! Lucky for him old Rhydic stays at his post. Sword in the Stars! Ha, who'd have thought? There'll be trouble in Tryllium. Maybe in Fen too. Better tell 'im right quick, or he'll toss old Rhydic out a window, like as not."

Rhydic made a few more notes on the star chart, tucked it under his arm, and scurried down a ladder through the trapdoor.

R hydic rubbed the back of his hand so hard on his stubbly chin that it burned his skin. He hated the throne room. Every time he parted those tall slab doors, it felt like death leaked out…a vaporous presence writhing, reaching— Rhydic shook his head. No, nothing would be worse than not telling him. Rhydic knew King Morlan had special ways of dealing with those who crossed him. Agonizing methods of prolonging the pain of death without allowing his victims the relief of crossing its threshold.

Rhydic shuddered and put his right hand upon the throne room door. A vaskerstone had been cunningly inlaid on the brushed granite door: black but gleaming red in the torchlight. The vaskerstone warmed immediately to Rhydic's palm. Within the doors, a stone latch scraped into place, sounding much like the lid of a crypt sliding and locking above a corpse.

The door separated, and dust rained down on Rhydic's sleeve. He brushed it off and pushed the throne room door in a few inches—just wide enough to stick his head and one shoulder inside.

Dark. Utterly dark. It was the kind of suffocating darkness of the inside of a tomb. *Why does he always sit in the dark?* Rhydic shrugged. *Kings do what kings do.*

The darkness was pierced from above. Thin knives of white moonlight stabbed down upon the throne and splashed the broad shoulders of the immense figure seated there. The king's helm and mantle shifted forward and the moon's light traced the intricate designs of his armor like rivulets of silver blood. Beside the throne sat another menacing shape. Sköll, King Morlan's pet blackwolf.

Rhydic wanted to slam the door. He wanted to flee, shrieking down the hall and the stairs to the stables, and lash a warhorse until it bore him far from Vulmarrow and this castle of horrors. But Rhydic did not flee. Under a compulsion he could not resist, he stepped inside and shut the heavy door behind him.

A great deep breath exhaled in mirthless laughter, and luminous yellow eyes opened beneath the helm. "Speak, soothsayer."

The king's voice, like icy wind slithering between the cracks of shutters or under a door, sent chills careening down Rhydic's spine. He felt his heart begin to seize, and he croaked out, "C-couldn't we have a bit more light?"

"Very well." The king grasped the black silhouette of an enormous table. Its opaque surface became translucent as a film of ghostly green light began to swirl within. King Morlan stroked the side of the table, and the thin bands of moonlight raining down began to widen. It was a vaskerstone table, of course, but of a vein so pure and a design so cunning that its likeness could not be found in all of Myriad.

Soon the throne room was lit in an eerie half-light. It was precious little comfort to Rhydic, for now he could see King Morlan more clearly. He was tall and broad-shouldered and wore a mixture of silver and coal-gray armor. But like the fur of blackwolves that roamed the kingdom after dark, there was a strange hint of blue in Morlan's armor whenever he turned at a certain angle. His hair was long and streaked with premature gray, and it swept back behind his head like a cape. He wore a very thin beard, cut to the skin. It knifed down from the corners of his mouth and ran along his jawline almost to his ears. Above his brow, he wore a thin, sable crown encrusted with red diamonds.

Sköll, thankfully, looked sleepy. His normally piercing eyes blinked shut and he his head lay on his forelegs. But the creature yawned, revealing rows of jagged teeth and wickedly long canine fangs.

King Morlan's yellow eyes dwelt heavily upon Rhydic, and he could feel the king's impatience growing like the tightening of a rope. Maybe even a noose...

"It-it's happening," Rhydic blurted out.

The king removed his hands from the table and leaned back in his tall chair. "Are you certain?"

"The charts confirm it, lord."

"Where?"

"Tryllium," Rhydic said. "Northern Tryllium. In Ardon, Carrack Vale, m-maybe Thel-Mizaret."

"Maybe?" The king leaned forward, and Sköll—his yellow eyes open and glowering—growled fiercely. "Have you any idea how many might die due to your 'maybe?' The prophecies those zealots cling to tell that the Halfainin will rule over all other authority. I am such an authority, Rhydic. And I will not suffer even the smallest encouragement to those who call the First One their master. Many will die. Are you certain you can do no better than 'maybe?'"

Rhydic began to tremble. He had the distinct impression that he was now standing at the edge of a great precipice, that he was losing his balance, beginning to fall... "By all my divinations... that is, as close as I can tell. If...if I still had the—" Rhydic's mouth snapped shut before he made the fatal mistake.

"The Star Sword," King Morlan said dryly. The yellow eyes narrowed. "Pity its loss, soothsayer. More blood must be spilled in its absence." The king leaned forward once more and the yellow in his gaze kindled. "I will consult the Table."

The king gripped the sides of the table and closed his eyes. He began to tremble. A shrill ringing filled the chamber. Rhydic clutched his ears and cringed, but he did not take his eyes off King Morlan. The king shook. Veins appeared on his neck and arms. The moonlight dimmed, and suddenly Morlan tore his hands from the table. In that moment, it seemed to Rhydic he'd heard the echo of a horrific scream.

"Your skills with that spyglass are considerable," King Morlan said, his voice low and thick. "Northern Tryllium—I have seen it. But not Ardon. Not Carrack Vale. There were mountains, mines, and fortified armories…Westmoor, Stonecrest, or Thel-Mizaret."

Rydic nodded. "Truly, lord, the Black Table gives you sight beyond men."

"Report your findings to Shepherd Alfex in the library," the king said. "Then return to your roost. If you observe anything of importance while I am away, alert Cythraul in the Bone Chapel."

Rhydic felt the tightening in his heart again. If there were any place in Vulmarrow Keep worse than Morlan's throne room, it was the Bone Chapel. Cythraul would just as soon gut a man as look at him. And Cythraul was always more ruthless when the king was away. "Lord, must you oversee the…" Rhydic swallowed… "business in Tryllium?"

"I won't be going to Tryllium. Velach Krel will lead my Wolf-guard. He is very…efficient. I have business of another sort in Anglinore." Morlan's eyes narrowed to slits. "Important business. I shall return in three weeks' time. Now, depart from me." King Morlan slashed his finger across the table. The moonlight vanished from the throne room, and Sköll howled.

Rhydic fled and desperately squeezed between the tall stone doors. They shut a heartbeat after he was through. As Rhydic raced down the corridor he heard thunder from below. It was the thunder of hooves. Rhydic stole a momentary glance from a tall arched window. A sliver of star-strewn night appeared through the always-swaying black trees in the direction of Tryllium. Rhydic muttered all the way to the library.

CHAPTER 3

LOOKING FOR A HERO

My Halfainin will be born into sorrow.
Wise beyond his years.
No blade will daunt him.
No blade will pierce him.
His eye will be keen.
He will tame beasts with a touch.
And he will bring fire from a stone.
From Canticles (XII.iii)
Barde Gray (r. 919 AS)

7 CELESANDUR 2212

"I don't much like the looks'a ye, dat's a fact," said Old Binik Gelsh, Thel-Mizaret's ruling steward. He leveled a loaded crossbow at Alastair's chest. "Just ye stay right there."

"If I stay at your door," Alastair said, "then it will be impossible for us to do business." He jangled his coin pouch.

"I like the sound a'dat," Binik said. "But yer business might be cuttin' me throat and fillin' yer satchel with *my* silver...comin' here this timea night."

"I apologize for the late hour," Alastair said. "But I've come when I've come. If you don't want my gold—"

"Did you say gold?" The crossbow shifted off center.

"Yes, and more than a fair amount. I'm looking for someone, you see. I don't know who exactly, but I know he's in Thel-Mizaret. To find him, I will need to hold a special kind of tournament."

"Gold, eh?" Binik echoed dreamily. "Ye best take a seat then." He lowered the crossbow to his side and motioned to the chair opposite his desk.

The parlor of Hazzlebrim, Binik's cottage manor, was large and roughly round, filled with rusty suits of armor, dusty paintings, and dozens of trinkets. In the center of the room was what had once been a very impressive desk. Now it had lost its color and had been scratched innumerable times. Binik sat behind the desk in a massive hide-covered chair. The chair across the desk was a mere stool.

Alastair sat down and shifted his weight to avoid crushing his seat. "Have you run tournaments before? You know, jousting, duels, archery—that sort of thing?"

"A tournament?" Binik scratched the few oily curls on his shining head—as if he'd not understood Alastair from the beginning. "Oh, dat kind'a tournament! Of course, of course. I'll make a decree et sun up. We'll have everyone in town attend…fer a small fee, of course."

Gazing at the collection in the parlor, Alastair had no doubt the fee would not be small. "Not a spectacle, mind," Alastair clarified. "I'd rather avoid drawing too much attention."

"But ye won't be able t'draw out the best dat way." Binik pursed his lips and worked his jaw. "We gotter' post signs and banners, offer prizes—make her known. Only way t'get worthy lads…uh…and lasses."

"So be it," said Alastair, letting his money pouch drop to the desktop with a rich thud. "You're sure we can get this all ready for tomorrow afternoon?"

"Of course."

"I'll need some supplies from your armory," Alastair said, nodding to the pouch on Binik's desk. "But I included a bit of extra gold. Will that do?"

Binik snatched up the pouch so fast and with such a broad grin that Alastair could just see plots and ploys bouncing on his sweaty brow. But when Binik opened the pouch, his jaw went slack and his eyes would have leaped from his skull if they were not internally attached. "This…" he mumbled, "this be kingsgold! Where—?" He almost asked, but caught himself.

"Your armory?" Alastair reminded him.

"Ah, yes…well, of course," Binik fell all over himself scooting from the table and waddling to the door. "Dagget!" he yelled. "*Dagget!* Get yer bitty feet in hey're with me keys!"

A handful of heartbeats later, a nervous-looking stonehand with exactly four hairs on his chin appeared in the doorway. Like most of the stonehand race, Dagget was only about four feet tall, stocky and muscular. He held up his meaty fist and showed the expected key ring. "Vis d'ring, bozz?" he asked, looking like a puppy waiting for a scrap from the table. "Ye called, and snappity-crack, Dagget's here!"

Binik Gelsh was a great many things, but he was apparently not in the habit of neglecting his help. "Yay, Dagget, ye didder's good, ye did. Here ye go." He tossed Dagget a piece of kingsgold and took joy in watching the dwarf's eyes bulge, much like his own had just moments before. "Now, get ye to the armory wid' mister…uh…?" He glanced nervously at Alastair. "'Fraid I don't know yer name, dere. Not that I need to know yer name, mind. It's jest I—"

"Tolke," Alastair said, laughing inwardly. He'd used the old Anglish word for "Caller."

Who are you?" Alastair asked, one eye on the first of the potential champions, the other on the crowd gathering upon the length of the city walls. Binik's signs and banners had worked as promised. "Your name, lad?"

"Jonasim Kindle, Mister Tolke, sir," the nervous teen replied.

"Well met, Jonasim!" Alastair cried out, eliciting an unwanted cheer and a few lusty boos from the crowd. Alastair glowered at the city walls and then turned back to his first candidate. The kid certainly looked heroic. Sixteen, maybe seventeen…tall, broad-shouldered, lean, solid as an oak. Large, piercing green eyes and a chin hewn from granite. "Well now, Jonasim, you've brought your own bow, I see."

"Yessir. Arrows too."

"Good, good. Well, let's put them to use then. You see the target there? Three shots. Three bull's-eyes. Think you can do that?"

"Aye," Jonasim said. "I think I can."

Thwip. Thwap. Thwip. The arrows leaped from the lad's bow, and one-two-three, they plunged into the bull's-eye.

Eyebrows raised and lips pursed, Alastair nodded to Jonasim. "Not bad. Nice grouping too. You advance. Wait over by the alder tree."

Next up was a dark-skinned lad named Duskan Vanimore. "Please, Sirrah Tolke," he said, ducking his head as if Alastair were some kind of royalty, "would it be obtuse for me to inquire as to the nature of the prize?"

"Gold," Alastair said. "Among other things too great to reveal to anyone but he who stands victorious at the end of the day."

"Or she!" came a fierce voice from behind Duskan's broad back.

When the speaker emerged, she at first seemed a child. She stood no more than five feet tall, with large eyes and cute puckered lips. She wore a motley combination of light leather armor and fancy attire. She might have been comical if her voice weren't so womanly and serious.

"The poster did not disqualify women from the contest." She gestured behind her. "I know most of these…boys…and I can best about all of them."

Some of the lads behind her laughed openly. Duskan remained silent.

Alastair cursed himself for not making it clear that only men could compete. After all, the prophecy did say… *Wait,* he thought. Did the prophecy say who could…? He couldn't remember. No matter. "What is your name, lass?"

"Laeriss," she said. "Laeriss Fenstalker."

"Well, Laeriss Fenstalker, you need to wait your turn. Come, Duskan, let your bow sing, if it will."

"Yes, sirrah." Duskan took up his bow. The lad's features were smooth, as if carved and crafted by a master sculptor. In fact, everything about Duskan was smooth. His movements, the way he put an arrow to the bowstring, the way he held his form even after the arrow was gone—velvet smooth. Alastair wondered at him. Could this be the Halfainin? He had to catch his breath—hope and joy threatened to burst—but not yet. More tests remained.

Three arrows and three bull's-eyes later—the grouping not quite as tight as Jonasim's—Duskan had passed the first test…as Alastair thought he would and much to the delight of the thickening crowd on the walls. Some spectators had even grown so bold as to leave the city and venture into the fairgrounds.

Laeriss came next and, true to her word, put three arrows in the gold.

A strong pull, Alastair thought. He'd expected there'd be early success. In a mining town like Thel-Mizaret there were bound to be some talented warriors. But these first three were exemplary. One of them was bound to be the Halfainin. All the prophecies were coming true. Alastair silently exulted. It was more joy than he'd felt in a dozen years.

The next handful of candidates produced a much different result. First, there was club-footed Negis Gorber, whose initial shot plunged into the bull's-eye. His second shot, however, dove into the sod three feet in front of the target. In the process, he somehow managed to slash his forearm with the bowstring and was unable to continue. Then there was young Darius Nook, who couldn't keep an arrow nocked long enough to fire it from the bow. And worst of all was Carvel Ploddington. When Alastair handed him the bow, Carvel's first words were, "Can't we start with sumpin' else?"

"The bow," Alastair said.

"'Cause I'm really good with the sword."

"Three shots," Alastair said curtly. "Three bull's-eyes or you join the spectators."

Carvel grimaced and looked down at the bow as if it were a snake liable to strike. He nocked an arrow and took aim. Carvel panicked, yanked back the bowstring, and let the arrow fly.

And fly it did. Straight into the top of a nearby apple tree.

"Ahhgh!" came a sudden yelp from the treetop. Branches snapped. A person appeared, tumbling from bough to bough and finally dropping awkwardly to the ground. But clearly, he was not dead. This lad leaped to his feet. Both hands flew to his backside and he hopped around like he'd sat in a fireplace. "Ya shot me!" he yelled as he hopped. "Ya shot me! I'm dyin', I am! You've kilt me!"

Alastair was first to the lad, followed by many of the other contestants. And indeed, he had been shot through with Carvel's errant arrow. The point had penetrated the seat of the teen's breeches. The fletchings were visible on one side of the lad's rear and the arrowhead protruded from the other side.

"Hold still, lad!" Alastair yelled. "Hold still!"

Whining and muttering, the lad finally stopped hopping around. "I'm dying! You kilt me!"

"Oh, no!" yelped Carvel. "I didn't mean to!" He turned to Alastair. "He's not going to die, is he?"

"Not hardly," Alastair said. With a swift flicker of his hand, he whipped the arrow right out of the lad's trousers. He held the arrow up so that the lad who'd been shot could see it. "There now, not even a speck of blood."

"But?"

"It was close," Alastair said, "but the arrow missed your bottom entirely. You'll need these britches stitched up, but you'll have to wait another day for a 'heroic' death. What were you doing up in that tree, anyway?"

"Watchin'," he muttered, his face red. With his wild thatch of wheat-brown hair, he looked like a turnip that had just been picked. "Me mum said I wuz too young t'enter meself."

"What's your name, lad?"

"Tonsel," the boy said.

"Well, Tonsel," Alastair said, "if you believe you have the skills to enter such a contest now, I can only imagine what kind of warrior you will be in a few years when you're old enough. See, this…quest…that I'm on, well, I'm looking for someone a bit older."

Tonsel nodded bravely. "'Kay."

"Good show," Alastair said. "Now, off you go. Find a safer perch—on the city walls. I daresay you have nothing to fear from us there." Then Alastair turned back to Carvel Ploddington. "Sorry, Carvel lad, but I don't believe you'll be needing this." Alastair snatched the bow from Carvel's hand. "In fact, for the sake of all of our buttocks, I think it best that you never pick up a bow again."

The other contestants laughed, and Alastair immediately wished he hadn't been so demeaning. There was nothing quite as mortifying for a young man as being embarrassed in front of peers, especially if that group counted young ladies in its number.

Carvel looked at his shoes and then back up at Alastair. "I know I'm no good with the bow," he said. "It's swordplay or axes for me. Can't I just do that part for you?"

Alastair remembered how his mother had treated him when he'd failed, so he looked kindly upon the lad. "You're a brave young man, Carvel. You came out and contested, when so many others stayed on the wall or—" he drew close to Carvel and whispered— "or climbed trees to watch."

Carvel's chin rose a little. He grinned.

"I have a feeling about you," Alastair said. "I have a feeling you are very good at the sword. I should know, as it is my specialty as well. But for this contest, it's all or nothing. I wish I could explain more, Carvel. But do not walk away with a heavy heart. Remember, you stepped forward."

When Carvel walked away, he did so with his chin held high.

What had begun as a group of twenty-four contestants soon diminished to seventeen. After the javelin, eleven remained. The final event for the day, a race up a steep hillside while wearing a satchel full of stones, narrowed the group to five: Jonasim, Laeriss, Duskan, and brother and sister twins, Niar and Nairi Jaiktide.

"Get a good night's rest," Alastair told them. "I have a long night of…preparation…ahead of me, so we'll begin at noon. Meet me just outside of the city gate. Come ready, with sharp mind and blade. You'll need both."

CHAPTER 4

TAMING WATER

When first has become last
And old faith has passed,
The Halfainin, the Halfainin.

When evil comes callin'
And towers are falling'
The Halfainin, the Halfainin.

In times a'when all broke men despair,
Allhaven will send us a love and a care,
A warrior so valiant and rare,
The Halfainin, will save us.

A Myridian Folksong
By Dannal Newfellow

9 CELESANDUR 2212

"What's with the hole?" Niar asked, scratching at a dark brown sideburn that ran all the way down to his chin.

"And what's with the shelleck paddles?" asked Nairi, looking around. They had gathered outside the city walls in a patch of hardpan where the old stables used to be. "Are we going to play a game?"

"Not exactly," Alastair said. "You see, I am not only looking for a warrior with unparalleled skills, but he—or she—must possess wisdom well beyond his years."

"Well, that rules you out, Nairi," Niar said to his sister.

"Ha!" she replied, her dark green eyes smoldering. "Such bravado! But who was it who couldn't lace his boots without help this morning?"

Jonasim laughed and looked down at his own boots.

Duskan was silent, but considered the elements laid before them. There were two shelleck paddles: wide wooden saucers with leather-wrapped handles about the size of a normal sword haft. There was no net or ball. Duskan looked for a thread to pull that might unravel this mystery. He found none.

"What must we do?" Laeriss asked.

"Ah, a very good question," Alastair said. "I said you won't be playing a game. But to solve this conundrum, you will need to assume that you were indeed playing shelleck, but the ball escaped you and went down this hole."

The youths stared down at the ground. There was a perfectly round opening just large enough for a shelleck ball to fit down.

"So get another ball," Niar said.

"Ah, but you cannot," Alastair replied. "You see, this shelleck ball is the only one in the city. And you cannot carve another one."

"That's stupid," Nairi said.

"Nonetheless," Alastair said, "these are the rules of this challenge."

"What sort of hole is this, Sirrah?" Duskan asked.

"Another excellent question. It's more than a hole. Actually, it's an iron tube, two feet of iron tube, anchored in the ground by felstone. Your task is to retrieve the ball without damaging it. But all you may use are the paddles, the laces that tie up your boots, and your waterskins."

"Don't worry, Niar," his sister said, "I'll help you get your boot laces free."

Niar glared at her.

"Can we work as a team?" asked Jonasim.

"I'll leave that to you," Alastair said. "Begin."

"YAY!" came a high voice from above. It was Tonsel, sitting on the edge of the city wall. Apparently he'd gotten up early just to watch.

Alastair waved and received a very enthusiastic wave in return.

"Duskan, will you work with me?" Jonasim asked.

"Certainly," he replied. "You are kind to ask." He turned to Laeriss. "Will you join us as well?"

"Uhm, uh...sure," she replied. "Twins too? Maybe just one big team?"

"No," Niar said. "I can do this myself."

"Not before I do," Nairi said.

Alastair shook his head. "You have one hour."

"Time!" Alastair called out. He summoned the youths back. Niar and Nairi stood about three feet apart, both with arms folded, frowning. They looked like angry mirror images. By contrast, Duskan, Jonasim, and Laeriss returned with smiles. They were uncertain, nervous smiles, but smiles nonetheless.

"Now then," Alastair said, "you will take your turn."

"Sir Tolke!" Nairi said. "I'd like to go first."

"So be it," Alastair said.

"Me next," said Niar.

"Fine." Alastair looked to the other three. "Did you remain a team? Or did you split apart?"

"We stayed together," Laeriss said.

Alastair nodded. "You will go last then. Nairi, remain. The rest of you, enter the city and wait for my command."

When the others departed, Alastair walked over to the hole. "I am ready to see your solution, Nairi."

Nairi looked at the hole and back to Alastair. "Honestly, sir," she said. "I don't think my solution will work."

"Why then did you volunteer to go first?"

"Well, I knew none of the others could watch the first one go, right? Otherwise, they could see what the other had done. I just didn't want anyone to see me mess up. Especially my brother."

"I have to admit," Alastair said, "I had my doubts about the two of you...the way you've bickered so much. And your independence, while admirable in some ways, could become a prideful disaster. I know something of this."

Nairi frowned pensively.

"However," Alastair went on, "you were clever enough to think this through—and courageous enough to admit your shortcomings."

"Thank you, sir."

"Still, you must show your solution."

Nairi nodded and picked up the shelleck paddles. She had already removed the laces from one of her boots, and now she went to work tying one end of the lace to the handle of one of the paddles. She tied the other end of the lace to the other paddle so that the lace now hung between the two handles in a kind of loop.

Nairi looked up to Alastair for a nod or some other sign of approval. She received none, and so went back to work. The iron pipe was narrow, perhaps three inches in diameter—just large enough for the shellack ball to slide into it. Nairi held a paddle in each hand and let the lace-loop dangle into the pipe opening. She lowered the lace-loop into the pipe until she felt some resistance. It seemed the right depth, about two feet of lace. *Now for the tough part,* she thought, fishing in the loop so that it would drop beneath the ball.

She twisted the paddles this way and that, one higher, one lower and then tried from different angles. It didn't seem to be working. There just wasn't enough space between the shelleck ball and the inner surface of the iron tube. "Ah, wait! I feel it. Just a tiny bit of weight on the loop." She looked at Alastair. "Ready for this?"

He nodded.

"Okay, here it comes!" In a swift but controlled movement, Nairi drew her hands apart, causing the lace loop to withdraw from the pipe with a snap.

Alastair heard the clatter of the wooden ball as it ricocheted within the pipe. The lace came out...but the ball did not.

"Oh," Nairi said sadly. "Do I get another try?"

Alastair nodded. "If you wish."

Nairi did wish. She tried again...and again. But each time the result was the same. The ball would travel a few inches up the tube, and then the bootlaces would slide out from underneath it. Not once did the ball come within a foot of leaving the tube.

"I am sorry, Nairi," Alastair said. And he was. What had begun as a contest full of hopefuls, any one of whom Alastair thought could be the young Halfainin, had diminished to a tiny field. Of course, it had to. Only one could end up being the hero the sword in the stars had pointed to.

"Wait over here," Alastair said, and he went to fetch Niar.

When they approached the hole, Niar ran to his sister. "Did you..." But Niar never finished the question. He could tell from Nairi's expression. "I'm sorry, sister."

Niari trudged to the foot of the alder tree and sat down to watch her brother.

"Proceed, Niar," said Alastair said.

Niar picked up the shelleck paddles and saw how his sister had strung them together with the laces. *That was clever*, he thought. But he would never tell her so. He untied the laces and dropped one of the paddles. His plan didn't involve the laces at all, so he dropped those as well.

He looked up at Alastair and then fell to his knees near the pipe. Then, using the shelleck paddle like a spade, Niar began to dig. *Two feet down, that's all. If I can loosen the pipe from the stone down there, then I'll have it!* As he suspected it would, the soil around the pipe came free easily. Mr. Tolke had prepared this the night before, so no matter how hard he packed in the dirt, it would be easier to dig through than normal, more established soil.

Kkuuurrrrssst! The paddle struck something hard. "Awww, not the felstone already," Niar groused. He tried the paddle from a different angle and, after an inch of uninhibited digging, crunched into the stone once more. Niar glanced up to Alastair, who sighed and raised an eyebrow.

Niar dug feverishly, but managed only to scrape the edge of the shelleck paddle to splinters. He threw down the paddle in disgust and rose to one knee. At the last moment, he seemed to have a brainstorm. Without looking back at Alastair, Niar put his mouth to the pipe…and began to suck.

"Uugh—uck!" Niar fell away from the pipe and landed smartly on his rear end. His mouth wide, he coughed and hacked and spat until, at last, a blue beetle flew out of his mouth.

"Not sure how that got in there," said Alastair, trying hard not to laugh. "I don't suppose the shelleck ball is in your mouth as well?"

Red from chin to crown, Niar shook his head and joined his sister.

Alastair left them to gather the other three youths. When he returned, he noted that a few more sleepy townsfolk had joined young Tonsel on the wall to watch.

"C'mon, you guys!" Tonsel yelled down. "How hard can it be?"

"Oh, you think you could do it?" Laeriss called back up to him.

"Well..." Tonsel made a face. "Maybe I could."

Laeriss grinned at Duskan and Jonasim.

"I hope you've come up with something," Alastair said.

"Uh, we have an idea," Jonasim said. "We think it will work."

"Did they get it?" asked Laeriss. "Did they get the ball out?"

Niar and Niari stared in opposite directions. Alastair shook his head.

Alastair handed Duskan the paddles, but he handed them back. "Thank you, Sirrah," he said, "but our plan does not involve the paddles at all."

"Really?" Alastair stretched the word out. And all at once he felt the strange joyous anticipation again. Surely one of these three would be the Halfainin. But which one? Duskan? Jonasim? Laeriss? Laeriss was certainly impressive, but still, Alastair couldn't admit to misinterpreting the Books of Lore. He took a deep breath. "Well, show us your solution then."

"It was Jonasim who first put us on to the thought," Duskan said. "He has played shelleck often and remarked at how light the ball was...made with dimpled cottonwood, he thought."

Laeriss approached the pipe and removed a waterskin from her belt. "So we wondered if the ball might just be light enough to float."

The twins gasped. Laeriss misunderstood and a chill ran up her spine. *Oh, no, they've already tried this...and it didn't work.*

"It'll work," Jonasim whispered. "Go on. Pour it in."

Laeriss pulled the stopper and poured her waterskin into the pipe. "Glad I didn't drink it," she said, stepping out of the way for Duskan.

Duskan carried two waterskins, and he poured them both in. "I believe I can see the ball in there now," he said. "Jonasim, the ball floats!"

Alastair grinned. They had it. They'd figured it out. Well, almost. But the last obstacle shouldn't hinder them.

"Well," said Jonasim, "here we go." He poured in his water-skin. The shelleck ball rose with the water level. They could all see the ball clearly now.

"Can you reach it?" asked Laeriss.

"I...I think," Jonasim said. He poked his fingers into the pipe as far as they could go. Then he sighed. "I can't reach it."

"Let me try," Duskan said. "I am certain my fingers are longer." Duskan tried, but while his fingers were indeed longer, he still could not reach the ball.

"Let me try," said Laeriss. "My hands are smaller." And they were, but not small enough to reach into the pipe far enough to reach the ball. "Oh, no."

The three youths stood around the pipe and faced Alastair.

Alastair looked to the skies. They were so close. How could they miss that final—

"Wait!" Laeriss said. "Wait, we didn't think this through."

"Sure we did," said Jonasim. "We needed to get the ball out of the pipe with only the paddles, our boot laces, and our waterskins."

"Right!" Laeriss said, exulting. "Mr. Tolke said we could use *our* waterskins." Without another word, she walked over to the flummoxed twins and took their waterskins. First, she poured Niar's into the pipe. Then, Nairi's. The shelleck ball rose to the top of the pipe and fell harmlessly to the ground. Laeriss picked up the ball and said, "We have solved the riddle."

"Hoorah!" Alastair said. "Brilliant!"

"You did it! You did it!" Tonsel cried. "Just the way I thought it should be done too!"

"I told you we should have worked together," Nairi said as she and her brother walked slowly back to the village gate.

"Oh stuff it, Sis," he replied. "You said no such thing."

"So what happens now?" asked Jonasim. "Do we all three win?"

"Nay," said Alastair. "This tournament will have only one champion."

Jonasim, Laeriss, and Duskan looked at each other uncomfortably. "Well, Sirrah," said Duskan. "When is the next event?"

"In the courtyard in one hour," Alastair said. "That is, if Masters Binik and Dagget have erected the palisades as I requested. I shall see to it. Rest now. Oh, and one more thing: wear old clothes."

"Why, sir?" asked Jonasim.

"Because you are going to get dirty."

CHAPTER 5

TAMING FIRE

The Star Sword was first discovered, or forged, depending on who you ask, in 2147, just after the Wight Wars. Synic Keenblade claimed to have found it—in a dream. Synic said he heard strange music, that he floated a great distance through the air and found the Star Sword beneath the pure white waters of a falls. Only, when he woke up, he still had the sword. Most folk think Synic forged the blade and made up the whole mystical story just to make the sword more valuable.

Of course, no one told Synic to his face that he was lying.

Jacob Shrewsbury, *Weaponry of Historical Significance*

9 CELESANDUR 2212

"The winner of this tournament must go above the typical mastery of weapons and battle tactics." Alastair did his best to ignore the crowd gathering in the courtyard beyond the newly constructed palisades and focus his gaze on the three remaining warriors. "Above courage and wisdom; above strength of mind and body. One of you, and only one of you, must possess something more. And perhaps this quality is something you have not even guessed because you have had no need of it thus far in your short lives. Dragons are not very common in these parts."

"Dragons?" exclaimed Jonasim. "We have to fight dragons?"

"No," Alastair said, pointing to a massive crate at the other end of the fenced-in area. "Just one dragon. And you don't have to fight it. You just have to tame it."

"Tame a dragon, Sirrah?" Duskan's eyes were wide, but more curious than fearful. "But breaking a dragon can take months or even years."

A menacing, low growl rumbled out from the crate.

"True," Alastair said. "The older they are, the harder it is to break them. This is a young dragon, like yourselves—a teenager. But as I said before, you will not accomplish this task through the regular means."

"How then?" asked Laeriss.

"That is for you to determine," said Alastair. "This will be dangerous. If any of you wishes to—"

Somewhere in the crowd, a baby cried out. Alastair looked and saw a young mother holding a child to her shoulder and patting it on the back. She looked up at Alastair but did not smile.

"As I was saying," said Alastair, turning back to his wards, "if any of you wishes to drop out now, I will not blame you. Facing this dragon is likely not what you expected. You will receive three gold pieces for your effort and remarkable success thus far. And know that all three of you will make fine warriors one day. So, will any of you carry on?"

"I'm not quitting," said Laeriss.

"Nor I, Sirrah," Duskan said.

Jonasim was quiet a moment. "Honestly," he said, staring at familiar faces in the crowd of spectators, "I didn't expect to get this far. Mi-Da is working in the mines, of course, but Mi-Ma and my sister are watching. If I stop now, I know they'll still be proud of me. And three gold pieces would feed us for six months. But… if I quit now, I guess I'd always wonder, always feel like I left a little bit back here, if you get my meaning. So, I'm in."

"Excellent, Jonasim," Alastair said, and the crowd surrounding them clapped. After all, it meant more entertainment for them.

"But one thing, Mr. Tolke," Jonasim said. "If any of us can't tame the dragon, you won't let it eat us, will you?"

Alastair chuckled. "No, I won't let it eat you. I might let it take a few bites, however."

The three contestants laughed, but nervously. All grins disappeared when another angry growl issued from the crate.

"Now then," said Alastair, "who would like to go first?"

"I will, Sirrah," said Duskan.

Alastair nodded and handed the lad a length of rope. *Duskan is the Halfainin,* he thought, feeling a slight chill. *He will tame this dragon and all questions will be answered.* Then, he had an odd thought. *What if he does tame the dragon? Jonasim and Laeriss won't even get their chance.* He shrugged. *No matter. The ancient scriptures were clear: there would be only one Halfainin.*

Alastair escorted Jonasim and Laeriss out of the fenced area. Then he circled the palisades until he came to the end near the crate. He grasped a lever with both hands. "Remember," he said to Duskan, "save the sword for a last resort, and even then, use only the blunt pommel. Thump it on the bridge of the nose—that will be enough to make it whimper and flee. We don't want to kill it…rare creatures, they are. Rare and beautiful."

"Bridge of the nose, right. Thank you, Sirrah, I have it. I am ready…I think."

Alastair pulled down on the lever. The door on the crate opened. And for a moment, there was nothing visible but strange sparkles in the dark interior. The rumbling growl came again. It rose in volume and became a sharp roar like that of an angry jungle cat, only more gravelly and scraping. There was a small burst of white flame, like the kindling of a torch, and the beast emerged from the crate.

Lizard-like in shape, seven feet long from tail to snout, the dragon was covered in purple scales so dark they almost looked black. It had large, slanting white eyes, deeply set within a prominent, bony brow. Its jagged cheekbones tapered slightly to wide jaws filled with innumerable narrow white teeth. Bright yellow shards, increasing in size, ran from the center of its snout along the back of its neck and torso, all the way to its thick tail.

As the creature emerged fully into the sunlight, Duskan couldn't help but be awestruck by the beast. He'd seen dragons before. But not this kind. This one had no wings at all, but sweeping back from its muscular shoulders and the backs of its arms were what looked like spikes of crystal. In fact, embedded everywhere in its scales were all manner of sparkling jewels. "This, this is a dragon?"

"A cave dragon," Alastair said. "Took me half the night to find one and capture it."

Hope it doesn't take that long to rescue me, thought Duskan.

Apparently getting used to the sunlight, the dragon blinked and shook its head. Then, it focused its attention on the teenager eighteen feet away.

"Okay," Duskan whispered to himself. "Tame the dragon. Can't be too different from other beasts, can it? Just get on its back and slip the rope on its neck. That's all. That's all I have to do—"

The cave dragon covered the eighteen feet in an instant, the crystal shards on its forelimbs grabbing the soft earth and allowing the creature preternatural traction and speed.

It was all Duskan could do to leap up in time to avoid the creature's teeth. Duskan held on to the top of the palisade and swung his feet up off the ground, and the beast snapped at the air beneath him. "Whoa!"

"That was close!" Alastair clambered up the outside of the fence and prepared to leap in if necessary.

But Duskan held his own. Showing incredible agility, he pushed off of the palisade and landed directly on top of the dragon. The only problem was that he was facing the dragon's tail end.

The cave dragon bucked its hindquarters and took off at a full-on sprint. Duskan groaned with each jolt and bounce but managed to turn himself without falling off. Now he rode the creature like a man might ride a horse. But this was no horse.

Ducking and throwing himself out of the way, Duskan narrowly avoided the creature's crystal shards. He fished for the rope at his side and tried to loop it round the creature's neck. But the cave dragon drove its crystal spikes into the ground, causing it to stop very suddenly. Duskan flew off the beast's back and slammed sideways into the fence. He rolled over with a groan and lay on his back.

Alastair felt a heavy pang in his stomach. *It's got to be you. Get up, get up!*

Duskan did get up, but the way he did it drew a gasp from the crowd and even made the dragon back up a step. Duskan reared back on his shoulder blades and put his palms to the ground on either side of his head. Then, he kicked out with his legs and flung himself up onto his feet.

Amazing, thought Alastair. *Now is the time. Reach out. Touch the beast and he will be yours!*

Duskan took a step toward the dragon. It ducked its head left and right and growled under its breath. Duskan seemed to draw courage from the beast's backing away. He held up his hand and approached the creature. It blinked lazily at Duskan and sniffed curiously at the lad's hand.

He's doing it! Alastair felt himself rising, as if standing on a platform climbing into the air. *It's all true. I am the Caller and Duskan is the—*

The dragon roared and snapped at Duskan's hand. Duskan yelled and pulled his arm back. For a moment, all feared that the creature had bitten his hand clean off. But it was not so. As

Duskan took off running at a sprint, pumping both fists, it became clear that he had avoided tragedy…barely.

Alastair stood very still. His eyes stared beyond the pen, beyond the gasping spectators, to a place unseen. Only his mouth moved, opening and shutting slowly, speaking without words.

"Mr. Tolke!" Laeriss cried. "Do something!"

Alastair snapped back to the moment, saw Duskan's danger, and leaped down between the dragon and Duskan. "Get out, Duskan! I'll distract the beast."

"Yes, Sirrah!"

The dragon seemed all too willing to let Duskan go. It eyed Alastair as if it remembered him…as if it might be thinking, "You're the one who took me out of my comfy hole in the mountain!" It bared its teeth and spewed forth a stream of liquid white fire. Alastair raced for the fence gate and slipped out right behind Duskan. The fiery spray fell short of Alastair and hissed when it hit the soil.

Though panting and huffing, Alastair couldn't take his eyes off Duskan.

The youth stared at the ground. "I am most heartily sorry, Sirrah," he said. "For a moment, I thought the creature might come around, but…I suppose a wild thing will not submit so easily."

Alastair shook his head. His shoulders drooped. And with a touch of anger in his words, he asked, "Who will face the dragon next?"

Laeriss and Jonasim stared at each other.

"Well?" Alastair asked.

"That thing's vicious, it is," Jonasim said. "But I'm not so ill-mannered as to push a young woman into harm's way before I'd be willing to face it."

"Good man," Duskan said. "Just so."

Alastair liked that Duskan remained to watch the rest of the contest. He liked it even more that Duskan was an encourager. In fact, there seemed to be a growing bond of camaraderie between these three.

Laeriss bowed and thanked Jonasim, but her eyes flashed. "You are very kind," she said, her words carefully restrained, but betraying a hint of frustration. "But look, gentlemen, this isn't some puddle you're throwing your cloak over so I can walk across, not some chamber door you're holding open for me. This is an untamed beast, and I am just as much a warrior as either of you. So I won't have it said that I shied away from a fight."

Jonasim's eyebrows rose. "So you wish to go next, then?"

"No, you go ahead, but I wanted you to know I wasn't afraid."

Alastair opened the fence gate, and Jonasim strode in.

Nervous chatter rose from the crowd.

The cave dragon was sniffing and snuffling around its crate home and didn't turn to see his new visitor. Jonasim used the time to think. *Jumping the creature didn't work. Nearly impossible to get a noose around its neck.*

The dragon sniffed the air and spun round. Jonasim's thoughts began to ricochet into a chaotic babble of ideas. *Wait!* He thought then about how he'd once coaxed a stubborn packhorse into a mine shaft.

Raawwwwarrrrkkchh! The beast charged.

Jonasim's hands flew from pocket to pocket, from jerkin to breeches. *C'mon, come on! Ah!* He felt something. With the dragon bearing down on him, he pulled out a strip of dried meat and tossed it to the dragon.

The creature pulled up short and sniffed the jerky repeatedly. Its very thin tongue flicked out and snatched up the smoked meat. It craned its neck and seemed to be tossing the jerky around in its big maw. Then its jaws snapped shut and the creature made a very different kind of growl. Almost a purr.

That was when Jonasim made a huge mistake. He thought he'd earned the beast's trust, so he reached out his hand to pat the creature's head. It happened so fast, just like with Duskan. A growl, a blurred vision of teeth, but this time, there was no question that the dragon's teeth had found flesh. Searing pain climbed up his forearm.

Jonasim released a kind of half-grunt, half-scream, and Alastair was over the palisade a heartbeat later. He smacked the creature's snout with the blunt end of his sword, but it wouldn't let go. Its jaws had closed like a bear trap on Jonasim's forearm. Rivulets of blood streamed from dozens of tiny wounds. The crowd pressed in. Then, the cave dragon began to twist, throwing Jonasim onto his back and turning his arm in an awful angle.

Alastair had seen this before. A cave dragon would lock its jaws onto a victim and use its crystal appendages to turn until its prey was dismembered. Alastair had no choice. He'd have to stab the creature...maybe kill it. He planted his feet and rotated his upper body to put maximum force into the strike. He plunged the Star Sword into the dragon's upper thigh. The beast writhed away from the blade, but did not release Jonasim's arm.

Suddenly, Duskan and Laeriss were there. After several failed attempts, each grabbed one of the creature's legs and tried to keep the beast from gaining enough traction to spin. But the cave dragon was perilously strong, and the two teens found themselves battered between the creature and the hard ground. Alastair reared back, aiming to drive the sword under the beast's left fore-limb and into its heart, a killing stroke.

"Wait!" Jonasim screamed and held out his free hand.

There was something desperate in his voice and gesture that stopped Alastair short. And when Alastair saw Jonasim's eyes, he took two reflexive steps backward. Jonasim's eyes had gone from dark brown to a milky, marbled gray.

Just as some of the spectators rushed in to the fenced-in arena, the cave dragon released Jonasim's arm. Alastair and the others gaped at what they saw. There were still streams of blood on Jonasim's forearm, but the blood was now blue. And the skin on Jonasim's arm...there was no other way to describe it...the skin had turned to stone. The moment his arm was free, Jonasim backhanded the creature. The beast yelped, rolled into a heap, and whimpered all the way back to its crate.

"Jonasim!" one of the townsfolk cried out. "You have the Shepherd-gift!"

"We've not had a Shepherd-born 'ere in an age," said another.

Jonasim's forearm slowly reverted to soft human skin. The fresh puncture wounds from the dragon's teeth were only pinkish scars now. He blinked slowly until his eyes were brown once more. "I don't know what happened," he said, his voice tremulous. "It hurt so bad, and then...it didn't hurt at all. I felt stronger."

Alastair gaped. The Halfainin would have many Shepherd-gifts. The prophecies had declared this. But not this Shepherd-gift. Not stone-skin. Alastair had discovered a new Shepherd-born, but not the Halfainin. Despite the wonderful discovery, Jonasim had failed to tame the dragon. That left only Laeriss.

Alastair trudged out of the fenced in area. *What...are...you...doing?* he admonished himself. It was not his own voice, but the sneering, castigating voice from the night he'd first seen the sword in the stars. *In your desperation to find this legendary—mythical—being, you've thrown teenagers in front of a dragon? Jonasim could have been killed. Any one of them could have been killed.*

"Mr. Tolke?" Laeriss called to him. She appeared a moment later, followed by Duskan.

In that moment, Alastair made up his mind. "Laeriss, I will not let you face the dragon."

"I might have argued...earlier," she said. "But now, I don't think I want anything to do with dragons."

Jonasim appeared a moment later. His mother and sister stood with him. "Mr. Tolke, sir?" he said tentatively. "So what happens now? I...I failed, didn't I?"

Alastair swallowed back his self-hatred for a moment and turned to the lad. "You did not fail," he said. "You willingly stood your ground against a fearsome beast. And now, look at you, you've discovered you're Shepherd-born. Huzzah to that, I say! Use your gift well to keep the people of Thel-Mizaret safe."

"I will, sir," he replied, standing up very straight and very proud.

"But what of the contest?" Laeriss asked.

Contest? thought Alastair. *The contest was over before it began.* But there was one last strand of hope. And however foolish it might be, he decided to follow it. "The gold is yours already, all three of you, for coming this far."

"Thank you, Sirrah," Duskan said. "You don't know what this means."

"But there is one more thing I'd like to see." He drew the Star Sword from its sheath. "Maybe this was the wrong kind of dragon. Maybe I misunderstood the prophecy."

"Wrong kind?" Laseriss repeated.

"Prophecy?" Duskan echoed.

"Bah, nevermind," Alastair said. "I want to see how you each handles a sword."

"And if one of us is good enough?" Jonasim asked.

Alastair allowed his inner hopes to kindle once more. "If one of you can wield a sword to my standard, then you will earn much more than gold. Fetch your blades and meet me in the pasture just south of the city."

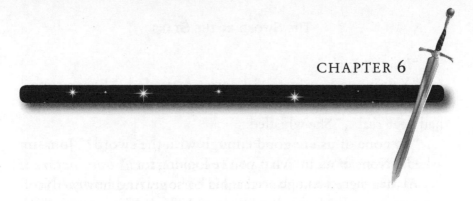

CHAPTER 6

FOOL'S GOLD

The Wayfolk, Prydian or Vespal, are the longest lived
of all the free peoples of Myriad, 700 years.
But no one exactly knows about the pureline branch.
Some say they're immortal.
Letti's Almanac, 2105

9 CELESANDUR 2212

They need not have bothered going all the way back to their homes for their swords. In a matter of seconds, Alastair had assessed their sword craft. It was poor. Very poor.

Jonasim's sword slipped out of his hand and nearly beheaded a cow grazing in the pasture. Duskan's sword stroke was very heavy, but also very slow. Alastair's quick slashes had the poor lad so turned around that he spun and drove his sword straight into the dirt. Laeriss was the best of the three, but she was undisciplined and left so many openings in her defense that Alastair could have taken her out with a wooden spoon.

In the end, all three panting, awed youths turned to Alastair.

"I've never seen anyone use a sword like you do, Mr. Tolke," Jonasim said.

"Nor I, Sirrah."

"You move...so fast..." Laeriss marveled. "Every time I thought I could strike, you slid away...out of reach. If this fight had been real..." She whistled.

"So none of us are good enough with the sword?" Jonasim asked. "None of us are what you're looking for?"

Alastair sighed and glanced at his horse grazing nearby. "No... no, your swordcraft is not at the level I was hoping to find. With some training, I've no doubt you could—"

"Please, Sirrah," Duskan said. "Really. I'm just grateful for the chance to try. Two days out of the mines and three gold pieces to show for my efforts. Not bad."

"Thank you, Mr. Tolke," Jonasim said. "Thank you for the chance. If it hadn't been for you, who knows when I'd have discovered...well, it feels so strange to say...that I'm a Shepherd."

Alastair climbed into the saddle of his horse and took the reins. He smiled grimly at Jonasim and nodded to Duskan. Even as he turned his horse to ride away, he felt Laeriss's eyes on him.

He was just a few yards away when she called out. "Mr. Tolke?"

He stopped his horse.

"Just what kind of super warrior are you looking for?"

One that doesn't exist. But Alastair found himself unable to speak the words, so he just shook his head and kicked his horse to a trot. He knew a good tavern on the way back to Ardon.

"Here now," the barkeep hollered from across the counter. "You in the corner: you goin'a order somethin' er just take up a table?"

Alastair looked up from his reading. Six tables in the tavern. His was the only one occupied. Still, he flipped a coin to the barkeep, and the shaggy man wandered happily away.

Alastair had entered the tavern intent on purchasing Witchdrale, but instead, he'd fallen into a chair and opened up his old copy of Canticles, the Words and Deeds of the First One. Even now, he pored over the text. *I must have missed something. The error can only fall to me.*

Flipping from section to section, page to page, Alastair ran through what he knew of the Halfainin. Born in sorrow, a mighty warrior who could wield any weapon at will. He would have many Shepherd gifts—taming beasts with a touch and bringing fire from a stone chief among them. The Halfainin would be brilliant beyond his elders and make fools of the wise. And there would be other distinguishing characteristics. When full into manhood, the Halfainin would cast out the Wicked King and put an end to the Convergence.

Manhood, Alastair mumbled. *I should have remembered that before putting Laeriss through all the trouble.*

Alastair had always assumed Morlan would become the Wicked King. Allhaven knew Morlan had already murdered thousands. Alastair thought surely Morlan would be the one to initiate the Convergence.

He shuddered at the thought, but turned to the end of Canticles to the Book of Last Things. He began to read in a low whisper, "'And it will come to pass when all Myriad will forsake me, the crowns I have given will be hoarded and withheld from me, and my sanctuaries will crumble. And so, by the will of all my free peoples, darkness will fester and breed. From distant lands and even from across tempestuous seas, vile things will be drawn nigh. From shadowy wood and hidden caves, evil will issue forth. From slithering tunnels and out of stagnant dark waters, foul things will emerge. Even the very sky will rain down pestilence and despair. Nothing will stand against the encroaching black tide, and even the high seat of all free peoples will be left empty."

Alastair shook his head. This was not the part he meant to look at. Just a few verses later, he read, "'Behold,' says the First One, 'I will not abandon Myriad to its own desires. I will bring forth my Halfainin, who will stand in the way of the Wicked One and turn back the tide. They will rail and curse the name, but my Halfainin will purchase peace at a cost beyond mortal reckoning. Then, the cursed deeds of nations will be forgiven. And I will cleanse their hearts forevermore."'"

Alastair went to turn the page, but found his hand trembling so much that he could not manage even that simple task. He felt as if there were inside of him a kind of living black stain; that if he could reach into his throat and grasp it, he might be able to rip it out. But this stain was burned into his being like an internal scar, and nothing Alastair could do would relieve it. He wanted so desperately to be cleansed…to know peace. He wanted to believe that he was the Caller, the one who would find the Halfainin and call his name to the world. More than anything, Alastair wanted the Halfainin to be real.

But it just wasn't true. Thousands of years of history and no Halfainin. The sword had appeared in the stars. Alastair had used the Star Sword to pinpoint the location, but no one had come forth…no one who fit the other prophecies. *Perhaps I am not the Caller, but the Halfainin lives. Maybe the real Caller has already found the promised hero. Or maybe the Halfainin still remains in Thel-Mizaret, but I did not find him. Perhaps he isn't supposed to compete in a tournament, but show his strengths in some other way. Perhaps I tested for the wrong things or in the wrong ways.*

Alastair slammed shut the book of Canticles and strode to the counter. "Barkeep!"

"Yessir, what'll it be?" asked the man, his voice somehow emerging from behind a thick mustache and beard. "We've a nice Prydian apple-wine, deep and satisfying. Or, if ye have a mind, there's good lager from Chapparel."

"Witchdrale."

The barkeep scanned the empty tavern just to make sure. "Look, mate, I know yer money's good, and I can tell by yer face you're in a rough patch. But you sure you want to sample this demon?"

"We already know each other quite well," Alastair replied.

"Ye won't tell anyone where ye got it, will ye?"

Alastair shook his head. "Just give me a bottle. This should cover it." Alastair slid two gold coins across the counter.

"That it will," said the barkeep who then disappeared into another room. He returned with an unlabeled black bottle and handed it to Alastair. "May the First One return your hope."

"Hope?" Alastair muttered. He tossed his book of Canticles into a rubbish heap and took the bottle back to his table. "There's no such thing."

CHAPTER 7

THE HAMMER AND BOW

Gorracks are manlike in shape; broader but not always taller.
They are very well-muscled, often more than twice as strong as
a man and nearly as strong as a Windborne Sky Captain. Their
skin is tough, scaled in all open places like a dragon and covered
with thick pelts of fur in all other areas. They move about in
packs, so to see one Gorrack is to know there are more abroad.
They are fierce but reckless combatants. When engaged, they will
often become frenzied and lose any semblance of strategy. That is
when they are most vulnerable. But they are never an easy fight.
What they lack in ploys and technique, they make up for in brute
force and sheer numbers.

Taken from the *Military Journal of the Anglish Guard*
By Anders Stormkin, 2105

10 CELESANDUR 2212

They waited in the shadows among the dense pines until deep into
the night, when the hardworking folk of Westmoor were sure to
be heavy in sleep. Sixty grim soldiers waited, yet not one of them
bore any token or insignia that could trace them back to their
home country or estate. No, if indeed any of the villagers survived

to tell what they had seen, they would report that a warmongering band of Gorracks had attacked Westmoor.

These warriors wore dark armor and, as is the custom of Gorrack-kind, cloaked themselves in all manner of fur tunics, mantles, or capes. Black hoods covered their heads and, beneath those, they wore helms carefully crafted with the pronounced brows, huge eye sockets, and gaping jaws that made Gorracks so fearsome. And each monstrous helm had false reptilian eyes painted below the real eye slits.

But these warriors did not attack in the blunt way of the Gorracks. They sent stealthy men ahead, archers and scouts, to dispatch the watchmen at the town gate. Once inside the city walls, their company fanned out into ten teams of five and one team of ten.

Velach Krel led this greater team, for their mission required special thoroughness. *Velach*, King Morlan had said, *find the sanctuary. Make sure.* "I like clarity," Velach whispered to himself as he led his team west along a shadowy cobbled stone road and past darkened windows and doorframes.

They crept past a small manor with gilded runes above its expensive polished cedar door. The door suddenly opened. The man who appeared in the doorway didn't even have time to inhale a full breath of fresh night air. Three soldiers were on him in an instant. A pike flashed. The man fell limp, a dark stain spreading rapidly on his moonlit white tunic.

Even as two of the soldiers dragged the body into a thin alley between buildings, three more warriors entered the home. It wasn't their charge, but someone inside might notice the man missing, call out, and rouse the city guard. These Westmoorlanders were miners by trade, and though the invading soldiers were trained assassins, they had no desire to face a hundred angry villagers armed with pick-axes.

The warriors emerged from the home. Weapons glistened for a moment only, then were wiped clean and sheathed. Ten shadows crept away, leaving a silent home behind them.

Brayden Arum, the proprietor of the Hammer and Bow, West-moor's most popular tavern, had been up late mending the chairs and stools that his more energetic patrons had happily disfigured. His candle guttered in a silver dish by his workbench and went out altogether just as Brayden heard a strange sound. It reminded him of the faint patter his three cats made when they trotted across the floor. But this sound came from outside and was slightly louder and heavier than anything his cats could muster. And...whatever it was sounded like more than three.

Brayden glanced at the stairs leading up to the inn above the tavern. *Full up,* he thought with a grin. His wife and two young daughters had even given up their rooms for paying customers. The family slept on cots in the basement storeroom. He had a mind to join them, but something about those sounds...well, he wasn't sure.

Against his first instincts, Brayden navigated the maze of chairs, tables, and snugs and went to the soot-smeared window at the front of the tavern. It was chilly outside, and Brayden's breath fogged the glass. He rubbed it clear, but still couldn't see. No road. Not the Sovereign's Cottage across the road. Not even the city walls or the stars above. Just black. *What in the First One's name is—*

His thought froze on his lips. The black wall in front of the tavern window slid slowly away. Two more similar shadows passed in front of the window, and stealthy footfalls patted across the tavern's porch. Brayden fell back from the window, upset a stool, and barely caught it before it crashed to the floor. Brayden backed quickly away, his sweat chilling to icy droplets on his flesh.

Katya. He saw a flash of his wife's almond brown eyes as he hastened toward the back of the tavern. *Little Adeline and sweet Mari*—he had to get them out of the storeroom...had to get them to safety. Brayden had seen the invaders' dark cloaks, but that was not all. He'd seen the ragged furs draped on their dark armor. And he'd seen the glint of an iron pike.

Brayden's heart pounded as he ducked behind the wall of barrels in the back of the tavern. There'd been another sound. Something was clicking the latch on the tavern door.

Westmoor Sanctuary was built on the highest point of the town's geography so that all could see...so that all could find their way to the First One. Velach Krel wasn't seeking forgiveness, restoration, or health. Nonetheless, he was happy with the ease with which they were able to find Westmoor's sanctuary.

The moon turned the building's gray façade an eerie stoney blue. The rune for the First One, a broken half circle with a stem plunging down, was illuminated also, like a strange glowing key pressed into the stone and mortar. Velach had never understood the image—why would the followers of the First One use a severed half circle? It was incomplete. It was broken.

Darkness shrouded the rest of the edifice except for one arched window toward the rear that radiated golden-yellow light. A slender elm tree waved in the wind, shifting back and forth forlornly in the light. For such light to burn at this time of night was peculiar. It meant the clerics were busy.

And just what might you be doing? Velach smiled. He thought he might know.

He gestured to his team. Four knights split away from the group and stood like sentries at the sanctuary's massive doors. Velach led the remaining soldiers outside the reach of the window's light and up a narrow wrought-iron stairway that spiraled up to a small rear door. Velach waited a count of ten and nodded to his largest comrade.

Gundara Shorn slowly freed a long bludgeon from his backhanger. The head of the hammer-like weapon weighed an ingot more than eighty pounds. Gundara wheeled it around and slammed it into the door. The feeble hinges buckled and the door collapsed. Velach and his men poured in.

They ascended another flight of stairs and burst into the sanctuary's main hall. There they found seven startled clerics crowding protectively in front of an armor-clad youth.

"Who are they, Mi-Da?" Adeline pleaded, pressing her cheek into the side of her father's knee.

Mari bit her lower lip and hid under his waistcoat. They stood huddled together near their cots just ten feet from the storeroom ladder and the trapdoor above. An oil lantern hung on a post and cast weak orange light on their faces. Brayden had startled his family awake as he banged the trapdoor shut and dropped hard to the storeroom floor. Now they all listened to the footfalls on the creaking floor above their heads.

"Mi-Da?"

Brayden shushed Adeline and patted her curly hair. But his wife, Katya, the same question burning in her dark eyes, was not so easily assuaged.

"Gorracks," he finally whispered to her.

Katya grabbed his wrist. "Gorracks? In Westmoor? They haven't come this far south in an age."

"I know." Brayden gently pried her fingers from his wrist and drew her near as well. "They'll wreck the place, take casks of ale… whatever they can carry. But don't fret, they're not smart enough to find us down here." Inwardly, he wasn't truly convinced of his own comforting words.

Katya's eyes widened. "But Brayden…the patrons?"

"I…I had to choose," he said, a quiver in his voice. "If I had gone up to warn them in the inn…the Gorracks'd cut me off from you."

Katya cupped his stubbly chin in her hand. "You chose rightly, husband. But I fear for—"

Brayden held up a hand. "Listen!"

Adeline and Mari clutched his legs so hard it hurt.

The storeroom filled with the unmistakable sounds of booted feet moving furtively above. Brayden heard them climbing the inn's stairs. But something was wrong. There should have been more noise: the shatter of glass, the crack of wood being broken and splintered. There should have been scuffles, the ring of blades, shouts, and screams. But there was nothing…just footsteps, and silence.

"What—?" Katya started, but Brayden's expression cut her short.

"They don't move like Gorracks."

Katya looked at him questioningly, but before he could explain, the footsteps crept across the tavern floor and stopped near the trapdoor. In the dim light of the oil lantern, Brayden watched the trapdoor move slightly, a tentative first pull. The bolt-latch would hold but not for long. Brayden turned down the lantern's wick, and the room plunged into darkness.

"Mi-Da!" Adeline and Mira both squeaked.

"Quiet!" he whispered urgently. He pulled his daughters free from his leg and dragged them deeper into the storeroom.

Katya stumbled behind them. "Brayden?"

The trapdoor shuddered, rattling the latch. For a moment, narrow bands of dust-choked light rained down from the outline of the door above.

"They are coming," he said.

"Then," Katya said, her voice flat and hopeless, "we are trapped."

CHAPTER 8

WIND, BLOOD, AND SWORD

The village cries
out for the children.
But they are no more.
Tree-lined lanes where laughter
once rang out and sticks and hoops
once clattered…now vacant,
strewn with dead
leaves and echoes
of whispered fears.
And beneath
the leaves and
soil, the trees' roots grasp
and clutch, remembering
the taste of blood
all too well.
From *A Dark Witness* (vol. 3)
Talonette Sindelair, Grand Poet of the Wayfolk

10 CELESANDUR 2212

Three hundred miles from Westmoor—a hundred leagues as the Wayfolk reckon it—Shepherd Sebastian Sternbough sat in his study and felt an inexplicable terror.

The voices on the wind had spoken.

Nothing specific—the voices never were. Oft-times the wind brought glad tidings or tingles of excitement. But tonight the invisible fingers of air brought only chilling notions of dread, unsettling whispers, echoes of agony from the horizon. *Echoes?* Sebastian wondered. *Or foretellings?*

On a clear, moonlit night, Sebastian's seat in the highest chamber of the highest tower of Anglinore Castle provided an unsurpassed view—from the Naïthe; with its quilt of deep forests, misty valleys, and ever-swaying grasslands; all the way to the Gray Mountains of Ellador. But on this night, in spite of all his gifts, Sebastian felt virtually blind. *Something is happening,* he thought, peering desperately into the twilight sky from his window. *Something we will all come to regret.*

Sebastian shook his head. *I am High Shepherd of Anglinor, chief advisor to King Aravel and Queen Maren, the First Lord and Lady of Myriad. Next to Mosteryn the Old, leader of the Order of Shepherds, I am considered most wise...and yet, I still feel utterly helpless.*

"No," said Brayden, exhaling a breath he'd held so long it had burned his lungs. "We are not yet caught." The trapdoor shook harder this time. There came a hacking sound as a blade bit into the wood. "Come!"

In the pitch black void, Brayden led his family around a corner into the farthest recess of the storeroom. Katya heard her husband grunt and then the whump of something heavy hitting the floor. Several thuds later came the groan of a heavy door on old hinges.

"This way." Brayden's voice urged from the darkness. "Duck your head." He ushered the girls through.

But Katya stopped. "Brayden, what is this?"

Kerrack! The trapdoor sundered at last. Heavy boots fell upon the rungs of the ladder.

Brayden did not answer his wife. *I don't have time to confess all the lies,* he thought. *After all these years, how do I tell her I've secretly delved a tunnel to the cove so I could smuggle in casks of Witchdrale? How do I tell her I've put the whole family at risk, violating the village elders' statutes by selling the black brew to the Hammer's more questionable patrons?*

"Brayden?"

"Not now," he whispered back. "We've got to move."

There were footsteps on the storeroom floor. Harsh torchlight shone from the corner and illuminated the suspicion in his wife's eyes.

Brayden gently pressed her head down and pushed her into the passage. He slammed the door shut behind him and rammed two bolt locks home. Then he led Katya and the girls a few steps, turned, and released a lever recessed into the side of the passage. They heard the clink of chains and a sudden metallic clang as the five-foot portcullis dropped into place and locked. "That'll keep them," he whispered.

As he ushered his family down the tunnel, Brayden could feel the weight of his wife's trust pressing on his shoulders. But heavier still were the questions plaguing his mind. *Why would the Gorracks come to Westmoor? And since when are they so clever an' stealthy?*

Axe blades hacked into the tunnel's wooden outer door.

"We'll have an hour or more before they're through." Brayden hurried his cherished wife and two precious daughters into the unknown darkness.

The startled cleric who stood closest to the rear of the hall was swift to react. He raked his staff toward the Gorrack intruders—but found himself suddenly impaled on the long shaft of Velach's pike. The cleric dropped his staff, gaped, and fell to his knees.

As if wiping refuse from his boot, Velach kicked the cleric off the end of the pike. His men came forward. The six remaining priests readied their staffs and kept themselves between the invaders and the youth.

"Let me fight!" cried the lad. "My nuncle taught me how to deal with Gorrack-kind."

"Nay, Saren," said the cleric closest to the lad. "These aren't Gorracks. These are worse. Stay behind us."

As per their orders, Velach's men didn't utter a single word. Jabbing with their pikes and slashing with their jagged short swords, they drove into clerics. One by one, the assassins cut down the ministers of the First One. Blood pooled beneath the fallen clerics and began to spread across the sanctuary floor.

The youth called Saren had already drawn a sword and gave no hint that he might try to run. Instead, he brandished his weapon. When Velach approached, he found that the young knight could indeed fight.

Saren lashed out with a flurry of jabs and then slashed as he stepped backward. "Get back! Whoever you are…you will pay for this!"

Velach would not underestimate the youth or his weapon. Especially not this weapon. Saren wielded a rare and very expensive Wyrm Blade. Such swords were made to puncture dragon scales. They were crafted from blackseed iron, the hardest metal in Myriad. They were sharpened to a long, nearly unbreakable, razor-sharp point that could plunge deep into a dragon's innards…even reaching its leathery heart. Velach found his own pike scoured with notches and dents just from Saren's first series of attacks.

Velach would attack strategically. He lunged with a feint to Saren's side and spun a slash high at the youth's neck. But just as

Saren blocked Velach's lethal shot to the throat, Gundara Shorn came at him from the side and slammed his bludgeon into the young knight's chest plate.

Stunned and struggling for his next breath, Saren dropped his blade. Gundara struck again, this time sending Saren flying backward. He sprawled on the sanctuary floor and lay still.

Seeing the horrible way Saren's chest armor had collapsed, Gundara didn't bother with another stroke. He turned and picked up a piece of wolf pelt and turned to Velach. "This yours?"

"Yes, but leave it. Leave yours as well." Velach reached down for the Wyrm Blade. "I will, however, take this as a souvenir."

Velach and his men searched every room and every chamber in the sanctuary. Once they were sure there was no one left alive, they systematically wrecked the interior: shattering windows, splintering benches, shredding tapestries, and smashing such relics and sacred things as they could find. If there was any skill or knowledge the Gorracks possessed, it was how to destroy.

Just before dawn, five of the six teams under Velach Krel's command met in the center of the village. Many were nicked or wounded, but only one team had lost men. They carried their two fallen comrades and laid them on the road at his commander's feet.

"What happened?" Velach asked, for Grahl Zander was a capable lieutenant. In more than a hundred raids or assassinations, he had never lost a man.

Grahl shook his head. "An early riser...militiaman. Came at us from a darkened barn. He swung a wicked axe."

Velach looked at the bodies, each scoured with deep glistening gashes. "So I see," Velach muttered. "What became of this militiaman?"

"I strung his entrails from one end of the barn to the other."

Velach nodded. He noted that the dead men were missing their helms, but Grahl had them. They dangled from a hook on his belt. Velach nodded again. He scanned his men. One team was missing. "Where is Sarius?"

No one knew. "They were to take the eastern quarter," Grahl said. "The cottages by the city wall—and the tavern."

"Perhaps they're sampling some of Westmoor's best vintages," suggested one of the men. No one laughed.

"If they are," Velach said, "then I will personally drown them one by one in a vat of Witchdrale."

As if hoping to avoid such speculation, Sarius Wrethmander and his three men arrived, trotting rapidly up the road to the rally point. Sarius dragged a large cloth sack behind him.

"You are late," Krel said.

"Following a rabbit trail," Sarius replied with no apology. "You said to make sure."

"And did you?"

"The tavern had a passage delved, leading from his basement stores to a cove beyond the walls."

"Outside of the city?" Velach barked. "Someone could have—"

"No one escaped," Sarius said. "We followed the tunnel, searched the cove for sign. There was none. They all died in their beds at the tavern." Sarius did not mention the worrisome traces he'd noticed inside the storeroom: the sacks of grain recklessly cast aside, the doors locked from the inside. *If someone got out, so be it. What would they tell?*

Krel scanned the faces of those who had returned. "What happened to Bachall?" He pointed to the sack.

"Witchdrale merchant in the inn had a dagger," Sarius said. "Bachall should'a been payin' attention."

Velach's gaze lingered on Sarius uncomfortably for a few moments.

Don't look in the bag. Don't look in the bag, thought Sarius. If Velach looked, he's see the body without a helm. He'd ask about it, maybe make him go all the way back to search for it in that cursed tunnel.

Velach snorted and pointed to the city gates. "First light will bring travelers, tradesmen. I won't risk anyone discovering us or our horses. We've a three-day ride to Stonecrest and much cover to find along the way."

"We travel by shadow, eh?" Gundara Shorn said with a wink.

"Always." Velach turned to Grahl and Sarius and gestured at the bodies. "You've got extra baggage. Try to keep up."

Any who would venture into Westmoor in the coming days would find wind whispering down empty streets and the darkened windows staring out from vacant homes.

CHAPTER 9

The Cold Blade Unsheathed

*On this day, Atervast the 42nd of the year 2202, be it known
to the Way Children of Llanfair and all who follow the Ways of
the First One by the wisdom of the hallowed Prydian Branch: It
is hereby decided that Witchdrale, and all brews fermented from
witchroot, shall not be consumed any longer. Such draughts are
forbidden.*

*The fruit of this vine is a blight over all the realm of Myriad and
a very great danger to our families and livelihood. The purchase or
sale, trafficking or trade shall not be suffered within our borders or in
any law-abiding nations.*

The Prydian Charter, King Ealden Everbrand

17 CELESANDUR 2212

Horses thundered over a winding path in the forest a few miles
from Thel-Mizaret. On the first horse, a white country mare
with surprising speed, rode a young woman. She held the reins
in one hand and protectively nestled a bundle to her chest with
the other.

Behind her, closing fast, were six huge warhorses. Upon them rode knights wearing dark armor, matted furs, and horrible mask-like helms. They dug their spurs harshly into the flanks of the horses and yelled for the woman to stop.

But she did not heed them. She raced on.

Her pursuers closed the distance until one of the knights leveled a crossbow and fired. The dart slammed into the woman's shoulder.

She screamed and lurched forward in the saddle. Her white mare seemed to sense the urgency of the wound and sped forward, for the moment leaving the pursuing knights behind.

Alastair banged his fist upon the counter in the little woodland pub. "Mawer Witchdrale, now!"

The burly barkeep appeared instantly. "Go easy on the Witchdrale," he said. "Too much of that dark fruit, and it'll own your soul. So they say."

Alastair slid a couple of gold coins to the man. "I've not yet 'ad my fill. Gem'me another bottle."

The other man looked at the gold and, shaking his head, did as he was told. Alastair stumbled back to his table and filled his tankard. He took a long drink and winced. It burned going down. *Maybe it will take my soul. Might as well...all it's good for.*

He shook his head, stared into the black liquid, and began to mutter. "Ten years of my life...searchin', studyin', and waitin'— for what? That's right, nothing!"

Two men at another table stared at Alastair. He cast a suspicious eye at them. "You want t'know wot I was waitin' for?"

The two men shook their heads vigorously. "Nossir, we just came for a wee drink and—"

"I was waitin' for the Halfainin," Alastair blurted out. "A mighty hero who's comin' to save the world! First One's sendin' him. Do you believe that, lads?"

The older of the two men said, "Nay, we don't go in for old myths round 'ere."

"Good!" Alastair shouted. He banged his tankard down. "'Cause that's all it is…a myth. I waited, I waited so long." He took another long drink. "Funny thing, though. The sword did appear in the stars. Did you see it a few weeks back?"

"Look, mister, we don't need to hear this. Why don't—"

Alastair leaped up from his chair and glared at the two men. "*Did you see it?*"

"N-n-nossir."

"Well, I did." Alastair swayed a bit. "No question about it… the sword was up there." He raised his tankard almost to the ceiling. "Turns out…it…meant…*nothing!*" In a blur, he hurled his mug at the wall, spraying pieces of hardened clay in every direction.

"Here now, sir!" the barkeep cried out. "Beggin' yer pardon, but there'll be none a' that here. You take your bottle and go on home!"

"S'allright," Alastair said. "I was just leaving." He grabbed the bottle and staggered out of the pub.

The late afternoon sun lit the clearing around the tavern and sliced into the surrounding trees. Alastair held his arm up to shield his eyes. Even so, his head throbbed as if Gorracks were taking turns hammering great bells in his mind. He had no idea how long he had been in the tavern. It seemed like forever.

He turned a blurry circle. There were three paths into the woods ahead of him and for a moment he didn't remember which one led back to his home.

The pounding in his head was suddenly much louder than it should have been. A white horse thundered into the clearing. It charged up to Alastair and gave him such a start that he threw the Witchdrale into the woods. "Watch where you're rid—"

A woman swayed in the saddle of the white mare, and the garments on her shoulder were soaked with blood. Alastair heard a strange, high-pitched cry that didn't seem like it came from the woman, but he couldn't be sure.

The woman leaned, almost fell, forward and stared weakly at Alastair. "Please, sir, help me."

"M'lady what has happened?" he said, wishing he had stayed in the pub.

"Beasts coming," she whispered, and then she leaned forward and handed a cloth-wrapped bundle to Alastair. "Please, save him, kind sir."

Alastair stumbled backward a step and blinked down at the bundle.

"Hold right there!" a deep voice bellowed from the woods. Heavily armored soldiers on dark horses stormed into the clearing. The woman on the mare spurred her horse and rode away down one of the paths. Two of the warriors sped after her.

Alastair staggered out in front of the others and held up a hand to ward off the collision. The horses slid to a noisy stop a few feet from Alastair.

"Here, now!" Alastair cried out. "You could have ridden me down!" He took several steps toward the riders, but stopped when he saw them. *Gorracks?* Alastair squinted at them, scrutinizing them.

"Be off, drunkard," one of the warriors said. "We have no quarrel with you."

"Drunkard I may be," said Alastair, looking them up and down. "But even with my blurred eyes, I can see you aren't Gorracks. What are you playing at? And why are you chasing that poor woman? She's grievous hurt."

The lead warrior gestured, and the other three horsemen rode forward, nearly surrounding Alastair. The warrior lifted the monstrous face guard on his helm, revealing sharp green eyes and a golden moustache and beard. "She is an enemy of King Morlan," said the man. "And now, so are you."

"Her?" Alastair laughed. "Morlan afraid of unarmed womenfolk now, is he?"

"You've earned your death already," said the warrior as he drew his sword.

"You had better put that piece of metal back in its place," Alastair said. "Do it now, or you won't leave this glade unless it be in the back of a caretaker's cart."

Something in the bundle squealed. Alastair had almost forgotten he was holding it. He looked questioningly down and then back to the threats around him. One of the other men pointed.

The soldier with the golden beard scowled, and fury darkened his brow. He made to strike, but one of his companions said, "Captain, wait! Do you know who this man is? He's the Iceman."

The other knights gasped, but the knight with the golden beard glared at Alastair and grinned. "Alastair Coldhollow?" he said. "This is what you've amounted to? A sot? A witchdrale-swilling fool? I don't care who you were. Give us what you hold in your hand!"

Alastair wasn't sure what was in the bundle. He didn't really want it when the woman handed it to him, but now, now that he had been provoked, he was ready to kill for it.

Suddenly, from somewhere deep in the forest, there came the piercing scream of a woman. It was cut short abruptly, and the woods filled with an eeric quiet. Alastair knew the other knights had ridden the poor woman down, and anger kindled in his heart.

"King Morlan would give any of us thirty kingsgold if we bring the Iceman back to the castle," the captain of the knights said. "Fifty if he's dead."

Just then the other two warriors came trotting up behind Alastair and closed off any hope of retreat. "What have we here?" one of them asked.

"I'll tell you what we have," said the captain. "We have enough kingsgold to feed us good beef for a year!" Suddenly, he leaped from his horse and slashed his sword at Alastair's neck.

But Alastair had moved aside and drawn his own weapon. Its blade glinted blue as Alastair whipped a blurred double slash across his attacker. The knight with the golden beard was dead before he slammed into the ground at Alastair's feet.

The other knights attacked together, using their horses and their blades as weapons against Alastair. Enemy swords thrust, hacked, and slashed, but Alastair wove in and out of the barrage like a sleek fish confounding the grasping fingers of clumsy children. In less than ten seconds, Alastair slew them all—and he did it one-handed.

He sheathed his cold blade and finally unwrapped the bundle to see what was inside. As he peeled back the cloth, there appeared a small round face with gigantic blue eyes.

A child? Alastair's thoughts raced. He glanced back at the pub. Then he looked at the openings to the three paths, and suddenly he remembered which one led home.

CHAPTER 10

ASSASSIN'S DREAMS

*The difference in their uncanny eyes could not easily be discerned.
For in the rays of the setting sun, both Aravel and Morlan's eyes
appeared gold, while in the pale light of the moon their eyes gleamed
yellow. Such inscrutable likeness is the way of things with identical
twins. But all who knew the two brothers well came to recognize an
unmistakable difference, a peculiarity felt rather than seen. For those
who stood before King Aravel's gaze felt the glad firelight of a banquet hall or the warmth of the sun on bare flesh. But those who fell
under Morlan's stare felt the frosty gleam of winter moonlight on jagged steel or the cold, white stone monuments in a bone yard.*
　　　Testimonies of Ezekiel Trinnet, Royal Barde, 2092 AS

"No, I have not changed my mind," the King said from his high,
black marble throne. He stroked the hackles of the wolf pup in
his lap and stared down at his military captain, who waited on
one knee at the bottom of the stairs. "Snuff out the life's breath of
every man, woman, and child."

"But King Morlan," said the captain, "Bryngate's folk—"

"Alastair," the King of Vulmarrow said in a voice that was
quiet and yet stern. "Since when does my dependable Iceman balk
at orders to kill?"

"If they remain your orders, Sire," Alastair replied as he stood, "then I will not hesitate. But after the slaughter at Avington, the peasantry will not rise up again. They have learned their lesson. These peasants can no more mount a rebellion with spades and pitchforks than I can spear a fish with a potato!"

The wolf pup growled. "Easy, Sköll," said the king. "We must always think before we react." He eased back in his seat and dwelt in pensive silence for a few moments. His piercing, golden-yellow eyes—wolf's eyes—weighed upon a man like a parching desert sun. Just a few moments of that menacing gaze was often enough to leave an enemy as limp as a boned fish. The king focused those terrible eyes now on Alastair. "Just let them be, eh? The peasants have had enough? Alastair, do you know the hope that those fools cling to in their so-called faith?"

"Nay, m'lord," Alastair replied. "I try not to entertain such foolish notions."

"Foolish? Yes. But make no mistake, Alastair, they are sincere. They look to stars for a sign that the Halfainin will arise. And this champion's only purpose is to lead a rebellion so complete and so final that all nations will be enslaved to the myth of the First One. They speak peace but prepare to conquer. And you know where it will start, don't you? My throne, Alastair"—this he whispered, but the bitterness within each word hit Alastair like a smack in the face. "No, these people need clarity. They must be taught that if there is to be only one king of this world, it will be me."

"Your brother might have something to say about that," muttered Alastair. He respected Morlan's power, but did not fear him.

"*Aravel?*" Morlan stood up so fast that Sköll leaped to the black stone table. "My brother is Overlord of Myriad by…by wretched fate. Eighteen seconds! But for those heartbeats, I would sit in Anglinore Castle."

Alastair knew his words had been rash. It was best not to antagonize a man who could, with the snap of his fingers, have your innards decorating the Bone Chapel. "Forgive me, Sire, I misspoke," he said. "But another slaughter in the realm of Fen could force Aravel and the armies of Anglinore to investigate."

"Aravel is as weak as he is naïve. He knew all about the massacre in Avington, and what did he do? He came to me. 'Brother Morlan, word has reached my ears that a tragedy has befallen the realm of Fen. Look into it for me, would you?' Fool. He wastes his position and allows his enemies to muster."

"All too true, my lord," Alastair said. "And yet the peoples of this realm remember Aravel's victories in the Battle of the Verdant Mountains and the Wyrm Wars."

"Not *all* the peoples remember so fondly. Many besides me chafe at his decisions and wilting backbone. Many have come to me in secret urging me to do something about the Gorrack threat since Aravel will not. Myriad is a wondrous land, wondrous but wild beyond reckoning. It deserves a king with the strength to tame it...for the everlasting good of all."

With Sköll trotting at his heals, the king went to a tall cabinet, one of many behind his throne, and pulled out a long wooden staff. The wolf pup growled and leaped at this strange new object. "Take this!" Morlan threw it down.

Alastair caught it in one hand but immediately recoiled at the acrid smell. "What is this?" Alastair asked, holding the staff at arm's length.

"A new device of Cythraul's," the king replied. "Always coming up with new tools, that one. He calls it a wolf's head."

Alastair knew more than he wished to know about Cythraul and his tools, but this was new. He kept the staff at arm's length but looked at it closely. It was sharp like a stake at one end and as long as Alastair was tall. The other end was covered with a burlap sack and tied off. It seemed roughly shield-shaped.

"When they are all dead," the king said, "stab this deep into the earth and remove the covering. Cythraul has soaked the head of the staff with some concoction he claims will draw blackwolves from miles around and whip them into a frenzy. As you can see from Sköll's reaction, it seems to work. You know how territorial blackwolves are. No one will live in the village of Bryngate for years to come."

Alastair and his mounted knights, the best of King Morlan's Wolfguard, waited on a hilltop far above the sleeping town of Bryngate. They wore dark anonymous armor, and every soldier carried a flaming brand.

"Are we really going to kill them all?" asked Sir Grannick, who had only just risen to the rank of Wolfguard Knight.

Mar Falred rode forward to be even with the newest addition to the guard. Mar, a grizzled warrior whose blank expression belied untold horrors seen in his many years of combat, said, "If we don't, then someone knows what we done. Word might reach High King Aravel, and then it'd all be up."

"Surely not the children—" Grannick argued, but he was cut short when his commander, Alastair Coldhollow, rode up beside him.

Alastair turned and said not a word, but his pale blue eyes were as cold as winter stone. He pulled down the mask of his helmet, spurred his horse, and flew down the hill.

Sir Grannick swallowed, and he and the rest of the soldiers rocketed after their commander. The storm broke upon the village of Bryngate with no warning. Torches arced high in the night sky and fell like a hail of deadly comets onto the roofs of the villagers' roofs. Made of thatch and rope, the huts burst into flame. Fire raced from rooftop to rooftop, and choking, dark smoke filled the air.

Terrified peasants, awakened by thunderous horses or sudden harsh orange light ran screaming from their homes—right into the blades of the waiting Wolfguard. Swords and axes flashed, and dozens of villagers went down. Blood pooled darkly on the dirt roads.

Many of the unmarried women of Bryngate lived in the huts near the woods close to a stream where they would gather water or wash clothing. Awakened by the carnage, they tried to escape under cover of darkness, but Wolfsbane's crossbow archers did not let them escape. Poisoned darts filled the air like a swarm of bees. The peasants had no chance. They all fell and lay still just a few steps from the trees.

Suddenly, a war-horn rang out, and a group of about two dozen peasants burst through the gate of their stables. Each one was armed with a crude, jagged sword or a notched axe. They came unexpectedly upon a small cluster of Wolfguard. Their blades met with clashes and clangs. At last, the Bryngate defenders overpowered their invaders and turned their steeds to look for more.

"So, they do have weapons!" Alastair said aloud to himself. Besides flinging his torch onto the roof of a small house, he had not to this point shed even a drop of the peasants' blood. He had simply watched the spectacle from the saddle of his massive black warhorse. But now he saw a a bit of a challenge. He stabbed the Wolf's head hard into the ground and charged into the battle.

It was dizzying to most knights: a hundred fires burning and spreading, arrows and darts streaking from all directions, horses galloping between the huts, trampling the unaware...smashes, thuds, screams, smacks, and horns! But for Alastair, everything slowed down and he could see clearly the path he should take and his best angle of attack.

Battle seemed to be an elaborate dance to the Iceman. He drove his immense horse into the mounted peasants, and many tumbled to the ground and were ridden over. The others tried to raise their crude swords against Alastair, but he was too swift and too skilled. In one swipe of his long, cold blade, he knocked the swords out of three of the peasants' hands. They turned their steeds to flee, but Alastair rode them down and slashed them from their saddles.

Alastair led his rank of Wolfguard and cut through Bryngate with little further resistance. But one of the peasants had defied the icy finger of death. This one man deftly avoided Alastair's attacks, each time riding just out of reach. Then he rode behind a burning cottage and seemed to disappear. Alastair wheeled his horse around and watched the rooftops, lest this man leap down on him from above. But the peasant knew the alleys of Bryngate far better than Alastair did. He spurred his horse from an unseen avenue and drove at Alastair.

Even so, Alastair was not wholly caught unaware. And such was Alastair's tremendous hand speed that he was able to flick out a weak but well-aimed attack. His peasant enemy blocked the swipe easily and countered with a blow so heavy it made Alastair's right arm tingle. This peasant combatant rode with great skill, high in the saddle, and faced the Iceman defiantly. In this moment, Alastair thought he recognized the other man.

Large, dark eyes shadowed beneath a protruding brow. An unruly shock of straw-colored hair and a long brown beard— Alastair felt certain he'd met this warrior before. This peasant raised his sword so that the blade divided his face and the cross-guard spread like a mantle beneath his eyes. The man's gauntleted fist was massive...as big as a gourd.

"Rhys?" the Iceman asked, growing more certain of the man's identity. He had been one of the Wolfguard. Alastair had ridden with him on several missions years earlier. But Rhys had disappeared in a skirmish with Gorracks on the border of the Felhaunt. Everyone had assumed he had perished.

Aparently not, thought Alastair. *Not yet.* But before Alastair could aim another stroke, the gourd-fisted peasant slammed his blade against Alastair's shoulder. The armor deflected the blow, but Alastair nearly fell.

"You cold, murderous devil!" the peasant yelled. "You seek to destroy what you do not understand!"

"*Rhys?*" the Iceman called. "Rhys Vanador?"

"That was my name," he replied. "But I no longer serve Morlan Stormgarden, Wolfking of Vulmarrow. I no longer serve myself."

Rhys glanced sideways. His defiant expression dissolved into a mask of fear. He slashed awkwardly at Alastair and then raced to one of the small homes across the way. One of the Wolfguard knights was setting fire to the building. Rhys came up fast, his sword already halfway through its arc, and hacked the knight's neck. The soldier fell like a tree. But Alastair swooped in right behind his former comrade. Rhys turned, fended off several of the Iceman's lightning quick attacks. Then he slashed at the belt that held Alastair's saddle in place upon the warhorse. The saddle began to slide, and Alastair with it.

Alastair leaped off just in time. He hacked at the knees of his opponent's horse, and the creature buckled. Rhys too leaped off in time.

He stood in front of the dark open doorway of the crude cottage as if he was guarding it. And then, Alastair saw why. A woman stood back in the shadows, and she carried a baby in her arms—a baby and a thick book.

"Stay away, Coldhollow!" Rhys yelled, but his voice was high and desperate. "Please...don't!"

Alastair rocked back on his heels, and lowered his blade. Rhys had always been a proud man, a capable warrior—utterly fearless. But not now. Now Alastair could see the whites of the man's eyes. Sweat streaked down Rhys' face. He trembled as a potent combination of fear and rage mastered him. Suddenly, he charged Alastair.

"No!" Alastair cried out. But Rhys was too far gone. His blade glanced off Alastair's late block and drove hard into Alastair's shoulder. It was excruciatingly painful but far from a lethal blow.

The Iceman's battle-honed instincts took over. Alastair rolled his shoulder and turned, detaching himself from Rhys' impaling weapon. Still rotating, Alastair flicked his wrist and slashed his blade across Rhys's sword hand. Before Rhys could even drop his weapon and cry out, Alastair finished his spin and drove his heavy sword into Rhys' chest.

Alastair, confused and still angry, withdrew his blade and staggered backward.

Rhys dropped, wide-eyed, to his knees, turned to the woman, and exhaled her name, "Yasmina…" And then he collapsed.

The woman in the hut shrieked and went to her fallen husband.

But Alastair came forward and raised his blade.

The woman placed the baby in a sling on her chest. She held up the thick book, but not as a shield. "Please, Sir Knight," she screamed. "It is not too late! The First One will show you forgiveness! Turn now. Heed the prophecy!"

Alastair gaped. *I have just slain this woman's husband, and yet she speaks of forgiveness? She should be cursing me right now. Nay, she should be running away.*

Alastair brought his sword crashing down upon the book. So sharp was his blade that the book was cloven in two. In a scattering of half-pages, the pieces dropped to the ground. The woman Rhys had called Yasmina grasped her child in both arms and backed slowly into the small home.

Alastair followed. They disappeared into the inky darkness of the smoldering building. And suddenly, a child screamed…

a child screamed…

a child screamed…

19 CELESANDUR 2212

A child screamed somewhere in Alastair's home. Alastair fell awkwardly out of his bed and stumbled across several dark bottles that lay on the floor.

Why do I hear a child? Alastair raced here and there searching for the source of the noise. Finally, he shook the sleep from his mind, and he remembered.

He ran up the stairs to his kitchen and found the child lying in a breadbasket and wrapped in the same blankets he'd been in when the woman—the child's mother?—had handed him over to Alastair two days earlier. The child's face was as red as a Stonecrest tulip and his cries sounded angry and hoarse, as if he might have been crying for a long time.

Not knowing what else to do, Alastair picked up the child and shouted at him. "Stop that infernal noise!"

And the baby did stop crying. He looked at Alastair and let out a strange gurgling laugh.

Then Alastair smelled something awful. "By the Stars!" Alastair put the child on the kitchen table. "Oh, that is horrible." He looked around the kitchen. *What do I do?* Then he saw an old rag he'd been using to wipe dishes. "Well, I cannot leave you sitting in that filth!"

Alastair carefully opened up the blankets and peeled off the child's cloth diaper. The sight of the diaper's contents, combined with the rancid stench, almost made Alastair ill. Still, he took the rag and did his best to clean the baby.

"Well, at least it's a boy."

And suddenly, something sprayed up from the child and hit Alastair in the eye. "Ah, you hideous creature! What have you done to me?"

The baby just stared up at Alastair and giggled. Soon, Alastair was giggling also. Laughing like he hadn't laughed in many years.

THE WHITE ROOM

All men are full of holes that cannot be filled
by clutching, grasping, or taking.
Myridian Proverb

24 CELESANDUR 2212

Stepping over empty black bottles—or, when less patient, kicking them—Alastair Coldhollow paced across his den. "What am I to do with a baby?" He cast a glance at the child, asleep now in a nest of rags upon a chair. "Whatever possessed me to accept him from that woman? None of my business!"

But in a corner of his mind as cluttered and dank as the cellar of his keep, he knew why he'd taken the child. He knew why he'd fought and killed King Morlan's knights. Spite. It was pure spite. He had been furious that Morlan's knights were harassing a woman and a child. He'd been outraged when they dared to threaten Alastair Coldhollow.

The child snorted. His eyelids fluttered, but still he slept. "What did Morlan's guards want with your mother and you?" Alastair wondered aloud. "I cannot imagine you are the criminal type."

Alastair scratched the stubble on his chin, turned to leave the room, and stopped short. He felt the most unusual sensation of curiosity. It was like a door had opened in a dark room, but no one entered. Then Alastair realized there was another reason why he had fought off those guards. *The Books.*

Long had he studied them in the years after he deserted Morlan's secret army of assassins. And the Books had taught him much. They had changed him, really—awakening feelings he had not known since he was a small child.

Come back to the Books, Alastair. There is a place for you at the table here.

"What did the Books do?" he asked the empty room. "Took years from my life, that's what. Had me searching all over the kingdom for someone who doesn't even exist!"

You saw the Blood-red Moon. You saw the Sword in the Stars. You are the Man of Ice, Alastair.

"Ahrgh!" Alastair yelled, kicking a bottle so hard it crashed into the wall and shattered. The baby awoke and began to cry. "A pox on the Books!" Alastair roared, glaring at the baby, whose tiny fists were shaking. "A pox on the Man of Ice! None of it is real."

Alastair sat down on the bed and put the swaddled baby into his lap. He immediately stopped crying, but his eyes were still needy. "Child," Alastair said, brushing a wispy lock of brown hair on the baby's head, "I have nothing to give you." The baby's eyes brightened and followed the movement of Alastair's fingers. Then, to Alastair's complete surprise, the baby reached up and grabbed the end of Alastair's pinky.

"Strong grip, lad!" Alastair freed his finger from the child and waved it around in front of the child's face. Alastair laughed. The child caught his finger again and again.

"A fine swordsman you would make!" he said, but inwardly, he doubted the child would live much past infancy. Sickness, famine, accidents, and even predators waited for all those born into this time. Even in the chief cities of the kingdom, the survival rate of children was little better than six in ten. And that was with loving parents who knew how to raise a child. It was even worse in small villages and isolated cottages like his.

Alastair shook his head and sighed. *What chance does this child have with a friendless, washed-up swordsman?*

The baby boy grabbed Alastair's finger again and cooed. Alastair knew he had to do something for the baby. But what? He scoured his brain for some memory that might help. He had precious few memories of his parents. There were none of his father, who had ridden off on an errand for Morlan's predecessor in Vulmarrow, King Mendeleev, when Alastair was just two years into life. Alastair's father had never returned.

His mother had not lived many years after that, and Alastair shook away the memory of her fate. He chose instead to dwell on the one vivid memory of his mother that he would permit himself to remember. The White Room. Well, that was what he called it. It was the corner room of his mother's cottage. Alastair had always loved coming into that room, but he remembered one day in particular.

Alastair couldn't have been more than five or six at the time, and he was hot and sweaty from lugging kettles of water up from the well. He had not finished his chores, but wanted a break—more than anything, he wanted to check on his mother. He carefully turned the glass knob of the dark maple door. He knew his mother loved him, but he also knew she would tan his hide for leaving chores undone. Having to raise Alastair alone, she had toughened by necessity.

Slowly, little Alastair pushed the door inward. White light spilled out into the shadowy hall and he felt the familiar cool breeze. The cottage was nestled on a sparsely wooded hill that overlooked a deep grassy valley on the eastern border of Fen. Even in the hottest weather, a cool, life-giving breeze swept up the hill and into the two windows of the White Room.

Alastair peered in, saw the white drapes billowing in the wind, the sunlight glittering on the bright stone floor, and then, his mother's bed. She lay still, with a lacy white sheet pulled up to her chin. Her chest rose and fell slowly, and Alastair could not help but stare. He'd always thought his mother was the most beautiful woman in the kingdom—especially when he saw her sleeping. Like a Wayfolk queen she looked, with thin arched brows and lush, dark lashes.

She stirred. Her eyes fluttered open. "Alastair," she said weakly, and he thought she would scold him.

"I'm sorry, Mum," he said. "It's just that I'm so tired from the kettles."

But to Alastair's great amazement, she did not rebuke him. "Come here, my young champion."

He came close to the bed and looked at the pristine white sheets. "But, Mum," he said, "I haven't washed yet. I'll dirty the sheets."

"We'll wash the sheets later," she replied, pulling Alastair into the bed and holding him close.

He looked over her shoulder at the sunlight on the white stone of the window sill and the gently billowing curtains. He felt his mother's warmth and wondered for the first time if that might be a little of what Allhaven might be like.

That was Alastair's last peaceful moment with his mother... the last moment of true peace in all of his life since then.

He looked down at the tiny boy in his lap. The child looked back, again with those wide, needy, eyes. And then, feeling very awkward and uncertain, Alastair picked up the child and hugged him to his shoulder. In just a few moments, the baby was asleep.

Alastair gently lay the child on his bed and sighed. In spite of his success comforting the child, he knew the care of a baby was beyond his skill. What would he even feed him? Goat's milk? Oatmeal porridge? Smoked staghorn jerky? No, keeping the child was out of the question, that much he knew. But who would—

It came to him. There was someone who might…if he pulled the right strings. *Yes,* Alastair thought, *she would do it.* That settled it. Alastair would take the child to the small village of Edenmill. And if all went well, he knew an establishment there that had a goodly supply of Witchdrale, for the right price. Alastair jangled his coin pouch and let the sound of gold push any thought of his mother, any thought of the Books, far from his mind's reach.

CHAPTER 12

A WICKED PROPOSAL

You've no doubt heard of the Thistle and Owl.
It's the very best inn by cheek and jowl.
Everyone there will know your name,
Or if you like, forget you just the same.
You can come in winter, spring, or fall.
You can bang your head against the wall.
But summer's when the time is right
For singin' and dancin' through the night
While the moon is high and glowing bright
The Thistle is a merry old sight.
Author Unknown
(though every Thistle and Owl tavern
keeper claims to have written it)

25 CELESANDUR 2212

Alastair found a sturdy leather satchel that he slung over his neck and shoulder. He placed the still-sleeping child in the satchel and mounted his horse. The first few trots were tense, for Alastair could not imagine having to endure a crying child all the way to

Edenmill. When the baby did not awaken, Alastair risked a faster pace. Soon, he had his horse at a full gallop, and still the child slumbered.

The forest paths went by in a blur as Alastair's mind wandered. He thought of Abbagael Rivynfleur living with her uncle in the village of Edenmill. Twenty-three, maybe twenty-four, but just a girl, really. She had been smitten with Alastair ever since he'd first come to Edenmill seven years earlier in search of a blacksmith who could mend a notch in his extraordinary blade. She was pretty. Emerald green eyes, a sprinkling of freckles on her nose and cheekbones, and coppery red hair that bounced as she walked. Very pretty and very interested in Alastair.

But Alastair had rebuffed her from the beginning…or at least from the very moment he'd discovered her history. Abbagael had been born in the small township of Umber, west of Vulmarrow and unfortunately close enough for Morlan to notice. A thriving sanctuary and a few hundred faithful followers of the First One were deemed a very present threat, especially since they refused to pay tribute to Morlan. The Lord of Vulmarrow gave an order, and Umber was completely destroyed. Abbagael had survived only because she had gone to stay with her uncle by the lake.

Alastair had not been among the knights on that raid. Had the order come on another night, he would have. He knew he could never explain that he had served King Morlan and led many raids like the slaughter that took the lives of Abbagael's parents.

In spite of Alastair's clear refusals, Abbagael seemed to seek him out whenever he came to Edenmill. Alastair thought he could perhaps still leverage her feelings. He felt guilty for that, but the child needed a mother—not some half-wit sot who could barely manage his own affairs. A sudden knot in his stomach threatened to lead Alastair into a closer look at his motives, but he expertly cleared his mind. He rode on for many hours in mental silence.

At last, he saw the timber arch that was the Edenmill gate. The sun was already well into its evening descent, and the villagers were closing up stands and shops for the day.

Alastair went to Abbagael's cottage first, but her Uncle Jak hadn't seen her for hours. He'd said, "If'n ye see 'er, tell her to git home fer supper!"

Alastair searched everywhere he remembered ever seeing Abbagael, but could not find her. Eventually, he rode up to the leaning fence of a building he knew all too well. For a time the Thistle and Owl had been a sort of second home to Alastair.

Alastair clambered carefully down from the horse. To his amazement, the child still slept. He tied off the horse and looked up at the Thistle, as it was called by the locals. Its dreary façade was all weathered gray stones, oddly shaped and somehow cobbled together to form a wall. Dark stains trailed down from the seams, as if the whole building had wept black tears. A thin, cracked wooden doorframe led up to a placard whose image was so faded it was barely discernable. But Alastair remembered it from when it had been newly painted: a scowling owl clutching a thorny thistle stem.

Alastair didn't really want to take the child into such an establishment, but the Thistle was the only place he felt sure someone would be willing to help...one way or another.

Alastair winced at the smell as soon as he passed through the doors. It was a rancid, biting scent—one he had, over time, learned to endure, but he'd never gotten used to it. And he certainly didn't want the baby exposed to the stench for very long.

Fortunately, Alastair did not need to remain inside long at all. For a piece of kingsgold, the keeper had told him that he might find Abbagael by the small fountain past the stables on the other side of the village.

And that was precisely where Alastair found her. Abbagael sat on the edge of the fountain and seemed to be weaving something out of silver thread. A last bit of late sun kindled the hair on one side, and she smiled. *Rivynfleur*, he thought. *River flower, an apt name.*

She glanced sideways and saw Alastair but pretended not to notice. He walked up so that his shadow fell upon her. "You're in my light," she said crossly. But then she looked up, beaming. "Hello, Alastair." She drew out the syllables in his name and stood to meet him.

"Greetings, Lady Abbagael. I am happy to have found you."

"Why, Alastair, I think that is about the nicest thing you have ever said to me." She grinned up at him and her green eyes were keen with interest.

Alastair had to turn his head. He could not look her in the eyes and do what he was about to do. "Lady Abbagael," he began, "I have had a terrible quandary thrust upon me. And well, I…uh, well, just look here, would you?"

Alastair opened the satchel and showed her the sleeping child. He told her the story of how the child came into his hands and how at a loss he was as to how to care for him. "And so, you see," Alastair said, "I could think of no one I would trust to care for the babe…no one, but you."

"Me?" Abbagael exclaimed, clearly flattered. But then she eyed him more shrewdly. "I see what you're about, Alastair Cold-hollow. What you really mean is that I am the only woman you might be able to trick into taking the child off your hands. Sorry to disappoint you."

"But I have no means for caring for a child!" Alastair pleaded. "I have nothing but branmeal to feed him, and I often have to journey far from home."

"I'll sell you a couple of my uncle's goats," she replied, "so you'll have a steady supply of goat's milk. And as for your travels…I might be persuaded, from time to time, to care for the child until you return. But other than that, Alastair…you're on your own."

Alastair felt his plan crumbling beneath him like a bridge of sand. "But Abbagael, I have no crib...my home is dank, unclean, and the forest is unsafe."

Abbagael looked down on the child and brushed away a lock of his wispy hair. Alastair thought for a moment that she might be coming around. "Sweet child," she said.

"So you'll take him then?"

"I meant you," Abbagael quipped. "You're so cute when you beg."

"But—"

"But caring for a child is a big responsibility...you'll need lots of supplies." She jangled the coin pouch on his belt. "Good... we'll go to the market in the morning."

"In the morning?" Alastair's mouth dried up in an instant.

"You can stay at my uncle's. He'll no doubt have supper hot."

"No doubt," Alastair muttered.

"We have a cot in the den where you and the baby—what did you say his name was?"

"Name?" Alastair's eyebrows rose comically. "Why...she didn't tell me. I haven't, that is, I didn't—"

"That will never do. He must have a name. I'll stay up with you. We'll think of one together. And then in the morning we'll go together to the market to buy what you'll need."

Alastair didn't like the emphasis she placed on the word *together*. And to have everyone in Edenmill seeing them *together* with a child, shopping for supplies—well, he wanted none of that. "I'd rather we didn't go to the market here in Edenmill..."

"What? Why?" She frowned, and her freckles came together in the wrinkles on her cheekbones like tiger's stripes.

"Well," he stammered and looked down. The child began to stir. "It's such a small marketplace, really...very few artisans. We should go someplace more distant—er, developed. Keltingham...

or Gull'scry...yes, Gull'scry has a thriving marketplace. We should go there."

"All the way to the tip of Chapparel?"

"Why, yes, it's no more than a three day ride."

Abbagael paused but then considered that she'd never had so much time with him...alone. "All right, Alastair," she said, gently lifting the child from the satchel and holding him up. "I'll go with you on this little journey. Stars know you need my womanly wisdom." She cuddled the child and cooed to him, "And tonight, you'll have a name."

Good, Alastair thought, *she really is falling for him*. The way Alastair saw it, he could live with having her around for three days. After that, well, Gull'scry was a port town. Easy enough to get on a ship and disappear.

CHAPTER 13

HAUNTING MEMORIES

*Shepherds are right fond of my smoked meats and sausages, they
are. Me and my meat cart have been in and out of Shepherd's Hollow
every other week for nigh on seventy years, and I've been welcomed
as friend by many of their order...even Mosteryn the Old. So what
I know about Shepherds is more than most, I'll wager. They are a
clever, secretive lot, prone to whispering and plotting. But all of it for
good. All of it for our good. We're the flock, you see. Every living
being of Myriad...we're in the safekeeping of the Shepherds. And
they're capable, given gifts by the First One, gifts beyond reckoning.
Healed my bum ankle with a touch, one did! Mosteryn, I once saw
him grab lightning right out of the sky just to craft that beautiful glass
he makes. And all Shepherds can hear tales from far off. Voices on
the wind, they call them. Kind of creepy if you ask me.*

No, Shepherds are not to be fooled with.

From a letter from Tal Osbarden to his nephew
Fergal Moonbrooke, Avrill the 39th, 2202 AS

24 CELESANDUR 2212

The voices had ridden the wind to Sebastian Sternbough's ear for
a solid week. Some of them spoke strange tidings. Some of them
offered small breaths of hope. But most spoke of grief.

He heard them even now as he leaned on the windowsill of his high chamber and watched the procession of carriages arrive at the outer gate of Anglinore City. Kings and Queens, sages and warriors—all coming for council and the grand Ceremony of Crowns.

Sebastian wondered what the other Shepherds had gleaned from the voices. That was the rub. The voices were helpful only if one learned to discern their message. And such discernment could come only from many years of experience. Sebastian was eager to test his own theories on Mosteryn the Old. If there was any Shepherd in Myriad who might have more clarity, it was Mosteryn.

Not that Sebastian didn't have his theories. He suspected the trouble that had begun in Vulmarrow many years prior was the root of the recent voice activity. And yet there were too many inklings in the voices hinting at things yet to come.

"Bah!" Sebastian swiped at the air as if he could ward off the voices. He could not. But he did tear a vine of purple flowers from the window frame.

Meowr. A small orange and white cat poked its head out from a pile of scrolls on the floor. It looked up at Sebastian and repeated, *Meowr.*

"Ah, Krindle," he said, stroking the feline. "I believe I may have ruined the vine you like to swat at."

Meowr.

"No, I'm afraid I cannot pick you up right now. I need both hands free."

He walked past his personal histories, the scrolls glued together and bound in thick leather. His collection was huge and stacks lined the curving wall of the tower chamber. But certain books were not in plain sight. These sensitive documents he kept hidden behind a wall of feather ferns beside his roan wood desk.

He removed one particular volume. "Have I not always feared what would come of this?" He remembered the sorrowful day upon which he had penned the words on these parchments. A tear trailed down Sebastian's cheek as he read his own words and recalled that day.

53 MUERTANAS 2068

Queen Clarissant screamed and gripped my hand. I thought she looked very pale, and the midwives cast worried glances at each other and at me. I looked to the eastern window, out over the endless hills to the horizon. A brilliant golden border blazed beneath the clouds. Another sunrise without King Brysroth. This sunrise would see him miss the birth of his son and, I feared, maybe more.

"Shepherd!" Queen Clarissant groaned. "I, I...something is wrong! Help me!" Her eyes met mine, and in that moment we both knew. Still, I would do what I could so that she might see her child born.

I released the queen's hand for a moment, went to my wooden staff, and scratched until I pried loose a gray splinter. I walked to the queen and held the small piece of wood aloft. Queen Maren saw it and smiled. Then, using the power granted me by the First One, I whispered life into the wood.

A small green shoot rose from the end of the gray splinter. It curled once and unfolded into a pair of teardrop-shaped leaves. Two more shoots grew out of the sliver from my staff until I had a vibrant sapling in my hand. I broke off a pair of leaves and gently placed them under the queen's tongue. Immediately her eyes became less cloudy and more focused. She reached for my hand and held it.

"I see the head!" one of the midwives shouted.

Excited and anxious, the queen bore down. One of her fingernails broke off on my hand as she clutched against the pain.

"Stop!" cried one of the midwives. "Wait!"

"What's wrong?" The queen raised herself up to try to see but, weakening, she fell back into the cushions. She looked disoriented, and what little color there had been drained from her cheeks. "Shepherd…" she whispered. "Sebastian, what is wrong with my child?"

Releasing the queen's hand, I turned to the midwives.

"I do not know what to do," one of them said. And then she whispered. "The cord is around the child's neck."

I felt a terror then like a finger of ice gliding down my spine. "Uncoil it, then!"

"We've tried, but it will not come free," said one midwife.

"It's as if…" began the other.

"Go on," I demanded, urgent for the child's safety.

"It's as if something is pulling the cord…from the inside."

Suddenly, the queen shuddered and unleashed such a cry as I will never forget.

"He is free!" shouted one of the midwives, and she held the child up for the queen to see.

"He is marvelous!" I said.

"Aravel," the queen said weakly. "You will be a strong man…a strong king." Suddenly her body heaved. She arched her back severely and cried out.

"Here!" the first midwife exclaimed as she handed me the child. I nearly stumbled going around the corner of the bed. I held the baby, but my attention was fixed on the midwives.

"Your Majesty!" she exclaimed, "the First One has blessed you exceedingly. For you have a second son…a twin!"

The queen did not answer. She lay very still and her skin was white like alabaster. I looked back at the second son, and I wondered if he was indeed a blessing…or something else. For I shall not ever forget what I saw—though to my great sorrow I did not realize its import then. The second boy emerged from the queen and, for a moment, just a moment, I am sure that he held Aravel's cord in his shaking fist.

Sebastian was still lost in thought when King Aravel Stormgarden rapped hard on the chamber door.

"Sebastian!" The king's voice was rich and merry, but nonetheless jolting.

Sebastian sat bolt upright and closed the book in his lap. "Yes, Lord? Is it time already?"

The king frowned as he entered the chamber and fiddled with a blue button at the straining seam of his ceremonial shirt. "Sebastian," he said, "we have but one Lord, and may I remind you, I am not him."

"Of course, my liege," said Sebastian. "I have not forgotten."

"Liege?" King Aravel shook his head and laughed. "How can you call me such things? 'Lord,' 'liege'—bah! You are one hundred years my elder. You changed my diapers!" The king of the realm of Myriad guffawed so forcefully that the blue button popped off his shirt and ricocheted around the chamber.

Sebastian caught it just before it would have bounced out of the window, and handed it to the king.

King Aravel received it and looked down at his somewhat bulbous pouch where the button had been. "Oh, dear," he said. "I need to stay away from Daribel's truffles."

The High Shepherd's attempts to remain stoic failed utterly at this point. And while his quiet snickers lacked the quivering punch of the king's belly laughs, they were merry nonetheless. "If I may be so bold, your majesty," Sebastian said, raising an eyebrow. "It may not be Daribel's truffles but rather her truffles plus her muffins, sweet cakes, scones, and pies!"

Ten minutes before the High King Overlord of all Myriad, King Aravel the Great, would face the most important rulers of the realm, he lost another button from his shirt.

CHAPTER 14

AN UNLIT TORCH

Times change. Truth does not.
Prydian Proverb

24 CELESANDUR 2212

King Aravel shifted uneasily on his throne as he watched the dining hall fill with royalty from all over Myriad. He whispered into the delicate ear of his wife, "You will remind me of their names?"

Queen Maren did not laugh, but mirth flickered in her emerald eyes. "Surely, Husband, you do not suggest that you have forgotten even a single name from these, the most powerful leaders of this age?" Her rich, dark hair and skin the color of white silk made those eyes burn with glad green fire. She watched the lords and ladies enter and nodded to them, but her wry smile was for her husband alone.

The king turned to Sebastian, who always sat at his right hand. The Shepherd shrugged. He'd told Aravel once before that, in spite of all his wisdom and foresight, he could not fathom the mind of a woman.

Aravel turned back to his wife. "You torture me," he said, genuine alarm creasing his brow.

"Only because I love you, Aravel." She turned and looked at him kindly. He was one hundred forty-seven, and the years had not been unkind. Youth still lingered in his wide, golden-eyed gaze and in the ruddiness of his cheeks and probably would remain well past his first triniary. His face was broad and strong, bordered by fuzzy brown sideburns. And though his square chin had softened with a bit of surplus weight, he was still just a moment away from the fierce warrior he'd always been.

That was why it pained Maren to see her brave husband so anxious. The man who had trod alone in the Abode of Wights; the man who, with his bare hands, had torn out the throat of a dragon—this man was terrified of a few dignitaries? "Come then," she said suddenly and labored up from the throne. "Shall I play herald?"

Before King Aravel could stop her, Queen Maren waltzed down the four steps and across the room to a tall being dressed in gleaming silver armor. "King Ealden!" said the queen with just enough volume for her husband to hear. "Too long has it been since your Prydian wisdom enlightened this hall!"

"Venescence!" King Ealden replied, the traditional Wayfolk greeting. "May the First One grant peace to you and to all who enter here." He took her hand and bowed. His oaken brown hair, carefully braided and drawn back over his straight pointed ears, did not move. Ealden did not kiss the queen's hand but merely lingered a moment over it, a respectful custom of his people.

Ealden, King Aravel remembered. *I like him. Serious as the grave and a wit lethal enough to send you there.* Aravel shook the hand of the tall Prydian leader. "Well met, Ealden. What news from Llanfair?"

"Little news," the Prydian king said. "The flowers are near full bloom. Little else. That is how I prefer it. The First One smiles upon us."

Aravel cleared his throat. "Um, yes, well, very good. Maren and I shall have to venture out to—"

"Forgive me, High King Aravel, but there is a matter that has reached my ears." Ealden raised an eyebrow. "When you have ears this big, you do not miss much. But I have received word that you have removed the Sacred Altar from Clarissant Hall—"

"In good time," Aravel said. "But, ah, I seem to have lost my queen. Perhaps after our meal?" He bowed and took a rather hasty leave. He found his wife already deep in conversation with a young Elladorian.

It was Queen Briawynn, but King Aravel stopped short of greeting her, for there were tears in the Elladorian's huge eyes. He'd known Briawynn for many years. She was, of course, the sovereign of Anglinore's nearest neighbor to the south. But in all their meetings, he'd never seen her with anything but an enchanting smile. Most Elladorian women were beautiful—creamy white skin, large dark-colored eyes, faces framed into a heart shape by a fringe of tawny feather-like sideburns—but Briawynn's loveliness surpassed them all. Perilous beauty, some thought, and that was perhaps why she had never married. Seeing the sorrow now marring her perfect countenance grieved Aravel deeply.

"They were just children," she was saying as Aravel approached. "Can we no longer trust the territory within our own borders?"

"It is your borders that concern me," Queen Maren replied. "How could Gorracks cross three borders unhindered...or unnoticed? I will have such questions at the council."

"I have such questions now," Aravel said as he took Briawynn's hand like a gentle father. "Has there been another assault?"

"The worst yet," replied Queen Briawynn. "Just children and their gaffers out fishing on Lake Tal-y-Llyn just before dawn. A detachment of Gorrack raiders came out of the mist...and..."

"You're sure they were Gorracks?" the king asked.

"Old Bannick Gindryffl was out on the lake with his grand'lins," Queen Briawynn whispered. "It was dark yet, but he swears it was Gorracks. He'd have been caught too but for the fact that their little boat was hidden in a bank of reeds."

A heavy shadow fell upon Aravel as if a great monolith had risen suddenly behind him.

"Gorracks in Ellador?" thundered a voice, causing all to turn. King Drüst, Lord of the Windborne, flexed his iron gray wings and rolled his neck. He stood a foot taller than Aravel and, with the exaggerated muscles of his shoulders and upper back that were common in beings of his race, he appeared broader than two men standing side by side. "That's impossible. My scouts have reported no unusual activity in the Gorrack Nation. And as you are all very much aware, we watch the borders of Wyndbyrne Eyries with vigilance."

"Please do not misunderstand, Drüst," Queen Maren said. "We do not call the Windborne negligent. Ever we are grateful for our winged friends."

King Drüst bowed his head. His large, angled green eyes glittered on either side of a nose that would appear too large on any face but his. A great spearhead of sea-gray hair windblown back on his forehead, immaculately polished blue stag armor, and a long two-fisted broadsword sheathed in black leather intercut by bands of silver—nothing about his appearance was anything less than regal. "I am grateful for your confidence," he said. "But it is far more likely that aged eyes were deceived than my scouts missing Gorrack raiders."

"However," Queen Maren said, "evidence is mounting that Gorracks have found some other way...perhaps circumventing the Felhaunt altogether. It could be that they've overcome their fear of the water at last."

"That would be alarming news indeed," Aravel said. "But equally alarming is that you've noted no new movements from the Gorracks at all. If they are changing their tactics from blunt, open attacks to more stealthy raids, we all have cause for concern." Aravel paused and brushed a curly lock of hair off his forehead. "Conjecture and worry have their place. We will discuss this further once the council convenes. For now, Drüst, well met."

Aravel's hand shot out and the two kings clasped forearms and shook.

Queen Maren led her husband around the wide chamber, subtly reminding him of names before he spoke, bowed, or shook hands. There was Queen Savron, willowy and lithe, beautiful and beloved ruler of the Vespal branch of the Wayfolk. She brushed several reluctant strands of dark, silky hair over her angular, pointed ears and nodded often as she spoke to Mosteryn the Old, chief of Shepherds. King Vang, Lord of the Mining Clans of Tryllium; Queen Fleut, Regent of Keening on the Naïthe; Prince Navrill of the Marinaens; and Warden Caddock of Chapparel together formed a very royal party indeed.

Having exchanged cordial pleasantries with them all, King Aravel and his unsurpassed queen ascended the wide stairs to the throne. Aravel turned and noted that the torches above each seat at the massive oval table were all lit, except one. But the High King Overlord of Myriad would not allow personal matters to impose upon his duty.

"My friends!" Aravel bellowed. "Allies of old and rulers of Myriad, let the feast of welcome begin!"

Lady Daribel had been waiting for this cue. She was the royal cook or, as she liked to be called, "High Mistress of All Things Worth Eating." Anyone fool enough to enter her kitchen without her consent invited a caustic tongue-lashing and, likely, an assault with a wooden spoon as well. The cooks and scullers who served under Daribel obeyed her every command instantly and to the letter. And so they did as she barked out commands from the vestibule.

"Flagons of meade and fairywater! Remember now, one flagon for every three tankards!" She watched her team intently and beamed with pride as they worked. "Now, place the snordic apple slices. Yes, yes, one spiral per platter." She paused and tossed a withering glare at one of the servants. "Don't crowd the center, Beatrice! How many times—ah, yes, that's better!"

"My lord," Sebastian said to Aravel, "perhaps, if you need a break from ruling the realm, you might consider Daribel as a substitute."

"Ha!" The king nearly spat a mouthful of fairywater. "Do wait until I swallow next time! On second thought, spare me such humor. I can scarce afford to lose another button."

Bemused, the royal guests watched all the activity. Other dishes came forth: steaming, buttered ballyhoo spears; jiggling saucers of candicott julep; savory piles of scallion potatoes; and hot vats of herb gravy. The aromas sifting around that dining chamber were almost maddening in their culinary savor. But all attention and a roomful of gasps were saved for the main course.

"Go, go, go!" Daribel flicked her hands like shaking out a rug. "Mind the stairs! Drop the roast, and you'll be next in my oven!"

Seven servants were required to hoist, transport, and place the roasted staghorn. Even just a calf was that heavy with lean meat, and it was fresh from the oven, the largest oven in Anglinore.

"Look at that!" King Vang blurted.

"Absolutely marvelous," said Queen Briawynn.

"Oh, do carve the beast." Prince Navrill wiped the gill slits on his lower neck with his cloth napkin. "It smells heavenly."

King Drüst tucked his wings far behind his back and put the carving dagger to the steaming staghorn.

"Wait!" King Ealden called, tapping his goblet with his fork. "Certainly a feast so fine as this calls for thanksgiving. Do you not all agree that a blessing is in order?"

No one answered. King Aravel leaned to his wife. "Here we go..."

"Hush, husband!"

Seeing no objections, King Ealden continued. "Please tilt your head back and close your eyes." He waited for obedience. "To Him who provides all that is just and good in this life, we lift our inner eyes to thee. First One, Father before all others, it is to you alone we give thanks for the scandalous bounty upon this table. We live in a time of relative peace…a time when we too often take for granted such a feast as this, much less the more mundane details of this world. It is…"

"It is going to get cold," Aravel whispered. Maren shushed him again.

"How many ages have we prospered from your storehouses?" King Ealden asked in prayer. "How long have you protected this land from widespread scourge and pestilence? Forgive us, Father of All, for allowing our faith to wither even as we soak up the warming rays of your love. We thank you for life. We thank you for health. We thank you for this extraordinary meal—"

Warden Caddock cleared his throat rather loudly.

King Aravel proclaimed the prayer over with a hearty, "Amyn!"

Ealden frowned but took his seat. Then the meal began in earnest, and for a long while, conversation utterly disappeared. Knives and forks clanked on plates, flagons met goblets, and succulent meat found tastebuds.

Daribel watched from the shadows and silently exulted. *Success!* She turned to her crew and whispered, "Well done, lads and lasses. You've the whole day off tomorrow. Well done."

Eventually waistbands expanded far enough, and the royalty around the table found breath enough for some little conversation.

"What, Ealden?" King Vang objected. "Your goblet is yet empty. Have some meade!"

The Prydian ruler arched his back somewhat stiffly. "I do not drink."

Vang's eyebrows nearly touched his hairline. "What? Not even fairywater?"

"I do not drink," Ealden repeated. "It makes one…silly."

Warden Caddock leaned over far enough for his beard to ride up on the table. "What he means, Vang, is that drinking anything besides goat's milk is a violation of his silly code."

"The code you speak of is nothing short of the First One's will." Ealden spoke matter-of-factly, as if teaching a child the most obvious truth.

"Now, I am certainly no expert in Canticles or any other Lore of the First One," Caddock said. "But I do not think His law forbids anyone from eating or drinking anything, much less fairywater. Makes one silly, indeed. Sprightly and energetic, perhaps, but not drunk. This isn't Witchdrale!"

King Ealden shook his head but said nothing.

The larders of Anglinore castle had provided a feast of unprecedented satisfaction. No one in the room would even so much as entertain the thought of another bite…except for the High King of Myriad. Aravel was about to trouble Daribel for another truffle or two when he felt a solid rap of the queen's knuckles on his shoulders.

"My dear husband," she said, "I'm quite sure any corners that aren't filled…don't need to be filled. You wouldn't want to pop the rivets from your new armor, would you?"

"Goodness, no," Aravel said, his voice cheery but his expression pained. His gaze traveled round the High Table to the one empty seat and the one dormant torch. Aravel rubbed his fingers along the rich marble armrest and wondered if his exalted seat was worth so much discord within his family. *Of course it is,* he told himself. *Ruling Myriad was a great responsibility, a high calling. The crown came to me, and there are no accidents.* Aravel turned to his wife and shook his head. The pity in her eyes told him that, as usual, she was reading his thoughts.

Somehow, no matter how important the crown and the kingship were, Aravel couldn't shake the feeling that he'd missed something vital within his own family, that he'd left one critical stone unturned. He thought of one name: *Morlan.*

CHAPTER 15

THE SHORTCUT

Where have you looked?
They're not in the flowers.
Where have you looked?
They're not in the gardens.

Where are the pixie children?
Look in the willows my friend.

From *Glad Tales*
Delph Wittenger (w. 902)

26 CELESANDUR 2212

"I think we're lost," Abbagael said as she peeked in on the child bundled against her chest. Sound asleep...as he had been for many leagues of their journey. "I don't understand. Why wouldn't you take the northern trade road?"

"I know a shortcut," said Alastair, who sat before her. He kept his eyes straight ahead and his horse at a brisk trot.

"But the northern trade road is well-traveled." Abbagael unravelled a faded cloth parchment. "Look here at the map. See, there are small villages along the way, places for traveling comforts, don't ye know. And it's safer, isn't it?"

Safe to say I'd be recognized. Alastair ignored the map and shrugged. "What is it with women and directions?"

"What is it with men and shortcuts?" Abbagael fired back. "Once, my father took us three weeks off course just to save us a day's travel."

"Abbagael," he said, his words becoming clipped. "I have spent many years traveling paths few in Allyra know anything about."

"Oh, let me guess: this path you know…it's not on the map, is it?"

"It's on the map in my mind."

"What does that mean?"

"It means we will get to Gull'scry my way."

Abbagael harrumphed and put the map away. This was just another in a string of disappointments on the trip thus far. It wasn't that she'd expected Alastair to fall madly in love with her on the journey. Still, she'd hoped to at least peel away a few of the layers that encased his heart like the husks of a haskin nut.

But Alastair remained as guarded as ever. He spoke little to her directly, but mumbled to himself often. Mostly she couldn't make out his words, but she'd heard bits and pieces like: "the wrong gifts" and "can't wait anymore" and "foolish notions." Whenever she asked about it, his response was the same. "It's not important," he'd say. And then there would be more silence.

And while the ropey muscles of his neck and shoulders were pleasant to hold onto, riding so close to him hadn't given Abbagael much warmth either. At times she felt as if a cold statue sat in front of her rather than a man. If it hadn't been for the child nestled between them and the glow she felt every time she stared into his blue eyes, Abbagael might have demanded Alastair turn back.

"The child," she muttered. Then she spoke more plainly. "It occurs to me that you've conveniently fallen asleep every time I've tried to get your help to name this poor child."

Alastair let his head fall and made a loud snoring noise.

"Oh, no, you don't Alastair!" But she laughed in spite of herself. "We've a long stretch of riding. And you said yourself that you must stay alert on this winding shortcut of yours."

"Ah, exactly my point. I couldn't possibly focus on the child's name. One wrong turn could prove disast—"

"That's just nonsense. I'll come up with some names. All you'll have to do is say *yes* or *no*."

"But—"

"See? You've answered me twice, so it should be no trouble to listen and blurt out a yes or no."

Alastair sighed. Abbagael had the strangest ability to confound him like no one else had. "Oh, very well."

"Good!" She patted Alastair on the shoulder. "He needs a fitting name. I'm not very well versed in the old languages. Now, my great Auntie Hildegard, now she knew all the languages. Old Anglish, Sunderell, Plainspak—"

"*Abbagael!*"

"Oh, oh, I'm sorry. Lost in thought, don't ye know. Okay, okay. A name. How about Evander?"

"No."

"Why not? It's a strong name."

"You told me all I needed to do was give a yes or a no."

"Right." She exhaled loudly. "How about Beleth?"

"No."

"Sage?"

"Sounds like an herb. No."

"Deran?"

"Too weak."

"Sunion?"

"Sounds like 'onion.'"

"Valerion"

"Abbagel, I cannot think right now. My head aches fiercely."

"What about Faedan—"

"Shhh!" He reached back and gripped her knee. "I heard something."

"Alastair, that hur—" Before she could finish, she heard it too: an impossibly high-pitched scream, keening and desperate, coming from deep in the foliage far off the path. The scream trailed off, and Abbagael whispered, "What could make such a sound? A bird?"

"I do not know," he replied. They heard it again, but this time, as the scream climbed in pitch and volume, it formed a word: *Help.*

"Alastair, do something!" Abbagael smacked him on the shoulder.

"*That*—was not necessary. I heard you."

"But you aren't doing anything."

"What do you want me to do? It's just some dying animal."

"Animal? That's no dumb animal! It said, 'Help!' You heard it." She made as if to descend from the horse. "If you won't do something, I will."

"Don't be ridiculous," he said, grabbing her shoulder. "You can't run off into the wood with the child."

"What? You don't think I can take care of myself?"

I hate questions phrased like that. Alastair felt that answering was like walking through a thick meadow full of bear traps. "Well, you are certainly a capable young woman, but...there are things in these deep woods—"

"Then, you go," Abbagael said, one green eye flashing between locks of crimson. "Someone's in trouble out there."

Snap! Foot in trap. Alastair glowered at her and then slid off the saddle. "I have a feeling I'm going to regret this." He headed for the brush.

"Wait! Aren't you going to draw your sword?"

In the flashed moments before he responded, Alastair had the brief notion of disappearing into the deep forest...forever. But no. He could conscience leaving her in a town, but not in this part of the wilderness. Aside from the Felhaunt and the more remote Hinterlands, the forested border of Chapparel was the most mysterious—and perilous—region in this part of the world. He couldn't leave Abbagael and the child here. But he would answer. "Lady Abbagael, do not beg me to action only to criticize the way I undertake it."

"Beg you? Criticize you? You arro—"

Alastair held up his hand. "Shhh, you'll wake the child!" With that, he was gone.

"Aren't you going to draw your sword?'" Alastair muttered as he hacked through the foliage with the Star Sword. As Alastair charted a jagged course in the direction of strange high voice, each sweep of his arm kicked up a storm of granger leaf shreds and hunks of pulpy feckletree branches. He stopped for a moment and flexed his sword hand. Tiny muscles twitched on top of his hand and in the pulp of his thumb. It was disconcerting and unusual. Of course, Witchdrale was known to have strange and unpleasant side effects during and after drinking it.

Heeeeeeeelllp!

Closer than I thought! Alastair charged forward, his blade a blur. The foliage opened up into a kind of path. Without so much resistance, he plunged recklessly ahead.

Heeeellp meeeeee!

The path widened yet more, and just ahead there was a lush floral glade. Alastair's mind registered the odd shimmer in the scene a few moments too late.

Crack!

Alastair found himself suspended in a clinging, elastic mural of the flowering grove just beyond. He could already feel the pinpricks in his chest, thighs, and arms. Numbness crawled across his flesh, threatening to render him immobile. Alastair would have none of that. He knew all too well what would happen if he didn't move. He knew what was coming.

"Ahhrrrgg!" he groaned, pulling with all his might to free his sword hand. "Ah! *No!*" The sword fell from his clumsy, numbing fingers. At that moment, he heard a cicada-like clicking from above.

He looked up into two huge, slanting mantid eyes.

"Spirax!" spat Alastair. At last he ripped his sword hand free, swept a dagger from his belt, and plunged it into one of the creature's eyes.

Schreeeeett! The spirax coiled upward, its segmented appendages wheeling, trying to get the splinter of iron from its wounded eye.

Alastair pulled the second of his seven daggers free and began hacking at the canvas of spirax webbing. It shredded reluctantly and then snapped free from its unseen anchor point. Alastair fell to the ground and tore the rest of the sticky matting from his body. It had not been a moment too soon. Any longer and the toxins in the spirax web would have paralyzed him.

Stumbling to his feet, he clutched his Star Sword. He sensed movement, ducked and bobbed to his right. Then, he hammered the blade down, in one motion beheading the creature and relieving it of its two mantis-like forelimbs.

Blade leading the way, Alastair raced into the glade and spun round. Which way?

"Over here!"

Alastair wheeled around twice before he spotted the other spirax snare. It was a huge drape extended between a large alder tree and a nest of shrubs. A spirax—a big one—was closing in on its prey...a being unlike any Alastair had ever seen.

Outside of a storybook, that is.

CHAPTER 16

A Ceremony of Crowns

One beheaded by a long, heavy sword…the other bludgeoned by a massive warhammer, our sentries fell without uttering a cry. The Gorracks came on us without warning, Gorracks by the hundreds. With their heavy mail, plate armor, and long pikes, they drove us like cattle through the Felhaunt. Never has a rank of the Anglish Guard been so utterly routed. They hacked us down as we ran until we came at last to the high bank of the River Nightwash. It was there that King Aravel mustered his men for one last stand. Aravel proved his mettle in the battle, but it was Synic Keenblade, then just a Signet Knight, who delivered us. Synic went to the trees. From above, his swift sword came down on the Gorracks. He parted the Grunt Commander from his head. Three Gorrack Arm Lieutenants fell headless to the ground by Synic's hand as well. With the Gorracks in disarray, Aravel and Synic led twelve of us to finish the battle. We stained our blades livid green, slaying more than a hundred. We drove off the rest. But we lost 88 of Myriad's finest warriors. We searched nearly a league of the Felhaunt, found our men—even what was left of the sentries—and buried our dead in a clearing deep in the forest.

From the Journal of Galen Stormkin,
Captain of the Anglish Guard,
18 Muertanas 2160

25 Celesandur 2212

Standing every seven paces between pillar and torch, Anglish guards, usually confident and proud in their polished silver and blue armor, glanced nervously at the procession passing before them. These were not common diplomats and ambassadors coming to secure payment for new roads or seeking advice about new taxes. No, these were kings and queens, stewards and rulers of all the free lands of Myriad.

Each one had been born to power through royal bloodlines or risen to power through storied conquests in battle. It seemed to the guards that a majestic glow surrounded these monarchs. Some of the newest Anglish soldiers had never witnessed such nobility, for the Ceremony of Crowns happened only once every seven years.

King Aravel stopped at a pair of immense wooden doors, each three men wide and so high that the tops of them were lost in the shadows in the rafters. Making a great show of their entrance, Aravel turned and looked at the others. "Clarissant Hall, sacred meeting place, institution of introspection, assembly of absolution, and sanctuary of solitude. And more personally it was, I'm told, my mother's favorite place in this great castle."

Then, flexing his broad shoulders, he gave a great shove on the doors. They swung slowly inward, revealing the nave of Clarissant Hall, a vast aisle lined on either side with marble columns that reached from the etched surface of the granite floor to the intricately ribbed, arched ceiling seven stories above. If any of the nine rulers present had not been awed by the architecture alone, they were by the exquisite music: harps, lyre, dulcimers, pipes, and kettle drums—all came to life the moment the doors parted. The musicians played the Anglish Anthem, of course.

And hundreds of fortunate citizens, each holding a single candle, lined both sides of the great aisle. They had waited for more than a month to have a chance to witness the Ceremony of Crowns, which formally began the Festival of Crowns. They lifted their voices in a chorus untrained but beautiful nonetheless.

Hand in hand, King Aravel and Queen Maren went ahead while the others remained by the doors. The rulers of Myriad smiled as they passed by townspeople cheering madly and still singing. A few held up infants who were too young to ever remember this day. Oh, but they would be told, "You were there, my lad. The Ceremony of Crowns. The High King and Lady passed right by. Count yourself blessed!"

Five lush seats—gilded, intricately carved, and, for the moment, empty—waited on either side of the wide aisle as Myriad's high rulers proceeded to a square pedestal that stood about chest high. The pedastal's flat surface was lined with lush velvet, and golden sunlight poured down upon it from two lancet windows high above. It was an altar, but in spite of its artistic grandeur, this altar stood out among the other stonework of the Hall. For all their craftsmanship, the stonewrights of Anglinore could not simulate age. While the hall and most of its other contents had existed for ages, the altar was a mere six years old.

Aravel and Maren stood on either side of the altar, reached across, and clasped hands. All the while, the music rose like a gathering wave, and the peoples assembled in the nave roared their approval. Even from a distance, they could see the gentle love between their lord and lady. Their eyes locked together, King Aravel and Queen Maren loosed their hands, reached up, and removed their crowns. These they reverently placed upon the purple velvet.

Two great, elevated seats, monuments of marble, waited behind the altar, and as the cheering and applause and music continued, the king and queen sat. Immediately, the music changed. The processional part of the anthem was over, and a stirring theme, heavy with deep stringed instruments and drums began.

Queen Savron of the Vespal Wayfolk came forward, striding confidently, as was her way. At her side hung a long, thin sword in a priceless cyrium scabbard. Her eyes, a whorl of deep blue, green, and violet, danced with the candlelight as she approached.

She stopped at another altar, this one waist high and topped with a vast shallow platter lined with dark green silk. Spaced all around the wide disc were circular indentations. Queen Savron removed her own crown, a black methycet and silver entwined circlet set with a single blue gem. When she bowed to King Aravel and Queen Maren, her expression was proud, but there was also a childlike excitement bordering on giddiness. She placed her crown in one of the indentations on the low altar and bowed again. There was a chorus of applause, and Queen Savron took one of the ten lower throne seats on the aisle.

King Ealden traveled the vast passage next, but though the music and crowd created a charged atmosphere, Ealden approached slowly, almost reluctantly. And when he came to the low altar where Queen Savron had placed her crown, his expression was troubled. He looked up at King Aravel and Queen Maren's crowns, then at the king and queen, and then, oddly, he seemed to be looking behind them as if searching. A slight tremor in his hands, he removed his own crown and placed it on the altar in the lowest slot. Then, he took a seat across the aisle from Queen Savron. Their eyes did not meet.

One by one, the other rulers approached and laid their crowns on the low altar and sat down on their throne seats. The cheering escalated and the music built to a drum-ridden crescendo. A few attentive citizens noticed the empty chair. But only a few. The final note sounded with a blaring trumpet that, in another setting, might have been mistaken for a war horn. Then there was silence.

King Aravel rose. "Truly Myriad is built upon that which is stronger than the stone of castles," he announced, "deeper than the fathoms of the Dark Sea, and more brilliantly varied than the flowers in all the fields of Llanfair."

Respectful cheers and one *Huzzah!* came from the crowd. King Ealden's ears perked up and he nodded.

"For there are no greater wonders in this realm," Aravel said, "no greater treasures…than its peoples!"

Rousing cheers. Ealden frowned.

"Citizens of Myriad, from Keening on the Naïthe, to Lyrimore and the Verdant Mountains in Ellador, Ardon in Tryllium, Llanfair in Amara, Westhaven in Chapparel, the Wyndbyrne Eyries, and Shepherd's Hollow…I speak for the queen and myself and all of Anglinore City when I thank you for the gift of your allegiance."

When the deafening cheers died down, Aravel gestured to Queen Briawynn, who stood and faced the crowd. She closed her huge dark eyes and began to sing.

> Ana…Ana Wynduor, ven ardor aen virnew
> Theos vendurin so tu
> Halfainin ven mari senet emthalot fre
> Halfainin aen trinalor, samarikind so menelae
>
> Senesca amyn vanador, pourina mari fre amour,
> Tu saes crea son atoll athor.
> Ventres, Halfainin
> Ventres, Halfainin, ventres.

Few in the large audience knew the meaning of Briawynn's song, save that it was a prayer of some kind to the First One. But her lilting, mournful voice and the subtle trill of her Elladorian language pierced one and all, resonating in deep places within them. Many in the crowd, especially the young, felt quickened to action: to take up a walking stick and explore or a sword to fight valiantly against an unnamed foe. But others, especially the old, were stirred to tears. When at last the echo of Lady Briawynn's final syllable faded in the deep vaults of Clarissant Hall, there were very few left unmoved.

Lady Briawynn took her seat once more and thoughtfully traced a finger down her cheek along the soft ridge of her feathery side-burns.

As King Aravel again stood, he discreetly wiped the corner of his eye. "Servants of Myriad, you have witnessed the humility of your leaders. With that spirit, we begin the Festival of Crowns. You are—"

"Lord Aravel." King Ealden raised a hand and stood. His expression was urgent. "If I may?"

A murmur shuffled through the crowd.

King Aravel nodded, and the Prydian ruler bowed. "Surely, you have not forgotten it is tradition that we read from the Book of the First One prior to beginning the festival."

All eyes turned to the High King. "We have had the Song of Reverence," he said, his eyes communicating an unspoken command to Ealden to let it go.

But Ealden would not be dissuaded. "Yes, yes, of course. And Lady Briawynn surely has honored the First One with her voice and convictions. However, it is right and good that we bring the word of the First One to the people before they leave to make merry. I wish only to perform the reading that has always been part of this ceremony."

At this, King Aravel's cheeks reddened. *Ealden and his Prydish sanctity!* But he held his temper in check. "The people can hear the word of the First One any Halfinday in any sanctuary in the realm. We have much to discuss in Council, so let us be—" He felt Queen Maren's gossamer light touch on his forearm. He didn't even turn. He knew what her expression, what her eyes, would say. "Oh, very well. Have your reading."

King Ealden bowed low. He strode forward, stood before the crown-laden altars, and faced the assembly of Myridians. "Venescence, nuvim!" he said as he drew a thin leather-bound volume from an inner pocket in his dark green cloak. "A reading from the Book of the First One, Canticles chapter twelve."

He paused. His brow furrowed. Intensity burned in his eyes. But as he began to read, the slightest hint of a smile lingered at the corners of his mouth. "'And His crown will not be made of gold, silver, or precious cyrium. Rather, it will be forged of iron. Through great calamity and peril He will bear this crown. Walking many long and lonely paths, He will bear this crown. Even in the shedding of His blood, He will bear this crown. His crown will endure forever and be set in a place of honor above all the crowns of this—'"

Crack! One of the doors at the entrance to the nave was thrown back. Clarissant Hall reverberated with the jolting sound. A tall, cloaked figure stood in the doorway in the shadows. From somewhere in the crowds a small child shrieked, and then the hall became utterly silent.

The stranger came forward. His stride was long and sure. His cloak hid all but the ever-peaking tip of a sword scabbard and the metallic glint of boots. Guards appeared from the crowd and traced the stranger's movements, keeping several steps ahead of the possible assassin. Like an apparition, he traveled up the passage and stood before the first altar in the midst of the kings and queens and their thrones. He threw back the hood of his cloak. "Allow me to place my crown with the others."

The guards released a collective sigh and melted back into the crowd.

"Morlan," King Aravel blurted out, "you're late."

"Ever it has been, older brother," Morlan replied, a glint in his golden eyes.

Aravel ignored the slight. "But you missed the Feast of Welcome."

"When have I ever…" Morlan removed his crown… "been welcome in this place?"

"Nonsense, Morlan," Queen Maren said. "You are the brother of the High King, friend to Anglinore…and to me. You are always welcome here."

Morlan shrugged and avoided her eyes.

She saw his shoulders droop subtly. "And whatever you do, don't let Daribel find you. She fixed your favorite roast calf of staghorn. The gravy and scallion potatoes were all there waiting for you."

"Pity," Morlan said. "It has been a long time since I have had such a savory meal…a very long time. Perhaps I can persuade Daribel to provide me with the leftovers."

King Ealden, who stood flabbergasted beside Morlan, cleared his throat audibly.

"I'm sorry, Ealden," Morlan said as he brushed by the Prydian and took his crown to the low altar. "Did I interrupt something you were saying?"

"The reading."

"The what?"

"The reading from the Book of the First One."

Morlan gave an exaggerated bow and placed the Crown of Vulmarrow among the others. "Oh, that." As he stood, he backed into the high altar, jostling the crowns of the High King and Queen. Morlan quickly steadied the altar and then said, "Well, do carry on. Don't mind me."

Ealden began to read once more. "'His crown will endure forever and be set in a place of honor above all the crowns of this world. Hearken to the man of—'"

"Good of you to save me one of the last chairs." Morlan gestured toward the two empty throne seats, one at the end of each row. Then he turned his wolfish glare on to Warden Caddock of Chapparel.

Warden Caddock was a fisherman and a hunter. His weathered skin spoke of the former, while his stout build and bright archer's eyes spoke of the latter. Few struck fear into his old heart. But Morlan Stormgarden did. Caddock stood and slowly walked over to one of the empty seats.

"Thank you, good Warden," Morlan said. "Always good to sit closer to my…family." He looked up at King Ealden impatiently and gestured with a flourish of his hand.

Glowering much of the time, King Ealden finished the reading from the Book of the First One. Anglish Knights then escorted the citizens of Myriad out of Clarrisant Hall to the courtyard and the Festival of Crowns where they would, in very short order, begin to make merry.

Shepherd Sebastian Sternbough had said nothing during the ceremony, choosing instead to stand behind the thrones and observe. He'd seen, and heard, enough to feed the suspicions that nagged at his consciousness like a squeaking window shutter just out of reach. He risked a furtive glance at Morlan. The Lord of Vulmarrow might have been smug, having in one way or another humbled most of the mighty guests in the hall. But no, Morlan did not look satisfied, but rather thoughtful, focused, and calculating. Sebastian would have preferred smug.

The Shepherd of Anglinore turned his gaze to the head of his order and found Mosteryn the Old already staring back at him. A clear and urgent message swam in those deep eyes. *We need to talk...before the Council begins.*

Sebastian nodded. *Message received.*

He looked round the room once more. Queen Briawynn's huge eyes swam in tears. King Ealden's brow and forehead furrowed. Warden Caddock cringed on the edge of his chair. *All of Anglinore celebrates outside. Pity that when the Council begins, things will be anything but merry.*

CHAPTER 17

CAUTIOUS MEETINGS

*King Brysroth's death was a mystery that held Anglinore in its grasp
for close to a hundred years. Some believed he'd been assassinated by a
stealthy killer from the Hinterlands or the Gorrack Nation. Other less-
logical folk thought the Wights of Cragland Hills had come and snatched
the king away. Most believed it was grief over his beloved Clarissant that
drove him to take his own life. As for myself, I haven't made up my mind.
Too neat or too farfetched, I say. But I haven't another theory to offer.*

From the Journal of General Gorm Candlewick, Anglish Guard

26 CELESANDUR 2212

Queen Maren twisted a satiny edge of drapes in her fingers. "You
need to put an end to this," she said softly. "Morlan will undermine your authority."

"And you think I don't know that?" Behind her, Aravel paced
their bedchamber.

"I meant no disrespect."

"Nor I to you, dearest Maren." Aravel slammed fist to palm.
"He's haunted my footsteps and vexed me near and far for as long
as I can remember. But he has never been this brazen."

"You should go to him, call him out."

"I have tried before. But no sooner does my mouth open than his ears close."

"What will you do, then?"

"Maybe I should have him arrested."

Queen Maren spun around. "Aravel, you cannot mean that."

"Maybe I do. Fell things have happened in and around Vulmarrow. There are rumors."

"Rumors are dangerous things," Maren said. "They can be misunderstood…or manipulated. No city in Myriad knows this better than Anglinore."

"You speak of my father?"

Maren nodded and went to her husband. She grasped his upper arms. "But I do not believe those rumors either."

King Aravel's jaw worked as if he had something foul upon his tongue. "Would you consider talking to Morlan?"

Maren's arms dropped to her sides. "What good could possibly come of that?"

"He listens to you, Maren. He always has."

"Do you hold that against me?" she asked.

"Against you? No."

The hardness in her eyes melted away. "What would you have me ask of him?"

"Tell him to stand down his defiance and contempt."

"As a favor to me?"

"Yes, that," Aravel said. "But also as a favor to Myriad. Morlan must relent willingly, else I will have to command it."

"Then you would have to arrest him."

"Either that, or he would smile and play the part until he returns to Vulmarrow." Aravel stepped to the window and looked west. "But rather than submit to me, Morlan would do just about anything short of war."

I thought I might find you here," Maren said as she entered the courtyard. She crossed the distance between the gated arch and the well in just moments. "I am afraid I've never quite understood your fascination with that dark water."

Morlan did not look up from the well. "It is its darkness that I value…mysterious depth, limitless distance. I find its stillness comforting."

"You've come here ever since…"

"Ever since my father died, yes," Morlan said. "This place… it helps me think."

"And what is it you are thinking about now?"

Morlan looked up, his large pupils shrinking to reveal more and more yellow. "I am thinking I miss my pet. Pity that Sköll fares so poorly in such gatherings."

"Enormous blackwolves aren't known for their friendliness, are they?" Queen Maren smiled. "But surely, Morlan, you are pondering more."

"I am thinking about why the High Queen has bothered to pay me a visit…alone."

Maren gestured to the stone bench. "May we sit?"

Morlan shrugged but sat beside her. Clouds drifted far above. The sun was bright, but there was a chill in the air.

The queen took a deep breath. "What are you doing, Morlan?"

"I must protest," he replied. "I don't know what you mean."

"You are far too old and far too wise for these antics. You very nearly knocked down the altar during the ceremony, to say nothing of your rude entrance."

Morlan smiled. "I have never stood on ceremony."

"Do you see any mirth in my eyes?" she asked. "This is no game, not to me. Try my patience again, and I'll have the guards put you in stocks."

"Always so direct, Maren. An alluring quality…at times. Very well, then…say your piece."

Maren's eyes smoldered. "Your king, your *brother*, deserves your respect. He has fought and bled for us all. Enough of your posturing, your demeaning subtle retorts. Lead Vulmarrow well and lend your wisdom where you may, but do not dare to undermine my husband again."

"For your sake, Maren, I will do as you ask." Morlan stood up and went back to the well. "But now, I would like to be alone once more."

Queen Maren stood and watched Morlan stare down into the well. "Morlan," she whispered, "I never meant to hurt you—"

He held up a hand. "Don't. Intentions are merely fancy excuses for murder. But tell me something...tell me this one thing: would your choice have been any different had I been born eighteen seconds sooner?"

She fixed her eyes upon him in an unwavering gaze. "No." She turned and fled the courtyard.

Liar, Morlan thought, staring down into the well. *Dishonest and deluded queen. Truly, this* is *a game we play. A very serious game.* Then he whispered, "One I shall win. Don't you think so?" Morlan could almost see his father's face in the black water's reflection.

Mosteryn the Old was approaching his fourteen-hundreth year and, in these latter days, he always walked with a long staff. But to assume that the leader of the Shepherd Order was feeble of body or mind would be a mistake on the order of blindfolding one's self and dancing on a cliff.

When Mosteryn at last looked up from the pages of Sebastian's archives, it seemed that lightning kindled in his eyes and caused his bushy white eyebrows to bristle. "It would not be the first time that misery has flowed from Vulmarrow Keep," he said, his famous temper barely in check. "Mendeleev put hundreds of necks beneath his axe before Shepherd Veridian found him out and ended it." Mosteryn stood, grabbed his staff, and strode over to the west window of Sebastian's high chamber.

Half fearing that the incensed Shepherd would call down a bolt of lightning, Sebastian glanced anxiously at his flourishing violet belles and the trellis of happy idresses by the window. Sebastian vividly remembered having bested Mosteryn in king's gate for the first time, and Mosteryn had been so furious that he'd raised his staff. That profound bolt of light had reduced one of Sebastian's climbing rose plants to a disintegrating ladder of black ash.

"Fear not for your beloved plants, Sebastian," the old Shepherd said without turning round. "The sky is clear…as is my mind."

A smile curled briefly on Sebastian's lips, but vanished as Mosteryn continued.

"That place is accursed—was from the beginning. Did we not both urge Brysroth against giving Vulmarrow to Morlan?"

"We did, Mosteryn," Sebastian said. "It was pride and folly that led the old king to bestow such a dubious gift. But did Morlan find evil there or bring it with him?"

"He left Anglinore a bitter man, that much is clear. But any seed he bore there has no doubt been nurtured in the deep holds of Vulmarrow Keep. I do not know how Shepherd Alfex has endured it all these years."

"What of Alfex?" Sebastian asked. "Has he noted a change in Morlan?"

Mosteryn turned. "Yes, he has. But Alfex sees it as blind rage toward the Gorrack Nation for their attacks in the Felhaunt and beyond. And so it may be, but still, the utter contempt he showed during the ceremony—"

"Could be explained perhaps. Morlan has always wanted a more aggressive campaign against the Gorracks. He's made no secret of his discontent with Aravel's lack of action."

"On that score, I have had my doubts," said the old Shepherd. "If the Gorracks are indeed crossing borders to commit wanton murder, something must be done."

"If?" Sebastian swatted the air. "That is the question, is it not? The voices on the wind tell of horrors to come."

"We agree on that at the very least, Sebastian, and, for now, that is what we must take to the Council."

"But if we do not confront Morlan openly, should we not at least—"

The first rap on the door was exceedingly loud. It was followed quickly by several softer but still insistent knocks. A timid voice squeaked through the sturdy timber of the door. "Shepherd Sebastian, it's me, Paige Martin. I've been sent to tell you the Council is beginning.

Sebastian looked to the sunlight on his wall. "Already?"

"It seems to me," Mosteryn replied, his eyes half-lidded and red, "that it is long overdue."

CHAPTER 18

SPRYE AND THE WILLOWFOLK

"Really? I get to be mistmaiden?" asked Dara.
She poked her finger back in her mouth.
Then she asked, "What's a mistmaiden?"
From *Greenshire Tales*, Hans Fablemeister

26 CELESANDUR 2212

"By the stars!" Alastair gasped.

Snared in the center of the spirax web was a small person—no doubt a girl as she wore a dress of green, yellow, silver, and gold. But she was no bigger than a large doll, perhaps a foot tall. And... she had wings. But there was no time to gawk. The spirax was upon her.

Alastair lunged forward. He tripped, completed an ugly forward roll, and with a groan came back to his feet just in front of the web. The spirax didn't see Alastair...or so he thought. He went to impale the creature right between its strange knobby shoulder blades, but in a blink it contorted and swung its upper body into Alastair.

The impact was so sudden and so powerful that Alastair crashed onto his backside and nearly blacked out. He blinked and shook his head. But before he could unleash his sword, the spirax was on top of him. It lashed out with one of its forelimbs and caught Alastair's arm in its grip. Then it began to squeeze.

"Ahh, rrrahh!" Alastair yelled. The pressure of the hinged, mantis-like appendage closing was intense and made worse by the thorny ridges that bit into Alastair's arm like shark's teeth.

Alastair dropped his sword, but not to the ground. He caught the Star Sword in his left hand and flicked his wrist, shearing off the top half of one of the spirax's eyes.

The beast recoiled, swiping at the wound. Purplish blood oozed down its triangular face.

But this spirax had more heart than the first. It released its hold on the branch above and let its elongated body drop to the grass. Before Alastair could react, it struck, coiling around him and pinning his arms at his sides.

Alastair fell backward. The creature loomed above him, and there was nothing he could do. The spirax could impale him with its forelegs or strike at his neck with its clicking mandibles. Alastair squirmed against the segmented coils, but they constricted in response.

Quick as thinking, the spirax's foreleg unfolded and snapped at Alastair's face. He jerked away, and the prong embedded itself seven inches in the turf. Again and again, it lashed out with its forelimbs, but Alastair, jerking and wrenching his neck, managed to confound its efforts.

But the creature had dealt with squirming prey before. Using the muscle in its curling abdomen, it brought Alastair almost upright and wedged his neck right into the crook of its forelimb.

As the thorny growths bit into Alastair's neck, a thousand thoughts coursed through his mind. *This is it, then. I die in my guilt. No prophesied one to bear my marks. I—*

Screeet!

An arrow shaft stuck out of the Spirax's good eye. Alastair blinked and another shaft plunged into the creature's chest. It loosed its grip on Alastair.

His sword arm free, Alastair drove the blade into the into the beast right beside the arrow. He withdrew the blade and whirled around the creature. Now directly behind it, Alastair slashed the Star Sword, severing the monster's spine. It fell limp at his feet.

Alastair spun around and ran to the spirax web. The tiny winged being had closed its eyes, the toxin no doubt doing its foul work.

Suddenly Abbagael was at his side, the child in a sling across her chest, bow and quiver of arrows in her hands. "What was that...that thing?"

"Here," Alastair said, urgency sharpening his tone. "Help me get her from this snare!"

"How about 'Thank you for saving my life?'"

"Huh?" Alastair looked up from the webbing. "Um, thank you."

"You're welcome," Abbagael said with a wry grin. She nodded to the small creature in the web. "What is it? A pixie?"

With Alastair's help, they managed to peel the spirax's intended prey from the sticky web sheet. They lay her in the soft grass where the sun cast its golden beams.

Almost immediately, the fairy girl opened her large, sideways-teardrop eyes. "Honeybelle," she said in a high, sleepy voice.

"Is that your name?" Alastair asked.

"No," she replied. Her eyes shut as if she might fall asleep once more. "Flower."

"Oh," Abbagael said, standing up. "The flowers there!" She started to go for them, but Alastair grabbed her arm.

"Wait!" Then he slashed his sword twice and the shimmering web mural fell.

"Thank you," Abbagael said. "I would've run right into it."

She grabbed a fistful of golden, bell-shaped flowers and returned to the winged creature. "What do I do with them?"

"I don't know," Alastair said. "Hold it near her face."

Abbagael lowered a honeybelle bloom to the creature's face. The little thing's eyes popped open. She grabbed the bloom and shoved her entire head into it. There came the sound of munching and chomping. Alastair and Abbagael looked at each other and shrugged.

Finally, the creature removed her head from the flower. "Ah," she said, puffing wild locks of silvery-gold hair from her eyes. "That'sbetter." Her words were so quick they ran together.

"What are you?" Alastair blurted out. "A fairy?"

"A pixie?" Abbagael suggested.

"Neither," the little being replied. A long pink tongue flickered out from the corner of her mouth and, in a blink, licked a bit of pollen off her upper cheek. "Willowchild."

"Willowchild?" Abbagael repeated. "I've never heard of such a thing."

"Neither have I," Alastair said. "Nonetheless, here you are. Do you have a name?"

She nodded so fast it was a blur. "Sprye."

"Well, Sprye," said Alastair, "it is a good thing we heard you calling for help."

"You mean," Abbagael said, "it's a good thing that *I* heard her cry for help. If you'd had your way you'd have just kept rid—"

"Nonsense," Alastair said quickly. "Tell me, Sprye, how did you resist the poison? And *how* did you keep the spirax at bay until we arrived?"

"Toansweryourfirstquestionwillowfolkarenaturallyresistant-tonaturaltoxinsand—"

"Whoa, hold on! What? What did you just say?"

The willowchild blinked twice, sighed and then repeated, "Isaid…Toansweryourfirstquestionwillowfolkare—"

"No, too fast, too fast, little willowchild," Alastair said. "I cannot follow you."

"Oh!" Sprye shook her head. "PleaseforgivemeasIamnotusedtotalkingtobigfolk.Isthisbetter?"

Alastair laughed. "Some, but not enough. A bit slower, please."

"How about now?" Sprye asked with exaggerated slowness. "I don't think I can speak any slower without getting lockjaw."

"Yes!" Abbagael clapped. "We can understand you now."

Sprye clapped also. "Splendid!"

Alastair scanned the area. "Any more spirax around?"

"Spirax?" said Abbagael. "That big-spider-mantis-centipede thing?"

"Yes, Lady Abbagael," he replied. "Sprye, are there more of them here?"

"Idonotknow," said Sprye. "I mean...I do not know. I haven't seen any, but then again, I didn't even see the web I flew into before it was too late. We willowfolk are so impulsive...and well, honeybelles are our weakness."

"I haven't trod this way in years," Alastair said. "There were no spirax in this part of Chapparel then. Clearly, things have changed."

"Changed, indeed," said Sprye. "Fearful things are creeping eastward. But not all things have changed. Besides, this region is not Chapparel. It is Greenshire."

Abbagael stood and took a step backward. "Greenshire?" she said. "Are all childhood stories this day come to life?"

"What do you mean?" Alastair asked.

"Whatdoyoumean?" asked Sprye, her wings suddenly twittering to life. In an instant, she darted forward and hovered right before Abbagael's nose.

"Greenshire," Abbagael said, "is the land of bewitchment. My parents used to read me stories before...well, before. One of the stories was my favorite. I've even dreamt of it."

"Tellme," said Sprye, her eyes flickering with anticipation. "Ilikestories!"

Alastair stood and sighed. "Look, I really don't think—"

"Shhh," said Abbagael. "Well, the story was about a young girl who wanders into Greenshire where she drinks the dew off an elephant ear plant and falls asleep. When she awakes, she is surrounded by fairies. They make her a queen or something. No, not a queen…a mist princess, or mistmaid. Wait, mistmaiden—that's it."

Sprye gasped. "Mistmaiden!" she exclaimed. "Thatisnostory!"

"Slow down, Sprye, please."

"I am sorry," she replied. "But I am amazed now twice in one day. I am the mistmaiden of my kinship."

"Kinship?" asked Abbagael. "Is that like family?"

"For the willowfolk, a kinship is more like a community or a village. In my kinship, I am the mistmaiden."

"What's that mean?" asked Alastair.

Sprye flitted in front of him. "It means that I am beautiful and adventurous!"

"Oh, well, that's lovely," said Alastair. "And you certainly are both."

"Thanks be to you."

"Yes, well," he went on. "We've certainly enjoyed this chance meeting, but—"

"Chance?" echoed Sprye. "What is chance?"

"Oh, uh…like luck or fate. Kind of like an accident. But as I was say—"

"We don't believe in that," said Sprye, crossing her arms.

"Be that as it may," said Alastair, "what I mean to say is that we are on an important errand. And we must be go—"

"Yes," Sprye said, "we must be going, but not where you were going. You saved my life. You are willowfriends now. You must come with me."

"Ohhhhh, no," Alastair said, waving a hand. "No, we have an important errand. We have a child to look after."

Sprye looked at the bulge in the sling on Abbagael's chest and darted over to it. "Oooh, so cute. And sleeping? My goodness!"

"Yes," said Alastair. "So as you see, we have to get to Gull'scry for supplies."

"In good time," said Sprye as she zigzagged to a patch of honeybelle. She dropped down and popped off a bloom. "Mmmm… tasty!" She jolted up into the air and zipped forward a few yards. "Come, follow Sprye!"

"Come on, Alastair," said Abbagael, unstringing her bow. "Maybe they'll show us magic."

"Turn us into mushrooms is more likely," he grumbled.

"Very funny, tallbeard!" said Sprye.

Alastair felt his chin. *Too long since I've shaved,* he thought. "I don't think we can afford the time."

"But if you do not come you will miss Willow Dell, my home."

"Forgive me, Sprye," he said, "but what's so special about your home?"

"Many things," she replied. "There is no place like it in all of Myriad. But more than that. You see, no bigfolk have been to Willow Dell in two thousand years. It is hidden."

"Come on, Alastair," Abbagael said. "We won't stay long, I promise. But if it's anything like the stories my parents told me, I can't miss this. Please, Alastair. We've got to see it, don't we?"

The mention of Abbagael's parents tore the scab from an old wound, and Alastair winced. "I'll get the horse."

I don't know this way at all," Alastair whispered to Abbagael. "I thought sure we'd have come upon the Suskind River by now."

"We've been lost since you took us on the shortcut," she replied, with no little contempt.

"Well, it's no shortcut now, obviously," he said. "Unexpected adventures are bound to happen, but what's bothering me is the direction. I've lost it. And I *never* lose my sense of direction."

"Never?"

Not unless I've had Witchdrale. "I'm not boasting, Abbagael," he said. "It's just a knack of mine, since I was a child." He looked through the tree canopy to the sky. "But I'm well and good lost now."

"Did you say you are lost?" asked Sprye, suddenly buzzing right before their noses.

"Yes," Alastair said. "Most completely. Even the sun seems vague here. I can't tell where it's traveling or where it's been. The shadows are impossible to follow too."

"Don't get your armor all in a bunch, big stuff," said Sprye. "Everyone gets lost here. It's willowfolk enchantment."

Alastair wanted to press Sprye for details, but she whisked away, beckoning them to follow. She led Alastair, Abbagael, and the child on an even more meandering course, deeper into the Tanglewood Forest—if it still was the Tanglewood Forest. With unexpected sinkholes, entanglements of vines, and jagged clumps of stone, the trail was not easy by foot or by hoof.

The uneven terrain eventually ended at a huge fist of marbled, gray stone that seemed to punch up through the forest floor to block their way. Alastair gazed around either side of the rocky upthrust. He whispered over his shoulder to Abbagael. "It a long ride either way. I wonder why she brought us here."

"Maybe we'll have to climb," she replied. "I hope not. That's too steep for my liking."

With a percussive flutter, Sprye circled the riders. "You'll have to leave your horse here."

"I'd rather not," Alastair said. "This is a good stout horse."

"Noharmwillcometoyourbeast," said Sprye, growing excited. Then she caught herself and slowed down. "She will be well cared for. Friends, come out!"

At her word, a dozen or more winged willowfolk appeared from the surrounding greenery. "Hel-lo!" "Hey'o!" "Hullo!"

"Ello!" Each one called out greetings but each at a different volume, dialect, or cadence.

"Why, hello!" Abbagael returned their welcome. "Oh, Alastair, aren't they beautiful?"

"Iteesyouwhoarebeauteeful," said one of the male willowfolk who wore a silvery-green tunic and breeches. He circled around Abbagael's head and emitted a high purring sound. "Afetchingcreeeture,Sprye, butwhyhaveyoubroughtherandtheotherhere?"

"They saved my life, Bevin," she replied. "And do slow down your words. Big folk listen slowly."

The willowfolk responded by swarming around Alastair and Abbagael. Each one sang a different musical note. Combined with the flutter and buzz of their wings, it was a dreamy, hypnotic sound.

The whirling stopped and the willowfolk hovered before the visitors. "Hail, willowfriends," Bevin said. "You have come where no other of your kind has set foot for many a year plus one. Will you enter the Dell and be refreshed?"

"I...well..." Alastair hesitated.

"We will," Abbagael declared.

"Very good!" Bevin clapped his hands. "Dismount your horse, my friends."

Alastair and Abbagael obeyed.

Sprye rose a few feet above their heads. "*Transport!*" she cried.

There came a sound like wind, and a veritable cloud of willowfolk arrived from every direction all at once.

Bevin flew close to Alastair. "Just relax. This will be an odd sensation for you bigfolk, but pleasant by all accounts."

"What?" Alastair glanced sideways at Abbagael, who only shrugged in return.

Bevin and his group began to swirl around Alastair and Abbagael once more, but this time their music was different. More melodic and rhythmic.

"I feel dizzy," Alastair said, glancing at the baby in the sling. "Is the child all right?"

"Still sleeping," said Abbagael, swaying slightly. "And I'm doing well too. Thanks for asking."

Sprye buzzed right before their eyes. "We are singing the song of your kind," she said. "You will sleep soon."

"Sleep?" The word was barely off of Alastair's lips when he and Abbagael fell backward like hewn trees. They landed in a soft blanket supported on every side by willowfolk.

The beat of their small wings increased, and soon, with Alastair and Abbagael and the baby sound asleep, they took to the air, climbing above the trees and above the fist of stone.

CHAPTER 19

THE COUNCIL OF MYRIAD

The Treaty of 414 established friendship between Anglinore and the
Wyndbyrne Eyries.
An odd friendship, to be sure, given that a Windborne at most
will live fifty years…while men can last close to four hundred.
One wonders if generations from now, the Windborne will even
remember.

Stacke Beledain, Court Historian of Queen Davara

27 CELESANDUR 2212

Footsteps and hushed voices issued strangely from the chamber
ahead. It sounded as if a secretive throng approached from the
other side of the long hall. But the rulers of Myriad knew no one
else was in the area. They had been in the Hall of Council and
experienced its unique acoustics many times.

Still, as they entered the grand room and were splashed with
countless colors from the stained glass windows far above, it was
impossible not to be awed. If Clarissant Hall had been marvelous
due to its vast depth and its long aisle, the Hall of Council was

much more so because of its great height, furnishings, and incomparable artistry.

"Ah, this I must see while there is still a bit of light." King Drüst spread his iron gray wings.

"Watch it, Drüst," King Vang said, peeking out between the forefletchings of Drüst's right wing. "You could put an eye out with those feathers."

"Sorry, old friend," the King of the Windborne replied. He crouched low and sprang into the air. His vast wings lifted him quickly, and soon he hovered a hundred feet above them all. He seemed to float in the midst of all the stained glass windows. The golden light of the evening sun shone through them and bathed him in color. Each time he beat his wings or turned, the colors and patterns changed. From below, it was like looking into a gigantic kaleidoscope.

"I could stay a week in Anglinore," Drüst called down to them, "and do nothing but wonder at the artistry in glass. See, here is Elrain slaying the dragon Balroth on the outskirts of the Hinterlands. And here is the Lady, Queen Faylura, upon her white mare—I saw her once, you know. As a fledgling...I fell in love that day." He laughed. "As did all who saw her. Myriad will not see the like of her again...pity she died childless. And... wait! Is this new? Yes, Telan Ironfist leading the charge against fell Droll and the Sabrynite Army! Lo, it is by the same hand. Aravel, I did not know this artist still lived."

"Not the same hand, my friend. His grandson's. Celan Utherbrand is his name."

"Amazing," Drüst muttered, continuing his slow turn.

"Look at the pretty pictures another time, Wing-man!" Morlan shouted. "We have much to discuss at Council. Or have you forgotten?"

Even from far below, they could all see Drüst's brow lower. "Nay, Stormgarden," he replied, slowly descending. "I have not forgotten our Council. Nor have I forgotten the counsel of our past. Much we may learn of it if we dare to listen."

"Come, take your place at the table," Aravel said, casting a heavy glare at his brother.

Beside him, Maren stared too, and they both wondered if Morlan would stay true to his word.

Drüst landed in his chair. "I cannot fathom how Celan does it," he muttered to Queen Briawynn on his left. "Midians, azors, plenches, even gulsh."

Briawynn looked at him quizzically. "What?"

"Colors, my lady," Drüst answered. "Colors only my kind can see. I wonder how Celan crafts so eloquently with colors he cannot see and has never seen."

"Let us declare the invocation," Queen Maren said, earning a relieved smile from King Ealden and something slightly less pleased from her husband. The queen waited until the chamber was silent. She thought whimsically that she could hear the echoes of the invocation spoken over the long years by the lords of old. "To Him who was first, is first, and ever will be first, we bid thee welcome in this hall."

They spoke the familiar rite in unison. King Ealden couldn't help glancing at Morlan, expecting him not to participate. But the High King's brother did—perhaps not with the proper feeling, but still.

Queen Maren's deep womanly voice echoed gently in the chamber as she continued. "To Him whose hand crafted Myriad from nothing and called forth life to dwell in the sea, land, and air...we bid thee welcome. And to him whose wisdom is far above the minds of those deemed wise in Myriad...we bid thee welcome. May you judge between us and grant us wisdom in our time of need. Glor annas met."

"Glor annas met!" came their unified response.

Aravel leaned forward immediately. "There is much to discuss: treaties, new trade possibilities, the Anglish Army Tithe, and so forth. But, to my mind, there are recent events that require our immediate attention. Let us hear first from the Shepherds."

All turned to the high Shepherd, but he nodded in deference to Mosteryn.

The old Shepherd fanned his gnarled fingers on the tabletop. "In 2180 AS, those of Shepherdkind with the skill to hear the voices of the wind began to hear rumor of calamity. The massacres at Avington, Bryngate, Maiden Vale, Teris Falls, Sennec, and so on confirmed our fears, but in spite of the combined armies of Myriad, the band of marauders was never found. In the years that followed, bloodshed continued in the form of murder, ambush, and assassination. Again, no one was captured; no blame was laid."

Morlan shifted in his seat, his expression fierce and…eager.

"Now the winds speak of even greater sorrow," Mosteryn said. "As Shepherd Sebastian can attest, the threat is palpable. And Queen Briawynn brings word of a ruthless attack in Ellador." He nodded to the young Elladorian queen.

"My lords," Queen Briawynn said, her expression hardening into anger, "this was not some raid on a barracks full 'a knights. They murdered helpless children and old gaffers with nought t'defend themselves but walkin' sticks and fishin' rods."

"Who?" asked King Vang, fingering the pickaxe at his side.

"Reliable witnesses claim these be Gorrack raids."

"Gorracks?" blurted out Prince Navrill, ruler of the Marinaen people. The bluish flesh on his narrow cheekbones turned purple.

Several conversations began at once, but ended just as abruptly when Morlan spoke.

"Yes, Gorracks! Is this such a surprise to us all? How long have I been warning that they muster for a third invasion?"

"Isolated attacks do not necessarily indicate a pending invasion," King Drüst said.

"Don't they?" Morlan asked. "Perhaps the leatherheads have learned from the epic failures of their past. On their first two attempts, they blundered forward with no plan, no strategem, and found themselves on an anvil awaiting the hammer. But see how they entered the Felhaunt so recently as fifty years ago. It was just an expeditionary force, as my beloved brother can confirm. They have bided their time, and now they are probing, testing our defenses."

"Defenses?" Queen Briawynn exclaimed. "Did you not listen? They slaughtered children and old men."

"Who just happened to be in their path," interrupted Morlan. "It is a straight line from the Verdant Mountains to Lyrimore, no doubt their intended destination. I tell you, if I commanded the Gorrack Nation, I would measure my enemy before invading. I would find their weaknesses and plan to exploit them."

"Yes, brother," Aravel said. "That is tactically sound. But the Windborne have seen no tactical movements from the Gorracks. Do you honestly believe they could be so clever as to avoid the sharp eyes of the Skyflights and the rest of the Borderguard?"

"Yes," Morlan said, earning a grunt from King Drüst.

King Ealden sat up straight in his chair and lifted his hands to shoulder height in a pleading manner. "With all due respect to my lady of Ellador, we have nothing to indicate this was a Gorrack raid besides the vague and fearful descriptions of an old man in the twilight of dawn."

There was general muttering at this. The two Shepherds leaned forward.

"Who then?" Morlan growled. "Brutish invaders from the Hinterlands?"

"Perhaps," replied Ealden, maintaining his calm demeanor. "Or could it be that the Cult of Sabryne has returned to its bloody roots and taken up arms against followers of the First One?"

"Sa-Sabryne?" Morlan chortled. "Ridiculous! And why, pray, do you call them a cult? They have as much right to believe what they will as you or I."

Ealden bristled. "The Sabrynites are deathmongering usurpers who have twisted the words of the First One to their own wicked ends. Their history is littered with the corpses of innocent Myridians."

"That puts rather a fine point on it," Vang whispered to Warden Caddock.

"The Sabrynites are whitewashed sepulchers full of rot," Ealden said. "I for one would not be surprised if they were solely respo—"

King Ealden's words were cut short by a sudden clatter of metal on stone. Morlan had taken an iron pike and a helm and tossed them into the center of the Council table.

"My Wolfguard intercepted a band of Gorracks just east of my garrison at Cragfield."

All eyes turned to King Aravel and Queen Maren. It seemed a weighty decision hovered in the air. But before anyone could speak, there was a ruckus from the passage leading to the Council Hall: hurried footsteps and anxious whispers.

Paige Martin charged over the threshold, came to a sudden stop, and bowed low. Behind him was a man whose eyes darted to and fro like a trapped animal. He had stringy, copper-colored hair and beard and was dressed in a tunic and loose breeches, all torn and ragged, stained green from foliage and dark with sweat.

"My lords," Paige Martin said, puffing. "Please excuse the intrusion! But this is Brayden Arum of Westmoor."

At that, King Vang looked up.

"He brings terrible news from Tryllium," Paige Martin said.

Poor man, High King Aravel thought. *He looks like he's been washed down a mountainside and dragged across the Naïthe.* "Come, Brayden, you are among friends. You've no doubt traveled a long way. Tell us your tale."

Brayden bowed low repeatedly and came a few steps closer. "Oh, King Vang," he said. "You are here. I searched for you in Ardon."

"Aye, lad," replied the King of Tryllium. "We've met before… you…you run a tavern, the Thundering Boar…or some such, a fine place."

"The Hammer and Bow, Your Majesty, and thank you. Least-ways it was a fine place. Now, I don't know what it is. Westmoor, sir, it's under attack!"

"What?" King Vang and several others stood.

"Gorracks, sir, they came in the night, they were all over the main road, breakin' in t'places. They tore into the Hammer...my wife, my children, we just made it out of the city in time. But the others... Everyone else..."

"You're sure they were Gorracks?" asked King Ealden.

Brayden bowed again. "Yes, m'lord. I saw 'em out the window of the Hammer."

"Yes, yes, I assumed as much," said Ealden, king of the Prydian Wayfolk. "What I mean is, how do you know the beings you saw were Gorracks? Have you experience in the Gorrack Nation?"

"Wot, me? No, sir."

Ealden smiled. He knew there had to be a hole in this man's story.

"But I 'ave been in the Felhaunt. I do a little business in Graymere. Brew a fine ale, they do. But once, a hunting party come back from the Felhaunt with a dead Gorrack footsoldier. Hideous things, they are. I wouldn't forget the look of 'em."

"How much proof do you need, Prydian?" Morlan asked.

King Ealden fell silent.

"Lord Aravel," Vang exclaimed, leaving his chair and striding over to Brayden. "I need to return to Tryllium. Who knows what mischief the Gorracks have done in a fortnight?"

Aravel nodded slowly. "I understand, my friend." He turned to Brayden. "You say you went to Ardon. Did you alert the guard?"

"Yes, your majesty. Why, we met Shepherd Brogan in the courtyard there. He's the one who sent me. Gave me a royal escort, he did."

"There, Vang," said the High King. "Your doughty soldiers will have things well in hand—"

"But, what if it's as Morlan says?" asked Vang. "My forces are as strong as the bones of the mountains, but they'll not stand against the entire Gorrack Nation."

"They'll not be standing alone," Morlan said with a note of triumph. "Will they, brother? We must unleash the Anglish Army and put down the Gorrack threat once and for all."

"Open war, Morlan?" Aravel asked, his ruddy cheeks turning scarlet. "You advise me to declare open war on the Gorrack Nation?"

Morlan held up the Gorrack pike. "Nay, I advise you to answer the challenge, for they have already declared open war on us."

CHAPTER 20

WILLOW DELL

He who risks his life for a friend will be first in Allhaven.
Canticles, (XIV.ii)

27 CELESANDUR 2212

When Alastair awoke, he at first thought he was in the White Room. A light, feathery blanket covered his body, and a white curtain was drawn around him. There was even a similar silky white roof above. Golden sunlight made silhouettes of branches, leaves, and foliage dance on the sheer material. There was a sweet, floral scent in the air, and a delicious cool breeze flowed over and around him. A gentle rushing sound whispered somewhere farther away like wind stirring trees in a forest or small waves breaking on a shore.

But as Alastair lifted his head and looked round, he saw that his mother was not there. He was alone. It all came back: the spirax, Sprye, the strange music. He sighed and let his aching head drop back onto the pillow.

Thoughts jabbed at him like a horde of daggers. *What am I doing? I ought to be on a ship with a black bottle in my hand. I have got to get out of here.*

And down beneath his turbulent thoughts, like the potent tremors that triggered tidal waves, deeper pains throbbed. Scenes flickered in his mind's eye: townsfolk, blackened and burning, emerging from cottage infernos, corpses untangling themselves from a massive common grave, and howling dead, bloated and fleshy, clambering out of a swollen river of blood. Alastair knew he could not escape them. There was no help now. No hope. No one was coming to save him.

He pounded his fist on the bed. "There's nothing left!"

Somewhere nearby, a high voice: "Hey'oSpryethebighuman-wokeup!"

Soon there was a flutter outside, and Sprye buzzed beyond the curtain. "Wake up, sleepy!" she said, hovering just above him.

Alastair cringed under the blanket. "Leave me."

"No can do, tallbeard." Sprye tugged at his blanket. "Up, up!"

"I said leave me!" Alastair jerked the cover, sending Sprye tumbling in the air.

"And I thought *I* was grumpy in the morning." But Sprye did not give up so easily. She raced back and forth across the bed, grabbing every corner of the blanket until finally she was able to yank it off.

"Why you little winged—"

"No time for silly stuff. The lady is already being prepared. You must join her."

"Prepared? Prepared for what?"

"The greatest honor our people can bestow! Come!"

Alastair's protests were roundly ignored as Sprye buzzed away. Alastair sat up all the way, found himself still slightly dizzy, but was able to stand. Realizing Sprye could be far ahead of him, he passed through the curtain. An intricately embroidered, grayish-blue curtain waited beyond. Shrugging, he passed through that as well.

Intermittent beams of glorious sunlight greeted Alastair through a half-circle of deep green pines that formed a barrier around the tent he'd just left. But when he pushed his way through the evergreen boughs, Alastair was momentarily stunned.

In the Witchdrale years, Alastair had been mostly a nocturnal being, staggering around taverns and staggering home under cover of darkness. In the decade since, his life enriched by the teachings of the Books, Alastair had not changed his environment very much. He kept his house austere, furnished with only the absolute necessaries of life in Tryllium. When he did venture out into the natural world, he endeavored to pay little attention to the landscapes and environs around him. Even with the Books, and sometimes because of them, it was as if joy was off limits. His guilt remained. There could be no pleasure. And so, for many years, Alastair had existed in a somber, gray world.

But when Alastair emerged from the evergreens, the other-worldly beauty of what he saw shook his senses. Many of Sprye's folk flew hither and thither or hovered about in small groups. Strange motes of purple, blue, or rosy-pink whirled in the air like snowflakes. The sun was warm and golden, and just a few clouds, puffy and bright white, drifted across it.

Spongy green moss spread away beneath Alastair's feet and was so utterly soft that Alastair didn't notice that his riding boots had been taken. For the moment, it seemed that humans were meant to walk barefoot and no other way. Lying upon the moss, and half covered by it, were massive oval stones, dark blue-gray with a hint of rusty red, and wide enough that ten human maidens could lay upon them and sun themselves. Alastair stood, mouth slack, eyes bouncing from sight to sight. He felt like a half-starved man suddenly dropped into a banquet.

But perhaps more than any other part of this waking dream, it was the cascading network of waterfalls and pools that drew Alastair in and refused to let him go. Crystal clear water, bearded and whiskered in white, poured down from great heights all the way round in either direction. For indeed, the willowfolk's landscape was surrounded by a high wall made of thousands—nay, millions—of dark slabs of rock. These were piled so haphazardly as to seem accidental, but were so perfect in their directing of dozens of streams of water and so dense that it seemed the Master Stonewright of History must have placed each one just so, stone by stone.

Each waterfall flowed into a shimmering pool below, which in turn poured over its own lip to fall to yet another cistern another level down. And leaning over some of these pools like protective parents were massive weeping willow trees. Draped with long green strands of foliage that hung down like mops of wet hair, the willows danced and swayed in the breeze, some even managing to dip their roots in the water. Other trees grew in the dell: pines, oaks, red maples, and even wide-leaved sables. But the willows, ancient and vigorous all at once, clearly ruled this valley.

"Hey'o, Alastair!" Sprye cried out from up ahead. "How sleepy you are! Come on, now. Follow me!"

Alastair found himself lumbering after her, and with every step, he felt lighter and stronger than before. So mighty and agile did he feel that he soon raced across the moss and stone until he'd caught Sprye and even surpassed her.

"Ah, you are revived at last," said Sprye, "and light on your feet. A willowsleep has many curative powers."

"I don't know what you mean," said Alastair, slowing to a jog. "But I cannot remember the last time I felt this…well, young. I—"

Alastair halted. His words fell from his lips like coins dropped in a pond as he caught sight of Abbagael Rivynfleur. A living willow, seemingly grown over many long years into a throne, held her, and more of Sprye's kind hovered around her.

She wore a flowing lavender dress and reclined against the trunk with her legs extended but slightly crossed upon one of the tree's immense limbs. She hadn't seen him yet, for she held the child in her lap and gazed down upon him. Her glorious crimson hair, dotted now with tiny white blossoms, spilled down her shoulders and swayed in unison with the willow strands all 'round. Behind her a fresh, clear stream flowed, winding away from the lowest pools and traveling to some other happy destination.

Alastair stood haplessly gawking, for it seemed to him he witnessed a goddess, Rivynfleur as she really was. All manner of emotion drenched the parched places of his mind and heart. How tenderly Abbagael held the child, love shining from her smile. And though there was no resemblance in form or appearance, there was something about Abbagael now that reminded Alastair of his own mother. It was strange to recognize it here. And strange also to notice that the freckle-faced child he'd tormented for so many years had abruptly transformed into a woman.

"Pretty, isn't she, tallbeard?" Sprye whispered into Alastair's ear.

Alastair, nodded and reality crashed down on him. No matter her interest in him, he could not pursue her. He didn't deserve Abbagael. And if she ever knew how his past connected with her parents, she would flee from him, or worse.

"Ahhhh, so he has awakened from his hibernation," came a high, resonant voice.

Alastair turned and found one of the willowfolk hovering ten inches from his nose. This little being had a shock of blue hair that stood straight up on his head. He wore a tunic and breeches that were criss-crossed in deep blue and purple, with three yellow bars on each shoulder. A gold medallion hung down from his neck. He seemed important—small, but important.

"I am Alacritous Tracer," he said. "You can call me Alac, as my friends do. I am High Noble of Willow Dell. Is my speech appropriate?"

"Yes, yes," said Alastair. "Not too fast. Perfectly understandable."

"Good," said Alac. "Won't you take your seat?"

Alastair looked up and for the first time noticed that there was a matching willow chair right next to Abbagael.

"Come on, Alastair," she said, noticing him at last. "I won't bite."

Alastair risked a quick smile to Abbagael, but it vanished, overcome by anxiety. "I don't mean to be rude, Alac," he said, "but…what is this all about?"

"Oh, you've not been told?" Alac whirled and glared at Sprye.

"What?" She shrugged and seemed to bounce in the air. "He slept forever and nearly knocked me silly when I tried to rouse him!"

Alac spun back around, his face reddening. "Fearfully sorry," he said. "But this is your crowning ceremony."

"*Crowning?*" Alastair almost laughed.

"Yes," said Alac. "You are the Willow King. The lady there, she is Willow Queen."

"There must be some incredible mistake here," Alastair said as a dozen willowfolk ushered him to the tree-chair.

"Alastair, isn't this exciting?" Abbagael asked, bouncing the child on her knee. "It's just like my old storybook come to life."

"But, but Alac," Alastair said, "we're not royalty of any kind. And we're certainly not willowfolk."

"Ah, no and yes," he replied, mischief bright in his eyes. "You and the lady are much too big to fit into our ceremonial garb, true. But you *are* royalty…and the best kind. You see, our people have three laws: love the Maker, love each other, and protect life. We do not elect our rulers or have any sort of royal bloodline. We simply wait for a king and queen to emerge. As the Writings say, 'He who risks his life for a friend will be first in Allhaven.'"

"I know that verse," Alastair said.

"Do you?" asked Alac, a gleam in his eye. "Good, good. We seek nothing more than to honor it here in our home. You and the lady saved Sprye from certain and painful demise. And today we crown you Willow King and Willow Queen."

"Alac, we're honored," said Alastair. "Really, we are. And your folk are wondrous and kind, but…but we cannot stay here in Willow Dell. We have errands to attend to. We must leave for Gull'scry tonight."

"Are you sure?" asked Alac. "You would be turning down an unheard of privilege."

"Well…yes, I'm afraid we must. But again, we are hon—"

"Alas, for this turn of fate," Alac said. "But since you refuse to stay and rule as our king and queen…you must die."

"*Die?*" Alastair stood up and found no sword at his side. "What is this? How can—?"

A merry explosion of laughter interrupted him…led by Alac, but sprinkled with Abbagael's giggles.

"*Ha!*" he said. "Youreallyfellforit! Ha,ha,ha!" Then Alac caught himself and slowed down. "My good Sir Alastair, but you are gullible."

"You mean you aren't going to kill us?"

"Of course not," said Sprye. " Alac just explained our laws to you. Did you not understand 'protect life'? To slay one who rescued one of us…how ridiculous."

"But," Alastair said, "we really cannot stay."

"Abbagael told us already," Alac said, wiping a tear away. "And we would never confine you here! Today you will be king and queen, but tomorrow we'll begin our wait for new ones."

Alastair saw no way to argue, not without insulting their new winged friends. So he nodded and fidgeted rather stiffly on his throne.

Once more, the willowfolk began to sing. Nothing hypnotic or dreamy, but still beautiful. Again, there seemed no words. Either that, or the words were sung at such a pace that Alastair and Abbagael could not follow them. For their human ears it was enough, melody wrapped around melody, uplifting and satisfying. Teams of seven willowchildren flew forward bearing crowns woven of bright green willow whips. These they placed upon the brow of their ceremonial sovereigns.

Alastair glanced at Abbagael and was deeply troubled by the feelings that thickened within him. He'd felt himself wounded by her beauty before, but somehow, the addition of the living crown served only to make things worse. He turned away.

The willowfolk continued their song, and to Alastair's astonishment, there were many, many more of them than he'd seen before. In fact, there were airborne rivers of willowfolk descending from the huge weeping willows that ringed the dell. *They come to see us. Ah, but if they knew me, knew what I've done...*

His thoughts trailed off to wander dark places, paths strewn with long, cutting blades of grass and briars that stabbed. Old wounds, long scabbed over, bled afresh. But sudden warmth brought him back.

Abbagael reached over and took his hand.

He dared to look at her again and found her glad green eyes staring back...and the bright blue eyes of the child as well.

The song hung on a final pure note...and ended. With a sound like a swift downpour on a thin wooden roof, the willowfolk clapped. And clapped. And, when several minutes of applause had ended, they clapped some more.

"Arise, Willow King!" proclaimed Alacritous Tracer. "Arise, Willow Queen! The Hearth is strewn with honeycomb and cream! To the Hearth!"

"Wait," Alastair called. "Alac, before we go, could I please have my sword back?"

Alac buzzed close to Alastair's face and raised a blue eyebrow. "You bear us no grudge for our little joke, do you?"

"No, none at all," said Alastair, though in truth he had to fight back the urge to swat Alac right out of the air. "It was a jest well played. But my blade, it has great value...especially to me."

"Of course, of course," said Alac, and he sang a peculiar warbling note. "Hollyn Honeybred and Emma Hardgrave are bringing it now. We took the liberty of polishing the weapon. It, uhm, needed no sharpening."

Presently, two willowfolk swooped up the incline and delivered the blade to Alastair's lap. He noted that the two willowfolk, both female, looked very much like each other. Chestnut brown hair, large dark eyes, and button lips. *Twins,* Alastair thought. *Must be.*

Alastair pulled the blade a few inches from the sheath. "It looks remarkable." Alastair stood, put on his swordbelt, and bowed to the willowfolk. "Thank you very much."

"Hollynatyourservice," said one.

"Emmaatyourservice," said the other, her voice much deeper and more womanly than any of the other willowfolk that Alastair had met. It sounded odd coming from this little person.

"There, you see?" Alac asked. "Good as new." Alac flew away, melting into one of the streams of willowfolk coursing across the mossy field.

"C'mon, Alastair," Abbagael said, taking his hand once more. "It's a feast in our honor."

A feast sounded good. "I feel I haven't eaten in days," he said.

"That's because you haven't," Sprye said, buzzing by Alastair's ear.

"I wish she wouldn't keep doing that." Alastair thought he heard Sprye giggling as she flew off ahead. He shook his head. "You know, it's funny. With the willowfolk being so small, why do you suppose they had those big tree thrones? They fit us rather perfectly."

"I wondered about that," Abbagael replied. "Perhaps they used them for something else." She glanced back and gasped. "Alastair, look!"

Alastair turned. Where the thrones had been only moments ago, two majestic weeping willows stood, their trunks just like any other tree's, subtly curved, but certainly not shaped into chairs.

"D'ya think they move?" asked Abbagael.

"It wouldn't surprise me," Allastair said, looking around. "Not in this place."

CHAPTER 21

A Lonely Seat

*I know it is forbidden for anyone outside of the royal family, but I
once sat in the Seat of Kings. It was a clear day, and I saw an amazing thing. I saw the purple fins of the maratees out on the horizon. I
broke my leg trying to climb down from the seat.*

A story told by Lorilae Spiller at the Fireside Inn, Ellador

34 Celesandur 2212

The queen's cool hand caressed his shoulder. "You are restless
again, Aravel."

King Aravel covered her delicate, slender fingers with his
own thick palm. "Since the Council, I've not been able to sleep,
not deeply as I am used to. Ha, you used to say the castle could
collapse around me and yet I'd still slumber! Not anymore, it
seems."

"I am sorry, my husband. Your shoulders are broad and
strong, but you bear too much weight upon them. Won't you
share your burden?"

"It is far more than one burden," Aravel said gravely. "But
I will share them…in time. For now, I must sort through them
myself, come to some sort of decision."

"Must you do this alone?" she asked, leaning up on one elbow.

"It is the only way I know. I am High King Overlord of Myriad. There is no one above me with whom I might seek audience."

Queen Maren's thoughts drifted to Clarissant Hall and the missing altar. But to mention it now, she knew, would put her husband in a foul temper. "Still, your wife might offer some wisdom."

Aravel turned to her. "How shortsighted I must seem to you. Forgive me. In my life, there is no one I trust more than you, Maren. But you are too close to advise in this matter."

"Pity Sebastian's gone. He is wise."

"Yes...yes, he is. But in fact he already bears his own portion of this burden." Aravel stood up from the bed and grabbed a tunic. "I doubt he's getting much rest in Shepherd's Hollow, either."

"Where are you going?"

"I need to see the sea."

Like Morlan and the well, she thought. "But it's still hours before sunrise."

"That's the best time."

Anglinore Castle was dark and quiet. Drowsy guards standing at their posts were surprised to see their king wandering the halls. Aravel could be a bit mercurial—this they all knew—but still, to find him out in the dead of night seemed odd. They exchanged nods but spoke no words.

Aravel didn't want to talk. Once past the high chambers, he took seldom-trod passages and secretive routes to avoid contact as much as he could.

One hundred forty seven years, Aravel thought. As grand and massive as the castle was, it was still a long time to live in one place. *Like living in a museum of my life. Not just* my *life, really.* He passed the fencing room where he'd first learned swordcraft. How often had he and Morlan sparred there? He knew he could walk into that room blindfolded, go through any one of a hundred forms, dodges, parries, thrusts. He could almost feel Morlan's attacks. Outstanding with a sword. Good instincts and devastating strikes. He was powerful on offense.

Defense was Morlan's weakness.

He'd overextend and Aravel would win most of their sparring matches, if memory served. The king couldn't resist. He opened the creaky door. *Huh,* he thought. The door's brass knob seemed so much lower on the door than it had of old. Of course, it had been so many years. He smiled and passed into the chamber.

The fencing room's ceiling was forty feet up, and a series of narrow windows cast bands of ambient light across the dusty wooden floor. Aravel left whirls of dust motes and large manly footprints, traversing the room like he had so many times when his footprint would have been much smaller. He opened the door to the supply closet. It smelled like two hundred years of sweat and old, cloth body suits. But it was the inside of the door that mattered.

There, he and Morlan had carved tally marks for their wins. Aravel always had more and just wanted to see them again… after all these years. He counted once and cocked his head sideways. He counted a second time. "Morlan was much closer than I thought."

With slight disappointment, he left the fencing room behind. He climbed a narrow winding stair and came to a landing where the way split. He could take the passage to the left and make his way directly to the stables. Or he could take the slightly inclined way on the right, a seldom-used passage to Clarissant Hall, where the Ceremony of Crowns had taken place just a week prior. Once more, he felt drawn to visit, so to the right he went. The passage narrowed as it steepened, and for the thousandth time in recent memory, Aravel chastised himself for letting his midsection get so rotund.

At the end of the path, he passed through a heavy curtain and emerged from a corner in the front of Clarrisant Hall. Due to the massive stained glass windows, the cavernous chamber was filled with spectral light of many shades. Aravel paced a few moments, running his fingers along the altars and the deep shelves holding various relics and tomes.

He'd never known his mother, but he'd learned a lot about her over his first triniary. He'd learned how very much she'd loved this room. Quite the scholar, Clarissant Stormgarden had spent many of the years of her youth studying the lore of Myriad. Anything to draw nearer to the First One. Aravel's father, King Brysroth, had renamed the hall to honor his wife...after she died.

Aravel wondered how his mother would like the hall now... after the changes he'd made. Maren had been against most of the changes, and she was less devoted, by all accounts, than his mother. He could just make out the faded lines on the center stone wall several yards behind the new altars and the thrones. It had been the visual focal point of the room. Clear prismatic glass discs embedded strategically in the stained glass had captured noonday sun and sent it streaming in. Quite a spectacle, if not divine. How long had the old structure stood? He didn't know, but times had changed. In Myriad, as in his own life, it was time to move on from myth and superstition.

He left Clarissant Hall and all its ghosts behind.

Halbred, the king's horse, handled the cliffside terrain with ease. He tossed his head in the sea breeze and stormed ahead. He seemed to recognize that his master was in a hurry, that dawn would not wait forever.

As they thundered up the trail, Aravel remembered the first time his father had brought him to the Seat of Kings. He'd been eleven. King Brysroth had led him up the curl of stone stairs to the massive granite seat above the shore. It was not the highest point on the cliffs, but it was the best vantage point. The way the rocky upthrusts and the cliff's edge peeled away at the foot of the mighty chair gave anyone sitting there an unsurpassed view of

miles of shoreline in either direction and an awe-inspiring pan-
orama of the Dark Sea.

Brysroth, a strong man who required specially made armor
to suit his broad shoulders and chest, had sat upon the Seat of
Kings then, with young Aravel wedged somewhat awkwardly by
his side. They'd sat in silence for a very long time, Aravel coveting
every moment of closeness with his father.

As he gazed across the sea, the moment replayed in Aravel's
mind.

"My father sat here," Brysroth said. "As did his father and
the kings of old. When weighty matters of kingship threaten the
mind, you will find peace…and often clarity…when you sit in this
place and stare out upon the water."

"I like it here…being here with you," Aravel said.

His father didn't smile. He stared straight ahead, out to sea.
"Be not overly used to companionship, my son. For the next time
you sit in this chair, you will be king, and you will be alone."

Aravel sighed and the vision dissipated. Brysroth had been so
right. *Did he know then?* Aravel wondered. *Did he know what he
would do six years later?*

He spurred Halbred and tried to shake the memory away. He
arrived at the bottom of a greensward of crag-grass downslope
from the chair and turned Halbred loose to graze. A mantle of
slate gray clouds floated heavily overhead when Aravel ascended
to the Seat of Kings.

Now a broad man himself, Aravel sat in the great stone chair
and thrust his massive arms out upon the armrests. He flexed his
neck. Ever since the council, Aravel had felt even the simplest
aches much more keenly. *Look to the sea,* he told himself. *Look to
the sea and wait.* There was yet no hint of dawn at the horizon,
only the deepening clouds and endless black water.

It was a strange combination of calm and violence, the Dark
Sea. Miles and miles so still and serene while great waves crashed
on the shore. The tide was coming in, Aravel noted. He leaned

forward, trying to make out something some thirty yards inland from the water. *Was it? No, it couldn't be.* He smiled. It was a sandcastle, after all, and a proud one at that. No toddler had built this one. No, it was too large and grandiose. Built by a group of lads and lasses, no doubt. They'd placed it well on a mound where it could sit safely and spurn the waves.

Aravel looked from the sandcastle up the shoreline to the mighty walled city of Anglinore and its fortress of stone within. If he made the decision he felt he needed to make, would his kingdom stand? *But how can I not? In the past decade, the Gorracks have attacked my people dozens of times, increasing in frequency in the last six months. We* are *already at war. How can I just sit idly by without retaliating? But if I do...*

The Gorrack Nation was a violent and teeming culture, spreading across a landmass that stretched from the borders of Amara all the way to the Hinterlands—nearly a full quarter of the known world of Myriad. There had been skirmishes between the civilized races and the Gorracks before, Aravel knew all to well. But even the Battle of the Verdant Mountains had not led to full-on war. Fifty to sixty thousand Gorrack raiders had passed their borders and been diminished by Vang in Tryllium and Morlan in Vulmarrow before finally arriving with just ten thousand in Ellador. Seventy thousand troops united under the banner of Anglinore had assaulted the invaders. And yet that had still been a bitter fight.

What now? The Gorracks had had a hundred years to refine their warcraft. What if they had indeed abandoned their reckless, bludgeoning approach to battle? The attacks in Stonecrest and Westmoor, even in Ellador, had been carefully plotted and executed. What havoc could the Gorracks now wreak upon the civilized nations of Myriad in a world war? Aravel closed his eyes and slowly shook his head. It would mean hundreds of thousands of dead, perhaps millions...bloodshed on a scale never before seen in Myriad.

If there is any way—any way at all—of avoiding such an end, I must find it. The recent Gorrack attacks, while brutal and troubling, had been very localized invasions. Perhaps if he could discover the Gorracks' intentions, there could be some accord, some agreement. Aravel rubbed his temples and slammed a fist down on the armrest. *Father, if only you were here to advise me.*

But no, Aravel thought. *Such a decision might have proved too hard for him as well.* Aravel didn't even fight the thoughts that came next. On the night of his death, his father had come to this very seat. Some say Brysroth was grief-striken. That his mind had crumbled at last, and he had jumped to his death. Others claim that the old king was murdered. But in spite of a massive, year-long search, neither Brysroth's body nor his killer was ever found. The Dark Sea had a way of hiding things.

Aravel had his own suspicions.

It was well past time for dawn. The dark of night had lightened to a thick twilight. *The sun will not show its face in Anglinore today.* Aravel whistled for Halbred, and the horse came trotting up the hill. Fighting his weight, Aravel clambered into the saddle. He took one last look at the water. He had made his decision and knew not what would come of it. His last sight before riding away was the sandcastle being swallowed up by the dark water.

CHAPTER 22

DARK WINGS

Darkseed iron, there is no finer metal in all of Myriad.
Nor Longshanks, foreman at Central Mine in Stonecrest

27 CELESANDUR 2212

The Hearth was a pavilion, a wide expanse of grassy hills and moss-covered stones, nestled between a thatch of tall pines and a grove of more willows. A series of waterfalls emptied into a stream behind it. Golden sunlight rained down from the lip of the dell high above, turning the water to sparkling, emerald green and setting the spectacular wildflowers ablaze.

As Alastair and Abbagael approached, the willowfolk surged around them. They flew and changed direction in unison, their iridescent wings glimmering in the sunlight.

"Look at them," Abbagael said. "Up in the willow."

Alastair gazed upward. Each of the willows teemed with willowfolk. They flew in and out of the vines and seemed to be playing. Chasing, climbing, even wrapping themselves in the vine-like foliage. There seemed no end to their joy. And hanging from the sturdier branches were teardrop-shaped houses. Two to three feet in length, these suspended abodes held several tiny faces each—willowfolk children who watched the proceedings from their window perches.

While the willow trees seemed a focal point, Alastair and Abbagael realized that not all of the willowfolk lived in the trees. Some of the large stones had been somehow hollowed out and made into living spaces. Each one had a small oblong door, two or three even smaller round windows, and a crooked chimney.

"It's like the storybook," Abbagael whispered.

"You know," Alastair said, "many old stories are grounded in truth."

"It's so beautiful."

Just then, Alastair had an urge he hadn't felt for some time—not since before he had searched for the Halfainin and found no one. Certainly not since he'd fallen back into Witchdrale. But the urge was there nonetheless. It *was* the perfect opportunity. He'd dropped such a tempting hint about old stories being true. Now would be the ideal time to tell her about the Books. *Later,* Alastair told himself. *When we sit down to eat.*

"This way!" called Sprye and she led the Willow King and Queen to a wide mossy stone very near to the happily gurgling stream.

As soon as they were seated, other willowfolk floated in bearing platters stacked high with golden brown wafers of what looked like crusty bread or nooky biscuits. Others brought clay saucers full of cream.

"Silence! *Silence!*" Alac cried out. "The king and queen must taste the honeycomb and cream and tell us if it is good!"

"Take one," Sprye said to Alastair. "We made these extra large…just for you."

Alastair picked up one of the wafers. It wasn't actual honeycomb made by bees, but it had similar octagonal pores in it. A sweet smell wafted up from it, as well as the warm aroma of something recently baked. Alastair took a saucer of the cream and poured a little of it upon the honeycomb. Abbagael followed his lead and did the same.

"Go ahead, go ahead!" urged Sprye excitedly.

Alastair took the first bite, a big one, as evidenced by a most satisfying crunch. Again, Abbagael followed. They chewed in silence, and it seemed the whole dell waited breathlessly for their pronouncement.

"Well?" Sprye asked, her eyebrows raised timidly.

"Extraordinary," said Alastair and he took another—even larger—bite.

Abbagael licked cream from the corner of her mouth. "Scrumptious!"

As if a gale-force wind had blasted the Hearth, willowfolk took wing and streaked at great speed in all directions—all the while cheering and hooting and singing aloud. Many, many more platters of honeycomb and saucers of cream appeared, and as soon as they did, willowfolk children flew down from the trees or out from their mossy homes to join in the feasting.

Alastair felt as if he'd never in all his life eaten real food before this meal. Everything from roasted stag to duck fat fried andicots now seemed like eating clay compared to this. Flaky, savory, wholesome, and rich—each bite of honeycomb melted on the tongue and drizzled sweetly away. And there was nourishment too. If there weren't more honeycombs to devour, Alastair felt sure he would've leaped up and sprinted about the dell.

Abbagael dipped her finger in the cream and put a dab on the child's tongue. His blue eyes kindled and he grinned. "Look, Alastair, he likes the cream."

"So do I," said Alastair

When he looked at Abbagael, she burst into laughter.

"What?"

"Truly," Abbagael said. "Truly you do like the cream. You have a spot of it on your nose!"

It was more than a spot. Alastair reached up, and his fingers came away with a white glob the size of a strawberry. "I don't know how that could have happened," he said, taking another massive bite from a creamy honeycomb, which left a similar blob of white on his nose.

When the laughter and willowfolk frenzy had died down, Alastair felt the urging once more to tell Abbagael about the Books of Lore. "Lady Abbagael," he said.

"You mean Queen Abbagael, don't you?" she replied with a grin.

"Uh, yes, right," Alastair said. "Forgive my insolence, Your Majesty." This elicited a giggle, and Alastair thought he had chosen wisely to wait. She seemed to be in a very good mood. "I wonder if you recall a conversation we started just after the crowning. You said this whole scene, this Willow Dell and the willowfolk, seemed like something out of an old storybook you'd read."

"Sure, I remember, Alastair," she replied. "You told me that most old stories began with truth, right?"

"Yes, precisely," said Alastair. "You see, there's a very old book I want to—"

The pavilion darkened suddenly. Alastair felt like ducking. There came a harsh cry from above, and many of the willowfolk began to scream.

"*Rooks!*" Alac cried out. "Make safe our offspring! Guard-flight, make them safe! Singers, to the trees! Grapplers, to the air!"

On his feet with sword drawn, Alastair saw a dark curtain slide over the rocky lip of the dell high above and behind the Hearth. Not cloud cover, nor any phenomena of Myridian weather—they were birds. Hundreds of large birds, black eagles with glinting silver talons. They swept down into the dell, screaming and shrieking.

"Therookshaveeverbeenourenemy!" Sprye cried out. "Get to shelter! This fight is ours!"

"No," Abbagael said. "We'll fight with you. Where's my bow?"

"Abbagael, take the child." Alastair looked frantically from place to place. "There! Into that stone house!"

Abbagael held the baby close to her chest as she ran, then slid to her knees near the huge, moss covered boulder. She found the door to the little home unlocked, pushed it open, and saw no willowfolk inside. The door was too small for her to fit through but, propped up on her elbows, she was able to gently lay the child inside.

"Okay, there," Abbagael said, wriggling partway through the door so she could reach the window shutters. "I'll just lock these so you'll be safe in here." With some effort she slammed the shutters and threw the latch. It wasn't much of a lock, but it would have to do. Screams from the rooks, Alastair's grunting and yelling came from outside. "I have to go now, little one." She stared hard at his placid blue eyes. Always peaceful. Even with the chaos outside. She touched his chin and then wriggled backward out of the home. The door had no lock she could trigger from the outside, but she slammed it shut. Birds couldn't turn a doorknob.

Rising to her feet and spinning round, Abbagael found the pavilion had become a maelstrom of light and shadow, dark wing and silver claw. The rook and willowfolk tangled everywhere in the air. A low, vibrating hum drew Abbagael's attention to the willow trees. There, many of the willowfolk hung among the vines and…were singing. Many of the rook that flew toward the willows fell out of the air as if striking an invisible wall. They flopped around on the ground awkwardly, and other willowfolk pounced upon them with daggers.

But the rook were swift and cunning…and they outnumbered the willowfolk. The rook soared and dove, aiming always for the willowfolk's fragile wings. The rook tore with sharp beaks and sharper talons, sending many of their prey plummeting to ground.

Abbagael couldn't bear to watch these beautiful, dear creatures dying. She flung aside her cloak, but found herself without even a dagger.

"*Here!*" came a cry from above. Her bow and a full quiver of arrows fell at her feet. Abbagael looked up just in time to see Sprye buzz back into the battle.

Abbagael didn't wait. She strung the bow in an instant and nocked an arrow. The sky was so full of rooks she scarcely needed to aim. Pulling back hard on the bowstring, she grunted and released. The shaft pierced the air, took one rook through the breast and another through its neck and finally thudded into a third. Abbagael's second and third arrows did equal damage. She heard a loud grunt, and turned to see if Alastair needed help.

He didn't.

Abbagael nearly dropped her bow. She had always thought Alastair moved with a kind of athletic surety, a manly sort of confidence. It was something that had always attracted her to him. And she'd seen Alastair fight the Spirax, but only after it had him pinned. Nothing had prepared her for the skill she now witnessed.

The rooks whirled around Alastair in a vortex of claw and beak. But within that storm, Alastair was a one-man tempest. His blade flashed high, swept through the cloud of birds, carving a bloody Z-pattern in the air. Pieces of rook exploded in all directions. Wet clumps littered the ground near his feet. Alastair moved like a panther, planting his feet purposefully, ready to lunge.

With each step, Alastair rotated his body this way and that, whirling his sword—at times with one hand, other times with both. How the blade could move so freely and at such angles, Abbagael had no idea. It was as if the bones of Alastair's wrists came unhinged from his arm. Just when it seemed rooks were coming from too many angles at once, Alastair would crouch, throw himself forward, and somehow slash behind him.

Having wiped out the birds that pursued, Alastair launched into a kind of cartwheel with the sword flickering out like a cobra's tongue. Impaled, cut in half, and de-winged, the rooks fell in piles in Alastair's wake.

How did that spirax ever get over on him? Abbagael wondered mutely. The man used the blade with reckless abandon. It was a performance like a master painter whose seemingly haphazard strokes left marks in just the right places—every time.

A rook grazed the top of her head. Abbagael dropped to the ground and rolled to a knee. She came up firing and shot the offending rook from the sky. Rising to her feet, she saw that Alastair had slashed his way down to the grove of willows. There were substantially fewer rooks left in the air, but black clouds of them still lingered all over the dell.

"Ah!" cried Emma Hardgrave, her low voice plaintive and fearful. "TheGuardflighthasfaltered!"

"Singers,comeforth!" yelled Hollyn, her twin.

Abbagael spotted Sprye flitting spastically above the hill near the evergreens. "*Sprye!*" Abbagael called. "What's going on!?"

"Hurry! Hurry!" Sprye screamed. "Our children, the willowchildren, are endangered. The rooks have defeated our Guardflight!"

"What can I do?"

"Get Alastair. Follow the Singers from the great willows! We must go with all speed to the Nookery!"

Sprye whisked away above the pines. Abbagael glanced at the stone home behind her where she had hidden the child. The rooks had not threatened here. And Sprye needed help. She couldn't linger, and so she tore off down the hill toward the willows.

The child rested inside the stone cottage. He heard the commotion outside, and his blue eyes flickered. But he did not cry. His breathing slowed and his eyelids fluttered. Sleep danced upon his brow.

A sudden *whump* from outside startled him awake.

Scratching at the door. Then at the shutters. A piece of wood cracked then tore away. A shaft of light fired in from the new opening. The light faltered. Something black flitted back and forth outside and with renewed effort tore at the shutters.

Raaawwwwerrrk! A sharp beak rapped at the wood and tore away another piece. The rook drove its head into the hole, pushed and clawed, but could not get through.

The child still did not scream, but he raised his little hands and they trembled.

With some effort, the rook yanked its head back out and went back to work on the shutter. *Whump! Whump! M*ore scratching and clawing...much more. The shutters began to shake. Bits and pieces were torn away. Wood splintered and cracked. A claw appeared and withdrew. A jagged piece of wood disappeared close to the center of the two shutters...where the latch was clasped. More than one bird was attacking the house.

One of the rooks shoved its head in and screeched as the sharp wood jabbed its neck. But no matter the pain, it struggled to reach the latch with its beak. Shrieking and straining, the rook delved farther in. The shutters rattled as the creature applied all its weight and tried to squeeze in just a little farther. The angle was wrong, and the determined bird couldn't seem to crane its neck to flick the latch out of its clasp. A sharp thorn of wood had already drawn blood from its neck. Black feathers glistened.

Raaawwwwerrrk! The rook's voice gurgled to a wet choke. It drove itself against the sharp wood and flicked the latch. The creature breathed its last, and its head fell limp, its neck still impaled on the wood. But its dying effort had not been in vain. The latch swung loose. The shutters parted and flew open. Two more rooks screeched as they leaped in from the windowsill.

At last, the child cried.

CHAPTER 23

SABRYNE'S CALL

Blood is thicker than water…and often more bitter than poison.
Cardiff's Book of Anglish Wisdom

1 DRINNAS 2212

Morlan shook from sleep and found himself gasping for air and staring into his dying campfire. Two smoldering embers glared back from a face of black ash.

"After all these years," he whispered, forcing the words out.

His ears rang as if he'd endured an explosion. His heart raced. He could barely catch his breath. He clambered to his feet, swayed a moment, and steadied himself on the trunk of the old tree that leaned over his camp. Dark shreds of clouds raced overhead, obscuring the pale slice of moon. Heat lightning flickered red in the distance. The haunting vision from his dream still lingered and replayed itself over and over in his mind.

He had seen a path of many switchbacks climbing up the shadowy backside of a leaning mountain. He'd passed through a wall of briars with thorns as long as dagger blades and emerged to find a cleft in the looming rock wall ahead. Within the cleft stood a long-forgotten archway. And within this gateway swirled impenetrable darkness. In the dream Morlan had stood outside this door…until the voice.

Come.

Morlan was unused to being commanded so directly, but he was not tempted to wrath. He felt instead a kind of desperation he had never known. That old stone gate—Morlan ached to see it in waking sight, to caress its ancient craft and penetrate its inky mystery. Morlan knew well that mountain range, thought he recognized that leaning peak: Mount Gorthrandir. It was no more than half a day's journey west of Vulmarrow, two days from his current location.

He shook the last remnants of sleep from his mind. No, he could make the trip faster if he did not stop at Vulmarrow at all. It might kill his horse to make such a ride, but so be it.

A few hours past midnight the next night, Morlan stood at the base of Mount Gorthrandir and gazed upon the jagged path he had seen in his vision. Like a long, cruel scar, the trail carved its way up the foothills before disappearing under the shadow of the great mountain's overhang.

A grunt from behind disturbed him. He turned to his horse that lay sprawled in a dusty patch of brush. The creature panted unsteadily and pink froth issued from its nostrils. Morlan whirled round. In one motion, his sword was out, flicked below the horse's jaw, and was sheathed again. Morlan began the climb without looking back.

Even with a clear path, the ascent was difficult. Rocks broke free from beneath Morlan's boots, and more than once he found himself skidding on all fours. Huge, twisted hooks of roots from trees long dead snaked their way across the trail. Some were so massive and tangled that Morlan had to climb over them or hack through them with his sword. But after much toil, Morlan climbed to the brink of the shadow.

The change in visibility was staggering. Moonlight draped the entire downslope of the mountain in a gray-blue twilight. But the mountain's leaning peak covered the western slope in smothering darkness. Morlan looked up at the immense slanting promontory. It seemed a great beast that had once crested the original mountain had turned to stone and now loomed overhead. Ignoring the uncanny feeling that the monstrous peak could slam down at any moment, Morlan stepped into its shadow and continued the climb.

The deepening gloom held no fear for Morlan, for he loved the night and dwelt in darkness whenever possible. And while most beings in the wide realm of Myriad would be rendered sightless on the backside of Mount Gorthrandir, Morlan and his brother Aravel saw even the blackest night as dusk.

Morlan picked his way up the leveling path and entered a high thicket that closed in on either side and narrowed the trail to a thin band. Morlan charged through nonetheless and immediately regretted it. As in his vision, this briar had vicious, long thorns. One of them scraped up the armor of his upper arm and slid under the iron pauldron that covered his shoulder. It stabbed into the muscle and released a torrent of blood. Morlan cursed and backed himself off the thorn. The new wound throbbed, and Morlan took greater care the rest of the way through the deadly thicket.

Suddenly, he was through. Before him stood the rock wall from his vision, the shadowy cleft in the rock, and the ancient archway. But one thing was different from the dream: the doors within the arch were shut. Perplexed, Morlan came to the doorway and felt the stone for a handhold. There was none, nor even a seam where the two doors met. Morlan leaned against the door and strained. "Bah, might as well be trying to move the mountain itself!"

He backed away a step and glared at the door…and noticed the inscriptions: rune letters of a very old and obscure form gouged into the stone and running up one side of the arch, overhead, and down the other. Weather and time had eroded the strange symbols, but they could still be discerned if one had the skill. Born the son of the King of Myriad, Morlan had enjoyed the finest tutoring of any young student. But this language was not taught or spoken in Anglinore. And yet, Morlan knew it.

As a curious lad of sixteen, Morlan had had first seen the runes while peering over the shoulder of Alfex, Shepherd of Sidon in Ellador. Of all the Shepherds, Alfex had taken the greatest interest in young Morlan. Most of the others were too busy fawning over crown prince Aravel to notice his brother. But whenever Alfex came to the capital city, he went out of his way to be with Morlan. He taught Morlan many wondrous things…including the language of Sunderell.

Morlan ran his fingers over the inscriptions. "This is not a dialect," he muttered. "It has not yet been defiled by Gorrack scribes. Very ancient, indeed." But as he followed the language up toward the arch itself, he found deeper cuts in the rock…newer engravings left by unskilled hands. The Gorracks had come. Morlan was not surprised. Ages ago, the Gorrack Nation had usurped the Sunderell language—some of its culture and tradition as well.

Morlan began to read the text, even the Gorrack scrawls, and came away with a very strange message. "'Oceans of tears, wails on the wind, weeping in shadow, finds the jagged blade…'" He paused at a difficult phrase. "'The black'—no, 'the night finger bids you leave due homage. Feed the beast and enter.'" That last part was the most difficult. From the look of it, it had been hacked into the living stone by several different hands.

"Feed the beast?" Morlan stared at the blank stone wall within the arch. "What beast? The door is barren. Feed it what?" Then one of Alfex's lessons from long ago came back to Morlan, and he rolled his eyes at his own stupidity.

Morlan reached under his shoulder armor and scraped the clotting blood off the wound he'd incurred. The fresh blood pooled in his cupped hand and escaped in drops between his fingers. He placed his bloody, dripping hand on the wall before him.

He felt a sudden tremor beneath his feet and reflexively looked up at the looming mountain. No, the peak was not collapsing. But something was happening within, for there came a deep rumbling sound and the grating of stone against stone.

Morlan stepped away from the arch and watched the blot of crimson liquid leak into thin crevices that he had not previously seen or felt. Blood seeped downward, tracing the image of the open jaws and serpentine neck of a great beast. Sprawling bat-like wings appeared next. And finally, the blood ink completed its journey in a long, curling tail. The dragon image was revealed. The beast had been fed. With a shudder, the stone shifted and a crease appeared. The doors opened inward to a sea of swirling shadow.

Your wait is over, Morlan Stormgarden, came a dry, quiet voice. Quiet but powerful, resonant of waves crashing, of thinly concealed malice, and of unnumbered years. *Come and see.*

"Who are you, lord?" came Morlan's tremulous reply.

My name is long…crafted like a great chain over ages past… from the works of my hand. The darkness churned and eddied with each word like mists swirling on a black pond. *Were I to speak but a moment's worth in the Sunderell tongue, it would break your feeble mind.*

"Then what shall I call you?"

Sabryne.

Morlan's yellow eyes widened even as he fell to his knees before the door. He could not bring himself to speak.

Yes…you do know me, don't you, Morlan? And I know you. You have searched for me, searched for me and plotted. Your deeds have not gone unnoticed, and the time has come for reward. Long has Myriad languished in the absent hands of a false god. Long has the great tree of Sabryne's line withered from neglect. And yet my root runs very deep and stretches far beneath the surface of this world. *I, Sabryne, Finger of Shadow, Blade of Spirit, Weaver of Night...I live!*

His arms and hands shielding his head, Morlan bent low before the door. "What would you have of me?"

A perilous question, Morlan Stormgarden. Would you know?

A distant memory surged into Morlan's consciousness, a memory of the day he had left the castle of Anglinore to strike out on his own and rule a small fiefdom called Vulmarrow. He had just exited the long gatehouse and was about to lead his horse down the wide and winding rampart when he felt something.

He knew without turning that it was the weight of King Brysroth's gaze. For a moment, he thought that perhaps his father would beckon him to return, that they both might repent of the terrible words spoken the night before. Morlan turned and looked up to the high gate wall. There stood Brysroth Stormgarden, his aging face expressionless—even cold. But his eyes, the golden brown eyes that had once flickered with mirth in countless courtyard games of *pitch* or *king's stone* now appeared as dead as a boned fish.

For Morlan, the message was clear: *You are dead to me.*

It became a family creed for Morlan. He remembered fondly the day he'd shown his father how well he had learned the lesson.

Morlan blinked the memory away and answered quite steadily, "I would know your will for me, Lord Sabryne."

The darkness within the archway withdrew as if inhaled. Then, one by one, torches kindled on either side of a long passage.

Come.

Morlan rose to his feet and passed through the arched door. Burning torches showed the way, and Morlan followed their winding path. In places the raw stone floor of the passage gave way to dusty tiles. The path would often branch or open suddenly into a vast expanse of darkness. Morlan sensed that there were chambers and great halls delved in this mountain.

He entered a wide, square room. In the torchlight, the stone floor of this room glistened pale red, especially in the thin seams where a dark burgundy grime had been pasted inexorably between its square tiles. Morlan noted monstrous statues standing guard in each corner of the room. They were nine feet tall at least, stone renderings of the same beast inscribed on the entrance to the mountain. But these winged beasts leered out at the center of the chamber as if they might at any moment come to life and belch fire at someone trapped in their midst. At the base of the nearest statue, Morlan saw much more of the burgundy grime. Apparently, these beasts required feeding as well. But for what? Perhaps there would be time to seek such answers and explore later, but for now, the torches showed only one way, and Morlan dared not veer.

He exited the square chamber and followed the torches as they continued their winding route through the mountain. Noting the Sunderell inscriptions but lacking the time to read them, Morlan ducked under a series of arched doors and found the path beginning to incline. It curled up and around as if climbing a subterranean tower. He stumbled suddenly, slammed to the cold stone, and heard bones snap.

But they were not his own. He had tripped over the desiccated skeleton of a large warrior. With some effort, Morlan removed his hand from the dead thing's rib cage. In the flickering light, Morlan spotted the remains of a long pike. Gorracks. Morlan clambered to his feet. He kicked the skeleton out of his path, raising a small cloud of foul-smelling dust.

As he continued the climb, Morlan found more and more long-dead Gorracks. In fact the floor was littered with scowling ancient warriors. It seemed a great battle had been fought in this hall. And yet, Morlan did not perceive among the many corpses any body belonging to another type of combatant. Gorracks were a warmongering brood, Morlan knew, but they rarely fought among themselves.

Picking his way carefully around the dead, Morlan felt the passage level out. He came to another arch and no discernable light within. The torches ended and he turned around, wondering if he could have mistaken the path. No, he had not. He was sure. A chill wind blew from the door in front of him. Morlan felt compelled to draw his sword.

He stepped beneath the arch and experienced a sensation much like walking through a large spider's web. Only this web covered every inch of him and, though it clung to him for a moment, it did not grasp. As he passed through it, he felt it break free from him. There was an audible snap as if it sealed after he had come through it. Morlan turned 'round and could no longer see the passageway behind him. There was only the arched doorway and darkness within.

He found himself standing in a tall, arched chamber. Massive stone columns lined the walls on either side and large fires burned in wide sconces along the walls. It reminded Morlan unpleasantly of his father's throne room in Anglinore Castle. Seeing no immediate threat, Morlan sheathed his blade. He found a broad table carved from the living stone of the mountain.

Behind it sat a ghastly being.

It was a dead Gorrack, but was not skeletal like the ones in the passageway. No, this creature was yet in the early stages of desiccation. Its skin and muscle were livid and shriveled but looked bulbous as if all its life's fluids had not yet drained out or dried up. The Gorrack's face was the most horrible. Its head was lolled back and its wide jaws were frozen open as if it had died while howling in agony. And in its arms, clutched in its dying grip, was a massive book.

The light in the chamber dimmed, and a chill washed through the pillars like the cold fingers of invisible phantoms. *They sought to keep it to themselves…"* came the voice of Sabryne, *"and in so doing, they delayed my plans for more than an age!*

Morlan felt a heaviness weighing upon him as if the air itself had become deep water and he stood beneath it all.

This is my word, Morlan Stormgarden. The Prophecies of Hindred and…my will for you. Take…and read.

Morlan grabbed the arms of the dead Gorrack, winced at the flaccid feel of the flesh, and pulled. The Gorrack's fingers slipped from the book, and when Morlan slid the volume free the creature's arms snapped back toward its chest with such force that the grimacing creature flopped out of its seat and fell to the floor with an awful spattering thud.

The book was eight inches or more thick, bound with black skin and engraved with a single silver rune: a diamond pierced by a forking spear, the Sunderell symbol for Sabryne. It was the legendary *Prophecies of Hindred,* the book of future things proclaimed by Sabyrne Shadowfinger.

Morlan opened the massive tome. The skin covering was still supple but the parchment pages inside were stiff and crackled from so many years. How long had it been lost? Sabryne had said more than an age. Morlan craned his neck to look at the stricken Gorrack. How could it be that this dead being was so remarkably preserved when all the others beyond the chamber had been reduced to bone and dust?

"This mountain hides many mysteries," Morlan muttered as he carefully turned the page.

The sixth page was the first filled with text. It began with a gigantic Sunderell symbol, the equivalent of the letter "I" in Anglish. This letter was illuminated in the old style with red and blue ink. Hand-drawn creatures danced around it and serpents slithered up its shaft. Morlan reached out to touch it, and the instant his finger brushed the symbol, a wisp of smoke rose from the page. Flickers of angry orange appeared within the large rune like a hard log in a fire whose flame had died down but waited only for a breath of air to rekindle. Morlan had provided that very breath, for the embers within the rune flared. Fire leapt from the page and surged into Morlan's eyes.

His knuckles went white as he desperately clutched the book. He could not let go. The flames poured forth, and Morlan began to see with eyes he'd never had before. Moment by moment, a story unfolded before him with such intimate detail that it seemed he was living it and had known nothing else in all his life.

There appeared the curving white line of a bright sun yet hidden by the horizon. A dark landscape rotated slowly forward. Dark but alive. Shadows of great trees sprang up and heaved as if in horrific wind. The surface bulged, stretched, distorted, and at last burst as mountain peaks tore free and rose. Black rivers suddenly gouged the landscape, and things began to gather at its edge. There were silhouetted beasts, some on two legs, most on four—or more. They swayed and writhed but not in unison. Each seemed to hear a unique, discordant rhythm, and their movement became frenzied.

They suddenly became as still as old stone. A figure appeared on the horizon and walked slowly forward. Presently he was joined by a host of others, and they began to fan out over the whole landscape. Some disappeared in the shrouds of trees or behind the shadow of mountains. But the first one kept coming. He raised his hand and there was a blaze of light.

Morlan fell away from the book as if he'd been struck. The *Prophecies of Hindred* lay open on the stone table. Morlan had read more than half of it, though he did not remember turning any pages. He could scarcely fathom what he'd read. *Seen*, he corrected himself. He'd witnessed beginnings and ends, births and deaths, treaties and treacheries.

There had been wars where spears and shields glimmered from one end of the horizon to the other. He'd seen rampaging beasts and a tide of fire sweep across great walled fortress cities. Morlan had eavesdropped on the conversations of the wise in their secret councils. He'd seen lonely ships sail from winding shorelines and never return. Morlan had watched with rapt attention as a fleet of dark sails covered the sea and drew near to land.

And, through it all, like a black stake hammered into the ground, had stood the presence of Sabryne.

Do you see? Sabryne asked, his voice carried on breaths of chill air.

"You cannot mean me, Lord," Morlan replied.

I do.

"But that's impossible. No one can return."

You are already on the path. The firelight flickered. *You have chosen well thus far and will choose well in days to come. One task remains before you return to your throne.*

Morlan heard the *whoosh* of flame and turned round. Tall braziers burned where he had not seen them before. Their light revealed a short rise of stairs and a platform, like a stage, built into the back of the room. A long block of gray stone, engraved with more Sunderell markings, rested there. And upon it, wrapped in strange cloths, lay a body.

Morlan went forward, climbed the stairs, and stood beside this thing. It was a large being, mummified in strips of a material that glowed faintly blue. An overpowering scent filled the air: a combination of potent flowers and the foul bodily odor of sickness. Morlan wondered what task remained. Why had he been led to this corpse—

It moved. A jarring movement—a spasm—just below what must have been a shoulder. Morlan shook his head. No, it could not have moved. It was just his nerves—and no wonder, given the gripping tension of all that had transpired. Morlan exhaled a long-held breath.

The task waits for you, Sabryne said, seeming to be right beside Morlan. *Take the blade.*

Morlan became instantly aware of a dagger affixed to the wall behind the block of stone. The dagger had a black obsidian handle, barely any haft at all, and a swerving blade that glistened yellow on the edge as if it had been dipped in resin. Morlan took down the dagger. He liked its weight. He placed the tip of its blade beneath one fold of cloth near the mummified being's chest. Then, slowly, methodically, he began to slice through the strips.

Though the blade was very sharp, the cloths did not give easily. Morlan thought it felt like sawing through the hide of a fresh kill. Layer after layer, the strips of material peeled back until finally, Morlan made a cut near the being's neck. There was an audible popping sound as if Morlan had punctured a seal. The smell was so horrid that Morlan turned away and gagged.

He gathered his wits and turned back to the task. He realized he had cut through the final layer and, with the pulling away of each strip of cloth, Morlan found bluish-gray flesh. With one long cut, the face was revealed. A Gorrack. Morlan was not surprised, but this had apparently once been a Gorrack ruler. There was a thin silver crown resting on his thick gray brow. That's when it hit Morlan…the condition of the body. It was preserved to a degree that no mummy should—

The Gorrack's eyes came open and it exhaled a stale dusty breath.

Morlan stepped backward. *Impossible. No Gorrack could survive an age!*

The creature's eyes fluttered and it turned, suddenly recognizing it was not alone. It's gaze met Morlan's, and the Gorrack grimaced as if in sudden terror. It struggled desperately but was still mostly covered in its burial cloths. The Gorrack howled, but it was a thin, sad sound.

Morlan still held the dagger and wondered. He stepped closer to the thrashing Gorrack. The beast at last managed to free an arm. It held it up as if to shield itself from Morlan's approach.

Morlan saw the palm of its scaly hand. There was a very old scar there, but it was hard to see because the creature was so frantic. As Morlan watched, the Gorrack's flailing subsided. Its arm waved weakly and then fell limp at its side. Morlan watched the beast struggle to keep its huge eyes focused.

Kill him now. Sabryne's voice sizzled through the room. *Take him.*

Its jaws opened and shut even as it turned its head back and forth, still trying in vain to ward Morlan off.

Morlan placed the tip of the dagger blade just above the Gorrack's right collarbone. The sharp point sank in, found the creature's heart. He twisted it hard.

The Gorrack became still. Its eyes locked on to Morlan, but they no longer saw. One final breath came forth and with it, "Nagan," the Sunderell word for *No.*

Morlan slid the dagger into one of the belts at his waist and hoped to hear Sabryne's voice once more. *Why had he somehow preserved the life of this Gorrack king only to command me to kill it the moment I arrived?*

There came a thunderous roar. Wind blasted through the chamber. The fires in the two braziers and along the walls were snuffed instantly. Morlan was plunged into darkness, but his rare eyes allowed him to see still.

The eyes of the Gorrack were still open, and they glowed suddenly with yellow light. Morlan felt himself caught in this stare. He felt crushing pain in his head and fell to his knees. A fierce swirling yellow pattern filled his field of vision and his ears rang as if he'd been struck with a hammer.

Then, just as suddenly as the pain had come, it was gone. Morlan knelt there in the darkness, seeing only silhouettes and shades of dark gray. But on this occasion, Morlan desired more light. As if in answer to his silent request, fire sprang to life in the two braziers once more. The Gorrack's arm dangled over the edge of its stone bed. There was something written in Sunderell.

Morlan moved the dead Gorrack's arm and translated. "'Banthas Incasian, High Strider,'" Morlan whispered. "High strider?"

Morlan sucked in a gasp of stale air. "Not high strider. High-walker, the Gorrack word for Shepherd. A Gorrack Shepherd… I…I never knew."

Banthas was the last of his kind. But you still do not see.

Morlan ran his finger over the dagger's pommel. *Why preserve the life of this Gorrack king only to command me to kill it the moment I arrived?*

Return to Vulmarrow, Sabryne whispered. *The answer is waiting.*

CHAPTER 24

TROUBLED SLEEP

The soul is like a well. Everyone can come and draw something from it,
but secrets still remain in its depths.
Wisdom from Sidon's Archives, 1922 AS

27 CELESANDUR 2212

Abbagael had reached Alastair in time. Together with a squadron
of Singers, they raced to the Nookery and found the largest group
of black birds that yet lived. The Singers began their song and
slowed the rooks down. Alastair went to work with his sword,
shredding the lethargic creatures, even as they tried to fly away.

What could have been a tragedy for the willowfolk became a
great victory. Few rooks escaped. Those that lived climbed into
the air high above sward and bough and raced out of Willow Dell.
Several such streams of black trailed out of sight.

"Well done!" Alac cried, buzzing in a tight circle. He came to
rest on one of the Nookery's long, round windows. "Our children are safe! King Alastair, Queen Abbagael, we are forever in
your—"

"The *child!*" Abbagael exclaimed, and with no word of explanation fled in the direction of the pavilion.

Alastair sheathed his sword and tore off after her. They traversed the distance quickly, bounding over stones and streams and picking their way through the rook carcasses that littered the ground. Alastair had always been fast on his feet, but Abbagael pulled well ahead.

She tore around the front of the stone house where she'd laid the child and screamed.

The shutters were broken out…and there was blood.

She rammed her shoulder into the door and burst inside. She would never forget what she saw.

Alastair came round the structure a few moments later and found Abbagael clutching a bloodied bundle to her shoulder. Abbagael's eyes were shut, and tears streamed. She seemed to spasm with each breath.

"Lady Abbagael?" he whispered, placing a gentle hand on her shoulder.

"He…he…" she couldn't seem to get the words out. "Oh, Alastair…"

Alastair felt as if he'd been punched in the stomach. "Lady Abbagael, I'm so sorry, I—"

"He's alive!" Abbagael finally cried out. "He's okay!"

"Wha-what? But…the blood?"

"I don't understand it either, Alastair. But it's not his." She held out the child to him.

Alastair received him. "You live a charmed life, little one." He was caught by the child's blue eyes.

The boy gurgled and cooed.

"Alastair," Abbagael said, crawling halfway back into the stone willowfolk home. "Alastair, you've got to see this."

Alastair thought her tone revealed a worrisome mixture of fear and disbelief. He clutched the child to his shoulder and knelt carefully so he could look into the cottage's round window. He found one dead rook hanging from the shutter, its neck twisted at a hard angle, its body limp. The frenzied creature had killed itself trying to break through the shutters. But the puzzle within the building defied his feeble attempts to understand what had happened.

Several rooks had followed the dead bird's lead through the shutters and managed to get inside. Thinking of those predatory creatures inside this small space with the child gave Alastair a chill and filled his mind with bloody images of what might have been. But the child was unharmed, and the invading rooks all lay dead on the floor or draped over wooden furniture. Black feathers were scattered around their corpses. There was blood, but there were no puncture wounds or arrow shafts.

Then, something registered at last. The head of each rook was ruined, misshapen, glistening with fresh blood. And there were bright red splotches on the walls.

"What happened in there?" Abbagael asked.

"I-I'm not sure," he said, staring at the splotched wall. "Best I can tell is some of the willowfolk saw the rooks break in."

"But did you see the walls?"

"Aye, I saw them. The willowfolk must have far outnumbered the birds. It looks as though they rammed the rooks headfirst into the walls."

Blessed willowfolk, he thought. *Blessed violent willowfolk.*

A lastair lay wide awake on his bed in the tent among the pines. But for a small oil lamp hanging from the center tent post, it was dark. Wind whispered in the branches outside. But no night shadows, no music from the trees, would coax Alastair to sleep. His head pounded. Too many thoughts wheeling about.

He and Abbagael had told their tale to Alac and Sprye, and none of the willowfolk knew anything of the dead rooks in the stone house. If indeed some valiant pixies had killed those birds, they must have taken their secret to their own graves. Still, what other explanation could there be?

Hushed voices outside. Very quiet footsteps. Then, "Alastair, are you awake?"

"Unfortunately," he mumbled. "You can come in, Lady Abbagael."

Abbagael slipped into Alastair's quarters and held up a grinning child. "Someone wanted to say goodnight to you." She handed him the baby, and he placed him in his lap.

The child was wrapped in a gray blanket and was wearing something colorful. Alastair peeled away the blanket to find the child adorned in a dark brown tunic with a deep blue mantle. It looked like something a knight would wear...a tiny knight anyway. "What's this?"

Abbagael sat down beside Alastair and tickled the baby's chin. "Sprye saw that our child had little but rags to wear. She has a friend, a grappler, and rather overweight for a pixie, and she borrowed one of his old uniforms. He's a fine little warrior now, don't you think?"

Alastair laughed, but only to be polite. *Did she say "our child"?*

"Speaking of warriors," Abbagael said, looking down at her shoes, "I've never seen anything like today...like you today, I mean."

Alastair stiffened. He waited. He stared down at the child. The child cooed and stared back.

"You were brilliant," she said. "A one-man army, really. You wield that sword like it was...well like it was something you were born to do. You must have killed more than a hundred rooks all by yourself. Do you have any idea how many of the willowfolk you saved?"

Alastair shrugged. His face felt hot, like he was leaning too close to a bonfire. "You were strong with your bow," he said. "Fast and accurate."

Abbagael emitted a soft laugh. "I am...adequate...nothing more." Then she was quiet for a few seconds. The room felt very still. Even the pines outside seemed to have nothing to say.

Alastair risked a look at her and wished he hadn't. He found the green fire of her eyes staring back between wild vines of coppery hair. Alastair looked away, but his mind had painted a picture that would last.

"You were valiant," she whispered, as she picked up the child from his lap. Her face was now very close to his. "A hero to the willowfolk...and to me." She leaned in closer and pressed her lips to Alastair's cheek just above the beard line. The kiss lingered warmly for several seconds. "Goodnight, Alastair."

Abbagael stood up and put the child to her shoulder. She went to leave, but turned. Alastair sat very still on the edge of his bed. She thought he looked stricken. "What?" she asked, smiling coyly. "I never said it was the child who wanted to say goodnight."

Alastair's mind had been as busy as a hive full of hornets *before* Abbagael's visit. But now it was as if Abbagael had smacked the hornet nest with a branch. Focusing on any single train of thought was immensely difficult, like using a spoon to try to capture one particular hornet from the swarm. The willowfolk, the rooks, the miraculous defense of the child, and Abbagael—round and round his thoughts went.

On top of it all, scratching and biting at the edge of his consciousness, lurked a yearning for Witchdrale. He'd not had a drop for days, not since the night before he'd come to Edenmill looking for Abbagael. Frequent headaches and tremors in his hands told the story of his body's growing craving. The willowfolk certainly didn't have any Witchdrale. Gull'scry would be the only place he'd find some. He knew one or two taverns he could hit, places from which he might purchase a whole bottle for the long sea voyage.

But thinking of Gull'scry led to thinking about the problem of Abbagael. She vexed Alastair mightily. She'd been smitten with him for many years, beginning with a childish infatuation that Alastair had felt sure she'd grow out of. But she hadn't. Instead, she'd pursued him with even more vigor—a fact Alastair had intended to utilize to escape the burden of the child. But Abbagael had somehow found a way to be close to him for nigh on a week. There was more to the puzzle, something Alastair had not expected.

But how can I possibly have feelings for her? Alastair thrashed about on the bed until he lay sideways facing the darkest wall of the tent. He clamped shut his eyes, hoping that sleep might overwhelm his rampant thoughts. But even abject exhaustion was no match for a restless mind.

She's too young. She's ridiculously talkative. She's far too trusting.

But none of those arguments seemed compelling any longer. Abbagael was beautiful and kind, nurturing to a fault. She might love him, but more importantly, she honored him. She noticed his skills and drew attention to his finer points, rather than his far more numerous flaws.

"Ah, but what's the use of this thinking?" he muttered. Faced with the choice of abandoning her with the child or marrying her and keeping his past a secret from her—well, there was no decision really. It would destroy her to know…destroy any relationship they had built. And there would be no way to keep the secret hidden, not without Witchdrale. A flash of faces, frightened townsfolk, just before they died. Alastair's eyes snapped open.

"Even with Witchdrale," he whispered, "I cannot hide. Not really."

He stared up through the thin roof of the tent at the dark night sky. He could just make out a few stars. "How did it all go wrong?" he asked the sky. Just a few short weeks ago, he'd been convinced that the Halfainin would come. *It was all in order.* His thoughts flew like prayers. *I took the Star Sword from Morlan; I charted the stars; I watched; I waited. I saw the Sword in the Stars, and I followed it.*

All for nothing. The Books had been wrong. There was no First One. No Halfainin. Alastair sat up suddenly. It was as if the ground beneath him had crumbled away, leaving only a dark chasm beneath him.

He had spent these weeks after the failure in Thel-Mizaret in a kind of denial, resolving that it had all been a colossal lie. But no, he realized now with certainty. The Sword had really been in the stars. It had been so clear that anyone who looked into the sky that night would have seen it. And it was no ordinary constellation. The First One was real. Somewhere out there, the Halfainin lived. But Alastair hadn't found him. And while he may have suspected it for quite some time, Alastair finally admitted to himself the real reason.

"I am not the Caller." He collapsed into the bed. "I never was."

CHAPTER 25

THE BONE CHAPEL

When one believes that by controlling the death of others
he will gain control of his own life, he has left the path of reason.
Myridian Proverb

6 DRINNAS 2212

Morlan's return to Vulmarrow Hold had left him feeling uncertain. Velach Krel and his team had taken out Westmoor and Stonecrest, but the larger team he'd sent to Thel-Mizaret had failed. Utterly.

Whorls of luminous green still undulated within the black stone table from Morlan's recent search. He'd seen Thel-Mizaret in flames, but clearly not destroyed. He'd seen the flames quenched and his own army of assassins chased off. He'd seen mounted messengers ride out from the ruined city gates, and that fact vexed him most powerfully. What message would they carry? And to whom would they deliver it? For those answers, Morlan needed to go beyond the table.

"Keenan Wraithgard," Morlan said, "how could you allow this to happen?"

Keenan chafed at the rebuke. He'd never had to turn tail and run from a fight before. "Perhaps if we'd had some warning of their fortifications. And their likely response, such a…defeat…an ambush…wouldn't have happened."

Morlan sat up straighter, tilted his head, and cracked his neck. "You seek to shirk the blame?"

"They had a Shepherd."

"Nonsense," replied the king. "Thel-Mizaret hasn't had a Shepherd in fifteen years."

"Precisely why we were caught off guard," Keenan said. "Worse still, the city was wide awake—celebrating, it seemed. Even their deep miners had returned." Keenan figured he was as good as dead anyway, so he might as well speak plainly. "You should have told us what we were getting ourselves into."

King Morlan rose from his high chair. His shadow fell on Keenan. With very slow, deliberate steps, he descended. The king stood right before one of his finest assassins and fixed him with his golden stare. "The table spoke nothing to me of a new Shepherd in Thel-Mizaret, nor of their reinforcements from the mountains. But you have never failed me before, and there is no lie you could utter to change this…situation. Tell me of this new Shepherd."

"He is a stone-skin," Keenan said. "His flesh was harder than granite. Keval, Thandrum, Maraketch—violent and sudden men, as you know—rushed this youth, but no blade could pierce him."

"Youth?" Morlan spat the word like a hiss of steam.

"He couldn't have been more than seventeen. Others rallied to his side. They called him Jonasim."

"Leave me," Morlan said.

Keenan took a step backward. "It was not a total loss, my lord. We managed to retrieve all of our dead…by all accounts Westmoor will claim it was a Gorrack raid."

Morlan grabbed Keenan's upper arm just below the shoulder and shoved him away. "*Leave me!*"

Like the jaws of a beast snapping at air when the creature reached the end of its chain, the throne room doors slammed shut behind Keenan. *I've escaped,* he thought, absently rubbing a tender spot on his arm. It was beyond comprehension, really. He was the commander of a failed mission. *Guards should be cleaning up my headless body. Maybe he respects how I stood my ground? Or, more likely, he has more important matters on his mind.*

"What does it matter?" he whispered to himself. "I live another day." He coughed and swallowed back the phlegm. *Ah, must be the chill.* Keenan thought a warm tavern fire and tall mug of Witchdrale would do the trick. Feeling relieved but still a bit jittery, Keenan strode swiftly away from the throne room.

Morlan fell into his seat and rubbed his eyes. One swipe at the table and the moonlight vanished. *Ah, darkness. Rarely have I felt such need of thee.*
Jonasim.
No more than seventeen.
No blade could pierce him.
Others rallied to his side.
It...couldn't...be. And yet, Morlan could not deny what he'd heard. The King of Vulmarrow cleared his mind, forcing away conflicting thoughts and one icy fear. Deep into his inner being he delved, peering through a tunnel of shadows until he found that place where he could speak and hear.

"Sabryne," he whispered. "Lord Nightfinger...I seek."
Shame upon you, came a voice.
"Why?"
Your fear is misplaced. Fear only me.
"But what shall I do? If the Halfain—"
Do not say that name to me. Myths do not concern us.
"Still," Morlan said, "I must make certain. There must not be a leader for them. Thel-Mizaret must fall."
Your right hand.

"My what?"

Your...right...hand.

And then Morlan understood.

Keenan put down the mug and grimaced. The Witchdrale burned more than usual. Something was wrong. "Glenrick!" he called to the tavern keeper. "Glenrick, I feel sick."

"Can't hold the Witchdrale, eh?" muttered the barrel-shaped tavern keeper as he waddled over. "S'why I war'nt touch the stuff meself. One drop and ye' can't— Ah! Fates preserve us!"

Keenan's eyes had become cloudy black, and inky tears streaked down his face. His entire body trembled. "What's...ha-happening...to...me!" He screamed and slammed his clay tankard down, shattering it. Frothing black foam bubbling from his lips, Keenan lunged across the bar, clutching for Glenrick.

The tavern keeper jerked backward, crashed into mugs and glasses, and kept backpedaling. Something was happening to this young Wolfguard solider. Something horrific.

"*Help,* gak-kek, me!" Keenan struggled to reach out for Glenrick, for anyone. But every person recoiled.

Keenan could barely think, the pain was so unbearable. It felt like he was being burned alive...from the inside. He screamed again and slid to the tavern floor. With little strength left, he lifted his arm. His flesh, puckered with black ulcers, seemed to hang loosely on his bones. Keenan saw wisps of smoke and then no more.

The passage from Vulmarrow Hold to the Bone Chapel was one of many, Morlan knew. There were dozens of veins and arteries that led in and out of Cythraul's place of worship. How many and where exactly they were, only Cythraul knew.

That might be problematic, Morlan thought as he walked the sinewy, torchlit passageway. It might be a problem, indeed, were it not for the fact that, of all the soldiers under his command,

Cythraul was the only one he could trust completely. As obsessively loyal as he was obsessive in his…pastimes…Cythraul would not veer from duty. Not an inch. He absolutely followed orders. And no matter how long it took or what obstacles stood in his way, Cythraul completed every mission. He was the perfect man-at-arms, the perfect security general, the perfect right hand.

Morlan laughed as he rounded a snaking turn in the tunnel. A Fennish wolfhound was known to latch onto a thigh bone from its prey and not release it—even if other hounds were tearing it apart. Hinterland bloodhawks would strike their prey a deadly blow and then follow it from the air for a hundred miles, patiently waiting for it to die. Cythraul was like a fearsome cross of them both. How he'd gotten that way, Morlan never learned. Cythraul's past was shrouded in mystery. Morlan knew more than most, but it was still very little. *Cythraul can keep his secrets.*

The king stopped cold at the smell. Sickly sweet and stinging to eyes and lungs, the foul scent had stopped many in their tracks. Not Morlan, usually, but it was an important warning that he'd have to watch his step. The canal was up ahead, very near. It was a narrow cut in the floor of the tunnel, a stream of sorts that ran from the Bone Chapel to a distant swamp somewhere in the murky forest.

"Ah, here it is." Morlan carefully placed his feet and made an exaggerated step over the narrow channel. It wouldn't do to misstep and place a boot in that…filth. Morlan glanced down as he passed over. In the dim, flickering light, all he could see was a dull, slow-moving ribbon of dark, muddy red.

At last, Morlan emerged into the great hall of the Bone Chapel. It was a massive room with a high arched ceiling, and scaffolds held many red candles in each corner. But it would never be called a cathedral or a sanctuary. For this building was built, inside and out, of black mortar, Dark Sea limestone…and bones. Not from bird or beast, but only the bones of every race of human-like being in Myriad. The building's main structure was intact, but not finished. And, according to Cythraul, it never would be. There was always room for more.

"You honor me with your visit, my lord." Cythraul's deep voice startled the king. In many ways the voice was like thunder, but not a sudden blast. More like a long roll that rumbles sinisterly for many seconds then unexpectedly cracks. And, like thunder in a canyon, his voice had a subtle echo. If sound could have a shadow, that was how Morlan would describe his general's voice.

Morlan found Cythraul toward the front of the chamber near the stairs and raised dais. He had a piece of iron, long and thin like a sword blade, and was using it to scrape his wide stone work table clean. As Morlan drew near, he saw that the table was smeared with blood. "Been at work, I see."

"Yes, my lord," he replied, wiping his long fingers and muscular forearms on a stained cloth. "A moment." Cythraul reached down and pulled an unseen lever. Morlan heard the rattle of metal and a clang. "There," he said. "It is best to clean as you go, don't you think?"

"Of course."

"I want to show you something," Cythraul said. "Though I must confess, it vexes me."

Morlan didn't think Cythraul looked vexed. But then, his general's expression rarely changed. His pale face was long with a tall forehead and a full chin. High cheekbones and tendons stood like tapering columns beneath his cold gray eyes. But there was no expression. No beetling of his bushy gray brows. No frown on his thinnish lips. It was only his eyes that might show something, a flash of interest or rage. But now…nothing.

Cythraul walked to the corner of the room where a bloodied sheet covered something. "Tell me what you think." He removed the sheet.

Morlan was speechless. He recognized the thick, slightly bowed thigh bones—definitely Gorrack. And the long, flowing contours from the lower legs of Wayfolk, Vespal Branch perhaps?

He wasn't sure. There were small skulls at each corner like accent pieces.

"It is an altar," Cythraul said. "But see here, I need something longer. No derelict will do. I need a warrior."

"Then it is fortuitous that I have come," Morlan said. "Keenan failed in Thel-Mizaret."

There was a brief flicker in Cythraul's eyes.

"There is a Shepherd there now. His skin turns to stone. No blade can pierce him."

"Like the prophecy?"

Morlan ignored the question. "His name is Jonasim."

"I will bring you his head in a bag," Cythraul said. "And...if I may..."

"Yes, you may keep the rest...for your own purposes."

Cythraul adjusted the fit of his chain gloves and then threw up his dark hood. His felmount was restless beneath him, ready for the long journey...and the spoils of war. *Yes,* thought Cythraul, *there will be blood.*

He spurred the felmount and rocketed into the night with one name on his mind: *Jonasim.*

CHAPTER 26

A Seed of Hope

Scormount: a fleet-footed creature as tall as a horse but with ram-like horns and impaling talons protruding from its knees.
From Graymer Black's Bestiary

28 Celesandur 2212

Alastair awoke with a start.

His heart hammered. He couldn't stop his legs from trembling. An involuntary twitch spasmed beneath his left eye. And he could barely breathe. There was nothing he could see above or around him. The willowfolk tent was still dark. But he felt like he was in the squeezing clutches of a huge constricting snake.

What is happening to me? he thought desparately. *I must master myself. I must quiet my mind.* But even with all his might in battle, the best he could do was force air in and out of his lungs.

There was no way out. The Halfainin had come to bring peace, had come to forgive. *But he didn't come for me. I am beyond rescue.*

Alastair had felt such misery on only two previous occasions. The first was his mother's death when he was seven years old. The other was just after Alastair had left King Morlan's secret army of assassins.

Twisting on the bed and fearful, Alastair tried to push his mind back to that time. Why? He wasn't sure. It was just another agonizing season in his life. But while he could not yet see it, he felt that somewhere, buried in that memory, was a seed of hope.

It had been twelve long years ago. Having left the Wolfguard, Alastair had lost his reputation. He'd lost anyone he might have called a friend. And perhaps, he'd thought at the time, he'd lost his mind as well. The Wolfguard was lifetime service. One did not grow old and retire or simply leave to pursue some other life path. Once enlisted in the Wolfguard, the only way out was to die. But Alastair had left.

He knew that doing so had placed a "slay order" upon him—that any servant of King Morlan could expect his weight in gold for killing Alastair Coldhollow. Worse still, he'd taken the Star Sword with him. Morlan had lent it to his favored swordsman, but now that it was gone, he would comb every nook and crag of Myriad to get that relic back.

Alastair had known all this when he left, but no matter what, he could not continue to kill for Morlan. Alastair felt that indeed he had lost his mind. He'd lost everything.

But that one night, he'd drunk more Witchdrale than usual and found himself on his horse riding out of Ardon and into the hills of Northern Tryllium. He remembered very little of the journey—just snatches of dark green foliage, a stream where he'd stopped to get a drink, and the thicket of briars he'd fallen into and thrown up in several times. He'd awakened with a searing headache in a cave dimly lit by a small fire.

A narrow figure wrapped in gray cloth had watched him from the other side of the flames. "There is fresh water in the cistern by your elbow. Use both hands."

It was a female voice, pleasant to the ear but emotionless. Alastair turned, found the clay cistern and tried to lift it. It wasn't heavy, but his hands shook. With both hands, he managed to bring the lip of the jar to his face. The water was icy cold and felt good going down his throat. He put down the cistern and slumped against the cave wall. "Where am I?" he muttered, squinting against the pain throbbing in his temples.

"You are in the mountains of Stonecrest...in the Bryngate settlement."

"Bryngate settlement!" Alastair's eyes shot open and he sat bolt upright. He saw her clearly at last. "You!"

She nodded.

"You're Yasmina Vanador." His hands searched his side for the sword.

She nodded again. "Your sword has been placed elsewhere. For safekeeping. It is, after all, a very special sword." She stood and brought Alastair a small saucer of something creamy and steaming.

Alastair glared at her questioningly but accepted the bowl. "You could have slit my throat. But instead you look after me?"

Yasmina returned to her place on the other side of the fire. She seemed content to let the question hang. Her dark pupils grew large in the dim light, leaving just a thin perimeter of violet. Her hair was long and absolutely straight, falling in black cascades on either side of her slanting, pointed ears. Her skin was still the color of milk, but less smooth. Carelines bunched between her brows and in the corners of her eyes. Alastair knew why.

"Eat," she said, "if you can."

Alastair sipped the white stew. There wasn't much taste but, given the knots in his gut, that was probably for the best. After a night of Witchdrale, it was not uncommon to be unable to hold down anything solid.

"Why did you bring me here?"

Yasmina tilted her head and raised one eyebrow. The hint of a sad smile appeared in one corner of her mouth. "I did not bring you here."

Alastair forced down a swallow of the stew. "But how did I—"

"You arrived just before sunrise," she said, "spurring your horse just outside our homes and yelling, making more noise than a hundred roosters. You called me out by name, but you could barely stay on your horse." She paused and then asked, "What do you want?"

"What do I…? Really, I don't… I didn't—"

"Surely you knew we were here…the survivors, I mean."

"Well, yes, I…I suppose I did know, but still…"

"Then tell me, Alastair Coldhollow," she said, an edge on her voice now, "what does an assassin want with the widow of a man he murdered?"

The Witchdrale-induced trauma to his body had left Alastair striken, but that was nothing compared to Yasmina's question. Why *had* he come? He didn't remember choosing to come or taking the way to this place, but he could not persuade himself that it was some Witchdrale-conjured accident. Not even a series of blurred wrong turns. He had come to see Yasmina for a reason.

Alastair felt as if he were being ground between two shifting stones. So many years living by the sword, adeptly performing unspeakable horrors and then sinking in a deep mire of guilt. Despair had been his constant companion. But Yasmina Vanador knew something. She had to. Alastair could hide no longer. He had to know.

Alastair clenched his eyes shut, and ground his jaws. "Rhys's blood was still wet on my blade, and yet you spoke of forgiveness, not vengeance as you should. Why?"

Yasmina blinked. Her eyes darted to the floor. When she looked up again, her gaze was rock-steady. "Vengeance belongs to the First One," she replied. "And though I might wish your death as payment, I dare not withhold forgiveness. I have been forgiven a much larger debt."

"Larger debt!" Alastair spat words of astonishment, of doubt. "I slew your husband! I personally killed a score of your village. I led the raid that razed your homeland from the surface of Myriad! How can you possibly have a larger debt than mine?"

Yasmina stared, and it felt to Alastair as if her gaze sliced into him, carving flesh away from bone, filleting him until all was laid bare. Finally, she nodded. "Taela!" she called over her shoulder. "Bring me the book, please."

"Okay, Ma-Mae!" came a high sweet voice from somewhere back in the cave.

Moments later, a thin pixie of a girl appeared. She wore a threadbare brown robe, but the hood was down. She had a straw-colored pigtail sticking up from the top of her head like some strange root vegetable ready to be picked. In one hand she clutched a very thick book. *She's strong for 3 or 4,* Alastair thought. She sucked the thumb of the other hand and simultaneously held the shreds of a blue blanket.

The thumb came out with an audible pop. "Here go, Ma-Mae!"

Yasmina received the book and tousled her daughter's pigtail. "Thank you, sweet Taela."

The little girl tucked her chin into her chest. Huge violet eyes stared up at Alastair. "Who dat, Ma-Mae?"

Yasmina looked at Alastair thoughtfully.

In those moments, he felt something dark, something with many sharp teeth, gnawing away at his innards. Taela...Yasmina's daughter. Utter innocence. She had no idea she was in the presence of her father's murderer. But Alastair knew.

"This is Mr. Coldhollow," Yasmina said at last. "He's...he's a friend."

Alastair felt a strange release. The toothy jaws loosened their grasp.

"Das a funny name, Ma-Mae," said Taela, plopping her thumb back into her mouth.

"No different from Yasmina Vanador," Yasmina said. "Or Taela, for that measure. Thank you for bringing me the book. Now, I wonder what your dolls are doing?"

Taela's huge eyes grew larger, and she spun and fled back into the recesses of the cave.

Yasmina brought the book around the fire and knelt next to Alastair. He gazed down at the tome and saw that its cover had once been cloven in two but had been lovingly stitched back together.

"That…that is—"

"Yes." She opened the book and began turning pages, each page bearing a similar wound and mended with equal care. "In this world," Yasmina said, "your deeds are indeed grievous…to me especially. Equally so to others who once called Bryngate home. And I imagine the raid on our village was not the first you led?"

Alastair looked away. "No," he whispered. "There were others."

Yasmina paused, and it seemed to Alastair that she was calculating the number of lives he'd stolen. But when she spoke again, there was no condemnation in her voice. There was something else. Determination, maybe. Resolve. "By Myriad's standard, Alastair, you are more guilty than most. But you were following orders, were you not?"

"Yes. Every raid was King Morlan's command, but I will not shirk blame."

"No," said Yasmina, "nor should you. There is no solace in blame. No matter the order, your sword moved by your hand. Most do not understand this."

Alastair sighed. "I have never *not* understood. With every raid, every single innocent I slew, there was for me an irrevocable finger of blame pressed into my soul."

"Ah, and it is in your soul where you are most guilty. So am I. For the First One is not like other beings of this world. He does not keep accounts the way I do…like you do. And inasmuch as you are hideously responsible for atrocities in this world, we are both far guiltier of offenses beyond reckoning. Offenses of the soul."

"I do not understand," Alastair whispered. "What have you done that could level the scale with my own?"

"In Myriad?" Yasmina shrugged. "Nothing. But in my soul… there is ragged parchment gouged red with deeds as depraved and heartless as your own—in the sight of Allhaven."

"Maybe if there had been time between," Alastair said. "Maybe if you'd had time to mourn and grieve. To seek solace from…from the one you speak of. But in the moment after I'd killed Rhys and I was threatening you and your infant daughter… how could you speak then of forgiveness?"

"It is not what I felt. But a power mightier than my own spoke mercy through me." She was quiet a moment. "I might ask you a question as well, Alastair. After you killed Rhys, you pursued me and Taela into our home, but you turned aside. Why did you not kill us as well?"

Alastair had asked himself the question a thousand times, but never had an answer. Until now. "I followed you inside," he said, watching the scene from his memory. "I meant to kill you both. You were a task for me to complete and nothing more. But you'd spoken of forgiveness…I could not…even if there was a small chance—"

"Alastair," she said, and her violet eyes lost their hard edge, "there is hope for you."

Alastair, the former assassin, felt as if he had been split open by a blade far sharper than his own. He choked out something far short of intelligible speech but, at the same time, far more profound. Convulsions wracked his body, and he toppled to the cave floor.

As the memory bled away from his consciousness, Alastair found himself in tears. But the sounds of his weeping were lost among the chirps of nightfrogs and crickets that made Willow Dell their home.

CHAPTER 27

RELENTLESS

It was often said that if anyone was born to be the ruler of the Prydian Wayfolk, it was Ealden Everbrand. "Stiff from birth," some called him. "As rigid and unchanging as stone," said others. One must understand, these were considered high compliments in Prydian society, and Ealden earned those and many others. But unlike many of his peers, Ealden was altogether shy. Solitary...reclusive even. He'd lost his darling little sister, Silwynn Mae, and that had changed him. He withdrew and seemed to wither. His parents feared they would lose yet another child. But there was in that small Llanfair village one of those uncommon beings who seeks out those who are hiding or lost. Who refuses to be put off by the surly or unresponsive, but relentlessly pursues. One who gives everything and expects nothing in return but to have the honor of being called "friend." Xanalos Ven Velion took to Ealden like an older brother, and through the stormy years of scintelarious, their friendship became famous. Xanalos was a passionate Lore Adept and helped Ealden with his studies, never once complaining or resenting that Ealden soon surpassed him in mastering knowledge of the First One. That's what made it so heartbreaking when Xanalos vanished from Llanfair. And though, to this

very day, Ealden would not believe it, Xanalos was thought by most
Prydian Folk to be guilty of the worst crime in Wayfolk history.
Histories, compiled by Gilthanor Wren

12 DRINNAS 2212

They sat 'round several mismatched tables near a crackling fire in the great room of the Dragonjewel Tavern. But there were no gladsome looks to be shared. No tall tales or raucous songs. There was nothing but frigid water in their tankards. And while many of these grim, soot-smudged men were indeed the famed miners of Thel-Mizaret, they had not come to the tavern to toast full carts of ore or to celebrate their full pockets. No, these men had not been mining at all, not in more than a week. Not since the attack.

"Did they cross the sea, then?" asked Davin Turdlebor from the end of the table near the broken-out picture window.

"Aye," Duff Grayscale said, "they must've. There's no accountin' fer anythin' else. Ye don't think they trod in Wind-borne country, d'ya?"

Low mutters of agreement rumbled around the tables.

"Doesn't make any sense," Jonasim said. "Why now, after so many years? I'm nineteen and 'til now I've not so much as seen a glimpse of a Gorrack."

"Leastways we lived to tell the tale," Binik Gelsh said, his fingers lightly brushing the bandages covering his right eye. "Thanks to you, Jonasim. Those devils couldna' touched ya."

"Thanks be to the First One for that!" Duff said.

Jonasim held up his hand and watched his flesh change to stone and then back again. "I'm thankful for all of you who fought with me...by my side."

"Speakin' a those as fought with ya," Davin said, "when'll Duskan and Laeriss be back?"

"Soon enough, I expect," Duff said. "Next time ye can do the hunting if yer in such a rush t'eat as that."

"Shows what you know, don't it, old Duff?" Davin rose from his seat and wiped his hands on his shirt. "I'm just concerned for them's, that's all. The gate guards'll know. I'll be back, lads."

Davin left the tavern, and conversation turned back to the attack.

"What I don't understand," said Duff's cousin, Borland, "is how come they come back for their dead? Never heard no such things 'bout Gorracks before. Thought the brutes just left their dead to rot."

There was a strong chill in the air, and Davin hugged himself and rubbed his upper arms as he walked. *Be right glad to get to the gate and warm meself at the guard's fire*, he thought. *Might be first frost t'nite.*

He could barely bring himself to look at what was left of Thel-Mizaret. The township had never been a sprawling city like Ardon or Anglinore, but it had always had a folksy village beauty. And with the miners in and out and the traders always popping up, Thel-Mizaret had been a lively place. Especially at night. But now, most buildings were caved in or burned out. Windows that normally burned with glad light were now shadowy and dark.

Too dark.

Davin might have been called slow of wit in the Houses of Lore, but not when it came to hunting or fighting. Something was wrong. He drew his dagger with one hand and loosed his pickaxe from his belt with the other. Still walking toward the city gate, he turned in slow circles. Besides the now distant tavern, there were no candles or torches burning on this side of town. No lights at all.

He could tell before he reached the gate that the guard fire was out. Had the Gorracks returned? If so, why were things so quiet? Davin crept stealthily forward and into the dark gatehouse, then through to the other side. That was when he knew he was in horrible trouble. All nine nightwatch guards were dead. They lay at the foot of the city walls…cast aside and left in all manner of unnatural positions. They looked like toy soldiers that some angry toddler had thrown about.

Swish. Davin had barely heard the sound, but he knew it was already too late. He spun and raised his dagger, but something coiled around his arm like a constricting snake. He groaned, feeling a sharp pinch in four places at once. Then everything turned darker than night.

Borland stood near the broken-out window and took a sip of water. "Cold snap comin' and no mistake."

The words were hardly off his lips when there was a sharp crack, and Borland was pulled through the window. All at once, the taverns candles and torches went out. There were more harsh cracks, the ring of blades, and shouting.

"Something's got me—" Duff's words were cut short.

"Jonasim, *help!*" Binik yelped, and his voice seemed to bounce from place to place in the room. But then he spoke no more.

"To me!" Jonasim yelled. He drew his broadsword and willed his flesh into stone. "Rally once more to me!"

"I am coming for you," came the voice of thunder.

Jonasim kept his back to the window and the threat in front of him. "Stay your blade, Gorrack!" he cried out. "For I am Shepherd-born. You cannot pierce me."

"No," said the voice. *Crack!*

Something wrapped around Jonasim's arm and began to pull. But there was no pain, and Jonasim's stone skin gave him weight and strength beyond mortal men. He pulled back, felt resistance— amazing muscular power from the other side—but it was not enough. Jonasim would draw the villain in and crush him.

Suddenly, the tension went slack and Jonasim fell backward. In that split second, something barreled into him and he tumbled backward out of the window and fell hard on top of wood, glass, and other debris. His sword clattered away as he slammed to the ground with his attacker on top of him.

"I do not need a blade to kill you," said the shadow on Jonasim's chest. "I am Cythraul, and I know many other ways."

Jonasim tried to push him off, but Cyrthraul began throwing wild, heavy punches at his jaw. Jonasim still felt no pain, but saw pebbles and shards of rock blasting from his own face. Iron gauntlets, he thought. He began to feel dizzy, felt consciousness fleeing, and acted in desperation. Jonasim arched his back and grabbed his assailant's legs in his stony grip. Then, with astounding might, he threw Cythraul off.

But Cythraul landed on his own feet and began to flee...only, he wasn't running away to escape. Jonasim felt himself moving, being dragged.

There was little light to see by, but he could just make out a cord of some kind looped over his chest and under his arms, some sort of snare. Jonasim couldn't get a foothold or stop his progress. In fact, he began to be dragged faster and faster. His head and shoulders bashed into tree stumps and the corners of buildings. He twisted and turned, trying to loose himself from the cords, but he couldn't get free. And with each slamming, concussive blow, Jonasim felt his thoughts drift.

"Goodnight, Shepherd!" Cythraul rumbled.

And suddenly, the hard ground beneath Jonasim gave way. It was suddenly soft and immersive, but with his stony flesh, he didn't recognize the sensation. He was sinking, and then he saw it. Water.

Jonasim had no idea how far he'd been dragged, but with horrible certainty he guessed that his attacker had dragged him to the brink of Firstdelve Quarry. His stone-skin weight caused him to plummet below the surface. Jonasim knew how deep the quarry went, knew he could not keep his flesh as stone. He started to let it change back when a sudden splash blasted the water above him.

Cythraul was there, swimming swiftly down, and then clinging to Jonasim.

He's going to ride me to the bottom! Jonasim thought with panic, and he tried to rush his flesh to turn back to normal. But in his water-blurred vision, he saw that Cythraul brandished a huge, cruel knife. Jonasim let out a burst of bubbling air, a terrible mistake. He hadn't mean to, but his situation was dire. If he kept his stone skin, he would sink to the bottom and drown. If he turned back to regular skin, Cythraul could have his way with the blade.

There was only one thing Jonasim could think to do. He grabbed Cythraul's arms and locked his grip. *I'll take you with me!* He thought defiantly.

And he did. But Cythraul did not squirm nor try to break free. He simply let himself sink with Jonasim, far below the surface, down into the depths.

When Duskan and Laeriss found the guards at the gate, they dropped their satchels full of wild game and sprinted into what was left of the city of Thel-Mizaret. It was as if a great dark vacuum had sucked the very life from all that remained of the city. Everywhere Duskan and Laeriss turned there were more familiar faces…dead. Had the Gorracks returned?

Both too shocked for tears, they followed the odd scrape marks in the dirt and finally arrived at the edge of the quarry.

Laeriss screamed hysterically. "*No!* Oh, no! Not Jonasim! No!"

Duskan pulled her into his chest and gripped her hard. He choked back his own tears and the sickness that welled up within him. The ground had been soaked with dark blood, and there were globs of flesh and bits of bone. There was also clothing. Jonasim's clothing.

Duskan drew Laeriss aside and pulled his sword. "Did you hear that?" he said. "Wolves…blackwolves by the sound of it." Then he noticed the odd stinging smell in the air. It seemed to be coming from the strange gnarled stave thrust into the soft ground near Jonasim's body. "I think we need to leave."

"But…where will we go, Duskan?" Laeriss asked. "It's all… it's all gone."

"The holds in the mountains," he said. "It'll be safe there. We can think this through."

"Think it through?" Laeriss repeated. "They're all dead, Duskan…dead."

"I know that, Laeriss. I know."

"We can't go to the mountains. The wolves will get our scent."

"The river then," Duskan said. "We make due east to the river. Maybe we can catch a boat to Anglinore."

"Maybe we can find Mr. Tolke?" she said.

"I was thinking the same." He looked up suddenly. "We've got to go now. The wolves are getting closer."

CHAPTER 28

MEETING AT MIDNIGHT

Haskin Nut: feathery, tender, delicious meat pulp (pink when ripe).
Surrounded by an incredibly thick series of husks. Very difficult to get
through; so tough, in fact, that usually an axe or similar sharp blade
is necessary to get it open. Or one could set about to peel the husk,
one layer at a time—splintery danger.
    Beatrice Bettle's *Field Guide to Herbs, Seeds, and Nuts*

28 CELESANDUR 2212

"Thoughwehaveonlymetjustrecently…" said Sprye. "Oh, there I go again. I will slow down." She winked at Alastair and Abbagael. "Though we have only met just recently, I feel like I have known you far longer."

"I feel the same," Abbagael said. They were outside of Willow Dell in the cool of the morning. "Maybe it's the stories I read as a child. Maybe I always believed you existed. But I am so glad to have met you."

"You have been very kind to us," said Alastair. "I wish you greater victories over the rooks."

"We willowfolk wish to have no more fights against the rooks," said Alac, hovering over a patch of budding flowers. "But if we must fight them, then we will defeat them."

"That's the spirit," Alastair said.

"Hey'o!" Alac cried. He directed a team of more than a dozen willowfolk in leading Alastair's horse into the clearing.

"Look at the shine on him," Abbagael said.

"I daresay you willowfolk take better care of him than I do," Alastair said.

"I am quite sure you're right," said Alac. "By the way, he likes honeybelles."

Alastair smiled again. "You do have a way of lifting a man's spirits," he said. "I think we will both miss you—well, all three of us. Oh, and the horse."

"But this is not goodbye," Sprye said. "At least, I certainly hope not!" She stuck her pinkie fingers in the corners of her mouth and whistled louder than most bigfolk could.

Bevin and Emma buzzed down from the treetops. Each carried a black cord necklace with a dangling wooden pendant.

"Lord Alastair and Lady Abbagael," Sprye said, "in this moment you cease to be Willow King and Queen, and you cannot keep your crowns. But we willowfolk want you to have these." She motioned to her two helpers.

Bevin flitted to Abbagael's neck. He flittered in and out of her hair until he had the necklace clasped. "There you are, my lady," he said. He nuzzled under her chin a moment and sighed. "Ah, fetching creature."

Abbagael giggled. The child in her arms found the pendant very interesting and immediately put it in his mouth. Abbagael giggled a little more.

Emma delivered Alastair's necklace. "Hereyego!" she said in her strange deep voice.

Alastair looked down at the pendant. It was a mere two inches long, tawny-colored, and carved to resemble a willow. It had an opening on both sides like a whistle.

"You are forever friends of the willowfolk," Sprye said. "If you are in the area of Willow Dell and you need us, just blow on it. You will hear nothing, but we will. And we will answer the summons."

"You understand," said Alac, "that it will not work if you are far away. Blow all you want in Ellador, and we won't hear you. Hee-he!"

"I will miss the willowfolk," Abbagael said, seated once more behind Alastair on the horse. The child had been awake for hours after they'd left Willow Dell, but now he slept soundly. "I don't know what it is, but something about them, something about their home, makes me long to go back. It already feels like a memory of some time long past."

"I think I see what you mean," Alastair said. "It seemed to me, at least before the rook attack, that their home was somehow kept just right, unspoiled by the rest of Myriad."

A night and most of the next day later, Alastair, Abbagael, and the child entered the maritime village of Gull'scry. Alastair had them enter the town near the docks. Abbagael was exhausted from the journey, and Alastair felt her forehead on his shoulder. He said nothing but made special note of several ships whose captains looked like they'd do just about anything for a little gold... including taking a lone passenger far away.

In another hour, he'd found them a room at a leaning, creaky old inn called The Broken Oar. While Abbagael bathed and fed the child, Alastair went down to see to the horse. Only, he didn't spend much time in the stable. Instead, he ventured quickly to the docks and struck a deal.

Later, they shared a meal of cheese and summer sausage in the inn's noisy gathering room. Abbagael did her best to strike up a conversation—even suggesting a few more names for the child, but Alastair had become unresponsive. When she inquired, his only answer was, "Tired from the ride."

Late that night, their room on the second floor of the The Broken Oar was dark and completely silent except for the slow and regular sleeping breaths of Abbagael and the child.

Child, Alastair thought with some consternation. Nigh on a week he and Abbagael had sought to agree on a name for the little boy, and still they could not. *Why should I care? Let her name him. It won't matter.*

Alastair slid one leg out of his bed and lay still. He listened. No change in their breathing. They were indeed sound asleep. He slithered the rest of the way out of bed. He stood in the darkness and waited a few heartbeats. Then he crept across the room. His elbow brushed the drapes and, for a moment, a sliver of moonlight bathed the other bed in soft white light. Alastair froze.

He wasn't worried about waking Abbagael. He had plenty of excuses lined up. No, he found himself staring because her considerable beauty was somehow amplified in slumber. Her skin, normally creased in concentration at the corners of her eyes and above the bridge of her noses was now as smooth as polished alabaster. Her closed eyes, so soft and peaceful, revealed the lush length of her long lashes. And perhaps it was the play of moonlight and shadow, but there seemed to be a most becoming smile curling on her lips.

Alastair shook himself out of such thoughts, let the drape fall back into place, and stepped quietly to the door.

Once in the hallway and down the stairs he felt better. After all, he was doing the right thing. The child would have an adoring mother, not some half-hearted rogue who could barely keep himself afloat, much less care for another.

He passed like a ghost through the main gathering room and the tavern without seeing a single living being. Then he stepped outside into the cool night. The world existed only in distorted blue shadows. Crickets chirruped from the forest on the west side of town. The hypnotic rush of waves crashing to shore came from the east.

Alastair went to the stable. He'd conveniently left most of his personal gear and supplies in his horse's saddlebags. "Funny," he whispered as he brushed the snout of his old stallion. "I've never given you a name, either." The horse swished its tail and bobbed its head.

He led the animal out of the stable and behind the inn to a side street he knew would keep him away from town guards or any watchful eyes. The *clip-clop* of the horse's shoes on the cobblestone had a curious hollow echo. It reminded him of the night he'd left Vulmarrow, never to return. Alastair shrugged.

He looked above the uneven roofline of cottages and inns and saw the tops of masts and one or two crow's nests painted silver in the moonlight. *Where will I go? A quick sea jaunt around the Horn of Whispich and make port in Brightcastle? Llanfair, maybe?* He wasn't sure about that. Llanfair was a land fertile with opportunities, but the Prydian Wayfolk were serious about their ban on Witchdrale.

Of course Abbagael, as feisty and determined as she was, might come looking for him, might find him in either of those destinations...so close to Gull'scry. *She would come looking, wouldn't she?* Alastair blinked. Abbagael never gave up. He found himself admiring that trait in her...much like his mother in that way. *Well, if she finds a way to hunt me down,* he thought with a dry chuckle, *I'll know I've been bested and I'll stay with the copper-haired maiden, come what may.*

The horse snorted, and Alastair suddenly paid more attention to his surroundings. He had entered the section of town called Whitkirk, not the safest of places to stroll at night even for an accomplished swordsman. The place was full of cutthroats and derelicts, any of whom would be willing and able to shake down a lone passerby.

Alastair kept walking, leading his horse down the road, but he'd seen a shape move quite suddenly in the shadows of a side street to his left. And this wasn't some half-conscious sot bouncing back and forth between the alley walls. These were stealthy movements, well-practiced, and it was likely that anyone else would have missed them. But Alastair hadn't.

He kept walking without changing the width or cadence of his gait. But his right hand nonchalantly brushed his cloak away from his sword. He shifted the reins from his left to his right hand, freeing his sword hand. Still the dark figure advanced in the shadows.

Inwardly, Alastair cringed. This would-be assailant, whoever he was, had no idea that this thievery would cost him his life. Alastair wished there were some way he could ward off such attacks. He had never liked to kill, especially since learning the Lore of the First One from Yasmina. It was just something he was very, very good at. And this poor thief was about to discover his mistake in the most unpleasant fashion.

The cobblestone road narrowed up ahead and completely bottlenecked at a brick and mortar arch, the gateway to the docks. Alastair thought the thief would strike there. From the corner of his eye, he watched the dark openings to side streets, the clefts between buildings, and the overhangs. The figure moved quickly, barely visible. It seemed inevitable to Alastair. They would meet at the bottleneck. There'd be the sudden gleam of a short sword or dagger, and then Alastair would kill the man.

But then, Alastair had a thought. Why not warn the thief? Perhaps just letting him know that he'd been seen would be enough to discourage an attack. So Alastair drew up short. The horse stopped and snorted.

"I've seen you," Alastair called out. His voice, though not a yell, seemed loud in the night quiet, and it echoed in the empty alleys. "You move well, thief. But you'd best be on your way. I am not your usual quarry."

Alastair stared into every dark corner. No movement. Even the air was still. He hoped he had scared off the thief, but felt sure he had not. There was still a presence, a threatening heaviness permeating his senses.

"Look, I'm more than you bargained for." Alastair drew his long blade and slashed it about. "I have more than a measure of skill with a blade. What good is gold if it costs you your life? Depart from here in plain sight!"

Again, no movement. *This thief must consider himself my equal.* Alastair's ire began to bubble like a cauldron of stew. "I'm in no mood to kill, but I will if you press me." Alastair reached into his coin pouch. He tossed a few coins towards the shadows where he'd last seen movement from the thief. "Here now, I've left you some gold, more than enough to feed you and provide a night or two of pleasure. Take the coins and go your way."

Alastair waited impatiently, but there was no sign. He was half-tempted to charge the shadows and force the issue. Who was this impudent rogue to think he could go toe to toe with Alastair Coldhollow? Of course, the thief couldn't know who he was.

Harrumphing, Alastair turned and continued leading his horse toward the dockyard gate. Not ten steps later, a shadow darted from an alley to a recessed doorway just ahead. Alastair grumbled. What would it take to warn this fellow off?

"You keep this up, you've just minutes to live!" Alastair spoke again, exasperated and temporarily losing control of his tongue. "This is no empty threat! I do not want to kill you, but I will. I have military training. By the Stars, I am an assassin. For your own sake, leave me be!"

Once he said it, he immediately regretted it. That detail of his life was something he intended to keep close. But the gall of this would-be thief had gotten the better of Alastair, roused his anger. It wasn't the first time nor the last.

Alastair pressed on toward the gate. There was a whisper of sea breeze washing up from the docks, but no movement in the shadows. He kept his sword drawn as he neared the gate, but there was no attack. Once through the gate, he waited for a few moments on the other side, thinking the thief might be stupid enough to blunder through. But no one came. *Good. The rogue's come to his senses. Probably doubled back to pick up the gold.*

Alastair led his horse down the hill and to the docks. They passed several dark ships moored along the seawall. There were no lanterns lit on these, no one stirring on deck. But Alastair saw the twin-masted schooner just ahead. He'd spotted it as they'd first entered town. The captain of that vessel had seemed like the willing sort. For the right price, he'd said, he would take Alastair just about anyplace on the east coast of Myriad.

Alastair kept his focus on the ship and never saw the dark figure slip through the gate behind him.

Alastair passed out of the moonlight and fell beneath the shadow of the schooner he'd been looking for. He found the captain leaning over the port rail, not asleep but not exactly alert either. "Excuse me, good sir," Alastair called up to him. There was no response. "Good captain, as we discussed this evening, I wish to pay for passage on your ship." *Lost in thought maybe?* "Down here!" Alastair called a little louder. The captain's eyes were open and fixed. He didn't even blink. *He could be dead*, Alastair thought. *That would explain a lot.* "I have gold!"

"Whassat?" the captain replied at last. His voice was dry and gravelly, like a barnacled hull scraping against a sea wall. "Oh, hey dere. It's you, izzit?"

"It's about time," Alastair said, glancing over his shoulder. "I've been calling you and you didn't answer."

"I was finkin,'" he said.

Alastair highly doubted that. "As we discussed, I'd like to book passage on your ship. What's your next port of call?"

"Brightcastle," he said. "Be there a'coupla days. Then I'll be 'aulin' fish and spices to Anglinore port."

Alastair thought King Aravel might be interested in his brother Morlan's recent doings, but Anglinore held absolutely no interest for Alastair. Too many well-trained soldiers who might be curious about how Alastair came to such knowledge. Too many who might recognize Alastair Coldhollow…and offer the gallows as payment for his information. "Brightcastle is where I was hoping to go," he said. "How much to stable my horse and bear us both there?"

The captain tilted his head and scratched the stubbles on his chin and cheek. "'orse got sea legs, has it?"

"It'd take more than a few swells to knock my horse off his feet," he replied. "And I'm willing to take the risk."

"Two crowns then, and not a penny less."

Two crowns? Alastair marveled at the price. "Done then."

The captain practically leaped over the side, shimmied down a rope ladder, and snatched the two gold coins out of Alastair's outstretched hand. "Ah, thank'ee, sir, that'll do right nice, it will. I'll just be a moment with the gangplank so's your 'orse can come aboard. There's right fine salted beef in the larder if you have a mind."

"Thank you, Captain uh…?"

"Dagspaddle," he replied with a courteous bow. Alastair heard a strange sound and dared not guess what it might have been. "Filbert A. Dagspaddle, at yer service." Captain Dagspaddle clambered back up the rope ladder and disappeared over the side.

The commotion that followed sounded like the captain was having a bit of a time waking his deck hands. Alastair glanced once more over his shoulder—nothing there—and snickered to himself. *Two crowns! I would have paid three times that to get away from—"*

The shadow was there, coming hard toward Alastair from behind and to his right. Alastair wondered how he could have missed him, but it was a thought two seconds too late. The thief was on him. Alastair's sword was only halfway delivered from its sheath when—

Smack! It was not the prick of a dagger blade in the small of his back. Instead, Alastair's neck and right ear stung from a well-delivered slap.

"You conniving, lily-livered, firbolg! How dare you run out on me and this poor child!"

"Lady Abbagael, I—I...how—?"

Smack! Now, Alastair's left ear stung. "Never you mind how I managed to keep up with you! Oh, you have so much to answer for I don't even know where to start."

Alastair started to speak, but Abbagael's smoldering eyes silenced him at the first syllable.

"This was your plan all along, wasn't it? Bring me way out here, far from home where I might have had any help. Leave me and the child with no horse and no money? After all we've been through? Cruel, Alastair...that's just hard cruel." And then the tears started.

Alastair would have rather that Abbagael berate him over and over. The tears were torture. "Listen, I know it was a mean trick, but Lady Abbagael, I am no good for a child." He paused, lifted her chin with his finger, and said, "I'm no good for you either."

"Hey'a what's this, then?" Captain Dagspaddle called down over the rail. "You never said nuthin' 'bout someone's else comin' along, a dame even. That'll be an extra two crown, it will."

"How much would it be to drop us in Chapparel City?" Abbagael asked.

"Chapparel City?" Alastair blurted out.

Abbagael glared at him. "It'll make for a nice, *long* journey. Enough time to sort things out." She looked back to the captain. "So how much?"

"Right, then. We've got to sail t'Brightcastle, pick up me load. I was fixin' t'sail to Anglinore straight away from there.

Chapparel'll take me a fair sight out'a me way. I'd say…seven crown and three fer the whole'a both a' ye."

"Done!" Abbagael called, wiping her tears away. She grabbed Alastair's change-purse, shook out the coins, and tossed them up to the captain. "Oh, and here's a bit extra for your trouble, and for my friend's…deception."

"Oh, oh, oh," Captain Dagspaddle replied. "That's right fine o' ye. Well, come on, then. Gangplank's down. We'll get under sail in a finner. 'S what we sailin' folk call fifteen minutes, ye see?"

"Excellent, captain," Abbagael said. "We'll be right up."

"Abbagael, what are you doing?" Alastair asked.

"I thought it was obvious," she replied. "I'm going with you to Brightcastle. We'll spend a couple of days in a small cabin by ourselves. Unless you drown yourself, there'll be no chance of you running off."

"But—"

"And don't think this will be some pleasure cruise, Alastair. I have many questions yet, and I will give you no peace until you answer them to my satisfaction."

"More questions?"

"Yes, Alastair, beginning with what you meant by calling yourself an assassin."

Alastair felt his stomach twist into a pretzel and began to think that drowning himself was a distinct possibility.

CHAPTER 29

KING'S FOLLY

The events that follow did all occur early in the Age of Origin.
According to the most ancient of records, the first Shepherd
appeared between the founding of Anglinore in 333 and The Great
Tryllium Exploration in 561. Shepherd Fane was the first,
and he established their order in the summer of 708.
It wasn't until the first council in 1717 that their code was established.
The Shepherds have served according to three tenets of their code ever since.
And from these, they do not waver:
    1. Protect all Myridians.
    2. Never rule over them.
    3. Never reveal the secret lore.

From *Myridian Antiquities*
Sage Josephal (w. 2127, D)

37 CELESANDUR 2212

"You're sure it was Keenan," King Morlan said. "Keenan Wraithgard?"

Glenrick the tavern keeper swallowed hard. He'd never been within ten yards of King Morlan, much less standing alone

before his black throne. "My lord, it couldn't hardly be anyone else…he 'ad the Wolfguard epaulets, he did. I served him,
meself."

"And you're certain the Witchdrale wasn't tainted?"

"Tainted?" Glenrick chuckled. "That stuff's always tainted—
gut rot, some's us call it. Heh, heh." Morlan's stern expression
did not change, but Glenrick felt the weight of those yellow eyes.
"N-no, sir, it wasn't tainted. Seein' yer meanin' and all. It was
the end of a bottle, it was. Poured it for three other customers…
and they left right as rain. Well, right as they could be after a dose
a'that foul swill."

Morlan nodded. Even long ago when tutored by Anglinore's
greatest scholars, he was considered clever and most wise, but
here was a puzzle that even he could not solve. "And no one else
fell ill?"

"No, my lord."

"Not even in the days since?"

"Nay, sir. Fact is, some a' the regulars—Anor, Rissia, Mul-
luck—they've all been 'round since. Fine, far as I can tell. Certainly nothin' like poor Commander Keenan. Horrible, it was."

"Tell me again. Spare no detail."

Glenrick had been hoping to avoid a prolonged interrogation,
but, seeing no easy escape, he told his tale.

"Right, well, the commander, he came in 'round six. He didn't
eat nuffin. Just called for Witchdrale. I left what was left a'the
bottle wid'im and saw to the other customers. Few ticks later, he
yells fer me, tells me he's sick. Gave me a scare, he did, screamin'
fer me like he was. I came over, and wishin' I didn't. He started
frothin' at the mouth like a rabid wolfhound—meanin' no offense
to yer Sköll here. But this weren't rabies spit—Keenan had black
froth. Then his skin started *bubblin'* like he was on fire. Bubblin',
I say! Each time a blister formed and popped, there was a puff a'
smoke. Horrible smell. The commander slid to the ground like a
boned fish. Worst thing I ever saw."

Morlan sat back in his throne. "That is all for now, Glenrick. See Quartermaster Brund in the armory. Collect a deuce-stack—reward for such helpful information."

"A deuce-stack?" Glenrick bowed so low he almost fell over. "Thank you, m'lord. Thank you."

Morlan watched Glenrick slip through the throne room doors. Two silver, two gold, two thrainium, and two scarlet dulcium coins—a deuce stack—was a fortune for a man of Glenrick's station. But Morlan had learned long ago that tavern keepers were some of his most valuable spies. Inside or outside of Vulmarrow. The news of Commander Wraithgard's unpleasant demise had been valuable indeed. Morlan had yet to solve the puzzle, but he felt sure he had all of the pieces, except one. For that, he'd have to visit the Bone Chapel.

39 CELESANDUR 2212

Cythraul had not yet returned from Thel-Mizaret, but Morlan felt sure there'd be a few living subjects left in the cells behind the great hall. Carrying a large oil lantern, Morlan stepped out of the tunnel and into the Bone Chapel.

Without the multiple red candles lit, it was remarkably dark, darker even than his own throne room. Still, Morlan made his way without trouble. And though his lantern's light cast shadows upon grinning skulls and the room's other ghastly architecture, Morlan traversed the room with no trepidation. It was like a cavernous charnel house, but relics of death held no fear for Morlan. And Cythraul had shown the king all the traps and pitfalls he'd rigged for unwary trespassers.

Morlan passed Cythraul's new altar and found the stairwell he was looking for. Just six stairs to a formidable iron door. The king selected a long serrated key from his keychain and unlocked the door. A gray path stretched before him, and the smell smacked him hard. It was not as sharp as the acrid smell in the main hall, but more pungent, like that of ancient filth. Morlan stood at the mouth of the passage and waited several moments. At first, he thought his trip was in vain. But then he heard it: the miserable soft sounds of weeping.

41 Celesandur 2212

Cythraul returned to the Bone Chapel to find an intruder sitting at his experimentation table.

"King Morlan?" Cythraul did not look particularly surprised. He carried two sacks with him, one large, one small. "I've brought the new Shepherd Jonasim to see you."

"I thought you might have," said the king. "Thel-Mizaret is finished?"

"Yes. All dead. But Vang sent troops. Where the trade roads cross, I saw a legion at least traveling north at great speed. I suspect they would have arrived in Thel-Mizaret in a day."

"I presume you scoured the city, scraped it...clean?"

"They will find Gorrack slaughter. Nothing more."

"Good, good," Morlan said, but he saw the flicker in Cythraul's pale eyes. "There was something else?"

Cythraul nodded. "I rode west from the crossing. I found your six missing assassins. They were slain by a master swordsman. If I did not know better, I would have thought Synic the Keenblade had returned. I suspect—"

"Alastair Coldhollow." Morlan stared at his feet and shook his head. "That is ill news. I had hoped he would have drunk himself to death long ago."

"You persuaded me not to pursue him then...twelve years past," Cythraul said, adjusting the sacks on his shoulder. "I have always been...curious...about that."

"A mistake," the king said. "I wonder if, even now, you might be able to rectify my...error."

"If you command it, it will be done."

"That Alastair would stick his neck out now…after all this time…it cannot be coincidence." King Morlan sneered. "He has the Star Sword. He appears so close to Thel-Mizaret and dispatches six of my men—what were you up to, Alastair?"

"Your assassins were after a woman," Cythraul said. "I found her deeper in the woods, dead from a crossbow dart and a sword. Perhaps Alastair was after her as well."

"Perhaps," Morlan said. "Alastair always was willing to be a fool for a pretty face." He pondered that for a moment. "But if she was important to Alastair, why would he leave her body for the worms?"

"I do not know," Cythraul said. "Perhaps he was afraid more of your knights were coming. He might dispatch six by himself, but sixty?"

"Perhaps," said the king, pinching the bridge of his nose. "Bah! There must be more. All right, Cythraul, you have my order."

Cythraul did not smile, but the depression in one corner of his mouth deepened. "I will leave at once. I know where to begin my search."

King Morlan brushed his hands together as if wiping off dirt. "But first, Cythraul, put down your burdens and light your candles. I have something rather spectacular to show you."

"You look as though you have been here long," Cythraul said as, one by one, the red candles came to life.

"I have been here very long." Morlan gestured to the table. "I hope you do not mind, but I made use of one of your live specimens."

A brief flicker of eyes to the corpse laid out on the table. Nothing more. "You've made quite a mess here," said Cythraul. More red candles. "Not recent."

"Two days ago."

"You've been here that long?"

"Waiting for you," said the king. "Given your expertise in such things, I need you to take a closer look."

"Of course." Cythraul lit the last few candles and then came forward. There was a click, and a sharp blade appeared in his hand. He went to work on the corpse.

"Based on the blistering, I would have thought he was burned alive. But no, the worst burning is on the inside of the skin. That is most unusual. Wait, one moment. Now this I have never seen." He reached to a loop on one of his waist belts and removed a metal instrument that looked something like a fork with only two tines. Two long tines. He began poking and prodding. "How did you...? His bones...they are blackened and brittle as ash. The kind of heat needed to do this... I must know what poison you used."

"It was not poison," Morlan said.

"What then?"

"I touched him."

Cythraul looked up sharply. "You did this...by touching him? But that would make you Shepherd-born."

"You know that I am not."

"You are a latent then?"

"No, Cythraul, I am a convert." Morlan relished knowing something Cythraul did not. But even as king, he would not push his chief assassin too far. He told Cythraul about Sabryne's calling him to Mount Gorthrandir, about the ancient Gorrack Shepherd—somehow still alive, and about how Sabryne had commanded him to slay the Gorrack. Then Morlan told Cythraul of his suspicions after Keenan Wrathgard died so horribly.

"So you believe that Shepherds pass on their gifts as they die?" Cythraul's eyes narrowed. "If this is true, then the Shepherds have managed to keep it a secret for thousands of years."

"Tens of thousands," Morlan corrected. "Ages."

"But I slew Jonasim. His stone-skin ability did not come to me."

Morlan considered this. "Perhaps it was too new. Perhaps a gift must mature before it can be passed on." Morlan paused. "Perhaps it will come to you in time."

"Your disease touch," Cythraul said, "how does it work?"

"At my will," Morlan said. "If I wish ill to anyone and touch the skin, that person will die."

"How long?"

"Hours…at least with Keenan. More than a day for this one."

Silence devoured the great hall of the Bone Chapel. Red candles burned lower. Shadows grew longer, climbing the macabre arches as Morlan and Cythraul weighed their new knowledge. There was no whisper of wind outside or even a faint gurgle from the canal that flowed beneath their feet. No skitter of spider or buzz of insect. It was perfectly dead in that chamber.

Morlan felt it first: an extreme heaviness, as if the air itself possessed weight. But for the king it was not really a burden to bear. It was more a mantle of responsibility, of great deeds to be done. Done *though* him. It became a filling, bursting kind of exhilaration, something he could not restrain.

King Morlan drew his sword, the Wolfblade, screamed and held it aloft. There was a flash and a terrible crashing sound, and the shaft of the blade came to life with tongues of yellow fire. For several pulse-quickening moments, light danced among the bones and Morlan stood without peer in the world of Myriad.

The fire extinguished. Morlan sheathed his sword and diminished, breathing out a deep sigh.

But for Cythraul, there was no reducing the grandeur of his sovereign. "My lord," he said as he bowed his knee. "You are most favored of Sabryne Shadowfinger. Command me."

"Ah, Cythraul," said the king, "among the beings in this world, you are my most favored. Rise up. Take whatever time you need to prepare. Find Alastair Coldhollow. Question him. And then kill everyone who has ever loved him, aided him, or given him shelter. Make it as if Alastair had never existed in this world."

"So be it," said Cythraul.

"My lords?" came a high, frightened voice from one of the primary tunnels in the back of the hall. "My lords, is it safe? I saw lightning and heard things I cannot explain."

Cythraul stood and a long thin chain dropped down from his forearm. A talon-shaped blade dangled at its end.

"No," Morlan said, "that won't be necessary." Then he called out. "It is your king and his servant Cythraul. Who are you, and why do you disturb our privacy?"

"F-five thousand apologies, my king," screeched the urgent voice. "It is Pietyre. I have returned from Anglinore with a message I was told could not wait!"

"Very well, Pietyre, come!" said the king. Cythraul's chain had already disappeared, and he made as if to leave the great hall. "No, stay and hear the news with me. Stay and watch."

Cythraul nodded. A soldier dressed in the blue-gray livery of Vulmarrow picked his way forward to the altar. Fit and very muscular he was, but he seemed on the verge of exhaustion. He bowed to Morlan and Cythraul. His large dark eyes were wild and flitted restlessly from sight to sight.

"You were wise to bear us this news in haste, Pietyre," Morlan said. "Tell me, what news do you bring from my brother's throne?"

Pietyre swallowed and closed his eyes for a moment. "Aravel...he will not declare war upon the Gorrack Nation."

"*What?*" King Morlan drew a sharp breath and glared at the messenger.

"He will send an envoy," Pietyre said, "a diplomatic team bearing tokens of Gorrack aggression."

"Fool," Morlan muttered. "Thrice the coward." His yellow eyes found Cythraul. "My brother weakens by the day. He needs more persuasion, don't you think?"

"Yes, my lord," said Cythraul.

"I haven't done wrong, have I, my lord?" asked Pietyre.

"Think nothing of it, Pietyre," said the King. "Come, take my hand."

Later, in his throne room, Morlan closed the *Prophecies of Hindred.* He understood at last why the Gorrack Shepherd had been kept alive, waiting for Morlan Stormgarden to take its life. So many pieces suddenly fell into place. Morlan saw his part in the story woven before him. He knew at last how to bring all of Myriad to its knees. And he also knew the price he would have to pay.

CHAPTER 30

STORMY SEAS

Standing on shore and staring at the water won't
get you to the other side of the sea.
Captain Angus Kindred, Brightcastle Port, 5618 D

38 CELESANDUR 2212

Alastair leaned over the stern of Captain Dagspaddle's trade ship, the *Mynx*, and got sick. It was the third time and on an empty stomach. But it wasn't the rocking of the ship on the unusually rough seas. Alastair had spent plenty of time on the water, often in far worse weather. No, his stomach heaved because he had never felt this kind of internal turbulence before. He wondered about that—why Abbagael vexed him in such a way.

The *Mynx* slammed down into a trough, and gust of wind and sea spray from the bow blasted Alastair's face.

He wiped sopping hair away from his eyes. *What does any of this matter? No matter how caring, no matter how beautiful and smart—Abbagael is simply off limits. If she knew what I'd done, if she knew what I am...it would break her heart. And now, I've tried to abandon her, breaking her heart anyway, and now she knows more than she should. She has the tip of the string and, should she pull it, the whole garment will unravel.* Alastair's stomach lurched and he heaved over the rail once more. There was nothing left…it was empty, but still churning.

One of the ship's hands walked by, muttering something about lily-white, gutless mainlanders.

"I've seen many a man toss 'is lunch over that rail, I have!" called Captain Dagspaddle from the helm. "Many in lesser seas'n this."

Alastair offered only a weak wave in return.

"But somehow, I didn't fegger you fer a knee-knocker," Dagspaddle said. "Looks like woman trouble t'me."

"You've a keen eye, Captain," Alastair said.

"C'mon up 'ere, and let's have us a conversation."

Alastair ascended to the helm.

"Gave you quite a dressing down, did she?" the captain asked, his eyes on the seas ahead. Thunder rumbled in the distance.

"Well deserved, I'm afraid."

"What's gotten between you, then? Ye look like a nice famly."

"It's…complicated."

"What's so complicated?" asked Dagspaddle. "Ye've been blessed with beautious wife. Baby boy, cute as a button."

"She's not my wife," Alastair said. "And the boy's not my own."

"Oh. *Oh!*" said the captain. "So it's complicated?"

"Uh…yes, you could say that."

"Well, now, that does throw a reef in front've ye, don't it? Hold on. Tricky bit here." The captain turned the ship's wheel to the port. Alastair felt the movement and the *Mynx* rose high on a wave. Dagspaddle spun the wheel back to the right, and they coasted down the backside of the wave into its trough. "If'n ye take my word on the matter," the captain went on, "I'd stay clear astern of another man's bride. No good'll ever come a' that."

Alastair shook his head. "Oh, no, that's not what I meant. Lady Abbagael's not married. And the child's not the problem…well, not really." He paused, knowing there were details about his past he couldn't reveal. But still, it felt good to have the captain's ear. "Look, here it is: Abbagael's just a girl. I'm too old for her…too much of a lot of things. She doesn't love me. She loves a picture of me. If she really knew, she'd sooner see me hung than take my hand. And even if there ever was a chance, I've blown it to bits."

Captain Dagspaddle kept one hand on the wheel and rubbed his stubbly chin with the other. "Seem's t'me like you've given a sack a' reasons why she should stay away from ye. But she got on this ship, didn' she?"

Alastair made no reply. He had none.

"She's a growed woman and, no mistake, makin' growed woman decisions, I'd say." He snorted and scratched his backside. "S'pose you make some growed up decisions 'ere. Ye'd be better for it."

"But I don't love her," Alastair grumbled. "I can't love her."

"No such rules like that in love," the captain said. "She's a woman. Yer a man. And I've known far too many lyin' dogs t'believe ye don't love the lass. The way ye calls her 'Lady' and such? And threw yer lunch over the rail down there?"

Alastair shook his head angrily. "But what do I tell her?"

"Truth. Truth's a lighthouse through reef and rock, fog and foul weather. It'll steer ye through." Captain Dagspaddle slapped Alastair's shoulder. "Now off wit'ye. Last I sawr a'yer lady, she was in the galley."

"But," Alastair protested. "If I tell her my past—"

"Balderdash! Look lad, nothin' built on a lie ever lasts."

Abbagael was just pulling a blanket up to the child's chin when Alastair walked in. The boy was sleeping in a bread box on the only table in the ship's galley.

"You look wet," she said.

"I've been topside," he said. "Talking with the captain. He's a wiser man than he looks."

"That so," she replied absently, her eyes returning to the baby. "You know, we still haven't named him. You were going to leave me with a nameless child."

Alastair cringed inwardly. He'd been run through with swords that hurt less than this. He trudged to the table. "May I sit?"

"If you want."

Alastair sat across from her. He reached for her hands, but she pulled away and folded her arms. "Lady Abbagael, I have a lot to say, and I'm not very good with words."

"It seems to me," she said, "that you are all too good at words. You had me fooled."

"You're not making this easy."

"Nor should I. Alastair Coldhollow, you had this planned all this time. From the moment I refused to take the child, you hatched this plan, didn't you?"

"Yes."

"And you really were going to leave me and the child in that bleak little port town? Leave me so far away from my home? Leave us with no gold?"

"Well, I...I mean, it hadn't occurred to me about the gold, but yes, I was going to leave you there."

She stared at him, her eyes darting continuously as if weighing him. "How could you?"

More swords...the gut, kidneys, maybe a jab in the shoulder. Telling the truth was painful. "It's not that I meant to hurt you or the child. I mean, yes, it was horrible to leave you in this manner, but...it was for the best that I leave."

"But why, Alastair? Why do you have to leave?"

"*Because!*" Alastair looked at the sleeping boy and lowered his voice. "Because I am no man to raise a child. I know nothing of children."

"Neither do any new parents. There has to be more than that. What? Do you hate children? Do you never want children of your own?"

"No, it's not...well..." Alastair stopped short. He didn't know. It'd been so long since he'd allowed himself a thought so normal to others as perhaps one day having a family. He took a lightning quick inventory of his life. It seemed there was a red X painted across all that he'd ever once hoped or dreamed. That was all gone now for him. He was cursed. He could never have what he truly wanted...or needed. "I...I have a problem," he whispered finally.

"What is it?" Abbagael asked. She leaned forward, her eyes large and so genuinely concerned that Alastair ached.

"Witchdrale," he said. "It haunts me. I cannot endure life without it, not for long. And when I drink it, I...it's like a black spot in my memory. I do not know what I've done while in its grip, unless I am told after the fact."

"Witchdrale, Alastair?" Her lips trembling, Abbagael actually smiled. "I've seen the bottles in your home. I've smelled it on you. But I've seen you go weeks without it. Can its hold be so strong on you? Maybe I can help you bear the burden?"

Alastair slammed shut his eyes and shook his head. "No."

"Why? Why face it alone?"

"There...there's more."

"How much more can there..." Abbagael became more rigid. Her face went slack. "You said you were an assassin," she said, a tear already in her eye. "Tell me. Tell me all of it."

Alastair opened his eyes and looked reflexively over both shoulders to make sure no one else was in the galley. "You've known me for a long time, Abbagael."

"Since I was a child."

"Twelve years," he said. "Ever since I built my home in Ardon. But for ten years prior to that I lived in Vulmarrow."

She stared blankly. It hadn't sunk in.

"Vulmarrow, Abbagael. I was a Wolfguard Knight—in the service of King Morlan."

Puzzlement still in her eyes.

Of course, thought Alastair. *She doesn't know. No one knows.* He swallowed, took a deep breath and said, "King Morlan is not a noble ruler...not like his brother, King Aravel. Far from it. Morlan is drunk with power and has, for many years, strived for more. His Wolfguard has a secret branch...a group of elite soldiers who violently put down or eliminate anyone Morlan deems to be his enemy. He is particularly obsessed with the followers of the First One. Obsessed with destroying them, that is."

Abbagael squinted. "High King Aravel...he doesn't know?"

"I don't know what Aravel knows, but he is no fool. He must suspect something."

"Then why does he not act?"

"Morlan is his brother. Perhaps Aravel needs more proof. Again, I do not know."

"What does this have to do with you...with us?" She asked the question, but then looked up abruptly. She mouthed, "No."

"I was the captain of King Morlan's most ruthless assassins," Alastair explained. "For six of my ten years under Morlan's command, I murdered countless people: scouts, ambassadors, politicians—anyone Morlan reckoned as a threat. I led the slaughters of entire towns and villages, people who had done nothing but devote themselves to a faith Morlan abhorred...and feared. Avington, Bryngate, Teris Falls—"

"Stop," Abbagael whispered.

"Elderwood, Belhaven, Caster—"

"Don't!" she yelled. "Don't say any more."

"No, you need to hear this. This is the truth about me. This is what I did. I remember every single town. Every single face. Stoneford Bluff, Ingledale, Incleff, and Dorn—they are silent now, their blood on my hands. Not Maiden Vale, not your parents, Abbagael. But only by chance. Had I not been on other business that night, it might have been me."

For a long, breathless moment, Abbagael sat very still. Her haunted eyes stared out with incomprehension. A flat, but altogether miserable moan seeped out from her lips. Before Alastair could say another word, Abbagael erupted. She reached across the table as if she might choke him, but instead ferociously pounded on his chest and shoulders. She shook him and scratched at him, drawing blood on his cheek and neck.

Alastair knew a dozen ways he could have taken her down, but he didn't even cover his eyes. He was his own curse. He deserved this and more.

She screamed, her face a blistering red. There were words: murderer, cold, bloodthirsty, heartless, but they were swimming in a mighty current of wrenching shrieks and feral growls.

The child startled awake. His tiny hands shook. Weeping and coughing, Abbagael stopped her attack on Alastair and huddled the child close. She stood up from the table and turned to leave when the ship rocked suddenly on a blast from the unruly sea. She stumbled toward the midship stair. The ship rocked again, and Abbagael fell backward.

But Alastair caught her and helped her regain her footing.

"Don't you *touch* me!" she hissed. And then she was gone.

CHAPTER 31

Blood for Blood

The Three Ages of Myriad
The Age of Origin (AO)
The Age of Dissension (D)
The Age of Silence (AS)

41 Celesandur 2212

"I must confess," Velach Krel said, his voice echoing in the throne room, "I shall be very glad to kill Gorrack kind rather than my own."

Morlan raised an eyebrow at this admission. "Really, Velach? I had no idea you had even a shred of feeling for such things."

"A shred," he replied. "But that is all. It numbs you, really… the killing, that is."

"Yes," Morlan said, "it does. But it is necessary. Very few understand the edge upon which this world teeters. The Gorrack Nation grows unchecked, their numbers swelling 'til their borders are near to bursting. They now barely attempt to conceal their hatred of the Great Races. We must act decisively, and we must not wait."

"You have laid the groundwork for revolution," Velach said. "The Gorracks and Aravel will be thrown down. Myriad will have a real overlord at last. I am grateful to be a part of it."

"Your team has never failed me, Velach," the king said. "You understand your orders?"

"Yes, my lord. First we slay two or three townsfolk in Chapparel."

"They must appear to be military," King Morlan said. "Uniformed, bearing the livery of Chapparel."

"We'll wait until dusk, take them from the city gate...or the walls."

"Moon's bright t'night," Gravin said to his guard duty partner on Chapparel's outer wall.

"Right pretty over the wetlands like that," Vinceri replied. "I was thinkin' a takin' Emi out for a flatboat later."

"Ah, good call, mate. Good call. She'll like that. Maybe I should take Keya out. She's been giving me flack for pulling so much extra guard duty."

"There you go," Vinceri said. "Take your beauty out. Show her a good time."

"Who's relieving us at eight anyway?"

"Jort, I believe, and Ardis."

"I'd hate to be the poor fool to climb the wall when Jort's on duty." Gravin laughed.

"Heh, heh, yeah, that big axe a' his. No way I'd—"

When Vinceri didn't finish his sentence, Gravin turned around. "No way you'd what?"

His friend was gone.

"Vince? Vince? Where'd you go?" He thought maybe Vinceri had lost his balance and gone over the wall. He drew his sword just to be safe and prowled over to the spot he'd last seen Vinceri. "Hoy, Vince, you down there? You all right?" Gravin leaned over...too far. A crossbow dart punctured his throat, and he toppled over the wall.

"Preserve the bodies as best you can and bear them across the border of the Gorrack Nation." King Morlan traced a finger across the map. "Follow the River Nightwash. You will find Gorrack villages. Slaughter them. Leave the Chapparel guards for patrols that pass through there."

"I'll need more men," Velach Krel said, "even if it's just Gorrack peasants."

"Hand-select your teams."

"Thank you, my lord. That sort of freedom will allow me to assemble a large, proficient team...without sacrificing stealth. I know exactly who to bring."

"And Velach," Morlan said, "you will need to make this one messy. When the Gorrack raider patrols come, and they will come, they must be enraged by what they find, enflamed to the point of swift retaliation."

"I understand. But the timing will be tricky. We'll want to attack when the noonday sun is hottest and the village is sure to be sleeping. The raider patrol will come at dusk. Figuring in how long it will take the patrol to contact their local base... and then march to Chapparel, we cannot be sure to have the Gorracks and Anglinore's diplomatic team in Chapparel at the same time."

"The timing is not as critical as it seems," the king said. "Yes, I would like to see Chapparel wiped from the face of Myriad. Warden Caddock is a sniveling bootlicker, posing as some kind of royalty. But should Aravel's diplomatic envoy escape Chapparel and travel west before the Gorracks attack, then so be it. They will run right into the teeth of a murderous legion of Gorracks. It might even serve us better that way, for without Chapparel's ground support, Aravel's men will be doomed."

Their stream riders hidden in tangles of reeds along the Nightwash River, Velach's hand-picked forces clambered like a mass of spiders across the sparsely wooded terrain. They aimed for the greenish granite cliffs to the north. Velach's scouts reported a large Gorrack village there. It would not be an easy target, but so long as everyone followed orders exactly, success was virtually guaranteed.

They'd made very good time, a tribute to the athleticism of Velach's men. But that meant they needed to wait for the sun to catch up. It was a clear day, and the temperature was rising, but Velach would not attack until the sun was at its peak. Gorracks get sluggish in the heat. Velach wanted them as sluggish as possible.

Somewhere between one and two, Gundara Shorn came to Velach. The burly warrior was drenched with sweat and glistened even in the shade. "I think it's hot enough," he said to Velach.

Velach nodded. "Tell the other team leaders. We move on my signal."

Ten teams of Wolfguard soldiers, comprised of ten assassins each, moved into position among the foothills below the Gorrack village. Gorracks dwelt in caves, deep caves, with networks of tunnels and massive hollows in the cool innards of the mountain. Velach counted the number of openings in the cliff walls. He whistled under his breath. A lot more Gorracks lived in this village than he had hoped.

Velach rose from his crouch and pulled his arm back high, bending his elbow as if he were drawing a bowstring. His hand flew forward. The signal. Ten teams of men fled their concealment. They moved in spurts, from boulder to spindly tree to thatch of brush—any cover they could find.

Nothing stirred in the Gorrack camp, but Velach and his team leaders were not so foolish as to imagine the village absent of guards. They found pairs of sentries hidden in clefts of rock at relatively regular spacing eighty yards from the caves. Tenements and wood and thatch longhouses stood within this perimeter, adding another facet to the invasion.

Velach went first with Gundara at his side. Their targets were two sentries, seated, facing outward near a large shade tree.

Gorracks were massive warriors. Their gray skin was marbled with streaks of dark brown or black. Each had a huge, hard skull, thick mantle-like brow, and reptilian eyes. Scales descended every Gorrack's brick-shaped chin, down its neck, chest, and midsection. Kilts of hard level panels covered their upper legs, but these two wore no additional armor—probably due to the heat. Thankfully, they looked drowsy.

Gundara took his target out with one blow from his hammer. Skull caved in, the Gorrack fell like timber. Velach needed a little more finesse. The scales made its throat an unreliable target, so Velach went for the Gorrack's femoral artery. He slid below the startled sentry's errant pike swipe and yanked his dagger hard across its thigh.

The Gorrack doubled over, reached for the wound, and started to howl, but Velach was still behind him. He clambered up the Gorrack's back and pounded his dagger into the base of its skull. The Gorrack's voice turned into the sound of air escaping its lungs one last time.

Velach looked over to Gundara. "That was close."

"You were a little slow," Gundara said. "You'll pick it up with the next one."

The Gorrack sentries eliminated, Velach's archers took positions on the cave guards. These were Morlan's sharpshooters—the best from tens of thousands of Wolfguard soldiers. Morlan had given express orders that not one of these archers was to be lost in the battle. So their task was simple: take out the cave guards, then get well out of the way.

Three archers to each cave guard. Cobalt-tipped arrowheads. Aiming for the eyes. Bows sang, the arrows traversed forty yards of open ground, and Gorracks dropped to the ground or fell from cliff edges. It took four volleys of arrows, one immediately after the other, to fell all the guards, but Velach's archers managed it with no more ruckus than Gorracks thudding to the ground. Then, following orders, the archers fell back.

Velach and the other infantry moved swiftly in. Lighting fuses as they ran, the Wolfguard came to a hard stop at the cave mouths and heaved their explosives far inside. Velach heard the pops. Cythraul's poison gas would seep forth and drive the Gorracks out...out onto the blades of Velach's forces.

The time for stealth had ended. Growls, shrieks, and cries came from the caves as Gorracks coughed themselves awake. The torrent began at once, Gorracks bulling their way out of the caves. Some hit tripwires and fell over the edge of their own cliffs.

But many Gorracks broke free and engaged Velach's men. Pikes flashed in the hot sun. Wolfguard Knights dropped to the ground and died, but only a few. Velach had chosen only two types of men for his infantry: massive, powerful warriors like Gundara Shorn, who came close to matching the Gorracks' beastly strength; and much smaller, speedy men...men whose foot speed and quick reflexes enabled them to stay out of reach and dart in for a kill.

And kill they did. Gorracks littered the rocks and hot ground. The Wolfguard followed orders, squeezing the life out of the village and leaving behind unspeakable carnage.

"We should have taken more guards from Chapparel," said Gundara Shorn to his commander.

Velach looked disapprovingly on the bodies of the two guards. "Well...I suppose we'll need to make do," said Velach. "Get some axes and...spread them around a bit."

It was dusk when Diavolos eSkel, forward scremander of the Gorrack raiders, approached the southern village of Dwimrsin near the Nightwash river. All Gorracks could see better than cats in the dark, but Diavolos's vision was particularly keen. "Slar, veeshak, ny!" He halted his team still fifty yards away. Nothing moved in the village. Something was very wrong.

There should have been ridiculous noise and reveling. It was the Festival of Charlock, an age-old celebration of the gift of fire. Diavolos had thought he might lighten up on the rules and allow his raiders to join in the merry-making, at least the feast. But what was this?

"Jeskret, sezh vullah, ny, ny, ny!" Diavolos commanded his raiders to fan out. Gorracks were not stealthy or fearful, but they approached the village with great caution. Dwimrsin was the closest village to the border where the cursed Wingborne and the occasional human raiding party dared to tread.

Diavolos was flanked by two other raiders, but he saw it first. Massacre. Dark blood pooled, spattered, trailed. Bodies were strewn across great stones, left hanging in trees, and wedged into crevices.

But that was not all. Diavolos ventured farther into the village and saw the carnage. Farther in, he found the torso of another victim, but based on the red blood, it had to be human. He reached down and grabbed a fistful of the dead man's uniform. Chapparel. Diavolos reared back and unleashed a howl so dreadful that nearby wolves ran for cover.

CHAPTER 32

TURNING THE TIDE

Brimstone isn't the weapon of Sabryne. Deception is.
Author Unknown

48 CELESANDUR 2212

Abbagael lay on her bed with the child sleeping in the crook of her arm. It wasn't much of a bed: three netted crates laid end to end covered with six flattened burlap sacks, and overlaid with a stiff tapestry for a blanket.

Captain Dagspaddle had apologized profusely. "We're not much used to real lady types 'board the *Mynx.*"

It was a compliment, Abbagael knew, but it hadn't helped her back to ache any less. *If only my back were all that ached,* she thought. It had been a very long journey to Brightcastle on the southern tip of Llanfair. Over that time, Alastair and she had spoken exactly once, and that was in port.

"I'll get off here," Alastair had said. "You can have my horse and the gold. I've caused you enough trouble."

"No," she said. "We'll ride out the trip. I won't do to you what you tried to do to me."

And that had been it. Even now, Abbagael regretted those words. She'd meant them to draw blood, and given the way Alastair had slunk away, she had succeeded.

The sea had become much less turbulent on the return trip, and the trade winds had given them good speed. Dagspaddle had announced sight of land—Gull'scry, most likely. Then would come the Wetlands and Chapparel City. Abbagael turned her head to look at the child. She twirled a lock of his hair. "What am I doing?" she whispered. "He's a trained killer. A murderer." She'd thought the same thoughts a thousand times, but never reached a conclusion.

Abbagael remembered that beautiful morning…it would be twelve years earlier on Drinnas the 33rd. She'd stayed with her uncle in Ardon and had a brilliant time. She'd already been feeling guilty about the trip because it wasn't her turn. Her little brother, Nathan, was supposed to go, but at the last minute, he had come down sick and was deemed unfit for the journey. Abbagael's uncle had brought her home via the eastern trade road so they could pass by the marshes for which the whole region of Fen had gotten been named.

The vision hung above Abbagael like a mural painted on the cabin's ceiling. There was her uncle, his bright blue eyes gleaming out from his tanned, weatherbeaten face and a broad grin some-how visible in that tangled beard of his. Beams of morning sun-light shone through the swamp pines, turning the murky water into an enchanted world. Butterflies and dragonflies moved about, one graceful and bouncy, the other purposeful and zig-zagging.

Abbagael remembered her uncle telling her not to get too close to the water because of fennigators. Thankfully, she hadn't seen any of those, but just as they were leaving the water behind, Abbagael saw a golden heron. Tall and graceful, the heron waded with agility through a marshland pool. It became still and, for a moment, it looked like like a golden statue…until, in a blink, it speared a fish with its long, blue bill. Then it spread its wide wings and took flight. Beautiful…and so rare that some believed they were only legend. But Abbagael had seen one.

Then they had smelled the smoke.

Her uncle had picked her up and raced ahead. He kept a swift pace, but took a wide, sweeping route to avoid stepping into a trap. He needn't have bothered. The danger to them had long passed. The village of Maiden Vale had been utterly destroyed.

Abbagael halted the memory right there. She would not revisit that smoldering, silent cottage.

Alastair had not killed her parents, nor her brother. But how many families had he destroyed? He'd gone through that terrible, long list of villages and hamlets. Her anger ebbed a moment, and she thought of the Alastair she'd always known. A tall, muscular knight in glimmering mail. Alastair had come to her village for provisions and to get his blade sharpened and oiled by old Rygan Danneby. Abbagael had been a little girl and had looked up to Alastair with stars in her eyes.

But as she'd grown out of infatuation and entered her teen years, she'd begun to notice other things about Alastair besides his rugged, knightly looks. He was always so generous, paying more than the asking price in the market and tipping on top of that. He was also more polite than any other man in the village. Holding doors for ladies and the elderly, Alastair seemed always to put others first. Once, her uncle had invited Alastair to dinner, and Alastair had actually done all of the dishes. Abbagael smiled, remembering the soap suds battle they'd had that night.

"People can change," Abbagael said to the sleeping child. "Can't they? He may have been a monster once, but he's not that way now." The child stirred and made a sleepy baby sigh. Her heart ached to believe that he was a good man now. But how could such a change take place? It would mean a fundamental identity shift.

Tears flowed freely when she remembered that he had just recently abandoned them. No, he hadn't changed. Not deep down.

The ship's bell rang frantically. Abbagael heard heavy thumps overhead and on the stairs outside her cabin. Doors slammed. There was a lot of shouting. Abbagael thought about leaving the child, but didn't want to risk him rolling off the bed if the ship tilted suddenly. She took the child, left the cabin, and raced up the stairs.

Ship's hands were everywhere, scurrying around the deck, raising or lowering sails or dragging out crates. Abbagael had no idea there were so many people aboard the *Mynx*. There were others as well: a few women and children she hadn't seen before. They sat on the deck, backs against walls, and out of the way as much as possible. They were wet and frightened, especially the children.

Captain Dagspaddle's voice rang out above all the other shouting. "Break out those arms, lads! Ready the cutters! Get those 20-stone carronades to the bays!"

Alastair had been standing on the bow near the forecastle but ran through the criss-crossing traffic across the deck to get to Abbagael. "You'd better take the child and get below."

"Why, what's happening?"

"We've taken aboard survivors," he said, gesturing to the women and children. "The Gorracks have invaded Chapparel."

Abbagael turned toward the coastline. She saw the smoke, and her heart fell.

"How many?" Alastair demanded.

"When my family and I fled Chapparel?" Creedic asked. "I don't know…three, four thousand. Three thousand, for sure."

"Three or four thousand?" Captain Dagspaddle muttered. "That's not just a band a' raiders. That's an invasion, it is."

They'd fished Creedic, his wife, and his young son out of the inlet several hundred yards from shore where his cutter had capsized. He'd told a tale of a surprise attack in the still hours after midnight and the chaos that followed. The walls were breached immediately, and the Citidel fell an hour later. Warden Caddock and his family had been slain. Chapparel's famed spearmen had fought valiantly, holding back the Gorracks so that some could escape via the docks.

Alastair gazed out over the rail. He could understand getting the women and children to safety and was glad of that. But there were hundreds of small boats, canoes, and skiffs plodding across the water—and many men. As far as Alastair was concerned, they were men who might still fight. "Why do they flee?"

"Our warden's dead," Creedic said. "We can't stand against the Gorrack Nation."

Alastair burned inside. "Captain Dagspaddle, are you of a mind to do some Gorrack hunting?"

Dagspaddle spit over the rail. "Oh, I'm more'an of a mind. I've got friends in Chapparel City, I do. What's yer plan?"

"We've got to stem the tide, turn these warriors round. I'll take your best men. We'll go ashore and rally the spearmen, any who live. But I'll need you to catch these…these deserters. Take on the women and children, but tell the men to steel themselves and get back to shore. We can win this!"

"I quite like the sound a'that," said the captain.

"We'll drive the Gorracks out of Chapparel City," Alastair continued, "or kill them all."

"How can you be sure?" asked the captain. "Thousands of Gorracks?"

"Gorracks are pillagers. More than likely, half their army will be looting and stuffing satchels."

"Still…"

"And the sun is up. That'll slow them down some."

"So you say," the captain said, "and I won't doubt ye. But seems I should be doin' more, it does. The *Mynx* is no ship-o-the-line, but we've a fair number of carron."

Alastair scanned the armaments of the ship. There were dozens of weapons on deck, each one capable of firing twenty-pound iron balls several hundred yards. *Fair number of carron indeed.* He thought for a moment, recalling the geography of Chapparel.

"Ah, got it! This is what you'll do. Instead of me taking all your men, keep what you need to man your cannons and guns, carronades too. There's an inlet on the east side of the city—it cuts in deeper than this. Once you've done your task here, sail to the mouth of that inlet within firing range of shore. When I give the signal, I want you and your men to open up with everything you have."

"What sort of sign, will it be?" asked Dagspaddle.

"I don't know," Alastair said. "Maybe I'll launch a Gorrack a hundred feet into the air. But when you see the signal, you'll know it's time. Unleash the fury of the *Mynx!*"

"Aye," said Captain Dagspaddle lustily. "That I will!"

"Sir," Creedic said, "I'm not much of a hunter or archer, but I can use a sword all right. I'll fight for you."

Alastair smacked the man hard on the shoulder. "Good man, Creedic! Now, let's hope your countrymen have as much courage as you do."

CHAPTER 33

THE GATE OF FIRE

A hunter's greatest enemy is impatience.
Rene Althorn, Man-at-Arms for King Mendeleev

43 CELESANDUR 2212

Deep in the woods of Ardon, Cythraul prowled closer to a building he'd been searching for most of the night. The tavern keeper had been especially helpful. Extraordinary what people will tell you if they believe it might allow them to live. But Morlan's orders had been clear.

No one would ever find the tavern keeper's body, nor any of the tavern's patrons.

Coldhollow had built his home in an ingenious location. A heavily forested hillside surrounded three quarters of his property. Inside this natural wall was a nearly impenetrable patch of evergreen trees. Cythraul had never seen anything like this thicket, the way the boughs interlaced so that no one could see beyond. It forced Cythraul to tie off his horse so he could clamber through alone.

Enduring the branch slaps and dozens of small cuts, Cythraul was rewarded to discover Coldhollow's home. Within the pine perimeter stood a modest cottage attached to a single turret. There was a rugged stable for a single horse and patch of tilled earth the size of a drawbridge. But what gave the owner's identity away was a network of posts embedded in the ground at varying heights. Some of them had targets hanging from cords. It was a swordsman's scaffold and, given the height and spacing, a master swordsman's.

The horse was gone and the vegetables in the garden were dying. Alastair had been away for some time, probably more than a week. But Cythraul studied the home for close to an hour before going inside. Alastair had served as Captain of the Wolfguard. There was no telling what traps he might have set for trespassers. But after a thorough search, Cythraul turned up no traps at all. *Gone soft, have you, Alastair?*

Cythraul descended some roughly hewn timber stairs and entered through a basement door. He removed a vaskerstone from one pouch on his belt, clutched it tightly in his palm, and then placed it on a shelf on the wall. The stone glowed an eerie green before kindling to brighter light to see by.

The basement was a wreck. Dank, dusty, and dirty...strewn with old garments, bolts of cloth, empty crates and casks. But in this mess, there were some items of interest. Cythraul discovered Alastair's Wolfguard armor, far from polished, but intact. Interesting that Alastair had kept it.

In the rear of the basement, Cythraul found a table that was curiously tidy. Upon it, carefully stacked, were charts. Hundreds of charts. Each one was a painstakingly rendered diagram of the stars. There were many notes written in each margin, and in the bottom left-hand corner of each page was a notation for the date. But from time to time the slant was different. *He uses either hand to write,* thought Cythraul. *Might he also wield a sword with both hands? I need to remember that.*

He continued to scan the star charts and was astounded. Coldhollow must have charted the stars day after day for years at a time. Why? The sheer time involved would have been mind-numbing. He'd have been up half the night, every night, sitting very still. How easy it would have been to make a mistake, to lose one's place in the innumerable points of light.

Cythraul stopped suddenly on one chart. Alastair had circled a certain constellation. Elspeth Gawain, he called it. A month of charts later, there was a different constellation: Caedmon's Bow. Three months later, yet another. And another. But Cythraul could not imagine what these things meant. Seven charts in all had such notations. Cythraul removed them from the stack and pondered them.

He flipped from one map to the next. "What am I missing?" Cythraul was generally very attentive to detail, very good at drawing conclusions. He himself had shelves full of diagrams as detailed as Coldhollow's work. Of course, Cythraul's specialty was anatomy. Faster and faster, he flipped through the charts, growing more frustrated each time through, and then... he stopped.

He did not laugh or smile, but the irony was not lost on Cythraul. As he flipped the seven charts, the circled constellations seemed to fall together as one image: a sword. And all this time, King Morlan had assumed that Alastair had taken the Star Sword simply because it was a master blade. That was not it at all.

Cythraul rolled the seven charts, secured them with a leather lace, and continued his exploration. On a shelf in the corner, among all manner of other books, he found several volumes of the Lore of the First One. It was all the confirmation he needed. Coldhollow and King Morlan were after the same fellow: the Halfainin. Amazing that such a determined and ruthless soldier as the Iceman could be taken in by such foolishness. *He must be weaker than I thought.*

Cythraul took his glowing vaskerstone and left the basement behind. The middle floor was very bare. Rickety cot; small, nearly empty cupboards; a table and one chair—no luxuries at all.

Coldhollow had not spent much on himself…or had he? Cythraul found several empty black bottles on the floor. Even before he smelled one of the bottles he knew what it was. More pieces of the puzzle fell into place. Alastair Coldhollow, like many of the Wolf-guard, had developed an addiction to Witchdrale. Only Coldhollow had not been able to handle it. Broken and out of control, he had run away from his command, run away from Vulmarrow, and joined the very cult he had once persecuted.

And Coldhollow had the Star Sword. According to legend, that blade could help an astronomer pinpoint the place where the Halfainin would arise. And based on the six dead assassins who had been slain as they returned from Thel-Mizaret, Coldhollow must have gone to that city as well. That premise led to the possibility that Coldhollow had found the Halfainin—or someone he thought was the Halfainin—before the massacres. Cythraul didn't put any stock in such folk tales, but Morlan did. And though the news would be less than pleasing to him, Morlan would want to know of Cythraul's discoveries.

Cythraul found the stair to Coldhollow's turret and ascended to a trapdoor that opened out onto a high platform. No doubt this was where he made all those star maps, but there was nothing else of interest up there. Cythraul departed Alastair's home and had to pull hard to get the front door to shut.

The slam startled a snagrat near Alastair's front stoop. Cythraul watched the bulbous critter hastily drag something white under a ledge. It was probably nothing, but Cythraul was not one to leave stones unturned. He held the vaskerstone aloft, and it showed a den crudely formed out of branches, dead leaves, and vines. The cornered snagrat bared its pathetic little teeth and unleashed its best snarl…which sounded more like it was spitting and sneezing at the same time.

It still clung to its treasure: a wad of white cloth—a shirt maybe? Cythraul couldn't tell. He drew one of his swords, the long Wyrm Blade, and stabbed the snagrat an inch behind its left forelimb. He pushed the blade in, puncturing the creature's heart, and then lifted it out of its den. It struggled on the end of the blade for a moment and then fell limp, dropping its prized possession.

Cythraul flung the snagrat off his sword, wiped the blade with a rag, and sheathed it. With his gloved hands, he picked up the white ball of cloth and began to unravel it. It was certainly not a shirt. It was nothing Coldhollow could wear at all. Too small… and given the contents of the cloth, there was only one thing it could be:

A diaper, a cloth diaper.

After a bit of digging, Cythraul found that the snagrat had several such *packages* in its den. Given the still pungent smell, these were a week or two old, but no more, and that matched the timeline Cythraul thought most plausible. But a child was a very new development. Alastair Coldhollow was not exactly father material, certainly not while battling an addiction to Witchdrale. What had become of his wife? There were no womanly garments in the home.

The woman.

Of course. Morlans assassins had slain a woman. Alastair had slain the assassins. So now, Coldhollow was stuck with a child?

That presented Cythraul with new trails to follow.

Morlan had studied the *Hradavisk Canamor*, the Book of Whispers, ever since he was sixteen, when Shepherd Alfex had secretly introduced him to the outlawed text. The legendary writings of Sabryne Shadowfinger offered power and vengeance, both coveted by young Morlan, and so he'd become a disciple.

With discreet tutelage from Alfex, the text became a guiding force in Morlan's life. Among many other inspired decisions over his lifetime, the Book of Whispers had led Morlan to leave his family in Anglinore to rule in Vulmarrow. But now, the direction was unclear. He'd felt drawn again and again to the other book in Sabryne's Canon, the newly recovered *Prophecies of Hindred*. One particular prophecy would not release Morlan from its grasp.

The One who would return.

How can this be? He wondered. *No one returns.* He'd prayed to Sabryne and asked for wisdom, but had yet to receive any guidance.

"No wonder I cannot perceive the text, nor pray as I should," Morlan said as he pondered the text in his tower library. He leaned back in his tall chair and rubbed the corners of his eyes. "My mind is too consumed." And indeed, even as he closed his eyes, shutting out the candle's light, his thoughts swam. *If Velach Krel does his job...if the Gorracks take the bait...if my brother responds with war...if the Gorrack Nation weakens Anglinore's forces enough...*

Too many *ifs*.

Am I not your lord? came the bone-dry voice Morlan had been longing to hear once more.

Morlan slid off the chair to his knees and bowed his head. "Forgive me, Lord Sabryne. I have allowed my faith to waver."

Rise, master servant. Your faith is intact. And for that I am very proud of you.

Morlan hesitantly took his seat. "You can see me," he said, scanning the diamond-shaped chamber. "But I can't see you."

Look beyond the candle's flame. Fire has ever been the door-way to me.

Morlan stared at the candle. At first, he saw nothing unusual. A bubble of melting wax grew at the base of the wick, occasionally bleeding over the side and cooling into static dribbles and globs. The tiny flame pulsed on the wick, flickering and swaying to some dark music never heard by man.

It was as he stared at the flame that Morlan noticed a faint corona of light surrounding the top of the candle. This ghostly perimeter moved as the fire moved and grew when the flame kindled. To Morlan's astonishment, there was another corona spreading outward from the glow. It was an engulfing dark halo, but more than dark, more than black. There was a kind of empty depth to it, the kind a man might feel as he peered into a deep hole with nothing more than starlight above. Morlan squinted and moved his head to gain different vantages into this window of darkness. There was something within, a shadow and a shape—humanoid with thick shoulders, but the head was misshapen as if it had ram's horns. And the eyes...rotten, white eyes.

Morlan jumped back in his chair and gulped for a breath. "I-I see you."

Well met, Morlan Stormgarden. It is different face-to-face, is it not?

Morlan nodded. "Very much so."

We have been working side-by-side for so many years.

"Then why have you not spoken to me before this year, my lord?"

You did not then need my full voice...only whispers. You have been clever and absolutely determined. Your faith has not failed you, Morlan. But your plans are too small.

"My plans are too small?" Morlan blurted out. "Sm-small! I'm only plotting to betray my own brother to steal the throne of all Myriad."

Why be merely a king, asked Sabryne, *when you could be a god?*

CHAPTER 34

Fire and Ice

The past is gone. A man cannot dwell there or ever get it back.
But it doesn't stop him from trying.
Shepherd Kensey Rander

48 Celesandur 2212

Abbagael emerged from her cabin once more to find the deck bustling with activity. But this time there were women and children moving to and fro among the deck hands of the *Mynx*. The child, newly full of barley porridge, giggled as Abbagael turned 'round and 'round.

"Captain!" she yelled, spying him at last on the starboard side of the forecastle. She rushed over to him. "These people... are they—"

"From Chapparel," Dagspaddle replied, tying off a thick rope. "Gorracks didn't get all."

Abbagael gazed off to shore. They were farther from shore now and the city was in a different position. "Where are we?"

"Sailin' with all speed to the cove east-sou'east a' Chapparel to wait for the signal."

"Signal?" Abbagael echoed. "What signal?"

"I dunno exactly," the captain said, sliding his knee across the deck to reach another rope. "He said somethin' about hurlin' a Gorrack up in the sky."

"Who said?"

"Yer husband."

"Alastair?" She frowned. "He's not my husband."

"Oh, right, I keep fergettin'. In any case, he's one brave man."

"Where is he?"

"Why, that's wot I mean. He's gone ashore, he has. To fight thems Gorracks, kick'em out of civilized territory."

Abbagael's hand flew to her lips. She ran to the rail and gazed at the still burning city. Alastair was a skilled swordsman, she knew. But to face the brutal Gorracks? "Alastair," she whispered, clutching the child close. And though she didn't quite understand why, she began to cry.

B lack arrows and crossbow darts surged toward the boats. *Thok, thok, thok!* Two stuck in the bow—and one lodged in the stern where Alastair's hand had been a split-second earlier.

Between Captain Dagspaddle's efforts and his own, they'd managed to turn most of the fleeing soldiers back to the battle, but now he wondered about his decision. The Gorracks had fought through to the shore and now defended it with abject fury.

Men screamed as darts found them. *Thok! Thok!* Neither Alastair's boat nor any of the small watercraft with them were made for battle, and few of these men had shields of any kind.

"Stay down!" Alastair yelled to Creedic while rowing so hard he feared the oar might snap. More arrows whistled by. Alastair watched the lead oarsman of a nearby skiff take a dart in the chest. He slumped over the side, and the man behind him took a shaft in the shoulder.

This is suicide! he thought frantically. *We have no—wait!*

"Everyone to the stern of your boat!" He ducked an arrow. "Right now! To the stern! And keep rowing!" A black dart careened off the bottom of his oar. Alastair used his legs to drive himself backward into the stern. He and Creedic put as much weight toward the back as they dared, and the bow lifted up out of the water several inches.

Thok, thok! Thok, thok, thok! Arrows and darts slammed into the risen bow.

Alastair looked to either side, and it seemed the other soldiers had passed the word around; they were now all using their boats as shields.

"Now," Alastair said, "so long as these Gorracks don't have brimstone, we ought to be all—"

Pop...pop! Pop, pop! Alastair hadn't heard that sound in a long time, but it was impossible to forget. The superheated brimstone snapped and popped as it flash-cooled in the air. Fist-sized blotches of angry red blinked by the port side of the boat. One hit the water with a simmering hiss and threw up a cloud of steam. *Pop, pop, pop!*

"Keep rowing!" Alastair yelled to Creedic. "But get ready to swim!"

"Yes, sir!" Creedic stayed so low he could almost grab the lace of his boot with his teeth, but he somehow managed to row with power.

"Beware the skies!" Alastair bellowed, drawing every ounce of his voice so that he might warn the others. "Keep rowing! But watch the skies! They are raining brimstone fire down upon us! If your boat catches fire, grab your weapons and get in the water!"

Alastair and Creedic both felt the impact. Something had struck the bow, and it was no arrow or dart. There came a sound like the pulling of a long-toothed saw across rough timber, and a red spark appeared on the inside of the bow. Suddenly, as if a volcanic demon was clawing at the wood trying to break through, a fiery hole appeared in the bottom of the boat. And it began to grow. *WHOOSH!* Flames leaped up and began to consume the front of the boat.

"Into the water, now!" Alastair commanded.

Creedic went over the side to the left. Alastair went over to the right. He caught a glimpse of the reeds and the shore beyond as he plunged below the surface. The water was cold and deeper that he'd expected. Alastair refused to panic. He kept his breath and swam as far forward as he could. Something hit his back, bringing searing pain. He rolled frantically and forced the glob of flash-cooling brimstone to sink away from his body. He kicked his legs and swam on until his lungs burned. Up he went to steal a gasp of air.

He surfaced to chaos.

Arrows whistled and brimstone popped. Men grunted and screamed. But there was also the ring of metal and Gorrack howls. *Yes!* Some of the men had made it to shore. Brimstone whooshed into the water on his left. Alastair jagged right and went under again. But where was Creedic?

Harder and harder Alastair swam until he drove himself right into the tall reeds. There was sand beneath his feet. Alastair broke the surface and, staying low, he drew his sword and charged ahead. Most of the arrows passed overhead now, but Alastair was still mindful. The water around him became more shallow, and he found himself with a great expanse of white sand before him. To his surprise and utter joy he caught sight of Creedic. The man had beaten him to the shore and was already fighting a Gorrack.

"Ah!" Alastair winced. An arrow grazed his upper arm and was still stuck in his sodden shirt. He berated himself for not paying better attention and tried to jerk the arrow free. It didn't come, so Alastair yanked his shirt over his head and threw it to the sand.

In that moment, he looked up and saw the Gorrack crouch beside a dune forty yards away, too far for Alastair to reach even with a dagger throw. The Gorrack fired.

The dart rocketed toward him, and there was no way to dodge it. It was not a graceful defense, but Alastair slashed his sword across his body, and the dart struck the blade just below the guard. The arrowhead shattered and the shaft cracked.

That was too close. Alastair rushed ahead to battle. With preternatural clarity, Alastair Coldhollow, the Iceman, faced his first seven opponents and saw exactly how he would fell them all.

First, he assailed the Gorrack hastily trying to reload his crossbow. That brute looked up, realized Alastair was closing and, with his right hand, went for his pike. Alastair climbed the dune, leaped off its backside and plunged his blade into the Gorrack's spine.

Two Gorracks with hammers charged just in time for Alastair to slash their legs out from under them. Alastair came out of a roll and leaped at a Gorrack with an axe who stood near the base of a fat oak. The Gorrack lifted the axe high to block a chop from Alastair. The axe blade stuck in the low hanging bough for just a moment. It was enough. Alastair carved a deep slash into its gut.

Alastair charged the three remaining Gorracks, positioning himself to leap and drive both feet into the brute in front, slamming him into the two behind. They toppled like dominoes, and Alastair rolled and slashed, dove and slashed, and finally rolled and slashed once more. That left three shocked Gorracks grasping at their ruined throats. Unlike a plain sword, Alastair's blade, the Star Sword, sliced through Gorrack scales.

But Alastair could not relax. He turned to plot his next course and saw that a few of Chapparel's spearmen yet lived. There were others too: archers in strategic locations on the walls and towers of the burning castle and fierce infantrymen wielding axes. But these wore a different livery than Chapparel. The Wetlands, maybe? Alastair didn't care. For now at least, more dark green blood than red splashed the sand and stone.

Creedic stopped by Alastair's side. He was panting and was covered in blood. "I...I slew three of them!"

"Good lad," said Alastair, not daring to mention his total thus far. "We've picked a good time to assault them. We've got high sun, and the Gorracks are sluggish."

"Sluggish?" Creedic's eyes widened.

"Look there," Alastair said, pointing. "Those stonecasters have some of our lads pinned down near the fountain. I'll see to them."

"I'm coming with you," Creedic said.

"Nay, stay closer to the water. Keep the brutes from hacking our wounded!" Alastair kicked up a blast of sand and sprinted away toward the courtyard.

Creedic wiped the sand from his face and watched Alastair take out two Gorracks without breaking stride. "See how that blue blade flashes!" He heard a sound a second two late. The Gorrack punch hit square on his jaw and lifted him off his feet. He crashed onto his back and saw through blurry eyes the Gorrack raise his pike and leap.

There were only three Gorracks, but they had nine opponents cornered where two walls of Chapparel Castle met. The men held shields and tabletop sized pieces of timber, but the Gorracks had brimstone. If Alastair didn't do something, the Gorracks would burn them alive. Typical formation, thought Alastair. One with the cauldron in the center. The two casters on either side.

A blink of movement from behind. Alastair ducked, spun, and nearly beheaded a Gorrack who had run up from the shore.

Alastair raced around behind his three targets. If one of the casters turned and hurled a spray of brimstone, it would end quickly. Alastair swerved to stay out of the Gorrack's peripheral vision. He took in the details he needed: the Gorrack caster on the left was right-handed, even now dipping his ladle-like scoop into the brimstone. He saw what he would do, but he'd have to be fast.

Alastair laid stealth aside and rushed ahead. But the Gorrack caster on the right had noticed the movement. He turned toward Alastair and still had a smoking scoop full of brimstone.

Alastair adjusted his plan on the fly, but knew he'd likely die anyway. On Alastair came, and the Gorrack pulled back his arm, ready to hurl a spray of liquid fire. But suddenly, the Gorrack's arm fell away at the elbow. Alastair didn't have a split second to see who had saved him. He changed direction and went for the Gorrack holding the cauldron.

Alastair thrust his sword into the Gorrack's kidney, causing him to arch his back and lift the cauldron higher than usual. Alastair rammed into the Gorrack hard, between the shoulder blades, pushing him forward. The blow sloshed the brimstone in the cauldron and it splashed out onto the other Gorrack caster. There was nothing he could do. The brimstone burned through his armor and flesh like parchment.

Alastair spun and found a brawny, axe-bearing warrior with wild coppery hair and beard to match. "My savior, I presume?"

"Aah, savior?" the man said. "I wouldn't dare claim those boots. Hagen Kurtz is my name. And, ahhhh, just thought you could use a hand."

"Well met," said Alastair. "And I can definitely use the help. We've got to regroup what's left of this city's defense and drive them south of the city."

"To the cove?" asked Hagen.

Alastair nodded.

"Right then. Let's get to it." He started to run off, but stopped. "Uh, you mind telling me, ahhhh, how we're going to do that?"

Alastair walked over to the still smoldering Gorracks and pried the handle of the cauldron from the hand of its dead keeper and hefted it. Half full. Alastair had the beginnings of an idea. "It would be a shame to waste all this good brimstone, don't you think?"

CHAPTER 35

FIGHTING GHOSTS

The Verdant Mountains of Ellador are known to sing in the high summer.
That and ribbon storms make them worth the climb.
Cadfan Swancott, High Mountaineer of Ellador, 3105–3290 D

48 CELESANDUR 2212

"How much longer are we going to wait?" Abbagael asked, putting the child on her inside shoulder, away from the ship's rail. She had to walk fast to keep up with Captain Dagspaddle. He waddled quickly for someone of such girth. "It's been hours, Captain."

"He said to wait fer th' signal," Captain Dagspaddle said. "So we wait. Ye sure he's not yer husband?"

Abbagael whacked him on the shoulder. "Yes, I'm sure!" She paused a bit to make sure he saw her frown. "But just the same, shouldn't we have heard something by now? What if he's in trouble?"

"Agreed there, Miss Abbagael," he said, absently inspecting one of the cannons. "Sun'll be down in an hour. Gorracks'll be downright beastly when night falls. Still and all, he sure looks like he could fight a blue streak at need. I'd say yer man'll be all right."

Whack! Same shoulder this time. "He's not my man!"

"Ah, blast! Well, what is he, then?"

"He's…well, of course, he's…" The baby gurgled and looked up at her. "He's a friend." She looked back out to the broken and smoking walls of Chapparel's Citadel.

"Y'know," said the captain, standing close to her at the rail, "I've seen a fish net a' scoundrels in my time. Now, yer…uh, *friend,* he don't seem like that." Dagspaddle spat over the side and laughed gruffly. "Y'know, I don't even know 'is name."

"It's Alastair," she said softly. "Alastair Coldhollow."

Dagspaddle stood a little straighter. "Huh, sounds like I should know that name," he said, massaging the back of his head under the bandana as if he might find a memory back there. "Nah, just an unusual name, I guess."

Abbagael felt suddenly awkward. Alastair hadn't given his name to the captain. But before she could ponder it further, she heard something. "Do you hear that?"

"Seagulls, always this close to—no, wait, I do hear somethin' odd."

Distant at first, but growing louder, there was the sound of something in pain. A moan or a scream…a little of both.

"Look!" Abbagael said pointing to the darkening sky. "What's that?"

Captain Dagspaddle stared. "Well, call me Monkey Mc'crackin! He did it."

"Did what? Who?" But as she stared, the small object in the sky grew larger. It was humanoid in shape, but very thick. The screaming became more of a howl.

"Great waves a' sea grass!" said Dagspaddle, pulling Abbagael away from the rail. "This is going to be close!" He moved her across the deck and behind the forecastle.

"What is it?"

"Yer Alastair said he was gonna launch a Gorrack up in the air as a signal, and so help me, he did!"

They peeked around the corner just in time to see the flailing Gorrack fall out of the sky and barely over the port side of the ship. It hit the water with a crackling smack, and water exploded high into the air.

Captain Dagspaddle was out in a shot. "That's the signal, lads! Have at it! All we got! Let 'em loose! Cannons and carronades!"

Boom! Foom! Cannonfire erupted all over the starboard side of the ship.

Abbagael covered the child's ears, but he cried out.

Captain Dagspaddle looked with pride on the massive firepower surging from his ship. "Alastair Coldhollow," he said softly, "I hope you steer clear of the southern shore. Won't be much left there."

"Not one Gorrack gets through!" Alastair bellowed, charging away from the catapult. "To the sand and no farther!"

"Push them back!" Hagen barked. "Harder! Now for it!"

Having followed Alastair's crafty plan and, buoyed by the resourceful men of the *Mynx*, the warriors of Chapparel now outnumbered the Gorracks. They coated timber on one side with brimstone and it became a burning barricade. They forced the Gorracks to move south or burn. Still, their flaming blockade had holes, and Gorracks broke through. Alastair, with his flashing blue blade, and Hagen, with his broadaxe sprinted back and forth behind the line wherever Gorracks slipped through a breach.

Alastair heard something like thunder, but knew it was no storm. "Dagspaddle came through!"

Cannon shot began to pepper the beach behind the struggling Gorracks.

"C'mon!" Alastair yelled. He joined some of the men, pushing on an uneven piece of timber that looked like a corner from a demolished cottage. Flames curled around it. The heat was intense. Soon they'd have to drop it. "Get them to the slope! *Now!*"

They pushed the Gorracks south and east out of the court-yard. Just sixty yards behind the enemy the ground began a gentle slope. Twenty yards beyond that, the slope was not so gentle. But without the city walls to hem them in, the Gorracks had more room to work with and could pour around either side of the mov-ing barricades. Heavy blasts continued offshore. Fire and sand erupted behind the Gorracks. More and more rushed the weak side.

"*Hagen!*" Alastair screamed. "*Watch your flank!*"

"*I know!*" he yelled back, already in combat.

But too many Gorracks rounded that side. They came upon the soldiers pushing the barricade and slashed them from behind. Right in front of Hagen, a whole section of their burning barri-cade fell. Gorracks streamed in.

Alastair saw their situation worsening. He looked over the clamoring Gorracks to the slope. *Ah! We're so close!* "You can't let up!" Alastair yelled to the men around him. "I'm going to pro-tect our flank! But you *cannot* let up!"

Alastair peeled away from the burning timber and roared toward Hagen and the Gorracks now surrounding him. With each step Alastair took, he thought of the people of Chapparel. They were a port city, a flourishing center of trade. Artists, craftsmen, musicians—they were more weavers than warriors. The Gorracks had come without warning in the middle of the night. That so many had escaped or lived to fight was an absolute miracle.

His technique fueled by rage, Alastair bore down on the Gor-racks. But his anger burned in deeper places than just Chapparel. For as much as he wanted to push away the memories of his own murderous evil, as much as he wanted to call it "another life," he could not. While many innocent beings died in Chapparel, Alastair knew he had been responsible for many more in other villages. So, as Alastair crashed into the fighting, he saw every Gorrack as a dark mirror's reflection of himself. And Alastair wreaked vengeance upon them.

Two fell headless in one stroke. A third discovered a sharp pain in its chest and slid to the ground, still wondering why he hadn't seen the fatal blow. Gorracks did not show fear and rarely retreated. But these wavered and backed away from Alastair. The Iceman did not let them escape. Cannon fire continued to pummel the shoreline. Alastair continued his one-man onslaught.

Soon, the weakening side of the barricade became a strength, and men pushed the Gorracks back. They came to the gentle slope and the Gorracks lost their footing in the sand. There were no tree trunks or roots for the Gorracks to grasp.

But as they approached the steep decline leading to the water below, they went berserk. They rushed the oncoming blockade, running straight into the brimstone-fueled flames. Many died trying to get over the fiery obstacle. Some fell under the feet of other Gorracks and men.

But with each Gorrack to die, the enemy lost strength to withstand the barricade that approached. Men increased their speed, screaming as the heat seared their hands and arms. It became unbearable, but they pushed just a bit farther. Gorracks began to fall over the edge. They cartwheeled down the sandy slope and careened toward the water below. Some never made it. Cannon shot struck some of these poor souls in midair.

"We've got them!" Hagen yellowed, his voice raw and strained. "One last push!"

The men responded, shoving the remaining Gorracks over the edge and then pushing the burning timber over the edge after them. Very few Gorracks made it alive to the water, but those that did howled as if they had fallen into a vat of acid. They thrashed about, clawing at the surface, but seemed unable to force themselves out of it. With cannon fire raining down on top of them, they didn't struggle for long.

Overjoyed but exhausted, Hagen looked up and blinked hard. Alastair had said there would be a ship out there, but now there were several and more on the way. Hagen saw the dark blue standards, dotted with stars and knew. "Anglinore has come! Ah ha, *ha!* Anglinore!" Chapparel's survivors cheered even as they nursed their wounds and losses.

"Alastair, we are delivered!" Hagen spun to look past the survivors and the bodies. When he saw Alastair, Hagen caught his breath. *First One have mercy!* He ran to him.

Alastair was covered in blood from head to boot. Trancelike, with eyes vacant, he turned from the ruined body of one Gorrack and began hacking away at another.

Hagen had seen this man wield a sword, so he approached him carefully. "Alastair, my new friend, the battle...is over. Put down your blade. We have won."

Alastair took two more hacks at the body and turned to Hagen. "I...had to kill him. Don't you see?"

"I understand, my friend," Hagen said. "But the enemy is beaten. There's nothing left to kill."

Alastair stopped swinging. His face was a mess of dark blood, grit, ash, and sand. "There is one more. Always...one more." Then he dropped his sword and collapsed.

CHAPTER 36

AN UNKNOWN HERO

In 2699, during the Age of Dissension, Kulloth Thrangor, the Gor-
rack High Chieftain, nailed his famous Declaration of Sabrynaen
Faith to Marken's Spire near the river Nightwash. This infuriated
the mainlander Sabrynites, the dour miners of Scalavon, who rea-
soned that beasts have no soul and so could not have faith. In the
Sabrynite Civil war that followed, Marken's Spire fell and the Night-
wash ran red.

From *Histories*, author unknown; compiled by Shepherd Alfex

49 CELESANDUR 2212

"Someone in King Aravel's party sent for me?" Abbagael asked.
"Where's Alastair?"

Knights in the blue livery of Anglinore stood on the gangplank of the *Mynx* and beckoned for her to follow.

"I dunno, lady," Captain Dagspaddle said. "But ye don't keep
a king waitin', I daresay."

"But I can't leave the child unattended."

Captain Dagspaddle spat over the side. "I can watch him if—"

"No," said Abbagael.

"What about Pretina here?" he asked, gesturing to one of the ladies who'd come aboard.

"I'd be happy to, Mum," she said.

Abbagael hesitated. She felt rather awkward. "Well, all right," she said, gently placing the child in Pretina's lap. "He's sleepy. He'll probably just nap."

"Right you are, then," Pretina said. "C'mere ye big boy. Cute one, you are."

One of the knights reached for Abbagael's elbow to help her down

She brushed him away. "I can make it."

They led her on a meandering route through the wreckage of Chapparel City. Around fallen pillars and arches they walked, avoiding small fires and jagged pieces of rock. Thousands of other soldiers picked their way through the debris searching for survivors. Abbagael watched them gently putting bodies onto litters and carrying them away.

By the time the soldiers brought her to the Citadel, tears streamed down her face. She hadn't seen Alastair among the bodies, but she felt sure he must be among them. But even if by some miracle he'd survived, so many others had been slain. It was a sight she hoped never to see again. It resurrected far too many ghosts from long ago.

The roof of the Citadel had collapsed, but the debris had been cleared and the shell of the great chamber had become a command center. King Aravel stood at the head of a collection of tables. She'd only seen him once. Her uncle had taken her to see him when the king had visited Chapparel some years back. He looked older and a bit heavier, but still commanding and strong. Behind him stood one of the Wingborne and another man whose face was face was half hidden by dark hair. At the tables she thought there was at least one Elladorian warrior and several Wayfolk seated among a dozen or more human soldiers. They were talking when the knights escorted her forward.

"...suppose I, ah, picked the wrong time to go shopping," said a knight whose beard and long hair were red and as wild as a tangle of briars.

"I believe it was absolutely the right day, Master Hagen," said one of the Wayfolk. "The First One chose you for just this time. Wouldn't you agree, High King Aravel?"

"Yes, Ealden," said the king. "We've been told of your exploits. To drive Gorracks like that...you saved this city from annihilation."

"Well, your lordship," Hagen said, "it may have been the First One's doing. That I won't argue with any man. But, ah, my part was just to follow the commands of this man here. He's the one who saved this city."

The warrior called Hagen gestured to a knight sitting on his right side. He had long dark hair, pulled back and tied off in an inconspicuous tail. He wore the armor and colors of Anglinore.

Abbagael gasped and covered her mouth with one hand. It was Alastair, she was sure of it. He looked cleaner than she'd ever seen him, and she'd never seen him wear a uniform of any sort.

"Rise, hero," said the king, "and be recognized."

"I am no hero," he replied, standing reluctantly. "I did what I did because the Gorracks needed to be stopped."

"I agree," the king said. "But wanting to help and doing so are too often very different bargains...to say nothing about actually pulling it off. What is your name?"

"Belliken, Sire," he replied. "Belliken Tolke."

Abbagael looked again. It was absolutely Alastair: his voice, his posture. *Why did you give that name?*

"Well met, Master Belliken," King Aravel said. "And thank you for stepping in when another would have run. Chapparel... *Myriad*...owes you a great debt."

The man whose face was hidden by hair whispered something Abbagael could not hear.

Then King Aravel said, "Stand, Master Hagen, join your friend. My Shepherd here suggests that I make you both Knights at Large, honorary generals in the Anglish Guard. We have need of stouthearted men for the war that is to come."

"War?" asked Belliken/Alastair.

"With the Gorracks," the king said. "Already I have dispatched the call-to-arms to our allies across Myriad. We will muster in Llanfair and march on the Gorrack Nation as soon as we reach sufficient strength."

Mutters and muted conversation stirred, but the king interrupted it. "This is the Gorracks' largest transgression to date, but not their only one. I can no longer count on diplomacy. The freedom of our world is at stake. What do you say? Will you join us?"

"Ah, a general of the Anglish Guard, me?" Hagen asked. "I'd be honored, Sire. Honored. But, if I may, I have a new wife...back north. We just settled down in the Wetlands villages. I'd like a few days to spend with her."

"Take a week," King Aravel said. "Then sail to Brightcastle by the sea and meet us at the muster."

Hagen agreed, and the king turned to Belliken/Alastair. "And will you also join us?"

"I am already with you in spirit," he replied. "But, my lord, I need some time also. And I am not certain what my answer will be. My life has been turned upside down of late, and I have many debts to pay." There he glanced at Abbagael.

She flushed. She hadn't realized he'd even spotted her.

"If it is gold you require," King Aravel said, "the treasury of Anglinore will see to your debts. We owe you that and more."

Belliken/Alastair bowed. "You are more generous even than I have heard. But, my lord, these debts are of a very different kind."

King Aravel frowned. "Very well. See to those debts. Join us in Llanfair if you are led to do so."

Belliken/Alastair excused himself from the gathering.

He was barely outside the Citadel when Abbagael threw her arms around his neck and embraced him. Then she backed away and eyed him warily. "That was…that was just…just because you are still alive," she said. "And I am glad."

Alastair blinked and muttered, "You are?"

"Don't be foolish, of course I am, Alastair."

He seemed to awaken. "Shh! Do not say that name here." He darted in several directions and bobbed up and down. "No good. This place is too crowded. Your cabin. We can talk there."

Alastair shut and locked the cabin door. There was a loud belch from the baby. Alastair stared. "That lass Pretina, what did she feed him?"

"Some kind of vegetable paste," Abbagael said. "Potent."

"Yes, quite."

"Now tell me, Alastair, what's going on?" She patted the child on her shoulder. "What's with this 'Belliken Tolke'? Why did you hide your name?"

"If I had spoken the name of Alastair Coldhollow in that assembly they would have had me executed."

Abbagael's words caught in her throat. "E-Executed, after what you did here?" She sat down hard on her bed. "Would they not pardon your deeds of the past?"

"Should they?" Alastair asked. "Nay. Nor can they. Anglish law counts me as a dead man walking. My sentence cannot be amended."

"Then you won't go away with them, will you?" she asked.

He did not answer.

"Will you?"

"Lady Abbagael," he said, "nothing will undo the atrocities of my past. Should King Aravel…should any Anglish military officer… discover my identity and take due justice, then so be it. But here is an opportunity I never dreamed would come: a chance to help the people I once heartlessly destroyed. I do yearn to join this battle, but…"

"But…you have debts to pay."

"Yes," he replied, and he sat beside her. "One of the greatest debts is the one I owe to you."

"You're right about that, Alastair Coldhollow."

He smiled. At last, she sounded like the Abbagael he knew. That made it easier and harder at the same time. "When that woman gave me the child…I thought only for myself. He was a burden and I tried to take advantage of our friendship by pawning him off on you. When you wouldn't willingly take him, I deceived you. And then, worst of all, I betrayed and abandoned you." He ran a trembling hand through his hair. "For all these things, I am…heartfully sorry. Can you…will you—"

She kissed him. Though the child was nestled between them, she leaned over and kissed him. It was not a long kiss. Nor was it a kiss of great passion. But it was sweet and genuine…and it left Alastair Coldhollow virtually speechless. The child, on the other hand, giggled twice.

"That means I forgive you," Abbagael said. "You bear no more debt to me unless you wish to."

Alastair's face was a mask of relief and curiosity. "What do you mean?"

"It is my turn for confession," she said, a blush devouring her freckled cheeks. "I love you, Alastair Coldhollow. Ever since you first strode into Edenmill, I felt there was something different about you. No matter what you've done, what you fear about yourself, I know you are a changed man. How you have changed, I cannot explain. But you have changed. And I know you will be a good man. Not perfect…but good. I love you."

If Alastair had been caught off guard by the kiss, he was blindsided by Abbagael's declaration. Within him surged a hope he had not dared to hope before. But there was a stumbling block. "Abbagael…I don't know quite how to say this, but, while I am immensely fond of you, I'm not sure…that is to say, I don't really understand my feelings at all right now. But…I don't love you."

"That's okay, Alastair," Abbagael replied inexplicably. "You will."

Alastair almost laughed. "Somehow that's not how I thought you'd respond."

"I know you. You need time. Just make sure you sort things out by the time you return from the war."

"You think I should go with King Aravel and fight the Gorracks?"

Abbagael's expression hardened. "I saw what the Gorracks did here in Chapparel." Her eyes lowered. "And I know the kind of warrior you are. Look what you did to save this city! It was brilliant—and you led them, Alastair. I saw the look in Hagen's eyes. He'd run through a burning wall if you asked him to. I believe you are needed to fight this fight, so do it." She put a hand on his shoulder and gave him a fierce stare. "Only, you be sure to keep yourself alive."

"I will that," he said. "But what of the child? I cannot leave you with—"

"I will look after him. You have a noble reason now. It's not abandonment this time."

"But I could be gone for…for years."

"Then I will tell him his brave father is off fighting to make Myriad safe for him to grow up in."

Father? Alastair was silent. He'd stepped aboard the *Mynx* a broken, troubled man. And now, this…woman…had so filled him with courage he felt he could take on the entire Gorrack Nation by himself. "Before I do this, let us at least name the child."

"I think…" Abbagael replied… "I already know his name."

"Really? What will we call him?"

"My Uncle Jak is part Elladorian," she said. "There's a word in their language. I didn't think of it until just now. *Telwyn.* It means 'one who brings peace.'"

Alastair gazed on the child and tickled his chin. His blue eyes were brighter than ever and he smiled. "It is a perfect name."

CHAPTER 37

THE ABODE OF WIGHTS

*The temblors began in the summer. It was as if some titanic beast
awoke in the stone heart of Myriad and began to claw its way
to the surface. Queen Aelyrion urges calm, even as her beloved
Crystal Sanctuary has shattered. Her faith is mighty, so we will
be steadfast. Still…I wonder. A terrible quake struck Innspel to
our west.*

*And then, last week, another crippled Dawnseye Township, the
sister city we can see from the western walls of Grayvalon. It's as if
the beast lurks closer.*

From the journal of Taryn Silkynd,
Scribe of Queen Aelyrion, 4666 AO

47 CELESANDUR 2212

I know my scars, Morlan thought, *and this one is new.* He slowed
his horse to a trot and ran a finger along the strange ridge of tis-
sue that traced from beneath his right eye down this cheek to his
jawline. *Strange.* He shrugged and rode on. He would ask Alfex
about it when he returned to Vulmarrow Keep. There were many
more important things to think about.

Velach Krel's efforts had brought about the necessary results. The Gorracks had invaded Chapparel, forcing Aravel to declare war on the Gorrack Nation. Even now, the forces of Myriad were assembling in Llanfair, preparing for what would likely be the most cataclysmic war in the history of the known world. It was a war that would destroy one army and leave the other crippled. No matter the victor, Morlan's Wolfguard would bring ruin upon them, and the throne of Anglinore would fall into Morlan's hands.

Yes, Morlan thought, *I have played a strong opening.* But even as he brought his steed to a gallop on the vast prairie below the Cragland Hills, he knew the game had changed. Sabryne had shown him...had opened his eyes. Now there was so much more at stake. Morlan did not know what he would find in the Abode of Wights, but Sabryne had promised something of value beyond imagination.

Just as the sun was setting, Morlan tied off his horse at a gnarled black oak at the base of the hills. He stared up at Cragland Hills.

This was a place of legendary horror. Far to the west of Vulmarrow, in largely unexplored—mainly *avoided*—lands, Cragland Hills stood as a forbidding monument of days long past. It had once been the site of Grayvalon, the ancient capital city of Myriad and home to the famed Moon Terraces of Queen Aelyrion. But the city had fallen to greed and royal treachery, and was destroyed utterly by a series of savage earthquakes. Massive shards of stone, crossing and crisscrossing, had pierced the city a thousand times, killing tens of thousands, leaving barely a trace of the civilization that had dwelt there.

Of course, many came to believe that something still dwelt there. For ages since, to set foot near Cragland Hills during the Gray Hour of twilight or in the Still Hour past midnight would be considered lunacy.

Morlan still remembered Lyrae Thatcher, the chambermaid back in Anglinore, warning him to get to sleep. "Stay awake at your own risk, Master Morlan," Lyrae would say. "But the wights be drawn to open eyes...especially wee open eyes like yours." Morlan had never seen a wight...even when he'd stayed up well past the Still Hour...but part of him had wanted to.

Morlan was certainly hoping to see something more today than he had in his childhood. If there was anything to the legends and warnings, he would discover it in this place. There was a crevasse in Cragland Hills, a black gash that in the shifting layers of granite had somehow left an opening to the wreckage deep below. A broken city—the Abode of Wights. His brother, Aravel, had gone there once searching for Queen Aelyrion's powerful weapon, the Moonblade. He had not found it, and he would not tell of his travels. *I will find out for myself what dwells there,* Morlan thought as he took to the hills.

There was no path up into those hills, no easy approach. Nothing green grew there. Patches of yellow lichen and white moss lined the terrain, and small forests of red mushrooms in the shadier spots. There were barely three feet of flat terrain at a time due to hundreds of shifts in the stone. It was like trying to walk up a mangled stairway. Morlan's boots gave him good traction, but he was still cautious. And he marveled at the size of the granite spikes that rose up all around him. *I feel like a flea on the scalp of a wolf. No, more like a bloodworm looking for a wound to enter.*

Morlan found his wound exactly where Sabryne had said it would be. The gash in the stone was longer than Morlan had suspected, maybe forty feet, but it was only six feet across at its widest point. Morlan entered at the southern end of the enormous crack and descended into the gloom. The sun had set behind the hills and the distant mountains beyond, so Morlan found himself in darkness that would no doubt smother most men. Morlan wasn't troubled at all. He reveled in it.

He descended deep into the rock, watching shadowy ledges and jagged ridges rise above him and fade. The setting seemed impossibly quiet, every breath and footfall thunderously loud. But Morlan was listening carefully for a very particular sound. Thus far, there was no such sound.

At last the descent ended; his feet found more or less level stone to walk on, and he saw a gray tunnel ahead. This passage was not something made by pick, hammer, or chisel. No, this had been formed organically in the earthquakes and, like the huge shards protruding far above, the tunnel was perfectly imperfect. There were places where Morlan had to duck under a jutting blade of stone and others where he had to clamber over. And still others where he had to take off his cloak, backhangar scabbard, and belt and turn sideways just to fit through. On and on he went, hearing nothing but himself.

Since leaving the last of the sunlight far behind, his night vision had allowed Morlan to see a kind of gray shadow world, but suddenly he came to a place that defied his vision. The path in front of him seemed to disappear into a wall of writhing black. It was like looking down into a cauldron of some brew that absorbed all light as it boiled away. Then Morlan heard it at last. The whispers.

These were not hushed voices of those trying not to be heard. Nor were they the sounds of wind through evergreens or the rustle of leaves in a soft but persistent breeze. These whispers were the full language of something otherworldly, something that had no other volume or speech with which to communicate. The dying gasps of those poor souls splayed upon Cythraul's work table often sounded like that. Gasping, desperate hissing…all they had left.

Morlan did not tremble at the sound coming from the undulating black before him, but he suspected that only a moment of this would drive a weak-hearted man insane. He wondered if Aravel had made it this far. "But here is where you turned back, isn't it, brother?" he muttered to the darkness. "Pity. You might have found something of value. But no, you didn't know about the candles, did you?"

Morlan searched the floor for the crack. He was standing on it, a wild, branching streak of black lightning running across the floor up to the base of a nest of jutting sharp stones. It was like a tangle of thorns, each a yard long. Morlan reached into the snarl and removed a fist-sized box made of dark metal. A sound like an exhaled breath issued from the box when he opened it.

Take only one candle, Sabryne had said. *The rest are for others on other journeys.*

Morlan removed one candle, closed and replaced the box. The candle was small, not even the size of his pinkie finger. It might have been made of wax, but the texture was rough and scaly. Morlan stepped up to the darkness and lifted the candle. As instructed, he twisted the top of the candle's wick. There was a spark and a sizzle, and a tiny band of red rolled down the wick and disappeared into the shaft of the candle. Soon the candle began to glow, softly at first, but then with ferocity. It flashed. Morlan blinked, and the light went out. Or had it?

The darkness ahead had been pierced. Morlan held up the candle. Luminous beings waited on the other side of an arched gate of stone. Male and female, some clad in armor or mail, others in tunics, robes, and long gowns, they stood or moved slowly about. Many more joined the others at the gate. Twenty sets of pale eyes stared out at Morlan. The whispers continued, and Morlan watched their mouths work.

His hand involuntarily moved to the hilt of his sword, but Morlan nevertheless pressed forward. He walked among them now, and wherever he lifted the candle it illuminated more ghostly beings and structures.

The buildings were wrong somehow. Where windows should have been, there were doors. And where doors should have been, there were windows. Living spaces were piled atop other living spaces, as if a giant infant had stacked them to create an awkward, precarious city. In other places, keeps and cottages were pierced through or sheared by shafts of stone. These were the remnants of the city of Grayvalon.

Morlan passed through it, holding up his candle and searching. But the spectral beings were insistent. They gathered in greater numbers and closed in on him. Their expressions were haunting and desperate, but they made no move to touch Morlan. Out of curiosity, Morlan stopped among them. "What do you want?"

At this, they became agitated, raising their hands and swaying.

Morlan thought they looked like they were screaming... though the whispers continued on as before. *Wait!* Morlan thought. He turned his head this way and that, trying to filter out individual voices. What at first had seemed like endless sentences spoken in their peculiar language was not that at all. The longer he listened the more convinced Morlan became that each of these beings spoke only a single word. A different word for each being, but only that one word...over and over and over again.

How utterly strange, thought Morlan. And then, he understood. *Names. They want me to know their names.*

Morlan felt suddenly very uncomfortable. He moved forward, looking straight ahead and picking up speed. But he could not move fast enough to outrun his thoughts. *Are these beings wights? Spirits of the dead? Or something else? Why do they cry out their names—and why to me?*

Morlan pushed on, and soon the spectral visions began to fall back out of his way. It was then that Morlan saw the chains. He slowed and held up the candle. Ghostly and luminous chains led away from each of the wights. Some where shackled at the ankles, some at the wrists, some both. But all of their chains led away in the same direction. Indeed, the chains formed a kind of glowing path. Morlan followed it.

The chains led downward and around a gradual curve. Wights moved along the path, some climbing toward Morlan and others slowly traveling down. Morlan had grown used to the whispers, but as he descended farther the cadence and tone changed. It became a low but incessant wail. There might have been words, but Morlan could not discern what they were.

The path opened into a cavernous chamber. Morlan held the candle high and beheld a massive wall. Six stories tall and a wide as a castle gatehouse, the wall was the source of the wights' innumerable chains. They spilled out from a central point like sewage from a drainpipe. Dozens of wights were gathered along the foot of the wall. Some tried in vain to pull their chains from the wall. Others scratched at the shackles on their ankles. Most were on their knees clawing at the stone and throwing their heads back in nearly silent screams.

But even if Morlan had a single ounce of pity for them, he would not have shown it then. For the wall bore symbols and markings he knew to be of the Sunderell language. He read, moving the candle to progress through the lines. Halfway through the text, he found himself shaking.

"Dark Shepherds!" he gasped. *This is not what I was taught... Alfex, did he know?* Morlan read on.

When he finished, he removed a tablet from the satchel at his side and copied his translation. He walked away from the wall, following the trail of chains until he'd left the pitiful wights behind.

Morlan didn't remember any of the journey back to Vulmarrow, his mind had been so completely immersed. He spoke to no one at the gate of his kingdom and wordlessly strode past every guard in the halls and chambers. He entered his throne room and slammed the massive doors shut behind him. He fell into his throne and let the darkness wash over him.

Revelation after revelation from the Abode of Wights whirled in his mind. Certainly he'd known about the Isle of Lost Souls. It was the place of ultimate banishment. Kings and queens from Anglinore's past had used it for the most ruthless enemies of Myriad's free nations. Morlan had seen it utilized only once. In fact, it was the only time in his royal tenure that King Brysroth had implemented the capital sentence.

Death had been deemed too merciful a sentence for Manfred Drake, a mercenary killer who'd murdered eighteen Wayfolk maidens, including Queen Faylura the Pure. Brysroth had taken Aravel and Morlan on the long voyage to the center of the Dark Sea. Morlan remembered bits and pieces of the ceremony. Manfred's crimes were read aloud to the witnesses. Brysroth spoke. And then the ship bearing Manfred Drake was set adrift. Aravel had walked away, but Morlan had gone to the rail to watch.

He remembered the abject terror in the killer's eyes as the wind filled his sails and took him across the waypoint buoys. Morlan knew that the winds and the currents would carry Manfred Drake a thousand miles away, to the Isle of Lost Souls. He also knew that the wind and the currents would never allow Manfred to return. No one could return.

So the Dark Shepherds had been exiled to the Isle of Lost Souls, Morlan thought. They—not a natural earthquake, as the histories recorded—had been the cause of the destruction of Grayvalon. Morlan had learned so much from the wall. He knew now what had happened to the wights, why they were chained to the wall and, most importantly, why they were so desperate for Morlan to know their names.

Do you see now? Sabryne asked. *Do you see what is possible?*

Morlan leaned forward and bowed his head. "But...my lord, no one has ever returned."

Go to your library. Speak to Alfex. There is a Shepherd you must know about.

"A living Shepherd?"

Yesssss, said Sabryne. *His...gift...is very unusual. He tames the winds.*

Morlan sat up very straight. "I will go to Alfex."

Good, whispered Sabryne.

"If only I could call Cythraul home," Morlan said. "I have need of his talents."

Sabryne laughed. *Is there anything beyond my means?*

CHAPTER 38

DEPARTURES

Our calendars mark the year as 1 AS, but that is a guess of historians.
No one is quite certain when the Silence began…or why it began.
Shepherd Aurora Kinsage

50 CELESANDUR 2212

The sea breeze was fresh and clean along the docks of Chapparel. Abbagael closed her eyes and inhaled deeply. She could almost imagine that there had been no battle two days prior, that the coastal city of Chapparel had not been reduced to rubble, that more than a thousand people had not been killed here. But she knew as soon as she opened her eyes that the illusion would vanish like morning mist in the hot sun.

"My lord king," Alastair said, stepping out of the shadow of the Aravel's command ship, "I realize I am newly accepted as a member of the Anglish Guard, but I would like to make a request before we depart to Llanfair."

Some of the many warriors assembled there on the docks stopped conversations and turned to hear the king's reply.

"General Tolke," the king said, "if it is within my power to grant, you shall have it."

"Thank you," Alastair said. "I am concerned about more Gorrack raids in the cities closest to their borders. I was hoping my lady and…our child might return to Anglinore with the other survivors from Chapparel.

"Of course," said the king.

"What?" Abbagael exclaimed. "I cannot go to Anglinore."

"Why not?" Alastair asked. "You cannot go to war with me, not with Telwyn…"

"I understand that," she said. "It's Anglinore…I mean, I've always wanted to visit, but I won't leave my uncle behind in Edenmill."

"If that's your concern," King Aravel said, "then it's settled. I will send a cavalry detachment to escort your uncle to Anglinore to join you. Triebold?"

A tall soldier with squinty eyes and wild thatches of sun bleached hair stepped forward from the crowd. "Yes, m'lord?"

"Feel like a long ride?" asked the king.

"Always, m'lord."

"Good. Pick a team. Twenty men at least. Bring spare horses and satchels for cargo…uh, and for one uncle. See General Tolke for details and be off as soon as may be."

Triebold nodded. "Absolutely, m'lord. And thank you, Sire."

After providing Triebold with enough information to find Abbagael's uncle in Edenmill, it was time for Alastair to board the ship with the other Anglish knights.

Abbagael wouldn't let him leave just yet. She placed young Telwyn in his arms. "Anglinore, huh? You could've warned me."

"Now where would be the fun in that?" he replied, holding out his pinky for Telwyn to grab—which he did, repeatedly.

"Do you really think we won't be safe in Tryllium?" she asked. "Vang is a shrewd leader. And no doubt Morlan will help from Vulmarrow. Together, they should be able to keep the Gorracks out…won't they?"

Alastair shook his head. "I've talked to some of the Anglish Guard. Vang's had three cities destroyed already. Now that he knows the Gorracks are coming, he'll be more proactive. But still, I'm not willing to take that chance. And Morlan? Don't forget how well I know that tyrant. He despises Gorracks, but I think I would rather live next to the Gorracks than Morlan. And Edenmill is right between them!" Alastair became quiet a moment. "And there's something else I wonder about Morlan…"

"What?"

Alastair looked around and spoke in a whisper. "Well, remember I told you about the day that poor woman gave me Telwyn? Well, it was Morlan's knights who were after her, and—"

"Ahhh, General Tolke!" Hagen Kurtz called from the west end of the dock. "It's time to board. We, ahhh, have a war to win, you know."

"General Kurtz?" Alastair replied. "I thought you were going to the Wetlands to spend time with your wife."

"So I did," he replied. "But she…ahhh, wouldn't let me go… without her, that is. Allow me to introduce my bee-you-tee-full wife, Darrow."

A woman in leather armor came to his side. She was his equal in height, but her long straw-colored hair was perfectly straight and perfectly groomed. She was tanned and had light brown eyes and patches of browned freckles on her cheeks and arms. If she were standing in a tall wheat field, she might disappear from view.

"Darrow is a very good hunter," Hagen said. "She'll be joining the Archer's Core."

"Never met a Gorrack I didn't want to shoot," Darrow said.

"See why I love her so?" Hagen winked. "C'mon then. Kiss her and let's be off!"

"Easy for you to say," Alastair said. "This may be my last kiss for quite some time."

Once the happy couple was out of earshot, Abbagael said, "I'm a decent shot with a bow too."

"I'm alive to attest to that," Alastair said. "I deem you as skillful as most any archer I've known. But truthfully, I want you and Telwyn as far from harm's way as possible. Even if you could come, would you want to face the Gorracks?"

"No," she replied. He started to turn, but she touched his arm. "You've kept me waiting. Tell me, what have you discovered... something about Morlan?"

Alastair's eyes narrowed. "I am not certain of anything. But I need to put more thought to it before I open my mouth."

A final boarding call put an end to their conversation.

Abbagael took Telwyn back into her arms. "Look on him one last time. There's no telling how old he'll be when the war is over and you have returned."

Alastair did look. He drank in every detail of the boy: round blue eyes. Thickening blond hair, getting darker maybe? Chubby, dimpled cheeks and a nobby chin. Alastair would remember him.

He would remember Abbagael too. She was lovely, persistent, loyal, and vexing all at once. Fire burned in her emerald eyes, while a carefree spirit danced in her smile.

"It may be quite some time," Abbagael said with a devastating wink. "So..." She kissed him.

She kissed him hard, long, and passionately so that when the trumpets would sound on each and every battlefield, Alastair would know who he was fighting for.

Cythraul was beginning to lose his temper. He swallowed the bile that gurgled in the back of his throat and slowed his breathing, gradually subduing the growing fury. The last time he'd lost his temper, he'd found it necessary to dismember a forest manarbeast. *Such a waste of a noble creature.* But the way things were going, Cythraul thought he might have to go hunting again.

He spurred his horse. Alastair's trail had all but dried up. If his theory was correct, and Alastair had been left in charge of a baby, he would have sought some assistance—somewhere! But Cythraul had spiraled out from Alastair's woodland home, scouring every city and village. No one had seen anyone of Alastair's description. No stranger had come into town looking for baby supplies. Cythraul had just a few towns left before he ended up in Chapparel or crossed over the river into the Felhaunt.

Cythraul was just a few miles ride from Ardon City, probably his best bet. It was one of the few places where Witchdrale could be found, if one knew where to look. Alastair likely knew. Cythraul rode out of the woods into the sun on the open road. After Ardon City, there was only the small village of Edenmill.

If he didn't find Alastair's trail by then, he would definitely need to kill something.

"War is upon us!" cried a messenger, one of three riding slowly up the trade road that divided Carrack Vale. "The Gorracks have attacked Thel-Mizaret, Stonecrest, Westmoor, and now Chapparel!"

"Who is that, Duskan?" asked Laeriss, turning from the fruit vendor's cart.

"Those are warhorses," Duskan replied. "And they wear the colors of the Anglish Guard."

"Anglish Gua—"

"Shhh, listen."

"King Aravel and King Vang issue a summons to all military stationed here in Carrack Vale, indeed to all Tryllium! Report to the ships docked on the River Feyn! To any and all who wield sword or bow, enlist now, for the Gorrack Nation threatens all!"

"I think we should join," Laeriss said.

"What about finding Mr. Tolke?"

"We have tried," Laeriss said. "But here we have a chance to avenge Jonasim, to pay back the Gorracks for their murderous raid on our home."

"I do not think my mother would want me to join the Anglish Guard." Duskan stared at the ground.

Laeriss laughed sadly. "If my father thought I would join an army, he would have chained me to the basement stair. But Duskan, they're gone now. We have nothing left…nothing left to lose."

Duskan's chin rose. His brows lowered. "In this, you are right." He stepped out into the street. "A moment, Sirrah!" he called. "We wish to join!"

CHAPTER 39

TACTICAL ERROR

There is a strange and inviting peace that follows
any decision, even the wrong one.
A Proverb of the Vespal Wayfolk

4 DRINNAS 2212

Llanfair was the last place in the world one might expect to find a council of war. The capital city had been built ages ago in a vast, rolling meadow flanked by grand purple mountains to the west and the sparkling swift waters of the Nothgiel River to the north. Thousands of tents, warsteeds, and war machines were completely out of place among the endless fields of flowers. Acres of brilliant red, blue, purple, and gold tulips washed across the field of view in every direction.

Alastair leaned around the high back of his chair and gazed out one of the many windows in Jurisduro Hall, King Ealden's Court. *If I survive all this, I will build a house here and spend whole days doing nothing but watching the flowers sway in the wind.* Thinking of such things brought Abbagael immediately to mind. Alastair found it very easy to picture her crouching among the flowers.

"What of their movements, Drüst?" asked King Navrill of the Marinaens.

Alastair turned back to the assembly. King Aravel sat at one end of a long slate table; Ealden at the other. Drüst of the Windborne, Savron of the Vespal Wayfolk, and Navrill of the Marinaens were also present in the opulent, many-windowed chamber.

"They are massing in the Felhaunt," said the Lord of the Windborne. "They think the deep canopies of the Felhaunt will hide them from our eyes. They are wrong."

"How many, Drüst?" asked King Ealden.

"Forty thousand."

"That is roughly a third of their foot soldiers," Aravel said, motioning to one of the Wayfolk attendants. "They must have emptied their garrison at Scaldera Pass."

The Wayfolk attendant used a slender wooden rod to move a collection of tiny silver figurines across an extensive canvas map spread across the table.

"They prepare to crash like a storm surge into northern Tryllium," Drüst said. "They will overwhelm Vang's forces there, especially if Morlan's armies have already been sundered."

"Briawynn marches twenty thousand Verdant Mountaineers from Ellador," said Aravel. "Vang will not be overwhelmed."

"But will they get there in time?" King Ealden asked. "If Gorracks are already in Vulmarrow, might they not waylay Briawynn's troops? Vang could find himself cut off."

Drüst spread his iron gray wings and drew them back in. "My Windborne Skyflights have not recorded Gorracks marching to Vulmarrow."

"What are you saying, Drüst?" King Aravel asked.

Silence fell over the table like a hammer. A memory flashed into Alastair's mind. The day he'd staggered out of the tavern and been given Telwyn.

Even with my blurred eyes, I can see you aren't Gorracks. What are you playing at?

You've earned your death already.

Jagged pieces of a puzzle were falling into place. Morlan, his assassins, the Gorracks, Drüst's testimony—but it was far from a complete picture. *Still,* Alastair thought, *I know enough to destroy Morlan's credibility. But to reveal it now? I might as well put my neck on the chopping block.*

"Drüst?" repeated King Aravel.

The Windborne king looked away. "If the Gorracks cannot hide from the Windborne under the canopy of the Felhaunt, there is little chance they could bleed south in such a force as to overwhelm Morlan."

Much murmuring surged around the silver table.

A quiet voice drew notice as effectively as a shout. "King Drüst, worthy ally, protector—and friend," began Queen Savron, a nervous quiver in her voice. "I do not condemn you or your people. But from Westmoor to Ellador, the voices of the dead tell us that the Gorracks have found ways past even the keen eyes of the Windborne."

Drüst did not answer, but his people behind him spoke in whispers.

"With all due apologies to your family, High King Aravel," King Ealden said, "but what of Morlan? He has never hidden his hatred of the Gorracks. Perhaps he has taken his army into the Gorrack Nation to win glory for himself. Perhaps he goaded the Gorracks into invading Vulmarrow. While we rue the loss of his armies, we are not without strength."

"You are right there," said Aravel. "By latest count, we outnumber the Gorracks' initial number four to one. We will proceed with our plan. The Wayfolk and Anglish Guard will draw the Gorracks out of the Felhaunt from the north. Prince Navrill, rendezvous at the Nightwash River with Vang—and Briawynn too, hopefully. Draw out the Gorracks' southern forces. Divide and conquer."

Prince Navrill nodded and leaned back in his chair. "The Gorracks have never excelled at fighting two fronts at once." A bit of purple flared on his dark blue cheeks. "But there are at least sixty thousand additional Gorrack soldiers unaccounted for. We will need fly-overs."

"And you will have them," Drüst said, not hiding his annoyance. "I'm quite sure we can track sixty thousand Gorracks."

"Forgive me for speaking out of turn," Belliken/Alastair said. "But Prince Navrill, your people fight best in the water, do they not?"

Navrill put both hands flat on the table and flexed the wing-like fins beneath his arm. "More fierce in the water are we than sharks and fennigators combined."

"Then why have your men leave the water at all?" Belliken/Alastair gazed around the table, wondering if he'd just put a boot in his mouth before such warlords. "Why not combine the Wayfolk and Anglish Guard as one force and drive the Gorracks out of the Felhaunt into the strength of the Marinaens waiting in the Nightwash River? Vang and Briawynn, if she's able, can plow north and we will close on the Gorracks like a manarbeast trap."

"Your insights are welcome here," said Shepherd Sabastian at Aravel's right hand. "But driving into the Felhaunt plays into the Gorrack's hand. They are more at home in the trees. King Aravel was trying to avoid—"

"King Aravel was wrong," Aravel said. "Belliken's strategy is superior to mine. If this be the first battle of the great war, then let us strike with courage and assault their strength. Defeat them in the Felhaunt now and strike fear into their black hearts for all time!"

Kings, queens, generals, and soldiers cheered at this. Fists slammed to the table. Tankards and goblets were drained. And everyone sensed the importance of the moment.

But there was one last thing troubling Alastair. "My lords, if I may ask one more thing?"

"Please, Belliken," King Aravel said. "We speak freely here."

"Well," Belliken/Alastair said, "my question really is for King Drüst. Sire, I have been wondering…for, though my years are long, I have little experience with the Windborne. But now that I have seen your people both in flight and up close, you seem to me the most formidable warriors I have ever seen."

Drüst nodded. "Your words, General Belliken, are both wise and kind."

"So what I am wondering," Alastair said, "is why have we not spoken of how the aerial forces of the Windborne will attack? Even just five hundred of your kind would wreak havoc…on… on…" Alastair's voice trailed off at the flashing eyes and quick glances exchanged at the table.

This time, silence fell like a smothering blanket. Even King Aravel looked stunned.

Alastair wished he was on a ship sailing far away, or perhaps at the bottom of the sea—anywhere but this room. *What did I say?*

Drüst's green-eyed stare fell upon Alastair and would not relent as he spoke. "The Windborne civilization has survived, nay *flourished,* for ten thousand years for one simple reason: we do not take up arms against the other people of this world. We maintain. We protect our own. But in the face of a threat such as the Gorracks, we do not sit idly by. We supply reconnaissance. We provide medical attention and transport. We carry vital information from the field to command."

He stood, flexed his wings, and took a deep breath as if he were a dragon that might spew fire upon Alastair. "Know this, General Belliken: the heart of the Windborne beats fast. Our lives are short. We will not waste them in the wars of this world."

King Ealden cleared his throat and stood. "We have all heard the word of King Aravel, High King Overlord of Myriad. Now, let us petition the First One for his favor." He waited for everyone to bow their heads. He noticed Alastair was one of the first and Aravel one of the last.

"Mighty First One," he began, "you have given us this world and told us to enjoy its freedom and bounty. But now that freedom in in jeopardy. We raise our swords against an enemy who, for a thousand years, has made no secret of wanting to wipe us all from the face of Myriad. First One, we ask for you to protect us, guide us, and embolden us to complete the fell deeds that await. Amen."

I should have escaped while he was praying, Alastair thought.

"Now, go," Ealden commanded. "See to your duties. But then please, enjoy the riches of Llanfair…if only for one night, it will be well worth your time."

Alastair had to hurry. A Windborne messenger would leave for Anglinore within the hour. *Of course, after my blunder the messenger might just refuse to take it. Or he might just hit me in the jaw.*

Alastair shook those thoughts away and dipped his quill into the ink.

> My Lady Abbagael,
>
> I arrived safely in Llanfair, and it is the most beautiful city I have ever seen. Alas that I must leave it in one day's time. Perhaps I will bring you and Telwyn to see it when this is all over.
>
> I fear that many grim days lay between now and then. We have had our council, and tomorrow we leave for battle. You may not believe this, but King Aravel himself chose my battle plans over his own. I'm sorry I cannot provide details now, but I will write whenever I can.
>
> I have been most welcome among the royalty and military here…with one glaring exception. Still, I am amazed to be in this position. Amazed and thankful. I have questions, but there are many wise and faithful here. Maybe I will ask them.

There are flowers here, Abbagael, fields so full of flowers that you cannot see the end of them. You would love it here. See now, you are in my thoughts often. The Windborne bear this message. Please pray for me as I do for you.
Belliken

CHAPTER 40

HARD LINES

Long before Queen Savron and King Ealden traded barbs over Wayfolk traditions, the damage had already been done. It was the loss of the Vaskerstone Table that began it all. Blame and resentment die hard.

From the personal library of Threvithick Librettowit

9 DRINNAS 2212

Alastair approached the Prydian guards outside Jurisduro Hall with some trepidation. Perhaps it was because he was not Beliken Tolke, and execution was always just one slip of the tongue away. Or maybe it was the guards' rigid posture. They stood painfully straight on either side of the arched doorway. Even their facial skin looked taut. They stared at some mutual point, and their eyes did not seem to shift in the least as Alastair approached.

"I am General Tolke," Alastair said. "I am looking for King Ealden."

The guards did not reply. Their eyes still did not move.

Alastair waited. And waited. It was a dark, moonless night, but the torches provided some light. Alastair studied them, looked for movement, signs that they were breathing. He didn't see any movement at all. *Perhaps they are wax figures.*

"Forward guards are not permitted free speech, General," said one of the Prydians. "With this one exception, we may answer questions with yes or no only."

How quaint, Alastair thought. *But I'll play along.* "I am a stranger to Llanfair, and I do not know where King Ealden keeps his quarters. Is he perhaps still here?"

"Yes," the guards replied in unison.

"Ah, good. Is he in the main hall or somewhere else?"

Silence. No expression.

"Oh, right. Uh, will I find King Ealden in the main hall?"

"No."

"Is he on the main level?"

"No."

I've gotten more information from a brick. "Is he on the top level?"

"Yes."

"May I go and see him?"

Several moments of hesitation, then, "Yes."

The guards stepped aside. Alastair hurried into the building and began to explore. The first staircase led to several interesting rooms: a garden room next to a mighty bank of windows. Many plants and shrubs looked ethereal and mysterious in the gray blue tones of night. There was also a kind of military museum with swords and other weapons mounted on plaques and vast murals of glorious campaigns from the Wayfolk past. Alastair noticed that each chamber contained at least one engraving of a quote from the Books of Lore—from the Canticles, especially. *Looks like I've come to the right place.* But King Ealden was yet to be found.

Down one set of stairs and up the next Alastair found a long hall with rooms on either side. Within each was a plain, dark wood podium standing in front of chairs and slanted writing desks arranged in neat rows. But still, no sign of the king.

He almost missed it. The hall didn't actually end with the last classroom. It elbowed around a barely visible corner and led to an alcove full of books. Floor to ceiling books. Shelf above shelf, accessible by a rolling ladder. And to the right, at a desk illuminated by an inferno of candles, sat King Ealden.

Belliken/Alastair crept into the alcove, wondering if the king had noticed. He seemed so absorbed, muttering to himself, tracing a finger line by line as he read.

"King Ealden, Sire?"

Ealden looked up, his dark eyes clouded as if he still pondered some complex idea. He blinked. "Belliken, right? General Belliken?"

Alastair nodded. "I'm sorry for disturbing you."

"Not at all," Ealden said gesturing for his visitor to take a seat. "Just finishing my nightly readings in Canticles. You are certainly welcome here."

Alastair sat in a chair across the desk from the king. The chair wasn't low to the ground, but Alastair still felt like he was looking up at the king.

"You seem nervous," Ealden said. "Are you all right? Can I get you something?"

"I am nervous," Belliken/Alastair said. "I'm not certain that I am all right at all. But no, I don't need anything…except, perhaps, your wisdom."

Ealden leaned forward and crossed his fingers on the desk. "This sounds important. I will do what I can. Please, go on."

Alastair took a deep breath. There was so much he wanted to say, but he couldn't reveal too much. "Well, Sire, I am a follower of the First One. I have been for a little over ten years. During that time, I met with several very wise people in the Bryngate settlement, and we studied the First One's lore, especially concerning the Halfainin."

Ealden smiled. "So you too have been waiting for him, eh?"

"Yes, desperately," Alastair said, staring at the floor. He looked up after a moment. "I have spent many years charting the stars, searching for the likely location of the Sword, should it appear."

King Ealden raised an eyebrow and spoke "When the moon is blood red and the Sword is in the stars, the Man of Ice will call Him, the Hero from afar—you saw it then on the third of Celesandur?"

"I saw it," Alastair said, "and it heartens me to hear that you did also. But this brings me to my point. I saw the Sword in the Stars. It pointed to Thel-Mizaret. I went there that night and stayed there searching, nigh on a week. But I did not find him. I did not find the Halfainin, and now, Thel-Mizaret has been destroyed."

"Ah," said the king breathing out a deep sigh. "I see why you are troubled. When I saw the sword in the stars, I too went looking. I sent scouts all over Tryllium, but I did not find the Halfainin either. But let your heart be at peace, Belliken. The Halfainin has come, just as the First One said he would. But he has not come forward yet for us all to know him. After all, the Caller must find him first."

Alastair had suspected all along that this conversation might go this way. It was dangerous ground, but he had to press on. "That's just it, Sire." He swallowed. "You see...I believe I am the Caller."

Ealden sat up very straight. He said nothing at first but began flipping through the well-worn pages of lore. "Tell me, Belliken, what makes you think you are the Caller?"

"It was a possibility I did not believe myself at first," Alastair explained. "But others saw things in me. All the traits were there. I lost my parents at an early age. I was once an enemy of the First One. The Star Sword came to me—"

"The Star Sword!" Ealden's eyes burned. "It was stolen, stolen years ago from Synic Keenblade."

"Synic trained me in swordcraft," Alastair said. "I lived under his roof when he first received the Star Sword. I saw his broken heart when it vanished. I tracked down the thieves myself and took the blade back."

"You have it…you have it here?"

Alastair nodded.

"May I see it?"

Belliken/Alastair stood, unsheathed the blade, and handed it to Ealden.

For many moments—silent but for gasps and whispers—Ealden drank in the details of the blade. "It is the Star Sword. The holes in the pommel, the crossguard, and the blade…they are all correct… just like the pattern I saw in the stars that night. Remarkable."

"The Star Sword pointed to Thel-Mizaret," Alastair said again. "But of all the lads and lasses I tested, none of them had all of the gifts, and now I suspect they are all dead." Alastair choked on those last words, thinking of Jonasim, Laeriss, Duskan, and the others. If only he could have warned them of the Gorrack invasion. No one could've survived, he was sure of it.

"Belliken," the king said gently as he handed the sword back to Alastair, "I too have seen myself in the scriptures…the prophecies. And, like you, I have longed to play a great part in their coming to pass. I'll admit, the Star Sword is powerfully persuasive. But if you did not find the Halfainin, you cannot be the Caller. The Book of Canticles makes that perfectly clear. I suspect the real Caller went to Thel-Mizaret and led the Halfainin away before you arrived."

"You know the scriptures well, Sire?"

King Ealden smiled, and Alastair felt like a schoolboy who had just asked a very ignorant question. "Belliken, I spent the better part of twenty-five years studying at sanctuaries all over our world. I have committed much of the book of Canticles to memory, especially that wisdom which refers to the Halfainin. He is the hope of Myriad. There is no more important pursuit. Yes, I know the scriptures well."

Alastair released a long pent up sigh. "It makes me glad to hear your wisdom," he said. "I too came to the conclusion that I was not the Caller. It's just…well, it's just that…"

"What is it?"

"The Halfainin, Sire. Wherever he is now, I must find him. I... need him."

"We all do, Belliken. We all do."

Alastair shook his head. The slight relief he had been feeling boiled away in a vat of scalding fears. And though he felt a warning in his heart, he ignored it. "But sir, I need him with a desperation that I cannot put into words. For ten years while I was waiting for the Sword in the Stars, I swore off Witchdrale. But when I returned from my failure at Thel-Mizaret, I was so disheartened that I drank—"

King Ealden stood up. "Witchdrale! You drank Witchdrale? When?"

"It was the second week of Celesandur, I think. I know it was wrong, but I—"

"'Wrong' is quite an understatement. Witchdrale is Sabryne's brew...it destroys those who drink it. Do you, Belliken, know the scriptures well? If you did, you would know that the Books of Lore declare it absolutely vile to have one's mind distorted by such drinks. Do you know 2nd Statutes, where the First One says, 'That man who is filled with drink, his mind is untrustworthy, a plaything of the wicked. Such a man has no home in Allhaven.' Do you know that, Belliken?"

Alastair had to catch his breath. "What-what are you saying?"

King Ealden's expression was fierce. "What I am saying, Belliken, is that you need not be concerned ever again that you are the Caller. The Caller would never poison himself with Witchdrale. In fact, search the scriptures. You may want to be sure you are a follower of the First One at all."

"With all due respect, King Ealden, I came to you for wisdom—"

"And I have given you wisdom. Not my own, Belliken. This is the wisdom of the First One himself. 'Such a man has no home in Allhaven.' It couldn't be much clearer."

Alastair stood up and for a moment, though a span of six feet separated them, the two warriors were eye-to-eye. "Thank you,

King Ealden, for the reminder to search the Books of Lore. I will do that. There is a verse I won't have to look for. It's in Canticles. 'Whosoever would wear the mantle of the First One as his own, he must give an account of his judgments. Better would it be for such a man to drown in a deep lake than to be wrong.'"

Ealden bristled. "You misinterpret the context of that verse. It clearly—"

"You misinterpret the context of my life! I do not glory in my struggle with Witchdrale. I do not understand why I sometimes fail." Alastair's voice lost its angry edge and became something more akin to pleading. "I am ashamed of my past—more than you will ever know. And I have lost so much...dear ones gouged from my life! Have you no sense of that? Have you never lost someone?"

The king opened his mouth to speak, but his jaws snapped shut. As Alastair left the room, he glanced back once. King Ealden still stood very straight behind his desk. He was a narrow figure in the flickering candlelight.

King Ealden went to a low shelf on the bookcase nearest his desk. He removed a book bound in dark green. "I do know something of loss," he whispered as he opened the book. He stared down at the portrait he had drawn of Silwynn Mae, his young sister.

Tears blurred his sight.

He began to wonder about Belliken. There was much more to this warrior than his exploits on the field of battle. Much more even than his words revealed.

Perhaps I was too hard on him, King Ealden thought. *But truth is truth.* Still, he prayed to the First One that he would not push Belliken away...like he had Xanalos.

CHAPTER 41

UNEXPECTED INSIGHTS

*In the history of mounted warfare, there has never been a thunder-
ous clash like the one that day at Loch Raven Valley. Fell Droll
led the Sabrynite Army and their calamitous scormounts down the
side of Mount Gorthrandir like an avalanche. Telan Ironhand and
his dour Mountaineers rode their grayhoofs down the sheer side of
the dell.*

*They met in the valley, and nothing has grown there
for three thousand years since.*

Li-Saide of Ot, *Mountaineer Lore* Volume 716, w. 2318 AD

9 DRINNAS 2212

Alastair had been to Edenmill. Townsfolk, especially vendors in
the market, had seen him on several occasions—though not in a
while, they told Cythraul. The tavernkeeper even knew Alastair
by name.

"Alastair, yeah, I know 'im. He fancies young Abbagael
Rivynfleur," he had said. "Her uncle—that's old Jak Rivynfleur—
lives up on the hill. Big garden in the back. Can't miss it." The
tavernkeeper had twisted a strand of greasy hair around his finger

and offered one more piece of information. "Yeah, the last time I sawl 'im, he actually had a baby with 'im. Imagine that."

Cythraul could imagine it. It confirmed some of his recent suspicions. Now, he waited in a tall hedgerow across from Jak's cottage. He'd seen the old man chasing rabbits out of the garden for some time, but he hadn't seen the girl...or Alastair. It was time to investigate a little more closely. All the time and effort was about to pay—

Horses. Several of them coming this way fast. Cythraul faded back into the hedgerow and watched. *Warhorses?* Cythraul thought. *From Anglinore. What's this about?*

The lead knight dismounted and removed his helm, revealing matted locks of blond hair. The warhorses, more than a dozen, panted and glistened with perspiration. They had been riding hard for some time. The leader went to the cottage door and rapped hard. "Jak Rivynfleur, open your door. Anglinore has need of you!"

A sturdy-looking old man opened the door a crack. "What's that then?" he asked, eyeing the soldiers suspiciously. But then he saw their colors and opened the door wide. "Oh, oh, you lads *are* from Anglinore, eh? King Aravel have need of my hammer, does he?"

"Nay, Master Rivynfleur," the leader said. "Though, from the look of you, I'd say you wield a mean hammer."

"That I do," said Jak. "Or did anyway, fifty odd years ago. Alack, I am now two hundred eleven. My joints are a bit stiff. He hoo!"

The lead knight smiled affectionately. "I am General Triebold Swiftfeld," he said with a bow. "Though word may not have reached you here, Myriad is now at war. The Gorrack Nation has overstepped its bounds and seeks to conquer all the free peoples of this land. Your niece was in Chapparel during an invasion."

"What? My Abbagael?"

"Have no fear. She is safe. The battle in Chapparel has ended for now. The Gorracks were defeated utterly. Lady Abbagael dwells safely now in Anglinore Castle, but she would not rest until we fetched you to her side. As you can see, I've brought capable men and spare horses to help you."

"Me? Leave my home and come to Anglinore?"

"Is this disturbing to you?"

"Disturbing?" The old man cackled and performed an awkward hop. "Ha hoo, no! Lads, have at it! Dang rabbits are eating up my garden anyway. Who needs it?"

Triebold motioned for his men. They swiftly dismounted and filed into the cottage. "Just tell them what to pack for you," Triebold said. "But do not tarry. We have need of haste."

"Ah, general," Jak said, tentatively. "My Abbagael set off with a friend; Alastair was his name. What became of him, do you know?"

Cythraul leaned as far forward in the hedge as he dared.

Triebold squinted. "I cannot say. But so many were slain in Chapparel, it is likely that it was his fate as well."

"Ah, now, that is too bad," said Jak. "My Abbagael was fond of 'im. Very fond, I think."

Triebold tilted his head thoughtfully. "As I say, I cannot be sure. In any case, we must hurry."

Cythraul watched the old man and the knight enter the cottage. He considered killing them all. He wanted to. The old man knew Alastair in some way, and soldiers from Anglinore were always good sport. But no…no, he would wait on them. Cythraul vanished from the hedgerow and found his horse in the forest glade east of Edenmill.

Alastair's trail had finally grown warm again. Had he died in Chapparel? Cythraul rather doubted it, but Abbagael Rivynfleur would know, and she dwelt now in Anglinore.

Queen Maren knelt against a chair near the front of Clarissant Hall. She'd placed the chair against the wall where the old altar had stood for so many years. Aravel had been so adamant about having it dismantled and removed. *Maybe I should have pushed him not to,* she thought as she lowered her forehead to her clasped hands. *But,* she thought now as she had then, *I must choose my battles wisely. First One, forgive me.*

For the first time in several months, Maren had come to Clarissant Hall to pray. The world had turned upside down. After fifty years of marriage, fifty years of trying unsuccessfully to bear children, Maren was finally pregnant. She discovered this fact one day after her husband sailed off to Chapparel and to war.

"What shall I do, First One?" she whispered. "Aravel should know. I should tell him." But Maren knew her husband too well, knew his family history. *Aravel would put his armies in Sebastian's hands rather than miss the birth of our child.* His own father had been at war when he and Morlan were born. Brysroth had missed the birth of his two sons, as well as the last breaths of his beloved Clarissant. Aravel would not allow himself to repeat his father's mistake. "But if Aravel comes home, how many will die for lack of his leadership?"

It was an impossible dilemma. Both choices valid and pressing. Both choices dangerous and potentially life-changing. Maren was known to be a woman of great wisdom, but she knew she did not possess enough wisdom for this decision. At least, not enough wisdom untainted by emotion. That was why Maren had come to pray.

She kept her eyes closed and saw strange patterns of darkness and light, fuzzy images of nothing, something, and then nothing again. And still she waited, hoping for direction from the First One. She wondered if there was some secret to praying. Sebastian always spoke about prayer as if he'd just had a conversation with an old friend. *What am I doing wrong?* she wondered. "Ooh," she exhaled forcefully. The baby had kicked. Hit a nerve too, she thought. Painful, but still she smiled.

Hoping to feel another kick, Maren put a hand to her stomach, but the child had decided to go back to sleep. She rubbed the place where the baby had kicked and went to pray once a—

A loud squeal came from the back of the chamber. Maren opened her eyes and found a tall young woman with fiery red hair standing in the aisle between rows of chairs. She was holding a baby and looking as if she'd broken something and had just been caught.

"I'm sorry," she said. "I was told this was a good place to pray, but I didn't know anyone else was here."

Maren stood up. "You are welcome here, child. Wait, you are one of those who came from Chapparel."

"I'm from Edenmill, actually, but I was in Chapparel during the Gorrack assault. I'm Abbagael Rivynfleur, and this…" she held up the baby. "This little guy is Telwyn."

"Oh, ooh!" Maren dropped to a knee.

"Are you okay?" Abbagael rushed forward.

"No, no…fine," said Maren, regaining her feet and laughing. "I am pregnant, and my unborn child is…quite active. Felt as though he jumped up and down just now. Whoo."

"You sure you're all right?"

"Yes, yes, child, I am fine. But let us sit." They walked slowly to the first row of bench seats. "Ah, Abbagael, where are my manners? You told me your name but I've not shared my own. I am Maren Stormgarden."

Abbagael's eyes widened. "As in *Queen* Maren Stormgarden?"

The queen nodded. "Yes, which doubles the shame of my discourtesy."

"Was this your private prayer time? Is this your room? Should I leave?"

"Nay, child, stay. I should be glad for the company." Telwyn cooed. "Beautiful boy."

"Do you hear that, Tel?" Abbagael said, bouncing him on her knee. "A queen called you a beautiful boy." Telwyn giggled and she held him out for the Queen. "Would you like to hold him?"

"Yes, very much." She gently accepted the boy. "Oh, he's a sturdy little man, isn't he?"

"He is that."

"Tell me Abbagael," the queen said, tickling Telwyn's chin, "what brings you to seek prayer?"

"There is a very difficult man in my life," she said. "And he has gone off to war."

Maren smiled. "We have much in common then."

"I met him once. King Aravel, I mean. He seems like a very good man."

"Oh, he is. A kind and just man too. The throne does not define him."

"I can see that," said Abbagael. "He seems to see right away what the best decision is, and just acts on it."

"Most of the time," said the queen. "What troubles you about your own difficult man?"

Abbagael felt strange talking to the High Queen of all Myriad about her trivial life. But, why not? She seemed kind and wise. "It's complicated," she began. "And I'm not sure if the damage is already done or not. You see, Al...*Belliken* is a superb warrior. And I know he'll do great things against the enemy. He offered to stay with me. He would have if I'd demanded it, but I could tell he felt...like he almost needed to go."

"You said he is off to war," said the queen, her interest waxing. "You let him go then?"

"Well, I remembered what my mother told me when I was younger." Abbagael's face grew peaceful and dreamy. "I asked her why she didn't stand up to my father more, and she told me, 'Abbagael, you can bend a man and make him soft, or you can bend yourself to make him strong. But you will never have the man you've dreamed of unless you let him lead.' So I let Belliken go, told him he should do what he needed to do."

"Thank you, Abbagael," the queen said, placing a grinning Telwyn back in Abbagael's arms.

"You're welcome. It's the first time Tel's been held by a queen."

Queen Maren smiled and stood. Holding the child had been nice, but that wasn't why she had thanked Abbagael. "If you'll excuse me, I have a letter to write."

"A letter?"

"To my husband. But Abbagael, I should like very much if you would join me for dinner this evening. Talking with you has been quite comforting to me."

"Thank you, Your Majesty. I will certainly join you."

Once the queen had left Clarissant Hall, Abbagael tickled Telwyn's chin. "You did that, didn't you? You made the queen feel peaceful."

Telwyn answered by blowing out a loud raspberry.

CHAPTER 42

THE BATTLE OF THE FELHAUNT

Chapparel has seen its share of bowmen, the proudest hunters in
Myriad, no doubt. But none surpasses the Archer of Silverglen.
Obert McAusland fought for many a high king, but lost the use of
his legs in the ambush in the Felhaunt. Obert found that his ruined
legs hindered his training. "I cut the confounding things off meself,"
he said. And he did.

If anything, his aim improved, but the elite hunting clans of the
Wetlands cast him out.

No one knows what became of Obert. He is sorely missed.
Warden Caddock's private journal, 7 Atervast 2165 AS

11 DRINNAS 2212

High King Aravel, ruler of all the free peoples of Myriad and
leader of an army nearly seventy thousand strong, rode beneath
the canopy of the Felhaunt and felt profound dread. He listened
to the hollow clops of their horses and gazed around at the foliage.

There were many tall trees: hemlocks, black oaks, skagmaple,
and fir. But dominating all others were the serpentwood. Their
black trunks, striated with shrouds of blue lichen, snaked up from
the ground and twisted in reckless spirals high overhead. Their

leaves were the size of a man's open palm and were roughly the shape of a dagger. And this time of year, the leaves turned from bruised purple to dark red. Loops of scaly vines hung down from the branches like so many hangman's nooses prepared for a mass execution.

Aravel wondered about this war and especially about the battle that was to come in this deadly wood. Would it be a mass execution? Aravel had more reason to wonder than most men. He had nearly been a casualty of a surprise raid by the Gorracks in among these very same trees just fifty-two years before. It felt like yesterday. He'd lost eighty-eight men in that fight and, had it not been for the heroics of Synic Keenblade, Aravel knew his own life would have ended then as well. Still, the Gorracks had been routed, and Xuth Rendquell, the Gorrack High Priest, had declared the raid a horrible misunderstanding, even paying reparations in gold and precious sorilcloth.

There had been an uneasy truce with the Gorracks since then, growing more strained in 2202 when Xuth Rendquell had died and the more militant Xabin Tarq had taken power.

"The past is the past," Shepherd Sebastian Sternbough said, riding up beside the king.

"Am I that obvious?"

"Only to me. And only because I know you well."

"I am grateful, Sebastian, for your friendship and guidance. I am certain I do not tell you that often enough."

Sebastian wiped dark curls of hair from his eyes. "You need not tell me at all. It is a rare person who wields the kind of power you do and yet still listens to counsel of any kind."

"That's Maren's doing," said the king, his easy laugh returning for a moment. "If I ever become too full of myself, she softens me up."

"I thought it was Daribel's baked goods that softened you up."

"Not anymore," the king said, laughing. "I've had nary a scone since the Council. I'm in perfect shape."

"So you are," said Sebastian. His mission accomplished—relieving the weight on Aravel's mind—Sebastian let silence descend once more.

The sun climbed as the massive army marched through the Felhaunt. Here and there they heard the mournful cry of the gray-strider, but little else seemed to stir among the trees. When they came to the edge of a clearing, Aravel held up his hand. Scouts appeared in the trees before them. They approached the king and shared whispers.

The news passed swiftly across the entire front line, and the army stirred. All eyes fell upon the king. At first, he said nothing.

He stared out into the clearing...at the grassy mounds. An ache somewhere within Aravel tightened the muscles in his stomach. "We have come to the Barrow Field," he said to his army. "See to it that you lead your horses around the mounds, for our comrades rest there, and we will not disturb them." He waited for the message to spread through the ranks. "But once we hit the other side of the clearing, we must ride with all speed. The Gorrack forces wait just a few miles on the other side, and we must come upon them like a storm!"

Alastair rode slowly through the clearing far behind the king. He looked respectfully on the mounds. *Those men who went forth that day...they had no idea it would be the last time they saw their loved ones. They had no idea they would never leave the forest.*

He wondered then about Abbagael and Tel. *What if today is the day I never leave the forest? I'll never see them again.*

The clearing became suddenly dark. Alastair looked up. The sky had been peculiar all day, but especially now. Clouds, some slate blue, some dark gray, moved slowly overhead. Wisps of white clouds at a much lower altitude raced in the opposite direction of the higher clouds. Gashes in the clouds opened and let flashes of sunshine in, but closed up just as quickly.

Alastair shuddered and looked suddenly to his right. Between two of the mounds and standing in the wind-waving high grass, was a shadow...humanoid in shape, but ethereal like mist. Alastair blinked, and it was gone. Other mounted knights rode through the place where the shadow had been. They seemed not to have noticed anything.

Then, Alastair sensed movement to his left, spun in his saddle, and caught just the glimpse of another shadow walking slowly down one hill before it disappeared.

A scream of agony blared from Alastair's right. The Star Sword swished out, and Alastair twisted 'round to find—quite possibly the shortest Anglish Knight he had ever seen. He was short, but as stocky as a tree stump, and he rode a rather stumpy horse as well.

The knight saw Alastair turn and looked up at him with eyes wide and fearful. "You're not going to hit me, are ya?"

"No, no," Alastair said. "Of course not. But...was that you... screaming?"

"Not, screamin', mate. Yodeling." He cleared his throat and let loose something like a mix of wolf's howl and a drowning moose. "There, see? Yodels. I do it when I'm scared...eases the nerves, ya know."

"I thought a banshee had come upon us," Alastair said with a laugh. "What's your name?"

"Pelham Frockenschlammer. But me friends call me the yodeling dwarf. 'Yodels' for short. And you're that new general— Tolke, is it?"

"That's right," Alastair said. "I have to confess, my nerves have been a bit on edge as well. The strange shadows among the mounds are enough to drive one mad."

"What?" Yodels looked among the mounds.

"Shadows. Shapes of men moving among the barrows."

"Don't you be playin' with me, General," Yodels said. "I may be young and small, but you won't fool me with such tales."

"I'm...I'm not..." Alastair's voice trailed off. It was no good trying to convince him. Having seen no additional shadows, Alastair began to wonder if perhaps what he'd seen had been a trick of his imagination and the light of the strange roiling sky.

The Barrow Field now just behind them, King Aravel gave a signal, and his army sprang forward. The forest floor was strewn with leaves and other deadfall, but there were paths and lanes for a skillful rider. The Anglish cavalry were among the best mounted warriors in Myriad, second only to the Wayfolk. And so the entire army charged deeper into the wood.

Alerted just moments before by the thunderous sound of so many hooves, the Gorracks rose from their daytime lethargy and tried to prepare a hasty defense. But it was too late.

Aravel and Ealden's forces exploded into the Gorrack camp, dropping hundreds of Gorracks in seconds. Gorrack tents collapsed and cook fires were extinguished by Gorrack bodies. For a few chaotic moments, the Gorracks fled.

In a state of shock, Alastair drove his horse toward the Gorracks as they retreated to more dense tree cover within the Felhaunt. But it wasn't their retreat that surprised him. Alastair had always believed that kings stayed well back from the fighting, coordinating and dishing out orders far from harm's way. Not so with King Aravel of Anglinore and King Ealden of Llanfair. These two sovereigns led their forces into battle.

Aravel himself had taken out more than a dozen Gorracks on his own already. He was a tactical warrior, analyzing his enemy, approaching from the perfect angle, and striking with precision. His bladecraft was masterful, if without flourish. His strokes were compact, no wasted motion or energy, and every strike's follow through carried his momentum into his next movement. The high king overlord had been trained by a master, Alastair knew. He was, perhaps, not as natural with a blade as some, but he was ten times more efficient than most.

King Ealden, on the other hand, was a holy terror on the battlefield. Like the other Wayfolk soldiers, he wielded a weapon his people called a glaive: a three-foot shaft with a hand-fitted grip in the center and a curving sycthe-like blade on either end. Ealden, who had seemed so reserved and polite in the council, fought like a madman. His glaive whirled from one hand to the other, dealing catastrophic damage to the enemy. His scormount, a fleet-footed creature as tall as a horse but with ram-like horns and impaling talons protruding from its knees, seemed to know exactly what its rider wanted to do, so Ealden was able to fight hands free of the reins.

Unlike Aravel's precision, Ealden rode recklessly into the enemy, swinging wildly in wide, powerful arcs. It seemed to Alastair that King Ealden's strategy was not to necessarily kill each enemy, but to render him unable to fight any longer. Ealden slashed off dozens of arms at the shoulders, hamstrung many other Gorracks, and even struck some of the enemy in the back—Alastair figured Ealden knew a certain nerve to hit—rendering the Gorrack useless. They would fall to the ground, twitching involuntarily and staring with wide eyes.

Alastair still stung from Ealden's hard counsel back in Llanfair, but he could not fault the king for his battle prowess.

With such leadership, the combined forces of Anglinore and Llanfair penetrated the Felhaunt and took the Gorracks by surprise. It was clearly not the Gorrack's full offensive force, not yet. It was as Drüst of the Windborne had said, forty thousand, perhaps a regiment more. *Count that as thirty-nine thousand, now,* thought Alastair.

But once the Gorracks recovered from the initial shock of the attack, they countered fiercely, and they were very much at home among the trees. They moved on two legs but had the speed and power of panthers. Grasping the huge sycamore trunks and propelling themselves airborne at their enemies, the Gorracks stopped the Myridian army's progress cold. Steeds buckled as they were cut down by the Gorracks. Combat became face-to-face and hand-to-hand. Wayfolk and Anglish soldiers fell under axe blades or were skewered with pikes.

Alastair leaped from his wounded horse and found himself in the center of a whirlwind of chaos. A seething line six Gorracks wide plowed towards him. Gorracks were in the trees as well, swinging from branch to branch and ready to lunge. Alastair knew he could retreat. It was just a fifty-yard sprint back to reinforcements. But Alastair did not retreat.

Like a chessmaster seeing a dozen moves ahead, he saw his path through the Gorracks, but it was not a clear path this time. If the Gorracks were smart, there was a point where they could have him, and there would be no escape for Alastair. That was if they were smart. He took the risk.

Alastair gathered as much speed as he could across the mossy forest floor and leaped up at the Gorrack swinging in from the left. The Gorrack was forced to jab across the bulk of his own body to get at Alastair with his pike. But his attack was far too late to do any harm to the Iceman. Alastair drove his Star Sword under the Gorrack's outstretched arm, plunging the blade between its thick, membranous ribs and into its leathery heart. The dead Gorrack crashed into the underbrush even as Alastair grabbed a branch and vaulted around the back of the tree.

Boots first, he bulled into the charging Gorracks' flank, slamming several combatants to the turf. Using two hands for certain penetration, Alastair plunged his sword into one prone Gorrack's chest.

Alastair planted his feet firmly, yanked out his blade, and drove the pommel beneath the chin of the next Gorrack, who had just risen to one knee. The creature released a kind of snarl-howl, and broken teeth and blood spilled out of its ruined jaw. The

Gorrack tried to fix its slanted reptillian eyes on his enemy and caught Alastair's elbow instead. Its head snapped backward and it fell. Alastair alertly lopped off the Gorrack's arm at the elbow, spun with the momentum, and dragged his blade behind another Gorrack's knees.

Every movement set up just as Alastair had predicted it would, and he continued his deadly dance through the enemy. But the sticking point was approaching, and so far, try as he might, Alastair could not see enough countermoves to avoid his fate. His only hope was that the remaining two Gorracks would not coordinate their attacks well together—or perhaps they wouldn't see the opening at all.

But as Alastair ducked an axe swipe, took a step, and drove his blade into the Gorrack now behind him, he saw that the two Gorracks ahead knew what they were doing. And worse, the bigger Gorrack of the pair had a combat net and readied to cast it. Too fast. No way to split them. No way out.

Alastair silently thanked the First One for a chance to fight for a noble cause. And, as the net fell around him, weighing him down, he took one final stroke, ripping his sword arm through the net and skewering the big Gorrack's throat. The other Gorrack would circle and plunge his pike into Alastair's exposed back.

Alastair whispered a quick but heartfelt apology. "I didn't find him," he said, as he felt the prick of the pike as it bit the flesh just above his kidneys. "I'm sorry I never found...you."

"Where are Briawynn and Vang?" yelled King Aravel, pulling his sword from the breastplate of a ruined Gorrack. "We need their pressure!"

"Perhaps they were waylaid by the enemy pushing east from Vulmarrow!" Sebastian called over his shoulder. He slammed his staff under the chopping stroke of a Gorrack, shattering the beast's elbow, then whirled his staff around and bashed the Gorrack in the back of its head.

For battle, most Shepherds favored staffs as the weapon to compliment their gifts. Sebastian had designed his own staff, choosing a massive hemlock limb and causing it to thin out on the shaft and grow thick knots on either end. It became a relatively lightweight bludgeoning staff, and Sebastian wielded it with authority.

"Bah, I wish Drüst had seen them," Aravel growled. "Wish he had their numbers. No telling if we'll receive any aid at all from Vang and Briawynn, to say nothing of Morlan." King Aravel winded his war horn and strode forward urgently. "Gelrod!" he shouted to one of his generals. "Take a cadre east! Keep the enemy from flanking us!"

Gelrod wiped blood from his forehead and waved his acknowledgment. King Aravel watched as close to a hundred knights peeled away from the main group to meet the Gorracks threatening their flank from the east.

He scanned back to the west and grunted. "Where has Ealden gotten to?" And then he yelled to his Shepherd. "Sebastian, where are the Wayfolk?!"

"Ealden drew them North!" Sebastian called back. "He went with some urgency, up a path through the thickness where the vines hang down!"

"There is urgency here also!" barked the king as he watched some thirty Gorracks burst through the trees up ahead. Led by their chieftain, they charged fearlessly down the bank of a dried-out creek bed and up the other side just forty yards from the Shepherd and his king.

The chieftain who led the Gorracks wore an animal fur cape and had black warpaint beneath his eyes. But more frightening still were the tattoos on his arms. A single red slash on the upper arm was given for each enemy kill. This chieftain had ten stripes on one arm and eight on the other.

"Sebastian!" the king said, his volume rising.

"I was hoping to save this!" yelled Sebastian, watching the Gorracks charge.

King Aravel found himself fighting off memories of another Gorrack onslaught in the Felhaunt. "Sebastian, now would be a good time!"

"Aravel, you may have to carry me after this!"

King Aravel watched with equal parts astonishment and admiration as his Shepherd kneeled to the ground and thrust his free hand into the black soil.

"C'mon," Aravel urged, watching the Gorracks close on his friend, "find a root! Find a root!"

Sebastian found a root.

Suddenly, the forest floor came to life. Massive tree roots twisted up out of the ground, forming loops and tripping the oncoming Gorracks. Once the Gorrack charge had been slowed, the roots went wild. They burst from the ground and wrapped around the legs or waists of the Gorracks like zephyr snakes or anacondas. But Sebastian wasn't through. He pushed his hand deeper into the soil and made a fist.

The Gorracks began to wail and howl.

Aravel winced as he saw the massive, entangling roots suddenly grow thorns as long as dagger blades. The thorns pierced thirty Gorracks at once. Last to fall limp was the Gorrack chieftain. He snarled and reached out, trying desperately to grab Sebastian. But it was no use. The roots held him fast.

Sebastian twisted his wrist in the soil, and the roots responded. Even King Aravel had to turn away.

Then Sebastian fell unconscious.

CHAPTER 43

LEFT FOR DEAD

There are impotent souls who, unable to create life,
will readily create death as an alternative.
From Sanguine Sayings by Rudolph the Hunted, 1412 AS

14 DRINNAS 2212

"Abbagael Rivynfleur?" the Anglish guard said, pulling at his gray mustache. "I dunno. Name sounds familiar." He turned to face the guard on the other side of the gatehouse. "Hey, Fez, you know an Abbagael Rivynfleur?"

Fez wiped sweat out of his eyes. It was a warm morning. "'Course I know her. Pretty thing, she is, eh, Skappy? One a' the survivors from Chapparel."

"So she is here in the castle, then?" Cythraul asked.

"Yeah," Fez said. "That's the way Lord Aravel and Lady Maren do things. They put all the survivors up in royal quarters, like."

"So what's your business with Miss Abbagael?" Skap asked.

Cythraul didn't miss a beat. "I lost friends in Chapparel. Some have not been found. I heard that Abbagael had survived… I thought she might know about my friends."

"Oh, sorry to hear that," Fez said. "Blasted Gorracks. I can take you to her. Think that'd be all right, Skap?"

The older guard shrugged. "Likely be at breakfast, I imagine."

"Thank you," Cythraul said. "You have no idea how this might unburden my mind."

Abbagael hadn't been in the dining room, which suited Cythraul well. He couldn't do what he needed to do with a crowd around. So, as he followed the guard called Fez through the labyrinthine halls and passages of Anglinore castle, Cythraul hoped that Abbagael would be alone in her chamber.

Fez rapped quietly on her door.

"Yes? Who is it?" came a muffled reply.

"It's Fezzel Crom, m'lady. I'm sorry about the early hour, but there's someone here to see you." He turned to Cythraul. "What's your name, then?"

"Banther," he replied. "Banther Coldhollow."

"He says his name is Banther Coldhollow."

The door opened. Abbagael held Telwyn in her arms and stared past the guard to Cythraul. "Did you say your surname is Coldhollow?"

Cythraul bowed. "Yes, Lady Abbagael."

Her eyes narrowed. She scanned his jawline, the bridge of his nose, his eyes...searching for points of recognition. Maybe, maybe the eyes. But he was older, approaching three hundred. Must be. "What do you want?"

"Only to ask a few questions. I understand you were in Chapparel during the Gorrack raid?"

"Yes. Yes, I was." Telwyn rubbed his eyes and whimpered a bit. "Where is my courtesy. Won't you come in?"

"Thank you," Cythraul replied with another bow.

"Wait outside your door, shall I?" asked Fez.

"Yes, please." Abbagael stepped aside so Cythraul could enter. Fez shut the door.

Cythraul didn't mind having the guard outside. It wouldn't hinder his work in the least. It might make departing a little difficult, but one more dead enemy didn't concern him. As Cythraul sat down, he was wondering about the child. Certainly this was the child Alastair had fathered with the woman from Thel-Mizaret. But how did this other woman, this Abbagael Rivynfleur, fit into Alastair's life? There were many questions to ask this woman. But Abbagael began the asking.

"Forgive my suspicions," she began as she bounced Telwyn on her knee, "but Alastair mentioned no living relatives."

"No, you are right to question," he said. "I am a stranger to you." He took a deep, dramatic breath. "I am Alastair's older brother by sixty years. I'm afraid he was never very…content. When our father disappeared, Alastair was yet very young. I think he resented me taking over the patriarchal role."

Cythraul went to the window of her chamber, stared for a moment into the gray sky. He let his head drop. "Maybe it was a role I should never have taken. I…I was never the man my father was." Cythraul let those words hang. He was certain Abbagael, compassionate soul that she seemed to be, would come and stand behind him. Maybe even put a hand on his shoulder. Cythraul twisted a peculiar silver ring on the forefinger of his right hand. Then, he slid its locket-like cover to the side, uncovering several tiny needles.

"And, I'm ashamed to confess," he went on, "that Alastair was more than I could handle. When mother became ill and was on the verge of death, I could bear it no longer. I abandoned them." Cythraul made a few gruff weeping sounds and let his head bounce. "Alastair's never forgiven me for it. Dead to me, he said once. Ironic."

He could feel her behind him, and the child still whimpered softly. He'd get her first, just a small dose. But a full dose for the child. A swift, quiet death for him…unfortunate, but Cythraul could not risk the noise.

"I'm so sorry," Abbagael said, standing just a couple of feet behind him. "Your...your family has endured such tragedy." She paused. "Tell me, Banther, how did you find us here?"

"'Us'?" Cythraul said with genuine interest. "You mean Alastair lives? He is here with you?"

Abbagael hesitated. "No...I am sorry. He was slain in Chapparel. I meant the baby and me."

Liar, Cythraul thought. *Alastair lives. He was in Chapparel with you, wasn't he?* Cythraul would find out for sure. He gave his ring one final twist. He would get her talking again, and strike when she was nearly empty of breath. Impossible to scream when inhaling.

"How did he die?" Cythraul asked without turning. "He was such a skilled warrior. He served under Morlan...on his Wolfguard, you know. Elite soldiers. Gorracks slew him? I do not understand."

"It wasn't the Gorracks," Abbagael said, feeling guilty for deceiving him. *What if he is Alastair's brother? It wouldn't be the first time he'd kept something from me.* She would ask him in her next letter. Something about this Banther felt wrong. So she lied. "And it wasn't in Chapparel. We were attacked by spiraxes in the deep forest outside of Edenmill. Alastair died protecting me and our child—"

Cythraul spun around and reached for Abbagael's arm.

The chamber door opened.

"Lady Abbagael, are you ready for our walk?" Queen Maren was flanked by Fez and three guards.

Cythraul froze.

Abbagael turned. "Yes, I am ready. You promised to show me the gardens."

"Oh, I'm sorry. I didn't realize you had a guest."

"High Queen Maren," Abbagael said, "this is Banther Coldhollow. He lost someone dear to him in...in Chapparel."

Cythraul closed his silver ring, grit his teeth, and bowed. "It is an honor, my queen."

"I'm sorry, Banther," Abbagael said. "Perhaps another time?"
Cythraul blinked. "Yes. Another time."

*C*lever girl, thought Cythraul. *Not very skilled at lying, but clever.* He stood in the cool night air, a shadow on the ledge outside Abbagael's window. Cythraul had tried things the easy way. He would have succeeded had the queen not appeared. He shook his head. He'd had half a notion of killing her as well. But that was not his mission, and Morlan felt somewhat differently about Maren than he did about his brother, Aravel. No, best to leave the queen to Morlan.

Though he'd been interrupted, he'd still learned a very important bit of information: Alastair Coldhollow was alive. Cythraul was certain of that. Unless he'd been jumped by a dozen or more, Alastair was too good to be taken down by Gorracks. And the story about spiraxes was pure fantasy. Cythraul truly looked forward to a chance to match up against the swordsman, so Abbagael's poor attempts at lying were welcome news. She'd all but revealed that Alastair had been in Chapparel for a time. Nonetheless, specific details still needed to be uncovered. And that was why Cythraul waited on the ledge.

She'd taken her sweet time to fall asleep, snuggling with the child in the huge four poster bed and shifting positions endlessly. Cythraul wearied of waiting…wearied of standing so still for so long. It had been an arduous climb, ten stories up from the courtyard now far below. His muscles still burned.

The longer he waited, the more conspicuous he felt up on that ledge. Fortunately, there was no moon this night and it wasn't the season for starshine. Guards might have noticed him otherwise. Still, he remained as motionless as possible, shifting his glance only slightly from Abbagael through the window to the castle entrance below. Once, he heard voices far below. He pressed himself between two pieces of ornately carved stone and watched as a small caravan—nine, maybe ten soldiers on horseback—came to the main gatehouse. After some boisterous conversation, punctuated by too loud laughter, the riding party entered the castle and all became quiet again.

Time passed and Cythraul watched as Abbagael shifted less and less. At last, he was convinced that she was sound asleep. He removed a compact leather case from a pocket in his vest, opened it, and selected a slender metallic tool. But as he leaned against the window and began to tinker with the lock, the pane of glass moved inward. She hadn't even locked her window. Foolish girl took too much for granted.

Without so much as the sound of a breath, Cythraul slid inside and closed the window behind him. A small oil lantern burned on the desk across from the bed. It cast weak but helpful light. He came to the tall bed and found Abbagael and the child both very much asleep. Kill the child first, then dose the woman—his original plan was still the best. So he twisted the ring on his finger and opened the covering. The small needles were there, sharper than a scorpion's sting and ten times as potent.

He watched their chests rise and fall…so slowly. He found himself wondering about the child. His face was so serene, and Abbagael doted over him as if he were her own. But why would she? If the child belonged to another woman—Alastair's former wife—why would she love the child so? Another question to ask her once she was under the venom's control.

Careful not to nudge Abbagael, Cythraul leaned over and stretched out his arm. He would prick the child's smooth cheek and listen for his breathing to stop. A few seconds was all that would be necessary. Cythraul changed the angle of his hand, the needles now just inches from the child's soft skin.

The boy's eyes popped open. His tiny body shuddered, and he grabbed Cythraul's middle finger and began to wail.

Cythraul cursed and tried to press the needles into the child, but hit his blanket instead. The child would not let go, and his squealing would no doubt wake—

Abbagael loosed a blood-curdling scream and launched a savage kick into Cythraul's gut.

He stumbled back a pace from the bed and drew a cruel thin dagger. His face still expressionless and cold, he reared back his arm to plunge the dagger when—the door crashed open.

Cythraul didn't even have time to turn. Something hit him so hard in the ribs just below his arm that he actually heard the bones breaking. A second blow lifted him off his feet and sent him cartwheeling through the window. Down he fell to the courtyard below.

"Uncle Jak!" Abbagael cried as the graybeard rushed in and hugged her. Two guards were with him.

"You all right, missy?" Jak asked her, pulling away to look at her. "He didn't get ye, did he?"

"No, no, I'm fine, thanks to you." She grabbed up little Telwyn and shushed him on her shoulder.

The guards went to the shattered window and looked down.

"Ah, he's ruined, he is," said Fez.

"Told ye I didn't like the looks a' him," Skappy said.

"That you did not!" said Fez.

"Don't matter much now, do it?" asked Skap. "Thanks much to Mister Jak's hammer. Ye fling that 'round pretty well."

"Fer an old goat." Jak turned back to Abbagael, concern still glistening in his eyes. "Are ye sure yer alright? That joker looked as if he meant no good business."

"Yes, Uncle, I am well. Frightened, is all."

"Who was he?" Uncle Jak asked, the two guards listening in.

"We'll talk of it later." Abbagael turned to the guards. "Would it be possible to have my things moved to a different chamber... one without an exterior window?"

"Course ye can," Fez said.

"And I want to be right next to her!" demanded Jak.

Guards had collected Cythraul's body from the courtyard and, per the queen's request, delivered it to the medical hold. She'd asked for Anglinore's chief physician, as well as the Knight-Captain in charge of security, to find out what they could of this would-be assassin. What the queen desired to know most was why anyone would go to such trouble to try to kill Abbagael Rivynfleur.

In the cold basement chamber, Knight-Captain Kask picked up his bundle of clues. "If you don't mind, Doc, I'm going to take this stuff upstairs. A bit too chilly down here for me to think straight. With this load of peculiar tools and such, I need to be able to think."

Doctor Mattys waved him off. "I don't mind at all, Kask. I've a fair amount of thinking to do myself." He looked down at the body. "Ye get used to the cold, ye do. And it keeps down the stink."

The security chief left and Doctor Mattys went back to work. "Gah, blood's poolin' again." He grabbed a cloth and soaked up the blood under Cythraul's misshapen head. He took a metal clamp. He wanted to look under the skin at the dead man's ribs. When he'd first peeled off the leather jerkin and the vest, he'd noted the severity of the wound. That hammer blow had caved in the right side of the man's chest. *Strange,* he thought, opening the wound, *there are fewer fractures than I remember.*

Cythraul's hand flew to the doctor's throat and closed like a vice. A sharp crack and a long, gurgling sigh, and then Cythraul let the doctor's body fall to the floor.

He felt a little dizzy as he stood. This fall was not the worst he'd endured, but every time it happened it took a toll on his mind. It would be an hour or so before he was fully healed. Cythraul found his clothing, put it on, and considered his situation.

While he'd been "resting," he'd heard King Morlan's voice in his mind. It was not a hallucination brought on by the trauma of the fall. Somehow, Morlan had used his vaskerstone table in a new way, to project his voice across the miles and into Cythraul's mind. Morlan had ordered him to return home. There was an urgent errand. More urgent than Abbagael or following Alastair's trail.

So Cythraul would ride to Vulmarrow. But first he would pay a visit to the Knight-Captain. Cythraul wanted his tools back.

CHAPTER 44

SHEPHERDS AND WOLVES

And the crown shall be torn from his grasp by the Usurper.
They will sear his flesh, and he will fall into darkness.
But he will return.
Book of Wrath, Chapter 12, verse 6,
from the *Prophecies of Hindred*

12 DRINNAS 2212

"Alfex, good of you to come," King Morlan said.

"Of course, Morlan, my son," the old Shepherd replied. "When you told me you'd been to the Abode of Wights, I was worried."

Morlan smiled and leaned back in his throne. "How many years has it been since you took me under your wing, Alfex? One hundred forty? A very long time." He laughed softly. "You called me 'son' just now. Indeed, you have been as a father to me."

Alfex placed his hand on Morlan's shoulder. "Your real father did not see your potential. I did. And while Aravel was being pampered, I saw to it that you were hardened. You are strong, Morlan."

"Yes," Morlan replied, looking up. "And so much of who I am is thanks to you. You fed me from the Book of Whispers and shared your wisdom with me. Now I am most favored of Sabryne Shadowfinger."

Alfex beamed down at Morlan with great pride. "You honor me too much, Morlan. I am grateful. But tell me, what did you learn from the Abode of Wights...that accursed place?"

"Many things," said Morlan. "And yet, I return to you with questions."

"I am not surprised." Alfex's hand dropped from Morlan's shoulder, and he sat on the top stair of the throne. "Many mysteries there, I am sure. Some are beyond my knowledge, but what I know I will share, of course."

"Of course," Morlan said. "I wish to know of one of your Shepherd brethren. I need to know where to find him."

"Who? What is the name?"

"That's just it. I don't know his name," said Morlan. "I know his gift...he has some power over the winds. He can call them to his aid."

"Oh," Alfex said, "then you don't mean 'he.' You speak of a woman. Draevan Zariac is her name."

"Draevan? Where can I find her, Shepherd's Hollow?"

"She would not be at Shepherd's Hollow this time of year," Alfex explained. "It is the storm season in Bell Farthing, her home province. She dwells in a castle on the moors near Loch Feymist. What do you want with her?"

"Do you know of the Dark Shepherds?"

Alfex stood abruptly and stared at Morlan. "Know of them?" He made a sharp grunt sound in his throat. "My family line descends from them."

"Yes," Morlan said. "But the rest of the Shepherd Council doesn't know that, do they, Alfex?"

"No, of course not." The old Shepherd began to pace in front of Morlan's throne. "If they knew, they would have sent me across the Dark Sea. Not to mention they would never have made me an officer in the Council."

"But why didn't they know, Alfex?" Morlan asked. "Surely the Shepherds keep genealogies? Family trees must be carefully charted and preserved."

Alfex did not respond.

So Morlan went on. "With such power in the bloodlines, the Shepherds would want to be certain of their descendants. Unless...*unless* the power is not passed on through the blood."

Alfex didn't stop pacing, but there was a momentary hitch in his step. "What do you mean, Morlan? Of course the power is passed through the blood."

Morlan shook his head. "Oh, Alfex. All these years, in all the many tutoring sessions, you never told me. And I know why." Morlan's right hand slipped to the side of his throne. "You didn't tell me how the power was transferred because you thought I'd try to take it for myself."

Alfex started to vanish, his form melting into the air. But Morlan was faster. His dagger plunged forward and upward into nothingness.

Alfex groaned and his body rematerialized around the dagger's blade. Blood trickled from the corner of his mouth. "You... you thankless...wretch."

Morlan forced the dagger in deeper. "You were right not to tell me," Morlan said. "If I had known, I would have taken it... as I am now. But no, do not die yet." Morlan kept the upward pressure on the dagger so that Alfex could not dislodge the blade. "Not yet. You see, I think I've figured something out. You do appear on the Shepherd's histories, don't you? You are a legitimate heir. It's where your vanishing skill comes from. But you are more than that, aren't you?"

Alfex groaned. His eyelids fluttered. "Just...be done with it."

"A moment more. A moment worth savoring." Morlan turned his face sideways near Alfex's eyes. "See this scar on my cheek? It appeared shortly after I took the power from the Gorrack

Shepherd in the mountain. It's a mark of thievery, isn't it? A mark very much like one on your shoulder." Morlan tore Alfex's collar, revealing a streak of mottled flesh.

Alfex squirmed and moaned. "I would have aided you, Morlan," he said, his voice sounding thin and far away. "As I always have. You didn't have to do this."

"Ever since the wights," Morlan said, "I've wondered what power you took to get that mark…I've wondered what your second gift is. But then, it was obvious." Morlan leaned forward so that his face was just inches from Alfex's face. "It's long life." Morlan twisted the dagger and tore it free, bringing with it a gout of dark blood.

Alfex slumped to the floor, his eyes staring…seeing nothing.

"And so, Alfex, you have helped me…so very much."

18 Drinnas 2212

"I expected him sooner than that," Morlan said, walking through the rubble in the courtyard of Vulmarrow.

"You are sure he was convinced?" asked Cythraul. "Drüst's mind is as keen as his eyes, maybe more so."

"Weren't you?" Morlan asked. "I didn't have my stonemasons tear down half the city for nothing."

Cythraul nodded. "You have a second scar on your face. But it looks old…how?"

"Alfex's doing. Unfortunately, he proved to be less than reliable." Morlan glanced wistfully up at the high tower. "Still, he gave his life for me. I ought to be grateful."

"There is more to that tale."

"Yes…much more."

Cythraul nodded, looking over the bodies strewn across the courtyard…festering in the hot sun. "How did you come by these dead?"

"Velach's team fetched a few Gorracks for me," Morlan said. "And I had to dispatch twenty or thirty soldiers who fell short in their Wolfguard training."

Cythraul nodded. "Pity I wasn't here to help."

"But you are now, my friend," Morlan said. "And I have great need of you. This mission is perhaps the most important of this entire campaign."

"Tell me."

Morlan did. He told him everything.

"When do we leave?" Cythraul asked.

"Now."

B ell Farthing was the westernmost Myridian outpost before the untamed wilderness known as the Hinterlands. It was a week's ride for most. Such was Morlan's urgency that he and Cythraul made it in six days. A vast thunderstorm raged overhead as they passed like phantoms through the sleeping town. Morlan sneered at the melodic chiming of the city's many bells. Bell Farthing had many sanctuaries dedicated to the First One, and the gusty wind kept their bell towers busy.

In spite of the pelting rain, Morlan and Cythraul raced across the rolling green terrain, which was barren but for blemishes of black shrubs and tall upthrusts of stone called tors. At the edge of the province, within sight of the Hinterlands, stood Bell Farthing Manor, a triangular castle with three turrets and a massive sculpture of the key-like symbol of the First One.

Morlan and Cythraul came to the manor's immense doors, which were darkened by the rain and more than twenty feet tall. In spite of the early hour—three in the morning, if the bells could be trusted—Morlan banged on the doors.

Two guards opened the gate. One older, but hale and strong. The other, young and powerful, with crafty eyes peering out from a tuft of unruly dark hair.

"What business have you here at so late an hour?" the older guard asked.

"We seek an audience with Shepherd Draevan Zariac," Morlan said.

"That's your wish, sure enough," said the guard. "But what be yer business?"

Cythraul stepped forward. "For the sake of the late hour, I will forgive your impudence. But before you speak again, consider that it is King Morlan of Vulmarrow whom you address."

The young guard wiped the hair out of his eyes and blinked. "King Morlan?" he said. "Brother of the high king overlord?"

"I see now your golden eyes, King Morlan, and your sovereign ring," the older guard said. "Please forgive our hesitance. These are troubled times."

Morlan inclined his head slightly. "Draevan is wise to keep guards of such discernment. But it is due to these troubled times that I have come. Now won't you please bring us in out of the rain and conduct us to see Shepherd Draevan?"

The guards instantly moved aside and let Cythraul and King Morlan inside the castle.

They found themselves in a wide chamber lit by oil lanterns in its four corners and flanked by two curling stairways leading up to the next floor.

The young guard poured each of the guests a flagon of wine. "It's 2101, our best vintage."

"We'll see to Shepherd Zariac," the older guard said, "if m'lords would wait here. We won't be but a moment."

Morlan nodded as he sipped his wine. Cythraul wandered the perimeter of the room. There were all manner of works of art: paintings, sculptures, engravings, and etchings. They all depicted landscapes or some piece of nature: the moors, a mountain, Loch Feymist, a tree, or a bird in flight. And each one showed the effects of the wind. Clouds swept over the moors in a painting. The sculpture of a dark tree leaned as if caught in a storm. An etching of the loch showed low schooners racing. And hanging from the arched ceiling at various heights were a variety of intricate wind chimes. One of these directly over Morlan's head began to tinkle softly.

He turned and saw an olive-skinned woman at the top of the lefthand stair. Her silver hair was braided and tied back, and her eyes were large and gray. She wore a gown of many colors: blues and grays, soft oranges and golds, like a fall sky; and gossamer ribbons fluttered softly all along the material.

She lifted a hand, and the wind chimes became still. But her gown still seemed to undulate. "You have grave news, Morlan Stormgarden. Or you would not have come so far."

"My lady, worthy Shepherd Draevan, I do bear grave news. And I seek counsel."

"Ascend to me, Morlan, and we will speak."

Morlan approached the stairs and turned to the guards. "Do not give Cythraul too much wine. It has a profound affect on him." He laughed as he jogged up the stairs.

The two guards watched Cythraul take a sip of wine. No one else laughed.

Shepherd Draevan led Morlan to the northern side of the castle and onto a wide balcony that seemed much higher than possible because it overlooked Loch Feymist far below. She waved her hand, and the whistling wind overhead changed direction, blowing the rain away from the balcony.

"That's convenient," Morlan said.

Draevan smiled and gestured for him to sit on one of the three stone benches close to the balcony's rail. "Please sit. You will find the stone quite dry."

Morlan sat and looked down upon the loch. The racing clouds above had parted for just an instant, and moonlight painted sheets of rain a ghostly, shimmering silver and glimmered on the loch's dark water.

"Please, King Morlan," Draevan said, "what brings you to Bell Farthing?"

"I need your counsel."

"Counsel? Shepherd's Hollow is far closer to Vulmarrow."

"I need *your* counsel." He leaned forward. "Lady Shepherd, Myriad is at war with the Gorrack Nation. This, you know." She nodded. He went on. "The beasts dared to attack Vulmarrow just two weeks ago. It was a small force, a raiding crew, maybe sixty Gorracks, and yet even with half of my Wolfguard at our defense, we were barely able to repel them."

"I am sorry to learn of this," Draevan said. "The Gorracks have grown strong."

"At least one of them has. He was a Gorrack princeling, and he had the Shepherd gift."

"A Gorrack Shepherd? Impossible."

"I saw him with my own eyes. He controlled the winds...like you do."

Draevan shook her head. "That cannot be. History records no Gorrack as part of the Covenant. No Gorrack could possibly be in the Shepherd bloodline."

"And yet, he exists. We drove him off this time, but he may return with larger numbers to support him. I need to know what he can do, the extent of his powers."

"Look, King Morlan, I don't know how I can—"

"Shepherd Draevan, you are the only other Shepherd with power over the wind," Morlan said, leaning forward. "I need to know the extent of your gift. Can you call a storm to your aid?"

"No, only Mosteryn can call storms."

"But if one approaches, can you divert it?"

"I...well, yes, if it is a local storm, like this one," she said, gesturing overhead. "But I couldn't move a hurricane, a blizzard, or a ribbon storm."

"What about ships?" he asked. "Could you give wind to a fleet?"

"Perhaps," she said. "But I don't see how—"

"With your fiercest gale, could you topple a stronghold…like Vulmarrow Keep?"

"No, not with my fiercest gale, not unless the structure is already weak, ready to topple."

Morlan traced a finger along the ridge of his thin beard. Cythraul had given him a flesh-colored putty to hide the new scar on his cheek. It had been a wise move. "Thank you, Shepherd Draevan," Morlan said at last. "You have provided just the information I was hoping for."

She stared at him hard. Her eyes narrowed. "There was no Gorrack Shepherd, was there?"

Morlan crossed his arms, leaned back, and smiled. "Actually, there was. In a forgotten temple within Mount Gorthrandir. But, of course, his gift had nothing to do with wind."

Draevan held up her hands, and sudden gusts of wind pummeled the balcony.

There was a glint of steel and Morlan vanished.

Draevan cried out and arched her back.

Morlan appeared behind her with one arm around her neck. "The blade that I have pushed into your back is a very special implement. Cythraul calls it a spine cleaver."

Draevan struggled. The wind howled, but Morlan held his ground. "There is a channel running up the middle of the blade," he said. "So right now, your life rests between two shards of metal. If I twist, your back will break."

"You won't have it!" she screamed. "It is no longer a gift if you steal it!" There was a sudden flash of lightning and a deafening blast of thunder. From the sky above came such a powerful downburst of wind that it drove Draevan and Morlan hard into the balcony rail.

Morlan had to let her go to keep from toppling over. Draevan tried to spin off the blade, to throw herself over the rail, but Morlan reacted too quickly. He twisted the blade.

She fell limp and the wind stopped instantly.

Morlan had his feet up on the large table in Bell Farthing Manor. He chewed salted pork, sipped wine, and moved just enough air to make the candle flames flicker. He heard Cythraul's boots behind him. "Is it done then?" Morlan asked.

"As you commanded," Cythraul said. "No one will ever find their bodies."

Morlan sighed and let his feet drop to the floor. "Thank you, my friend. Your talents truly are unmatched." He stood and joined Cythraul by the chamber door. He waved his hand, and every candle in the room blew out. As they left the empty castle, Morlan said, "As difficult as all this has been, I believe I dread the next stage more."

"Why is that?"

"There is no telling how long the conflict between Aravel and the Gorracks will take. Now we face the long wait."

CHAPTER 45

FLIGHT TO THE NIGHTWASH

Balroth swooped across the border into Fen and, unlike the great wyrms of old, he did not come to escape starvation. Addle, Wildbrook, and Ettindale burned to ash in his red flames. But Elrain Alriand stood undaunted at the Bryngate.

With his bladed sling, Elrain tore such a shard from Balroth's wing that the wyrm could not fly. Elrain tracked the beast into the Hemlock Barrens on the outskirts of the Hinterlands. And there Elrain clove the dragon's skull.

From *Wyrmlore* by Pyralis Mar, the Dragon Bard

16 DRINNAS 2212

Alastair felt the prick of the pike, but...that was all. Miraculously given a second chance, Alastair spun around with his blade and would have beheaded the Gorrack behind him, except that the Gorrack had already lost its head.

King Ealden wiped one of his glaive's blades on the Gorrack's leather jerkin. "Venescence," Ealden said. A host of his Prydian Wayfolk kin marched behind him. "It seems you took on one too many."

"Very true," Alastair said, holding out his hand. "Thank the First One you came along."

A gladsome look on his face, King Ealden shook Alastair's hand. "It is to Him that credit is due," the king said. "Don't you agree?"

Alastair found it hard to meet the king's eyes. "Most of the time."

King Ealden's eyes narrowed. "There is no 'most of the time.' If you belong to the First One, you must give glory to Him always."

Alastair nodded and smiled, but he wasn't quite sure whether King Ealden meant what he said as an encouragement or another criticism.

"Come, ally," King Ealden said, breaking the awkward moment, "we have a horde of Gorracks to drive toward the river!" Glaive whirling in his hands, the Prydian ruler raced away.

Alastair followed, rubbing at the sore spot on his back .

Before they could get very far, a shadow passed overhead. King Drüst and three Windborne soldiers landed before them. "You have pushed too far to the east," he said. "The Gorracks are racing back west toward their own border."

"Can we circle back in time?" King Ealden asked.

"To stop them from crossing into their homeland, yes. Aravel and the Anglish Guard are already closing on them, but you must hurry if you are to offer aid."

"What about reinforcements?" Belliken/Alastair asked.

King Drüst raised an eyebrow. "Many thousands of reinforcements have departed Lichbyrn Cleff, their capital city, but you have at least a fortnight before they come into play. Lead your men now. Lead them swiftly."

King Drüst looked directly at Alastair then. "However naïve you may be in some areas of knowledge, your plan of attack is strong. Follow it through." The Windborne king gave Alastair something of a nod and then he and his countrymen took to the air once more.

Belliken/Alastair and King Ealden led the Wayfolk soldiers west. They ran hard for hours, and the longer they ran, the more they began to understand a flaw in their plan.

The sun was setting. Darkness would embolden the Gorracks and quicken their thick hearts. When Alastair, Ealden, and the Prydian forces finally met up with the Anglish Army, King Aravel had reached the same conclusion.

"We must push our advantage now, while it lasts," the high king said. "The Windborne report that Navrill is in position in the Nightwash. We've got to use our superior numbers to force them south." He looked up through the trees at the crimson sky. "Nightfall will multiply their savagery."

"Lord Aravel," Ealden said, "how many of your men have war horns?"

"All of my generals, captains, and infantry commanders. I'd say a hundred men."

"Good, very good," Ealden said.

Alastair caught on right away. "Yes, yes, have them give blast after blast with those horns the moment we set upon them."

"It is not much," Ealden said, "but in the darkness, the report of those horns will confuse them, make our numbers seem more than they are."

The combined forces of Myriad moved swiftly through the southern Felhaunt. Their speed would have served them well if their opponents had continued to flee. But the Gorracks had ceased from their sprint to the border and now turned to fight. They slammed into the Wayfolk ranks like a rogue wave on a calm sea.

"Steady!" King Ealden yelled just before a Gorrack hammer knocked him off his feet. He fell into a wide oak and disappeared into the dense ferns at its feet.

He was not the only soldier to fall. In an instant, the Prydian and Anglish armies lost more men than they had in all the day's previous fighting.

King Aravel saw better in the dark. He dodged potentially lethal pike-thrusts and axe-swipes. He plunged his sword into a Gorrack, wheeled his horse about, and searched for Sebastian. The Shepherd was nowhere near, and Aravel felt their strategies unraveling. "Horns!" he yelled. "We must have them now!"

War horns began to ripple from the ranks behind them to the north. Aravel saw his new general, Belliken, speeding between the trees among his people like a ghost knight. And wherever he rode, the horns blared. *He understands,* King Aravel thought. *He's doing it!* They were intermittent blasts at first. But soon the horns coordinated and their triumphant song rang out, filling the Felhaunt with the report of imminent victory.

The sound emboldened the Anglish and Prydian forces, and they drove into the coming Gorracks. For a moment, the enemy ranks foundered, and Aravel's forces cut a deep swath through the middle of the Gorrack army. The horns continued, and some of the Gorracks did indeed become confused. They ran about searching for their own commanders, looking for direction.

The advantage was short-lived. The sun fell at last below the horizon.

"Come, my lord, to your feet," Shepherd Sebastian urged. "The horns sound! We must find Aravel." He took the Prydian's fist and pulled.

"Ah!" King Ealden winced and pulled his hand away. "Not that arm. Please! Blasted Gorrack hit me smart with a hammer."

Sebastian took the king's left hand and helped him stand. "How bad is it?"

"Dislocated, I believe."

"I can help with the pain. Let me fetch my staff—"

"No need," Ealden said. "But I do need your help. Take my wrist and my elbow, keep them steady. Be completely firm."

Sebastian did as he was told.

"Now, lift the arm and elbow. Yes, there!" With Sebastian holding his wrist and elbow, Ealden leaned forward and twisted at the hip. There was a wet, crackling noise, and Ealden gasped. Then he pulled his arm away and rolled his shoulder. "Ah, now, that is much better."

Sebastian squinted. "I don't know how you can bear that."

"It's just pain," Ealden said. "Come, let's find Aravel."

The Gorracks became otherworldly in the darkness. They forced the Myridian army to fall back all the way to the clearing. But there, something strange happened: the Gorracks did not pursue. In fact, they withdrew to the south.

King Aravel was puzzled. "Their strength waxes. They force us backward. We are almost done for. And yet they give up the advantage? What do you say, Ealden? Do we pursue?"

Anger burned in the Prydian ruler's eyes, but he shook his head. "As much as I yearn to ride on, there is much we can do with this gift of time. We must regroup and see to our wounded. There are many, and they will not survive without care."

King Aravel turned. "Sebastian?"

"Ealden is right, my lord. And we must wait for Drüst to return with news."

King Aravel slammed his fist against a serpentwood tree. "How foolish to hope that we would win through before nightfall."

"Your majesty, if I may?" said Belliken/Alastair.

King Aravel nodded.

"We may yet have many days of fighting, but we are winning. Prince Navrill is in place. And we still outnumber the enemy at least three to one. So long as they gain no reinforcements, they cannot hope to last. If they do not fight at night when they are strongest, it is to our advantage. We have only to wait until daylight to resume our attack."

"A battle of attrition," Aravel muttered. "That is what you mean. Alas, I had hoped for better."

Drüst did not appear the following morning, but close to a thousand Windborne did. They bore no news of the Gorracks, why they hadn't pursued the night before, or where they had gone. But they had brought strong salves and medicines, food, and other supplies. And when they were unburdened of their provisions, the Windborne took all of the wounded and bore them back to Llanfair.

Not wanting to waste any more daylight, Aravel gave the order for the army, now diminished to sixty thousand, to forge ahead back under the eaves of the Felhaunt.

For all that day and into the night, they followed the Gorracks' trail of wreckage. They found tales of battle. Vang and the forces of Tryllium had been there, for they found his men among the dead. Aravel thought surely it had been Vang who had drawn the Gorracks off the previous night. But still, there was no sign at all of the army of Ellador. Aravel feared that another army of Gorracks had waylaid Briawynn.

If that was so, he knew Anglinore might be in danger as well. The thought spurred Aravel on to finish the job here. So he commanded his troops to follow hard after the enemy. And they did, heedless of the darkness, but found no living Gorracks. The next morning, Aravel ordered his troops to halt and take brief provisions.

An hour later, King Drüst descended so suddenly that King Aravel spat a mouthful of beef into the fire. "Drüst!" the king said, "where have you been?"

"I followed a hunch and looked in on Morlan in Vulmarrow."

"Blast it, Drüst," Aravel said, "we need news of the Gorracks, not Morlan!"

"With all due respect, High Overlord, he is your brother."

Aravel bowed his head and expelled a deep breath. "What of him, then?"

"It seems I was wrong. Vulmarrow is in flames," Drüst said. "But it was not a rout. Morlan's Wolfguard took a hefty bite out of the invaders. Vulmarrow Keep still stands, but the battle was not without cost. Shepherd Alfex perished."

"That is dark news," Sebastian said.

"So I thought as well," said Drüst.

"What of Briawynn and Ellador?" King Aravel asked.

"She arrived in Vulmarrow just before I departed. She had heard of the assault on Vulmarrow and wanted to make sure the enemy did not press on to Anglinore unhindered."

"Ah, brilliant!" Aravel said. "I should have guessed. She defeated the Gorrack remnant from Vulmarrow then?"

"That is the odd thing," said Drüst. "Briawynn saw no sign of Gorracks heading east. I was wary of my time, but I searched as I could and likewise found nothing. It is as if they vanished…or went belowground."

Aravel pondered this long. "Did you divert Briawynn north?"

"Yes," Drüst said. "She will arrive in three days. But that should prove perfect timing, for Vang has nearly drawn the Gorracks to the Nightwash where Navrill waits. If you hurry, you will all arrive at the river at the same time, and the Gorracks will have no chance."

The Gorracks were down to a scant twenty thousand soldiers when Aravel's forces came upon them just a few miles from the Nightwash river. But the dense tree canopy blocked much of the sun, and the enraged Gorracks had inflicted heavy losses on Vang's armies.

"Now for it!" Aravel commanded his men. "The last push!" The king had been unhorsed once more and plunged forward on foot. Sebastian flanked him on one side, Belliken/Alastair on the other. Wielding his fierce glaive, King Ealden led the Wayfolk to the southwest, cutting off any Gorrack escape.

But the Gorracks did not have escape on their minds. They fought brutally, hammering away at men and Wayfolk alike. Even their wounded fought on until left immobile or killed. They inflicted heavy casualties on the oncoming enemy, but still they could not stop the inevitable.

After three hours of fighting, with the sun plummeting toward the western horizon, the Gorracks found their backs against the Nightwash River. And that was when their worst nightmares came to life. For it seemed to them that the river had given birth to an army of water beings who splashed up the bank behind them. There were suddenly four or five of these creatures for each Gorrack, and they dragged their victims back into the river.

"Prince Navrill and the Marinaens!" King Aravel exulted. "We have the enemy now!"

Where energy had been all but depleted, the Anglish Army became rejuvinated and drove the enemy backward, closer and closer to the river.

Alastair watched a Gorrack struggle briefly against a triad of Marinaen warriors. One of them clamped a webbed hand over the Gorrack's mouth and nose. Another drove a barbed spear-like weapon into the Gorrack's midsection. And the third dragged something that looked like a bird-of-prey talon across the back of the Gorrack's legs. The heavy Gorrack fell backward into the river. "First One, have mercy," muttered Alastair.

"On the Gorracks?" King Ealden approached on Belliken/ Alastair's left side. "It is too late for them. They have followed their false gods for generations and now have raised their fists against the people of the First One. There is nothing but judgment for them. Judgment and wrath."

Queen Briawynn and a massive army from Ellador arrived too late to do anything but tend to the wounded. The Gorracks had been wiped out. Prince Navrill's Marinaen Army had been as lethally efficient in water as he'd promised. And any who had escaped the water had been run down by Vang on the southern side and Aravel to the north.

Gathered now in a massive tent was a royal party indeed. King Aravel, King Ealden, Queen Briawynn, Queen Fleut, King Vang, King Drüst, and Queen Savron assembled around a makeshift table of tree stumps and planks covered with tanned leather. Shepherds, generals, and other military leaders were there as well. The maps and charts spread before them offered no answers. All eyes lingered on King Aravel.

At last, King Ealden asked the question on everyone's mind. "Will we follow through? Will we invade the Gorrack Nation and push for complete victory?"

"We 'ave surely dealt them a mortal blow," King Vang said. "Why wouldn't we pursue?"

"For precisely that reason," Briawynn said. "Twice now we have turned back their efforts. And unless the Windborne estimate is far wrong, the Gorracks have lost a third of their army. They must surrender."

"They will not surrender," Aravel said, rubbing his temples. "Tarq would rather see his race extinct from the face of Myriad than surrender to us. We are godless vermin to him."

"Ironic," said King Ealden.

"What then?" asked Queen Savron.

Queen Fleut removed her eyeglass and said, "If they will not surrender…"

King Aravel sighed. "We can no longer wait until the Gorracks cross the border. We cannot allow Tarq to scar our own land with war. We will invade the Gorrack Nation. We will destroy every city, every village, until we collapse the walls of the Gorrack capital city itself."

CHAPTER 46

LETTERS IN WAR

42 Marne 2212
Dear Belliken,
You've only been gone for a few months, but so much has happened. A man came to Anglinore, and I am quite sure he was searching for you. He claimed to be Banther, your older brother. I was very suspicious of him and told him nothing of any use. But later that night, he broke into my chamber. I am terrified to think of what he might have done, but my Uncle Jak came and struck him so full a blow with his hammer that this Banther sailed out of the window and fell to his death.

Unfortunately, the story does not end there. His body disappeared, and two men here were killed. It's as if he came back to life. Queen Maren and Uncle Jak call me foolish for saying such things, but I don't know what to think. In any case, this Banther has not returned, and Queen Maren has given me an incredible interior chamber. She has also tripled the guards in every area of the castle.

Telwyn has grown so much. I think we both have—since we're being fed so well. He's so responsive to me now laughing with me and mimicking the faces I make at him. Just this morning, he pulled up on an end table...and promptly slipped off. All that work and just a banged chin for the effort. But you know what he did as soon as I put him back on the floor? He went back to the table and pulled himself up again. He reminds me of you in that way, Alastair. He never seems to give up.

Uncle Jak tells me that King Aravel's forces are driving toward the Felhaunt. I'm afraid for you. That is a terrible place, even without Gorracks.

I pray for you often. In fact, Queen Maren and I meet in Clarissant Hall every morning to pray. It feels strange to pray. I pour out my heart until I feel it breaking, and then I listen...sometimes for hours. And yet, there is nothing in return. I wonder what it must have been like before the Silence. How wonderful it must have been to hear the First One speak.

Your faithful Abbagael

P.S. If you don't love me yet, I'm quite sure you will soon.

16 Solmonath 2213

Dearest Abbagael,

It seems impossible that so many months have passed since last I wrote. Forgive me for not writing sooner. I have read and reread your first letter so many times that the parchment upon which it is written has nearly become shredded.

I am troubled by the attempt on your life. Thank the First One ten thousand times for the timing of your Uncle Jak. I trust that Queen Maren has you and Tel under lock and key and heavy guard.

And as for this charlatan who claimed to be my brother, well, rest assured, I am an only child. If this "Banther" fellow yet lives, I will hunt him down and take from him what the fall could not. King Aravel assures me that the castle's security will maintain your safety. I pray that it is so. And what of Telwyn? He should be walking and talking by now. What nonsense has he gotten himself into? I find myself thinking of you both often.

You've no doubt heard of our victory in the Felhaunt. That was a harrowing adventure indeed, but we prevailed. Since then, King Aravel has led us into the Gorrack Nation. If you could only see an army of seventy thousand warriors on the move! Ten thousand cavalry on everything from horses to ramsteeds and Elladorian panthers! Once the sun shone down upon us all, gleaming off so many shields and blades. It was breathtaking. I do not love war. Truly, I wish it could end today and I could return to you this very night. But there is something inspiring about seeing so many warriors marching under one banner to defeat a common enemy. And we are winning, Abbagael. The Gorracks are vicious, but they fall before us like kindling wood under an axe. King Aravel pushes us from one city to the next, and we are systematically wiping out every military settlement. It almost seems too easy.

There is one final thing to mention. A great victory—though not on the battlefield. It was two nights ago. A soldier whom I will not name gave me a skin to drink from. It was Witchdrale. And Abbagael, I did not drink it. By the hand of the First One, I crushed the demon this one time. Please pray that there will be many more victories to come.

Belliken

10 Octale 2213

Dear Belliken,

I am so relieved to hear back from you. After all this time, I am afraid it is all too easy to fear the worst. I am glad for all the victories over the Gorracks, but not knowing if at any moment some great peril may befall you—that gnaws at my nerves. I try not to think in such terms, but late at night I have the most horrible visions run through my mind. A blade, a shaft, a fall...so much can go wrong. I know the First One has given you rare skill, but please...fight well, and do nothing foolish. You have much to live for.

Telwyn is two years old as near as I can tell. He is walking quite well and running a little too much for my wants. I'm chagrinned to admit his first spoken word was "father." All the time I've been alone with him—feeding him, changing his diapers, holding him, and playing with him, and still his first word is "father." Let that speak to you. It seemed to me in our time together that you felt you could never be a father, but you took this boy in. You defended him—kept him safe. And he thinks of you.

I feel terrible for Queen Maren and King Aravel. She lost the child she carried. It was a dark time for her, but she has come out of it somewhat. She likes to take Telwyn for walks in the garden courtyard. It snowed here once, and that seemed to cheer her mightily. She told me stories of her youth and how she loved the snow. She told of how King Aravel courted her. I wonder if we'll be able to tell such stories.

Abbagael and Tel

P.S. I am certain you must love me by now.

1 Atervast 2214

Dearest Abbagael,

I am so encouraged to hear of your safety…and of Telwyn. I wish I could be there for both of you. Take him fishing for me, would you? Show him how to bait a hook. Give him chores to do. He'll be stronger for it. Alas, I cannot say when I will return.

Things here have taken a turn for the worse. Twice now, our approaches to the Gorrack capital city have been turned back by tens of thousands of Gorrack raiders. They have flying beasts too—creatures bat-like and yet feline as well. They dive at us and force us to take cover at the worst possible moments, and they harass the Windborne and make it difficult, nay, impossible at times, for King Drüst and his kin to aid with our wounded…or bear us news.

That is, in part, why I have not been able to deliver you any new message until now. And the weather has delayed us even more. There is snow and ice now, not the delightful kind you spoke of, but rather miserable sooty snow that renders the terrain treacherous. At least the Gorracks are not fond of snow either. That is some comfort.

If I understand your last message correctly, then Telwyn must be close to four by now. I fear I am missing so much. And King Aravel feels the loss even more keenly. He wonders if he could have been at Anglinore, if maybe the child might have been spared. The loss of life here he feels so keenly, as if every single ally to perish is his sole responsibility. Such is the lot of the high king, I know, but it is a terrible burden…even to watch.

As time passes, I have had a recurring thought. And while I selfishly do not want to voice it to you, I feel I must. Often you have pledged your heart to me, but should that change while I am gone… should you find another…some Anglish knight who wins your love, then do not be burdened by memories and old feelings. I give you leave to go where your heart must go.

Belliken

7 Sedwyn 2216
Dearest Belliken,
We feel so helpless here in Anglinore, so far away from all of you. You will be victorious, I have no doubt, and I beseech the First One to that end. I am glad that King Ealden and the Prydian Wayfolk are there. Queen Maren tells me that, even as the world has changed around them, they have not forsaken the old ways. They study the Books of Lore from the earliest age. Of all the races of Myriad, they seem to be the most faithful. Perhaps it is because they are the longest lived? Their memories are long. And they cling to the prophecy of the coming Halfainin. I don't know if I believe all the stories in those old books, but I find myself wanting to.

Tel is five now and growing like an Elladorian oak. I did take him fishing. In fact, it has become one of his favorite pastimes. He caught a ten pound spotfish right out of the Dark Sea and drew it all the way to shore by himself. Strong lad, he is. Takes after his father. Speaking of the Books of Lore, I've been reading them to Tel. He is fascinated by the stories. In the past few months, his own reading skills have developed so much that he can read the books on his own. He is especially fond of Canticles. Ah, he is such a wonderful child. Polite, kind, strong, and wise.

And all that nonsense about me finding another besides you—no chance. No chance at all. I would not give my heart to someone else even if this war takes twenty years. And I won't give up on you, unless you return from this war and tell me you don't love me. But you won't tell me that. I know—even though you won't say it yet—that you love me even now.

Abbagael
P.S. I thought you might enjoy hearing from Tel yourself. So read on. Your son has written you a note.

Dear Mi-Da,

I am Telwyn. Do you remember me? Mi-Ma tells me you rescued me from very bad people and you changed my diapers. Thank you. I caught a very big fish. Queen Maren had the castle cooks make dinner out of that big fish. Did you know she's a real queen? She wants me to call her Grand Mi-Ma, but she's too pretty to be a Grand Mi-Ma. She's not as pretty as Mi-Ma though. When are you going to marry Mi-Ma?

Love and Honor,

Telwyn

43 Avril 2217

Dearest Abbagael,

So much has changed. Where once victory seemed assured, we have now been pushed back near twenty leagues from the Gorrack capital city. We've suffered terrible losses. King Vang and Queen Fleut fell in an ambush, and our number is whittled down life-by-life, near to fifty thousand. And I am grieved to report that, in our sudden retreat, Hagen Kurtz and his wife Darrow were captured and slain. We have made the Gorracks pay dearly, but their numbers do not seem to be depleted.

The rivers here have run dry in the summer heat, and so Prince Navrill and the Marinaens have not been able to aid us. Despair falls over us like a cloud. I don't know how to explain it. It is more than our losses. It is more than the heat. A shadow lies upon us. King Aravel is beside himself with rage and regret. He has spoken even of calling on the Shepherd Council, but they are a last resort.

The only light I've had is the letter you sent last. It was so good to read about Telwyn. You've done well to teach him to read and write at so young an age. Please tell him that I will come home one day, and he can show me how to catch the biggest fish.

Now, Abbagael, please do not share this with Telwyn. But I swore I would never deceive you again. The night we lost King Vang and Queen Fleut was a nightmare. We'd been driven like cattle into a ravine, and the Gorracks loosed landslides against us. I saw men…my friends…smashed right in front of me. I have seen death in all of its dark forms, but there was something so barbaric about the boulders—like we were just insects that might be crushed with rocks! We lost a thousand men before we clawed our way out of that ravine. Bloodrift, we have named it.

That night, Abbagael, I heard the whispers. I could not drive them from my mind. And I drank Witchdrale. I remember very little of what happened, but I am told that Hagen Kurtz saved my life. First he took my sword away and then the bottle. I have not touched the brew since, but I dwell in a house of shame. How could I…after all that has happened? Ah, it is maddening!

Tomorrow we will march once more for the capital city. I fear it will be like waves breaking on the side of a cliff. Perhaps, given enough time, the waves will prevail.

Belliken

12 Marne 2218

Dearest Belliken,

All of Anglinore mourns with you for King Vang, Queen Fleut, and the thousands of other men and women who have now fallen to the Gorracks. But don't you see? That is why you must be victorious. For our entire lives, the threat of the Gorrack Nation has hung over us. You must end it for good and all.

And listen to me, shame is no place to dwell. It is a sinking mire! You drank the Witchdrale. You paid the price for it. Shame will only drag you back to that bottle. Cling to the First One through this! Cling to me, cling to Tel! We love you. We love you with a desperation I cannot put into words. Leave the past where it belongs and allow seeds of hope to bloom. Trust that it will not always be this hard. Better days are coming.

You wrote your letter in Avrill, and it is already Marne. I can only imagine that your attack on the Gorrack capital has already begun. Perhaps it is over and the enemy is conquered at last. I long for you to return. I enjoy my walks and prayer time with Queen Maren. She is dear to me—and to Tel—but there is still an emptiness as conspicuous as a dragon in the kitchen. I know Maren feels it too for Aravel. Would that the First One would end this war.

I end this letter with the most amazing thing I have ever experienced. About a week ago, I took Tel to the garden courtyard. Queen Maren could not join us that day, so it was just the two of us. I was weaving a tapestry, and Telwyn wandered off. He's seven now and has proven himself responsible, so I thought nothing of it. He likes to explore and plays as if he's discovered a new world. Often he brings me back flowers.

But this day, he had lingered beyond my view for quite some time, and I was engrossed in the tapestry. It was just past noon when a shadow passed overhead. I looked up and saw just a glimpse of white wings. I knew enough to recognize that it was not one of the Windborne. But before I could crystallize my thoughts, I heard the roar, and it froze my blood. It was something ferocious and raw and reminded me of a fennigator. I flew from my bench and screamed for

Telwyn. He did not answer, and I sprinted along all of the normal paths searching.

I found Telwyn at last near the Fountain of the First One, what those in Anglinore call the Key Fountain. I froze in my spot. Not three feet from Telwyn was a snow drake! It was not mature, but was still three times as big as Tel. I drew a dagger and stepped toward the creature, and it growled at me, baring its saber-like lower teeth. I was not going to let this thing hurt my son, so I stepped forward.

But Telwyn held up his hand. "Please stay back for a moment," he said. Those were his very words, Belliken. And then Tel put his hand on the creature's snout, and it purred. It purred! Then it nuzzled Telwyn's chin and licked him. "It's okay now, Mother," Telwyn said. Guards came running in next. They had seen the creature overhead and feared for anyone in the garden. When they arrived, they found the snow drake on its back with Telwyn scratching its stomach. He calls it Icetooth, or Icy for short.

Belliken, I've never seen anything like it. The guards tell me there hasn't been a snow drake in Anglinore for over an age. It is a sign of a hard winter, they said.

I enclose this letter with a kiss. Surely you must love me by now.

Abbagael

CHAPTER 47

WINTER'S HAND

Chronologists have been searching the skies for ages, seeking the legendary Sword in the Stars. But to this day it has not been seen. Shepherd Fulham claimed to have seen it once during a shower of shooting stars. That led to the Great Hunt of 1515 A.S. And that colossal waste of time in turn led to Shepherd Fulham being banished from Shepherd's Hollow to live in a shack in the woods.
Thurber's Almanac, Winter 2014 AS

25 ADVENT 2218

Abbagael received the letter from the Windborne messenger. He shook the snow off his wings and looked at her strangely.

"Is there something more?" she asked him.

"Nay, m'lady," he replied. "Not from me. But you should go inside. The weather is worsening."

And so it was. The snow had begun three days earlier, but now it was falling at a ridiculous pace. Abbagael took the letter back to her chamber and sat down on her bed. She wondered absently where Tel had gotten to. *Playing with Icy in the snow, perhaps?* She shrugged and opened the letter.

So short! she thought with dismay. Only one extended paragraph of Alastair's flowing script on the parchment. With a deep sigh, she began to read.

25 Advent 2218

Dearest Abbagael,

At last we have a measure of success. We have taken Karchet, a Gorrack stronghold east of their capital city. It is a strategic victory, cutting the enemy off from supplies and armaments. But alas! We cannot pursue them any farther. The snow has put an end to our march. I was alive during the Shadow Winter of 2160, when the snow blotted out the sun, but I have never seen anything like this. Three, four, even five inches of snow falls each hour. The entire landscape of the Gorrack Nation is pristine white. The enemy is under siege in its capital city, but not from us. The snow will keep them digging for a month and keep them from mounting any kind of offensive for longer than that. Even their flying beasts will not take to the air. King Aravel was at first frustrated by this sudden stalling, but now he calls it a gift. For while the enemy has no way to fly, our Windborne are more than adept at soaring in the snowy skies. So you see. It is a gift. You do see, don't you? Why do you still gaze at the letter? Look up, sweet Abbagael.

Abbagael looked up from the letter, and there, standing in the doorway of her chamber stood Telwyn, grinning as if Daribel had given him all the cookies in her kitchen. But standing tall next to the lad was a lanky, dark-haired man with a full black beard flecked with snow.

"Alastair," she whispered, rising slowly from the bed. "I mean Belliken! I'm always forgetting!" She dove into his arms. "First One be praised…you, you're—"

He lifted her chin and kissed her. He kissed her as if contact with Abbagael was life itself.

How long he would have kissed her was anyone's guess, but after several minutes, young Telwyn cleared his throat audibly. Getting no reaction, he tapped Alastair on the arm. "Hello, Mi-Da?"

Alastair finally let their lips part, but before Abbagael could speak a word, he said, "Lady Abbagael, I believe you are a prophetess."

She looked at him sideways, happy but curious still. "I don't know what you mean."

"Truly? Perhaps the cold has hindered your thinking. Six years ago, you stood with me on the docks in Chapparel and foretold that I would love you. As a matter of fact, you restated this divine prediction in every letter you sent to me." Alastair went silent and beamed at her.

"And?"

He led her by the hand to sit on the edge of the bed. Bright-eyed Telwyn padded to the foot of the bed and waited.

"Warfare is a bitter, arduous thing. But there are often great lulls, time with nothing to do but think. I thought often of love and what it might mean to say 'I love you.' If it boiled down to simple attraction, then I could have told you I loved you back in Chapparel. Oft I looked at you and was undone, laid low by the hand-spun copper of your hair, curled like ribbons…and, and your tiger-striped feather brows and pristine, sparkling green eyes—ah! Every freckle on your cheek or the bridge of your nose is an alluring treasure to me. So if love were just attraction, then it has always been there."

She blinked and her smile became unsure. "But Alastair…"

"But love is more than that. I think I always suspected so. But I had to know. So I spent many hours thinking about who you are. I discovered this very strong woman, one who would risk her life for an anonymous cry of help, one who would sacrifice everything to raise a small child—even alone. I found one who was willing to let me go…to do what I needed to do—even though it might cost you. I found one who...who could forgive the unforgivable." Alastair shook his head and wiped his eyes. "That was the hardest thing, Lady Abbagael, the hardest thing...I don't deserve your forgiveness."

She lifted his chin with her fingertips. "But you have it."

Tears dropped into his beard. "It is a gift, my lady. A gift. You have helped me to understand what love actually is." He paused and looked into her sparkling green eyes. "And now that I understand, I can say to you, Abbagael Rivynfleur, I do love you."

She stared back, searching his face and waiting. He seemed to reflect a moment as if he had more to say.

"Abbagael, this snow will not last forever. The sun will burn bright once more, the trumpets will sound, and I will have to return to the fighting." Alastair slid off the bed to one knee. "I cannot risk delay. So I come bearing a question: Lady Abbagael, would you be...would you consider...if you will have me..."

Abbagael slammed a kiss into him with such force that Alastair nearly fell over backward. She drew him to his feet and held his face.

Telwyn's eyes grew wide. "Whoa," he said, and then he clapped.

In between a barrage of kisses, Alastair said, "I take that as a yes."

"Yes, yes!" she said. "You brave, strong, fierce, foolish man... yes!"

Alastair turned his face sideways a bit and looked at the boy. "Tel, now."

Grinning and bouncing, Telwyn handed Alastair a ring.

Alastair dropped once more to a knee and slid the ring on to Abbagael's finger. "The band is the purest Tryllium silver. The stone is a rare white diamond. This ring once belonged to my mother. I give it now to you."

King Ealden married Belliken/Alastair and Abbagael out in the garden courtyard...in the snow. They had only six guests—seven, if the snow drake could be counted. Uncle Jak gave Abbagael away. King Aravel and Queen Maren were there, of course. The queen was Abbagael's maid of honor. Hagen Kurtz was Alastair's best man. Telwyn was the swordbearer and presented the blade to King Ealden.

When Alastair and Abbagael knelt to receive the blessing of the First One, Hagen's wife, Darrow, sprinkled them both with strawberry blossoms. Icetooth ate a few of them before Telwyn gave him a soft whack on the snout.

So in the sight of the First One, kings and queens, and one snow drake, Alastair and Abbagael were married. Of course to all but Telwyn, the new couple were known as Lord and Lady Belliken Tolke.

And that is precisely what bothered King Aravel. For during the ceremony, right before the two kissed, there was a silent moment. Even King Aravel found himself caught up in the romance of that moment, watching them gaze longingly into each other's eyes. But then, Abbagael whispered something. If others heard it, they did not flinch. But Aravel heard.

She had called her new husband...Alastair.

I don't know, Sebastian," said the king, later that evening. "Everything about him seems noble and valiant. He's tactically brilliant and he's a terror on the battlefield. But he hides his name!"

"In these dark times," the Shepherd said, "a man might have good reason to hide his name."

"Ah, I know," said the king. "I don't know why I feel so troubled by this. I have this strange feeling... When I heard the name Alastair, I suddenly felt I should know him."

"Could it be he reminds you of Synic Keenblade?" asked Sebastian. "Belliken—Alastair—or whatever his real name is, certainly fights like Keenblade did. And the sword he wields, it is masterforged."

"That is true," said the king, "and yes, those details do make him more familiar. But there's something else. Something that worries me…"

"My lord, Aravel, I—"

"Sebastian!" cried the king, "just because we return to the castle you begin again with this 'lord' foolishness?"

"I apologize. *Aravel*, I suspect that something important lies beyond this question. There is a path to the answer, perhaps a path you have not considered."

"What path is that?" demanded the king.

"Ask him."

"Thank you, Sebastian. I knew I could count on you for profound, Shepherdly wisdom."

"I try to help however I can, my l— Aravel," the Shepherd replied with a grin.

King Aravel gazed from the tower window and watched the snow fall. "This snow cannot last. We will soon have to return to the Gorrack Nation…and the war. I must find out before we go back."

"That seems wise."

"But what if I do ask him, Sebastian? And what if I don't like the answer?"

Sebastian put his hand on the king's shoulder. "Aravel, you are a just man. I trust your judgments. But more than that, you are the high king overlord of this world. If this man, this Alastair, speaks the truth…you'll know what to do. But if he lies…then, there will be…a problem."

Guard high!" Alastair shouted. "Guard high! Once more. Good! Now strike!" He readied his onside block, dropping his blade into the imaginary slot where the blow would come.

But Telwyn spun off the block and slashed at Alastair's backside. He got out of the way, but just barely.

"Hey, whoa!" Alastair said, laughing. "You aren't allowed to do that!"

"Why not, Mi-Da?" Telwyn asked. "You told me to always look for a path to victory…to watch for the cues and take advantage. I saw you plant your back foot and shift your weight. I knew you would block onside, so…I took advantage."

"Ha!" Alastair said. "I think you just wanted to whack me in the rear end!" They shared a laugh, but Alastair was thoughtful. He'd been training seven-year-old Telwyn for two weeks, but in that time, the lad had absorbed years of learning. "Your reflexes are sharp," he said. "Your eye and your mind keen."

"Can I go to war with you then, Mi-Da?" Telwyn asked, looking up with earnest blue-eyed wonder.

Alastair nearly choked. "To *war?* Nay, son, you are yet too young to fight in this conflict. But please understand, I'm training you so that you can be ready should the day ever come. I just pray that such a day never comes in your lifetime."

"I think it will, Mi-Da." There was no fear in his expression. Just peace, as usual. Peace and curiosity.

"Belliken! I have news! Rare good news!" Abbagael ran from the door to the center of the fencing room. "I have just been with Queen Maren. She is expecting a child!"

"Pregnant?" Alastair laughed. "That is spectacular news, indeed!"

"Come, let us go to them!" Abbagael said, dragging Alastair and Telwyn by the hand.

They did not find the king and queen in the council chamber where Abbagael had last seen them. But after a search, they found them in Clarissant Hall.

"She insisted," King Aravel said with a shrug. He gestured to Queen Maren, who knelt at the chair where the old altar had been. Alastair and Abbagael leaned into one another and smiled.

"Have you already prayed?" Alastair asked the king.

"What, me?" King Aravel glanced nervously side-to-side. "Well… not exactly. I don't exactly go in for that kind of thing…not anymore."

"But surely with the good news today…" Abbagael suggested.

"Yes, you are right," King Aravel said. "And I *am* grateful. But, with all due respect for our friendship, I have to make clear that for every joy I've ever seen, I can point to a dozen tragedies. My mother, for whom this hall is named, would tan my hide if she heard me speak such things."

"What do you speak of, husband?" Queen Maren asked as she stood and took Aravel's arm.

"Ah, nothing to be concerned about," the king said. "Are you finished with your prayers?"

"Yes, yes, all finished," she replied, looking from Abbagael to Belliken/Alastair to Telwyn. "And I'm so glad you've come back. Isn't this exciting news?" She almost hopped.

"Oh, I am so happy for you both!" cheered Abbagael, matching the queen with a hop of her own.

Alastair looked at the king. He shrugged and beamed a massive smile.

"Would you like to know the names?" Queen Maren asked. "We've thought of both."

"Yes, please tell," said Abbagael.

"Well," she said, "if the child is a girl, we will call her Clarisse. If a boy…"

"Lochlan," finished the king.

"Glorious names!" Abbagael said with a clap. "Ah this is a splendid day! Shall we get some tea?"

And just like that, the queen and Abbagael were off, arm-in-arm, like sisters. Young Telwyn looked from the king back to Alastair. "Uh, Mi-Da, may I go play with Icetooth?"

Alastair nodded. "Go ahead, but no flying!"

Telwyn was gone in a shot, leaving the king and Alastair alone in Clarissant Hall.

Alastair bowed to the king and started to leave. "A moment, General."

"Yes?" Alastair said.

The king looked up at the stained glass windows and then back to Alastair. "You know, Belliken, the Windborne report movement in the Gorrack capital. The month of Alpheus is nearly spent, and Wenvier will be upon us soon. We will need to return to Karchet soon…to finish this war."

Alastair nodded. "I've seen the Windborne flights leaving by the hour with our troops. I…I've been trying to prepare myself for the time."

"You know, Belliken," the king said, eying Alastair closely, "Anglinore, nay, all of Myriad, is grateful for your leadership and valor. But before your field promotion, you had no obligation. You and Abbagael, you have a son to raise. You've done enough on the battlefield; you can remain if you wish it."

Alastair was dumbfounded. But he did not allow the shock and urgent hope to overcome what he knew was right. "A very wise man once told me, 'Faithless is he who says farewell when the road darkens.' I will see this fight through."

King Aravel found new respect for his general. "I thought you would say something like that. Very well then. We will return to the front in three days. Spend your time wisely."

Alastair said he would and began to walk away, but the king called out again. "One moment, Alastair."

Alastair stopped and turned around. "Yes, King Aravel?"

The king did not answer. His thoughts whirled. *He slipped up and didn't notice,* thought the king. *There can be no doubt. His real name is Alastair. But why? Now is the time to ask him. Now is the time to know.*

"My lord?" Alastair waited.

King Aravel looked up. "No…nothing," he said. "Another time."

CHAPTER 48

Stark Clarity

There are few things a man can count on. But one thing is certain.
Those who travel across the Dark Sea never come back.
High King Brysroth Stormgarden, 2043 AS

48 Solmas 2219

"The time has come!" Morlan announced from a balcony overlooking ten thousand soldiers, the elite of his Wolfguard assembled in the vast field beneath the arching boughs of the tall trees that surrounded Vulmarrow. "Our spies report that the ice and snow is melting in the Gorrack Nation. Their numbers dwindle. And though it may take months still, it is now a foregone conclusion that King Aravel and his forces will defeat the Gorracks."

Hisses of disapproval slithered through the Wolfguard.

Morlan drew his sword and raised it high. "This is victory for us all! Ending the Gorrack threat is long overdue, but at last, we will see the end of the Gorrack Nation!"

Cheers and great clamor rose.

"I charge you, Velach Krel," Morlan said, pointing his sword over the rail. "And I charge all of you to ride forward, to join the fray, and speed the inevitable end. Then march back in victory, all the way to the Naïthe. And there, on the very doorstep of Anglinore itself…the real victory will be won!"

The Wolfguard seemingly went mad as one, slamming blades on shields, pounding their marching drums, and screaming.

"Rage!" Morlan cried out.

"*Rage!*" the army responded.

"Vengeance!"

"*Vengeance!*"

"War!"

"*Warrrr!*"

Led by Velach Krel and the other generals, the Wolfguard streamed away from Vulmarrow.

"A rousing speech," Cythraul said when Morlan reentered the tower.

"Rousing, you say?" asked Morlan. "I am grateful you told me, for I can never tell by your expression."

Cythraul did not at first reply. He slipped silently around the room and glanced at the soldiers still filing into the trees. "I have some doubts," he said. "Ten thousand will travel to the Gorrack Nation and escort King Aravel to the Naïthe. You have thirty thousand troops in reserve, in the hidden bunkers within the catacombs. When the time is right, you will lead these against Aravel." Cythraul looked down at his hand and began to twist his silver ring. "Forgive me for asking this, but I have taken part in failed uprisings before. Are you certain you can defeat him, Morlan?"

"Cythraul, there is more at stake here than simple victory," King Morlan said. "Sabryne Shadowfinger has shown me how much more. When I ride out against my brother, I am assured of victory…of one kind or another."

"Even if Aravel kills you?"

"He won't. He doesn't have the stomach for it."

"But if he does?"

"Then I have underestimated my brother, and Anglinore will have a proper king." Morlan stared hard at Cythraul. "Now forgive me for asking a question of you. Given what you know of my plan and the potential consequences, are you willing to serve me?"

Cythraul did not hesitate. "I will serve you."

Morlan nodded. "Now, Cythraul, I will tell you the rest of my plan."

The two spoke until the moon began its long descent.

"Even if all goes awry," Morlan said at last, "preserve the black stone table. I will come back for it."

Alastair didn't much care for travel by windcarriage. Certainly it was preferable to the weeks-long journey to the Gorrack Nation by land or sea. A man-sized, aerodynamic tube constructed of lightweight metals and timber, the windcarriage was carried in flight by two Windborne soldiers. It was cramped for someone Alastair's size, and the ventilation/illumination tubes let in too much cold air. Worse still, Alastair felt guilty every time he went to the bathroom. After all, there was no way to see beneath the windcarriage, and it had to go somewhere.

Even by flight, the trip back to the Gorrack Nation was seventy-two hours, so Alastair had many hours to think. He spent some time looking at the new ring on his finger, feeling like his hand looked somehow more manly now. *And why not?* he thought. *I am married now, and not just to anyone.* He shook his head, thinking of Abbagael. Never in all his years had he thought he would have such joy. She was intelligent, wise, beautiful, and kind.

But there was something else. She had forgiven him. Not just for the incident in Gull'scry. But she'd forgiven him for all he'd done in Morlan's service. Somehow the burden that had weighed so heavily on his heart felt a little lighter because of her forgiveness.

"It is going to get a little bumpy!" came a deep voice from above. "Stormy weather ahead." It was one of his Windborne escorts, the one with red wings. Flan, they called him.

Bumpy…great, thought Alastair. *Just so long as they do not drop me.* He shook his head and went back to thinking about forgiveness.

Abbagael had every right to hate him—if not for being responsible for her parents' deaths, then for being a party to Morlan's murderous raids. And yet Abbagael gave up that right to blame, and she forgave him.

That led Alastair to think about the Halfainin. For it was ultimate forgiveness that Alastair sought. And only the Halfainin could provide it. Had Alastair somehow missed the coming of the Halfainin in Thel-Mizaret? King Ealden had said so, but it didn't seem possible. He'd tested all the potential heroes, and none of them had all of the characteristics. Some were expert marksmen, others were very strong or wise beyond their years. But none of them had tamed the dragon. None of them had swordcraft that could compete with Alastair's skill.

There was a possibility, one that discouraged Alastair mightily, but at least offered hope that the Halfainin might still be out there. *I might not be the Caller. But if I'm not the Caller, why did Yasmina think I was? Why did Synic Keenblade give me the Star Sword? Why did the sword appear in the stars and show me where to look?* It was maddening.

Whump! It felt like someone had hit the bottom of the windcarriage with a hammer. The whole contraption shook. *A little bumpy…right.* He went back to looking at his wedding ring. *But I'm not just a husband. I'm a father.* He thought of what a fine young man Telwyn was growing into. *As a matter of fact, I owe a lot to Tel. If it weren't for him, I'd have never involved myself with Abbagael. I'd have never gone to Gull'scry and ended up defending Chapparel. I'd have never been enlisted by King Aravel and given a chance to fight for Myriad rather than against it.*

Alastair thought back to the day Telwyn had entered his life, and he shook his head. He'd been so influenced by the Witchdrale that he couldn't even find his way home. *Wait a moment…*

Whump! This time the sharp blow was to the ceiling of the wind-carriage. But it had not come from stormy air outside. It had been Alastair's head striking the ceiling as he suddenly tried to sit up.

"Are you okay down there?" asked Flan.

"Fine, fine!" Alastair yelled back, rubbing the welt on his head. He struggled to remember. "C'mon, Alastair, think!"

He thought back to that day, suddenly urgent. He remembered the sun in his eyes. He remembered the noise of the horse charging up. He remembered the woman's face. But what direction had she come from? Was it east? It could have been. *No,* thought Alastair, *it definitely was east. Telwyn's mother had been chased from Thel-Mizaret by Morlan's Wolfguard.*

Could it...be?

He will be a bringer of peace. *Anyone who held Telwyn immediately felt calm. I remembered the way home.*

He will be wise beyond his years. *Telwyn was reading Canticles before age five and writing.*

He will be keen of eye, and his sword will be swift. *Telwyn saw my moves before I did them. He nearly crowned me, and he's only a child.*

He will tame beasts with a touch. *First the rooks in Willow Dell. They should have hurt Telwyn, but he drove them into the walls. And now the snow drake. He has tamed a dragon!*

Alastair shook his head. He'd misunderstood the prophecies all along. The Halfainin would be a conquering hero...just not at first.

The Halfainin had come as a child.

Whump! Alastair banged his head on the ceiling again. "That means...I am the Caller...after all!" Alastair rubbed his head and laughed. Then he laughed some more. Soon he was laughing like a lunatic.

"What's going on with you down there?" Flan called.

"I'm fine!" Alastair cried out. "Better than fine. I am...I am marvelous."

CHAPTER 49

Porous Defense

Without clear knowledge of the truth, there can be no justice.
Shepherd Traudain Kromel

2 Feftin 2219

The warming temperatures and thawing ice and snow had brought King Aravel and his armies victory after victory. Replenished lakes and trickling streams turned into coursing rivers that gave the Marinaens the environment they needed to devastate Gorrack reinforcements. Within a few months, the forces of Myriad had pushed all the way back to the Gorrack capital city.

King Aravel knew victory was at hand, but as the sun fell behind the mountains, he commanded his armies to make camp. He would not press into the city yet, not at night.

And there were other concerns besides the Gorracks.

King Aravel sat behind a table in his command tent. He was flanked on one side by King Ealden, and Shepherd Sebastian sat on the other.

A guard lifted the tent flap and leaned in. "General Tolke is here to see you, m'lord," he said, "as you commanded."

"See him in," King Aravel said.

Belliken/Alastair stepped into the tent and met silence and stern expressions. King Aravel, who usually kept a slight smile and a joke at the ready, looked worried—even grieved. Sebastian Sternbough appeared grim and thoughtful. But worst of all was King Ealden. The eyes of the man who had presided over his wedding to Abbagael were now heavy with judgment. It was as if every doubt Alastair had ever had about himself, every knife of guilt and condemnation he'd ever felt, were all present in Ealden's stare. Alastair could barely endure it.

"You wanted to see me, Your Majesty?"

"Yes, Belliken," King Aravel said. "Please come forward. There is a matter we need to discuss."

Alastair strode several paces until he was directly in front of the king's table. Something close to despair dried his mouth and made it hard to swallow. He'd seen King Ealden's hand move slowly to the glaive on his belt.

"Belliken, place your sword on this table."

It was not a request, and Alastair thought he knew what this was all about. He drew his sword and placed it lengthwise on the table. "Will it be hanging, then, or a traitor's pyre?"

King Aravel did not answer. He scrutinized the weapon from tip to pommel and then looked to Ealden and the Shepherd in turn. Each nodded, and all eyes went back to Alastair. "This is the Star Sword," King Aravel said, "discovered long ago by Synic Keenblade."

Alastair nodded. "Synic taught me swordcraft when I was very young. He gave me the blade."

"You told me it had been stolen," King Ealden hissed. "That you recovered it. But it was you who stole it."

Alastair could barely will himself to speak. "No…Synic gave me the sword. He believed I am the Caller."

"I cannot endure this!" Ealden said. "How dare you!"

"Belliken," King Aravel said, "is not your real name, is it?"

Alastair hung his head. It had finally come to this. He'd always known it would, and so he would not lie. "No, my lord. My name is not Belliken Tolke. I was born Alastair Coldhollow."

A haunted wind howled outside the command tent.

"The Iceman," whispered Sebastian Sternbough.

"Your name is infamous in Tryllium and Ardon," King Ealden said. "You are an assassin...a murderer."

King Aravel nodded. "It was my brother who uncovered your actions, put a price on your head. You are a cold-blooded killer."

"*Was,*" Alastair said. "I was such. I will freely admit. But the First One rescued me from that life. I have been waiting for the Halfainin and I think I have found h—"

"Bah!" King Ealden spat. "Men such as you do not change!"

Alastair had the sudden urge to reach for his sword, but he pushed it down. He would not listen to whispers.

"There were very few survivors from your raids," King Aravel said, scribbling hastily on a sheet of parchment. "But enough to place you as responsible for hundreds of murders. Do you admit this?"

"Yes," Alastair said.

"You were not alone in these...these massacres," Aravel went on. "Where are these other killers?"

"Dead, mostly," Alastair said. "A few are still at it, I suspect. I do not know for sure. It was nearly twenty years ago."

King Aravel looked puzzled. "Why did you do these things, Bel—Alastair? What bloodlust led you...?"

"It...it was my job," said Alastair lamely. "I was commanded to do these things. I followed orders."

"Whose orders?" demanded King Ealden.

Alastair met their eyes in turn. "The orders of King Morlan of Vulmarrow."

"*Lies!*" King Aravel rose abruptly. "You impugn my brother to my face?" Aravel pounded his fist and snatched up the parchment. "If it weren't for your recent valor, I would slay you right now. But this—" he held up the parchment to Alastair's face— "this is your warrant! Alastair Coldhollow, for your crimes against the free people of Myriad, you will stand trial. And once you are found guilty, you will be sentenced to hang by the gallows of Anglinore until you are dead. Guards!"

"There will be no need of a trial," Alastair said, as six soldiers poured into the tent and surrounded him. "I am guilty."

"Wait!" Sebastian said. "I have one question: why did you fight for us, Alastair? Why join us when you must have known you'd be found out? You must have known what would happen when we did?"

"I knew," said Alastair. "I knew I would be caught one day. And I knew my penalty would be death."

Sebastian squinted. "Then why?"

"It was right," Alastair said. "For a very long time I used my skills for evil purposes. But I believe the First One gave me another chance...a chance to use my ability to protect and to save. I am grateful to have had that chance."

King Aravel waved, and the guards took Alastair Coldhollow away.

At dawn, the forces of Myriad broke like a potent storm on the Gorrack capital city. A military base with natural defenses, Lichbyrn Cleff was surrounded by porous limestone mountains on three sides. Anglish Guard and Wayfolk smashed through a defensive perimeter only a few thousand Gorracks thick and raced straight through to their stronghold, the Skellery.

This crude, ancient castle had three squat levels, each built on top of the other. Six crenelated turrets bordered each level like fists. It was a marvel of stonemasonry. It was also empty. Soldiers searched every bastion, turret, and keep and found no Gorracks at all.

Queen Savron was at the castle's main gate when there came a series of popping sounds. A second later, a splash of fire hit the wall just above. The queen was not quick enough to get to shelter. A gout of flame spattered the armor on her leg. "They are in the caves!" she screamed even as she tried to rip off her burning armor. "It is a trap! They send brimstone from the caves!"

Thus with her dying words, Queen Savron saved thousands of lives. For the brimstone the Gorracks now employed was a particularly wicked variety called cendrite, which could be launched in a high arc over the castle where it would be blown into thousands of smaller droplets and fall as a rain of sticky liquid fire.

Wayfolk archers turned their bows on the cave openings and quickly suppressed much of the brimstone attack. Aravel and Ealden led their men into the foothills of those mountains and were confronted by a scarce number of defenders. Aravel and Ealden burst through their ranks and charged to the caves. It proved to be a deadly mistake.

In a matter of hours, the forces of Myriad had lost thousands of their warriors who could not see in the dark to fight like the Gorracks could. And not only that, but those caves had long ago been prepared for a battle of this kind. There were hidden traps, sudden falls, crevices where the Gorracks could hide. They knew every twist and turn of every tunnel, and they easily slew the men and Wayfolk who entered.

"They know this terrain too well!" Aravel yelled. "It could take years to dig them all out! Years and many lives."

Sebastian growled. The rocky terrain had little or no vegetation, and there was nothing he could use his gifts on to make a weapon. Then he had an idea. He turned to the king. "I need an hour."

"You have it!" King Aravel said. "But where are you going?"

"Trust in the wisdom of Shepherds, my king," he replied hastily. "I will return soon."

They had not carried a portable prison, so Alastair remained under house arrest in his tent, surrounded by guards inside and out. He was bound at the wrists and ankles. So when Shepherd Sebastian Sternbough entered the tent, Alastair said, "Forgive me for not standing."

"I am glad you keep your humor," Sebastian said. "But I must ask you to be completely serious. We need your help."

"King Aravel asked for me?" Alastair wriggled in his chains. "Get these stupid things off me, and I will fight for you!"

"Actually," said Sebastian, "Aravel does not know I am here."

"Regardless." Alastair held up his bound wrists. "Release me so I can fight. I will return to your custody when the battle is over."

Sebastian thought hard a moment, noticed the glances from the guards. He couldn't tell if they were nervous that he might set a dangerous prisoner free or if they were secretly hoping he would let Alastair fight for them. Sebastian suspected the latter. "I cannot unchain you, Alastair. But your mind remains free. I have come to seek tactical advice. Will you hear me?"

Alastair nodded. "I will do what I can."

Sebastian told Alastair of the initial trap and the fire weapon. He described the layout of the hundreds of limestone caves and how the Gorracks were decimating any forces they sent in after them.

Alastair listened intently and thought for a moment after Sebastian had finished. "Why are you going in after them?"

"We must draw them out," Sebastian said. "We must find their king and finish this war."

"No, I understand that," Alastair said. "But we're in their country. This is their capital city. They know those caves and, aside from sheer numbers, they have every tactical advantage. Why play their game?"

"What else can we do?"

Alastair edged forward. "Look, going into those caves is suicide. It's precisely what they want you to do. Forget about drawing them out. I say, seal them in!"

Sebastian's eyes widened.

"I know Vang is gone," Alastair said, "but we have thousands still from Tryllium—Carrack Vale and such. If there's anything they know, it's stone. And you said this is limestone, right? That's relatively easy to work with. Have Vang's men lead, and have every available warrior help collapse the opening to each and every one of those caves. My guess is that once the Gorracks figure out what we're doing, they flee from those caves right into our net."

"Thank you, Alastair," Sebastian said. "I won't forget." He turned to leave.

"Wait!" said Alastair. "One more thing. Send a legion, no, more than that. Maybe five to seven thousand troops. Have them patrol the other side of those mountains. The Gorracks may have some sort of escape route."

"Brilliant!" Sebastian said, and he was gone.

Sebastian returned to King Aravel with Alastair's plan. Only he didn't say it was Alastair's plan. "Why didn't I see this before?" King Aravel chastised himself. "We have been needlessly casting away lives. Truly the wisdom of Shepherds is great!" He scrambled to find his generals and set the plan in motion.

As Alastair suspected, the soldiers and engineers from Tryllium were indeed adept at breaking rock. Many of them used pickaxes for weapons, and they went to work immediately creating weaknesses in the limestone near each cave's openings. Others helped as they could, using metal or timber as wedges or levers.

"That is clever work there!" called a warrior in shining armor. It was General Cilion Silverfox, commander of Anglinore's seventh legion. He surveyed the collapsed opening. "Where'd you learn your craft?"

"Thel-Mizaret, Sirrah," the youthful, dark-skinned man replied.

General Silverfox blinked. "Thel-Mizaret?"

Duskan nodded. "Before."

General Silverfox nodded back. He understood.

A few feet away from the sealed cave entrance, a young woman put down her axe and said, "You could say we know our way around a mountain."

"What are your names?" the general asked.

"I am Duskan Vanimore." He bowed.

"My name is Laeriss Fenstalker."

"I won't forget your names," said the general. "If we all survive this, I want you to visit me in Anglinore."

"We will, Sirrah, thank you."

The general rode away. Duskan and Laeriss went back to work.

Soon, man-made avalanches began to cover the caves. The forces of Myriad could hear the Gorracks howling and shrieking inside. Where there were caves yet to be collapsed, Gorracks began to pour out like bats. They emerged into the dazzling sunshine and fought briefly before being overcome.

Outside the mountains, King Ealden led two legions of soldiers on a patrol. Just as Alastair had predicted, the Gorracks had several escape routes, even more than Ealden's troops could cover. That was when Bregolath, one of the Wayfolk commanders, ran up to the king.

"My lord," he said, pointing to the southeast, "an army approaches."

King Ealden's heart sank. He spun around and saw the soldiers, perhaps three legions or more. But they were not Gorracks. They wore black with silver and blue, and many of their tunics and shields had a golden eye in the center. It was an army from Vulmarrow…Morlan's troops. But why had they come now? And what was their purpose?

"Bregolath," said the king, looking at the position of his Wayfolk soldiers, "see to it that none of our teams guard any escape too long. When the Gorracks stop coming from one, move our men to a different exit."

"Yes, sir," Bregolath said. "But what will you do?"

"I intend to discover the nature of these newcomers from Vulmarrow."

King Ealden felt suddenly very small riding out alone to confront something on the order of ten thousand warriors. But as he drew near, a leader broke free from the pack and approached. He wore a broad smile and, as he rode to King Ealden's side, he immediately held out his hand.

"King Morlan sends greetings," the man said. "I am Velach Krel, First General of the Wolfguard."

King Ealden shook the man's hand. "What is your business here, General Krel?"

"Why, to defeat the Gorracks, of course," Velach replied. "We have had our hands full with Gorracks in Vulmarrow, but at last, we may help in the broader fight."

King Ealden eyed him shrewdly. "As it turns out, you could not have come at a better time. The capital city has fallen, but the Gorracks seek to escape. Think your men can plug those holes?" He pointed to the mountains.

Velach smiled. "I think we can do that!" He gave the order, and the Wolfguard raced toward the mountains with a sound like thunder.

King Aravel stood on the parapet of the Skellery's highest tower. He held aloft a jewel-encrusted staff so that the tens of thousands of warriors gathered below could see. "This is the ruling scepter of the Gorrack Nation! Until today, it was held in the massive hand of Xabin Tarq, high priest and self-proclaimed ruler of this land! Until today, this ruling scepter was held in the hand of the villain who unleashed his minions upon our people! Until this day, this symbol of power and authority was in the hand of he who dared to cross his due border to harass and murder in one unprovoked attack after the other!"

"Garbak-thra!" yelled one of the Gorrack wounded who had been taken prisoner. "Garbak—lies! You! Sagrin-tha! You murder us…first!"

One of Velach's men drove a spear into the Gorrack's chest, and he fell silent.

King Aravel went on. "But Xabin Tarq no longer holds this staff! I myself pried it from his dead hand! And by the power granted me as High King Overlord of all Myriad, I declare the Gorrack Nation dissolved. This is now *free* land!" The king broke the staff over his knee and cast the pieces down from the tower. "Victory is ours!"

Alastair heard the speech. He heard the cheering. And he was grateful to have played a part in it all. But he knew what the coming days would bring. A long march back to Anglinore.

To meet the gallows.

CHAPTER 50

A Reckoning

On my first and only journey to Anglinore, I can say with full assurance of heart that nothing moved me more than the Ceremony of Crowns. That the High King of all Myriad, together with the sovereigns of many other nations, would display such humility before thousands of plain townsfolk—that was remarkable. I will never forget watching them, one by one, placing their crowns below the key-like symbol of the First One on that tall altar.
A letter from Kieran of Braide Wood

7 Celesandur 2219

Months had passed since Abbagael had received news from her new husband. Windborne messengers had come and gone twice, bringing word of ground being taken and new victories, but nothing from Alastair. So Abbagael was noticeably distracted at her daily tea meeting with Queen Maren.

"In my last message to Aravel, I asked him to tell me of Belliken," the Queen said. "We should hear back soon. But sweet lady, I am sure your beloved is fine. He has even more to fight for now."

"That's what I am afraid of. What if he changes his manner of combat, becomes too careful?"

Queen Maren was silent a moment. "Once more, we are kindred spirits." She patted her bulging belly. "I wonder if this child will be on Aravel's mind too often. Ah, but these are things outside of our control. That is why we pray." She picked up the tall silver pitcher and began to pour. "This is delightful tea. Tell me if you taste raspberr— Oh, good afternoon, Fez, what brings you to tea?"

The gatehouse guard swiftly removed his hat. "Beggin' ye pardon, yer ladyship," he said. "But there's a Brayden Arum here to see you. He says it's rather urgent."

"Brayden Arum," the queen asked. "Why do I know that name? It's all right, show him in."

"Are you sure?" asked Fez. "Last time I let a stranger in, it didn't work out so well."

The queen smiled. "I believe we'll be safe this time, won't we?"

"*Yes, m'lady!*" thundered the voices of the fourteen guards standing at attention in the angles of the heptagonal room.

"There," Queen Maren said, "you see? Please bring Brayden in. I feel quite sure I know that name."

A few moments later, Fez returned, followed by a man in a dusty brown tunic and breeches. He had coppery hair that was rather unruly and reddish stubble on his chin. He held a leather satchel tightly in both hands as if afraid it might get away.

"Queen Maren," Fez said. "This is Brayden Arum to see you."

"I do know you, don't I?" the queen asked. "Years ago, you came to tell us about the Gorrack raids in Westmoor."

"Yes, that's right," said Brayden, bowing at least nine times. "I'm grateful as you remember me."

"Westmoor is a long ride. What can Anglinore do for you?"

"Well, as ye might recall, I run a tavern. Hammer 'n Bow, it is. Destroyed that night seven years ago, but I've rebuilt it." He squeezed the opening to the satchel repeatedly. "Fair amount a' work went into it, framing, roofing, foundation, masonry. And anyway, last week, part of the new foundation caved in."

"I'm so sorry to hear," said the queen. "Was anyone injured?"

"No, m'lady. Wife and daughters are all fine. No boarders were in. But I had to drop down in there—in the sinkhole, that is—and dig out. Whilst I was in there, I found this." He opened the satchel and took out a large piece of metal. He brushed it several times before placing it on the table between Queen Maren and Abbagael."

"Oh, *Oh*," Queen Maren said, hands moving to her stomach. "The baby just kicked." She shifted position in her seat and stared at the object. "I'm sorry, Brayden. I don't know what that is."

"Right," said Brayden. "It's sideways, and the way it's bent. Here." Brayden changed its orientation. "This here's the face mask. Hinge still works if you push."

Queen Maren sat up straighter. "It's…it's a helm? But its shape…it's odd, almost like…"

"Like a Gorrack skull," Brayden replied. "If ye look close here, ye can still see painted-on eyes above the eye slits here."

Abbagael caught her breath.

The queen caressed her belly. "I don't understand."

"Don't ye see?" asked Brayden. "This is what they wore that night."

"What do you mean?"

"The night Westmoor was raided. This is what they wore."

"The Gorracks…?"

"No, they weren't no Gorracks," said Brayden. "They just wanted us all t'think so. I wouldn'a remembered if it weren't fer Katya—that's me wife. She put two-an-two together, see. We was down in my storeroom when they broke in to the Hammer. I thought sure they were Gorracks, but they didn't move like Gorracks. They were quiet like, sneakin' around the place like spies or some such. I remember thinkin' then that they ought t'be smashin' up the place, not sneakin' around. Then, all these years later, I find this and, well, it hit me. Me wife, that is."

"Brayden, you're telling me that Gorracks *didn't* attack Westmoor…that someone—a group of raiders—disguised as Gorracks destroyed your town."

"I reckon that's what I'm sayin'," Brayden said. "I just thought you should know."

"Thank you, Brayden," the queen said. "You are a true patriot. That you would come all the way here once more with your findings…we are honored to have you. But I don't know that we can draw that conclusion from one strange helm and seven-year-old memories."

"It's more'n that, m'lady," said Brayden. "See, I did some pokin' around in Stonecrest and Thel-Mizaret."

"Were there more helms?" asked Queen Maren.

"No," said Brayden. "No more helms. But I got to thinkin', isn't it a little strange after those raids, there wasn't one dead Gorrack left layin' around? I mean, the Gorracks don't care much for their dead, do they?"

"No," said the queen. "No, they do not. You're sure of this, Brayden? In all of those raids, not one Gorrack corpse was left behind?"

"Not if those as had come back to rebuild the towns can be believed."

"Fez, take Brayden to the dining hall. Feed him the finest sirloin and ale. Then fetch him a ten-piece of gold as reward for his service. And find him a nice room. You'll stay with us for a while, won't you, Brayden?"

"Be happy to." He muttered something about sirloin as Fez escorted him out.

"This is grave news indeed," the queen said to Abbagael. "But I do not know what it means. That someone would masquerade as Gorracks and kill so many innocent townsfolk… Why would any—"

The look on Abbagael's face stopped the queen cold.

"Your majesty," Abbagael said, "there's something I have to tell you."

"Mi-Ma?" Telwyn put his hand on Abbagael's shoulder. She knelt at the steps in the front of Clarrissant Hall. "Mi-Ma, are you well?"

"I am, Telwyn," she said, and she rose and embraced him. "I was praying."

"Is something wrong?"

"I have a decision to make, son," she said. "You see, I think I have figured something out. Something very important. But if I reveal it to anyone, it might cause something terrible to happen. And if I do not reveal it, something else terrible might happen. I do not know what to do. That's why I was praying."

Telwyn smiled a little sadly and brushed a few red locks of hair off her forehead. "My father's book says, 'An honest word bears much fruit, but truth withheld begs for destruction.'"

Abbagael looked at him strangely. "Did you…did you say, your father's book?"

"Yes, Mi-Ma," he replied, his smile now more peaceful, content. "The Book of Canticles."

Abbagael sat with her mouth open for a moment, and then she understood. *Oh,* she thought, *he's talking about Alastair's old copy of Canticles.* "You are very wise, Telwyn," she said. "Thank you for reminding me." She looked up and saw Queen Maren in the aisle. "Now, Telwyn, go and play. I'll see you at supper. The queen and I must talk."

Telwyn waved and sped away. He smiled at Queen Maren as he passed her by and left the hall. The queen came to the front and sat in one of the long bench seats where colored sunlight shone down from the stained glass. Abbagael sat beside her.

"I have been troubled," the queen said. "I believe you are about to tell me something I will not like. But I too have prayed, and I am prepared to listen."

Abbagael took a deep breath. *An honest word bears much fruit, but truth withheld begs for destruction.* "The helm Brayden brought to you today. I believe I know where it came from."

"Abbagael," started the queen. "That is good news. We must—"

"I believe it was forged in Vulmarrow and worn by King Morlan's Wolfguard."

Maren stiffened. "M-Morlan? But that would mean…"

"That would mean that King Morlan's troops have been masquerading as Gorracks…to stir up hatred. To start the war."

Queen Maren shook her head. "No, no. Morlan has good reason to hate the Gorracks. He's always advocated taking preemptive action against them, but he would not do this. I know…him. He would not do this."

"Queen Maren, forgive me," said Abbagael, "but I would not speak this against the king's brother if I did not have compelling evidence."

"Tell on, then."

"You see, King Morlan has been using his Wolfguard secretly against his enemies for a long time. For generations. Bryngate, Avington…Maiden Vale. He put down any town or village in Fen or Tryllium he believed was dangerously devoted to the First One."

"This is blasphemy!"

"No, no, it is not. King Morlan has been behind the murders of thousands. And I believe his hatred of the Gorracks has led him to fake raids in Elladar, in Thel-Mizaret, in Stonecrest, and Westmoor in order to provoke your husband into declaring war upon them."

Queen Maren started to stand, but placed a hand on her stomach and slowly took her seat. "I have heard what you think, but I have yet to hear any proof."

An honest word bears much fruit, but truth withheld begs for destruction. Abbagael committed. "You have not heard how Telwyn came to be our son. Seven years ago—"

"Wait...*came to be* your son? How many ways can a child come to be a mother's son?"

"Telwyn is not my flesh and blood, Maren. Seven years ago, my husband stepped out of a tavern in the woods west of Thel-Mizaret. A woman, mortally wounded, rode up. She was being chased—by Gorracks, or so she thought. She had Telwyn wrapped in a blanket. In her desperation she gave him to my husband.

"Before he knew anything, great warhorses rode into the clearing and nearly ran him down. They were dressed in armor, cunning armor and furs that made them look like Gorracks. But my husband saw through the disguise. And when they removed their helms, he knew them. They were Wolfguard soldiers. They tried to kill my husband, but he slew them and went into hiding with Telwyn."

Queen Maren blinked. "But how did Belliken know they were Wolfguard soldiers?"

Abbagael swallowed. "He knew because he had once been a Wolfguard Knight. A general in Morlan's army. He knew because he had once ridden with these assassins when they murdered and plundered whole villages. My husband's name is not Belliken Tolke, Queen Maren. His name is Alastair Coldhollow."

The queen took a sharp breath. "I know that name! That is the name of the Iceman. He is wanted under penalty of death across the entire realm."

"Yes, but don't you see?" Abbagael pleaded. "Those warriors dressed as Gorracks had just returned from the destruction of Thel-Mizaret. They wore the same kind of helm as the one Brayden found in Westmoor. All this time, it has been Morlan's Wolfguard shedding innocent blood. Not the Gorracks."

"There are ten thousand questions that I would ask," said the queen. "Beginning with why you would marry a killer. And why you would tell me all this now."

"As to the first, Alastair is a changed man. You heard yourself how valiantly he's fought for Myriad. You've seen him, how tender he is with me and Telwyn. He is no longer the killer he was. But make no mistake: he was a killer. A killer following Morlan's orders. And as to why I tell you now, I didn't understand until Brayden brought that helm in and slammed it on the table."

Queen Maren was quiet for several tense heartbeats. "My husband will need to know all this, and I fear for Belliken...Alastair, that is, when Aravel finds out." She shook her head wildly. Tears beaded and fell. "But Morlan...I cannot...that he would sacrifice so many for his—!" The queen stood up and began to amble back down the aisle.

"Queen Maren," Abbagael said, "where are you going?"

"This madness must stop." She turned and her eyes flashed with anger. "If I tell Aravel this news, I know full well what he will do. And what if your theories are wrong? I must know. I must be sure."

"But how—"

"I will ride to Vulmarrow myself."

"Ride?" Abbagael held up her hands in a pleading fashion. "But the baby."

Queen Maren looked down at her stomach. "No...no, I cannot ride. Dangerous for my child and far too slow. But there are Windborne around. I will have one bear me to Vulmarrow in a windcarriage."

"But if it's true," argued Abbagael, "Morlan will kill you rather than let you tell Aravel."

"Morlan would not kill me," the queen said. "Not ever. I will make it clear that I have already told Aravel. Hindering me will do him no good. And Morlan, misguided as he is, has always heeded my counsel. He will listen to me. He must."

"But—"

"My mind is made up, Abbagael. You will not hinder me either."

CHAPTER 51

An Errant Queen

I have heard from reputable sources that I might find an adventure here.
Aidan Errollson of Corenwald upon first
entering the Venture Inn in Lyrimore

7 Celesandur 2219

Queen Maren hadn't worn armor for years, but for this journey she'd put on her old boots and greaves. The pauldrons and bracers were fine as well. But the cuirass was a lost cause. Her belly made sure of that. She'd been forced to wear just a hauberk of light mail. *A regular swordmaiden I am*, she thought. *And I will be quite heavy for the Windborne.*

She trudged up the winding stairs to the barracks atop the castle's main stronghold and found herself out of breath. "Quite heavy for myself too," she whispered. "Pity I've become so soft." She shook her head and internally vowed to resume her training—fencing and contact arts, mostly—once her child was born.

Maren took a deep breath and charged through the barracks, ignoring calls of, "Hail, my queen" and "Greetings, my lady." She approached a guard. "The Windborne, are they still here? Have the messengers departed?"

"Uh, no," mumbled one guard.

"Wot he means is, yes," said another. "At least a couple of 'em are here. One's departin' now, I think. Wait, m'lady, wot's wrong?"

Without a word, Maren navigated between the bunks, weapon racks, and soldiers and burst out onto the roof. She found two Windborne resting by a fire cauldron and saw that another had just taken to the air. "Windborne!" she cried. "Come back! I have an urgent message for King Aravel!"

"My queen," said a red-winged Windborne. He was instantly on his feet and already limbering his broad wings. "Shall I chase down Halvard?"

"Yes!"

He ran across the roof and leaped into the air. Moments later, he and the messenger landed on the roof and strode up to the queen. Halvard, a Windborne with large dark eyes and steel-gray wings, bowed before Maren. "You have an urgent errand?"

"Deliver this to Aravel himself," she said, noticing that Anglish Guards were collecting behind her. "See to it that he alone gets this and reads it immediately."

Halvard took the scroll and plunged it into a leather cylinder slung on his shoulder. "It will be done."

"I trust you always travel at great speed," Maren said, "but if you can go any faster without harm to yourself...please..."

Halvard nodded. "I hear your urgency, High Queen. I have fresh wings. For this task and for you, I will race the wind!"

"Thank you!"

Halvard launched from the roof and within moments was nearly out of sight.

"Now, you," said the queen, turning back to the red wing. "Have you a windcarriage?"

"Certainly."

"Good. I need you to bear me to Vulmarrow."

"Vulmarrow? But Queen Maren, we are in a time of war. And your condition. I cannot—"

"Yes, yes, you can," she said, her expression fierce. "It is to prevent an even greater war from erupting that I must go to Vulmarrow."

"I do not question your intent," he said, "but perhaps a written message could—"

"No. I must go personally to King Morlan. There is no other way."

He flexed his red wings. "I, Süven, will bear you. But I will not trust such a journey to my wings alone." He turned, strode to the still sleeping Windborne, and gave him a swift shove on the leg. "Awake, Kjell! We have need of your mighty black wings."

Kjell blinked and stared round at the unexpected gathering on the roof. "What's all this, then?"

Süven explained all. Kjell shook the sleep from his eyes. "It will be my honor."

"Your Majesty," said one of the Anglish Guards, "I don't know if this is wise. King Aravel—"

"King Aravel is not here," she said. "I lead in his stead. Delay me no longer."

The guards stepped aside. Maren boarded the windcarriage. Süven and Kjell clicked their harnesses to the carriage rails and began to flap their massive wings.

"You are light enough for one!" Kjell cried out. "With two Windborne, we will bear you swiftly indeed!"

The Anglish Guard shook their heads and muttered to each other as the Windborne took the High Queen of Myriad away from the safety of Anglinore Castle.

The queen had ridden in wind carriages before, of course, but she still found herself surprised at how smooth the ride was. "Do not sacrifice speed for my comfort!" she cried through the roof of the carriage.

"Fear not for that!" Süven called back. "We are already entering Ellador!"

"Good then. Very good."

Morlan, she thought and shook her head. If all this were true, then he had changed beyond recognition. He'd once been a gentleman…to her, at least. Maren knew he'd wanted her hand to join his. She remembered the look on his face when she told him she was betrothed to Aravel.

He is wounded deeply, she thought. *To lose his mother in childbirth, his father to murder or worse…suicide, to lose the crown and a coveted woman to his older brother—that could easily wreck even a very strong man. But it does not justify treason.*

She let her head rest on the pillow. Even with the baby kicking, Maren fell asleep for the rest of the journey.

The Windborne took a southwesterly route, avoiding a massive storm and its dangerous winds. They dipped into Ellador, raced past Shepherd's Hollow and across the border into Fen.

It had been wise to avoid the storm, but if they had flown a more northerly route, they would have seen a massive dark army—some thirty thousand soldiers—pushing hard to the east… toward Anglinore.

When Abbagael finished her letter, it was three full pages of parchment. She rolled it up, tied it with a leather lace, and put it in a satchel. Not trusting the message to a guard, she raced around the labyrinthine halls of Anglinore Castle and finally climbed to the top of the main keep where the Windborne would come. There she found a dozen guards, none of whom seemed to be doing anything important. Just standing around, talking in hushed voices, and pointing west. There were no Windborne.

"Excuse me," Abbagael said to one of the guards.

The man had a thick black mustache and looked like a silver pear. "Yeh? Yeh?" he said, stepping away from the other guards. "Pardon me, boys. What seems to be the trouble, m'lady?"

"The Windborne? Where are they?"

He scratched his stubbly cheek, making half of the mustache hop up and down. "Ah, yeh, the Windborne...they're gone."

"I can see that," Abbagael said. "Where have they gone and when will they return?"

"Queen Maren went with two of 'em," he said. "Off like a shot, she was. Even pregnant! Haven't seen nuthin' like that me whole life. Oh, and there was another one. She sent him off to deliver a message to King Aravel. That should do it."

"What do you mean?"

"Well, that's the last we'll likely see a' the Windborne 'til tomorrow afternoon. Y'know they've been comin' so much less frequently."

Abbagael looked down at her satchel. Alastair had to get this message. "If one comes, I need to know about it right away."

"Wait a minute," said the guard. "Yer Miss Abbagael, right?" When she nodded, he said, "Just a sec." He went over to the other guards, pushed his way through, and sifted through a number of bags and satchels of various size. He returned with one and handed it to Abbagael. "I'm sorry, Miss Abbagael, but with the queen flyin' off like she did, well, we've been a bit distracted. This came fer you earlier, just before the hubbub."

Abbagael whipped the satchel out of his hands, made a noise that might have sounded a little like *thank you,* and raced back to her chamber.

The message was from Alastair at last. And it was four pages long. Abbagael began reading.

Twenty minutes passed, and Telwyn came walking in. Abbagael looked up from Alastair's message and stared at Telwyn.

"What is it, Mi-Ma?" he asked. "What's wrong?"

Abbagael hugged the parchment to her chest. "Telwyn," she said, "why don't you tell me...about your father."

9 CELESANDUR 2219

The two Windborne assisted Queen Maren out of the windcarriage. They had landed in a courtyard on the third story of the main keep. She'd been to Vulmarrow only once, but she thought she could remember her way to the throne room.

"Stay here," she commanded the Windborne. "And keep out of sight."

"Are you sure?" Süven asked, rolling his head and flexing his wings. "You are with child. Perhaps, I can assist—"

"No, I'll go alone, and I'll be fine."

"You sure?" asked Kjell.

"Of course. The Gorracks have been dispelled from Vulmarrow. Morlan and his Wolfguard are our allies, right?" She swallowed.

Süven's eyes narrowed. "Then why do you wear armor?"

Maren didn't have an answer. She patted his massive shoulder softly and said, "Be ready if I call you, but please keep hidden."

"As you wish," they said together.

Queen Maren got herself turned around in the castle a few times, but eventually, she found her way to the throne room. *No thanks to the guards,* she thought. She'd passed more than a dozen Wolfguard Knights. They had stared, gawked even, but not one of them had said a word to her.

The throne room doors wouldn't open at first. Then she remembered the vaskerstone. Impatiently, she pressed her palm to the stone and waited. It warmed to her touch and the doors parted. Darkness bled out from the room and thickened when she entered. "Morlan?" she called. There was no answer.

The throne room doors closed behind her. Unable to see anything, she took a few tentative steps forward. "Morlan!" she called again.

She saw a faint glow up ahead. A step closer, and she saw that a slender band of silvery light shone down on a hooded figure seated on the throne. He wore intricately patterned silver armor. He leaned forward, casting an even deeper shadow over his face.

"Morlan!" said the queen stepping closer, "I don't know what you're playing at, but I want to know what is happening. Is it true? Are you behind all these raids—Ellador, Stonecrest, Westmoor, Thel-Mizaret? Is this your doing? Did you start this war against the Gorracks?"

"Yesss," answered a voice so low she felt the vibrations in her chain mail.

She tried to stifle her tears, but they were all too ready. "Morlan," she said, her voice high and pleading, "what...what has become of you?"

The figure lowered his hood, and Queen Maren screamed.

"I am Cythraul," he said. "Welcome to Vulmarrow."

"But you...you fell."

"And yet I am alive again," said Cythraul.

Queen Maren had heard the reports—the slain doctor, the guards—but still couldn't believe her eyes. "How can that be possible?"

"Do not be absurd. My kind cannot be killed in that way."

"Where's Morlan?" she demanded.

"He has gone on a little journey," said Cythraul. "Along with thirty thousand soldiers, he travels to Anglinore to take his rightful throne."

"This is madness!" She turned and ran to the throne room doors, but they would not move. "Release me, now!"

"No," Cythraul said as he stood. "The two Windborne are already dead. But I think I will keep you...as a prize for the new king."

Halvard had never opened a private message before, but as he passed over his homeland just south of the Wyndbyrne Eyries themselves, he felt the urge to see what Queen Maren had deemed so urgent.

"Of course not," he muttered to himself. He knew he would never violate his charge. But still he was curious. He had raced the wind, daring to fly directly over the Dark Sea into Amara without landing in Chapparel to rest. Lesser flyers, he knew, would have fallen from the sky from exhaustion. But having seen the queen's expression, Halvard kept flying.

He reached the border of the Gorrack Nation just as the sun was setting. Even in the gray shades of twilight Halvard could see the destruction wrought across this foreign land. Whole villages were blackened and silent. Strongholds collapsed and walls thrown down. Even as high as he flew, Halvard could smell the stench of the dead. Still, there was no sign of the Anglish army. Exhausted but determined, he flew on.

He arrived at Lichbyrn Cleff just after midnight. He landed behind a pointed palisade wall and found a temporary garrison near the perimeter of the city. Anglish Guards patrolled the wall and the new gate, but they were not startled by Halvard's arrival.

"Come, Windborne," said a soldier. "What news?"

"I bear messages from Anglinore," Halvard said, gaping. "But judging from what I have found here, I am guessing that the Gorracks have been defeated utterly."

The knight laughed. "Those that live have fled to the hills in the north. They will think twice before again crossing their border with ill intent."

"But where is King Aravel?" asked Halvard, scanning the area. "Where are the armies of Myriad?"

"Marching victoriously back to Anglinore," said the guard. "Four days ago. Why?"

"Ah, curse my initiative," Halvard muttered. "I missed them. I flew as direct as I could."

"You seem distraught. I ask again, why?"

"Queen Maren herself gave me a message for King Aravel. She was in great haste and fearful. I flew from Anglinore straight away."

"Without rest?" asked the guard.

Halvard nodded. "I am spent. I cannot get this message to Aravel now. Are there any more of my kindred in this camp?"

"I think so," said the guard. "Least there was. Up by the caves. A female. She was there an hour ago."

Halvard found her there still. "Hail!" he called to her as he landed. "I bear an urgent message from Queen Maren for King Aravel and for him only. But I am depleted of stamina from my journey."

She shrugged her snowy white wings. "This had better be important. I returned only a few hours ago from an errand myself."

"If you had seen the queen's face, you would know how urgent." He handed her the leather cylinder. "Now, go."

She slung the message and took to the air.

Halvard shook his head. *I hope the message is not too late.*

CHAPTER 52

DECLARATION OF WAR

The first step into treason leads inevitably to the last.
Ireth Silimaurë, Court Historian of Llanfair, 1489–2107 AD

8 CELESANDUR 2219

Abbagael walked alone in the garden courtyard. It was a bright and warm early summer afternoon. Trees and flowers were beginning to bloom and, though dark clouds seemed poised to creep in, it was virtually a perfect day for a walk. But Abbagael was not there to relax. She had come to think. Had it been a week? More? She could not remember. Everything after the letter from Alastair had been a kind of blur. And since that day, she'd asked herself the same question:

Could Telwyn really be the Halfainin?

Abbagael paused at a birch tree and watched a green owlet caterpillar building its cocoon in a knothole. It was a beautiful little creature, fuzzy with gold whorls along the length of its body, leading to the spectacular white spots on its head—spots that looked like owl's eyes. Of course its appearance now was homely compared to the brilliant moth it would one day become.

Her mind drifted back to her son. But was Telwyn really her son? She remembered what Telwyn had told her when she asked about his father.

"He talks to me sometimes," Tel had said. "Especially in dreams. There are other voices there too, but I know my father's voice."

"Have you seen him?"

"I think that I have, but it was a long time ago."

"What does he look like?" she had asked.

"I do not have the words," he had said. "But you would like him."

"I...I think I would," she had replied.

Thunder rumbled. Wind chimes began to tinkle their melodies. The clouds had finally covered the sun. Abbagael looked again at the little caterpillar and then up at the sky. *I hope the little guy will be all right,* she thought. *There's a storm coming and it looks like it's going to be bad.*

After more than a week of uneventful marching, the armies led by King Aravel finally crossed the Naïthe into Anglinore. As the last soldier crossed, the sun went behind a bank of dark clouds, the wind kicked up, and rain began to fall. Lightning flashed, and there came thunder like the splitting of a mountain. Then things happened so fast that King Aravel could not comprehend all he was seeing.

Just as the bulk of his army had passed into the last deep valley and into sight of Anglinore Castle, there was a great disturbance near the rearguard. There were screams and horns. More lightning flashed, and the rain began to pelt the entire field. Suddenly, men within fifty yards of the king fell dead, each with an arrow or two protruding from his chest or neck. His men raised their shields as more arrows fell with the rain. The army began to spread out into companies—owing to the training of their generals—but they didn't see their enemy. Neither did Aravel.

Horns rang out again and soldiers began pointing to the vast hill above them. The tall grass was yellowish-green, new grass mingling with the dead grass from winter, and swirled in the wind.

There, cresting the hill and trampling the grass, was a black serpent. Or so it appeared at first—just a thick dark coil stretching from one end of the hills to the other. But it was not a serpent at all. It was an army. The rain obscured the sight, but Aravel was stricken by his own estimate of their numbers. They poured down the hill, closing on Aravel and his armies.

"Who are you?" Aravel whispered.

They surged closer.

"Who are you?" he yelled.

And then they were close enough that he could see their colors. Black and silver-blue like a wolf's mane, and in the center of their surcoats and shields...a yellow eye.

Recognition crashed upon the king, tearing the scab off of every old wound, exposing every foolish decision, and crushing all hope of returning to life as it should be.

Aravel heard the shriek of a horse, and on the hill a massive black horse reared. Upon it was a warrior clad all in black. He raised a wicked axe as if in salute and then disappeared into the carnage at the base of the hill.

"Morlan," muttered Aravel.

Suddenly the king found himself in the midst of combat. Wolfguard soldiers parted around him as if he were a tall stone in the sea. Aravel's sword felt heavy, and though he knew he should lift it, he simply did not. He watched as Morlan turned his steed and began to slowly walk it down the hillside.

Aravel didn't even see it coming. A massive warrior with a hammer came barreling down the bottom of the hill. Pushing his comrades out of the way to make himself room to swing, he wound up to deliver a blow.

But a blur raced past King Aravel and intercepted the attacker. The hammer-wielding foe tripped hard, as if someone had cut off his lower legs.

And there was Alastair Coldhollow. He had dragged one of his guards along with him and used the chain between them to trip up the assailant. Alastair crawled onto the back of the fallen man, slung his wrist chains over his head, and pulled tight. The fallen warrior could not breathe. His eyes rolled back and he became still.

The Anglish Guard Alastair had dragged with him sat nearby in a daze, rubbing his head.

"Are you going to order this man to set me free?" Alastair asked, "or am I going to have to drag him all over this battlefield?"

King Aravel snapped out of his trance and looked for Morlan. Then he went to Alastair. "I am sorry," he said, thrusting a key into the locks. "I do not pardon the deeds of your past, but you were right about Morlan…and you have my respect now."

"Thank you, King Aravel," Alastair said, shaking off the chains. "When this is over, if in your eyes I still deserve death, I will go to the gallows willingly. Now, however, where is my sword?"

"Sebastian has it," said Aravel. "He is near the rearguard."

Battle moved in between them, and Aravel waded in sword-first. As he slew a Wolfguard Knight, he called out. "Alastair! If you find Morlan, do not kill him! Bring him to me!" Aravel wasn't sure if Alastair had heard or not.

The last thing Alastair heard the king say was that the Shepherd was near the rearguard. The only problem was that Velach Krel and his ten thousand soldiers from Vulmarrow *were* the rearguard!

Ducking blades and dodging cross traffic, Alastair threaded his way across the battlefield. Someone came at him from the side.

Alastair dropped into a crouch and kicked the attacker's legs out from under him. He slammed the knuckles of his fist against the back of the man's head. He did not get up.

"Sebastian, Sebastian," he muttered, "where are you?" Then he saw something he could not at first believe. Through the sheets of rain, Alastair watched as a patch of grass some twenty yards wide suddenly grew twenty feet tall. "There you are!"

Alastair sprinted toward the long grass and dove into it— which was like trying to dive into a hay bail. It didn't budge. It was so thick he couldn't even slip his hand in past his wrist. *I feel sorry for the poor folks Sebastian caught in there,* he thought as he raced around the perimeter of the giant grass.

He found Sebastian barely standing, leaning up against the grass and holding the Star Sword up. Three Wolfguard soldiers stalked warily closer to him. He didn't stand a chance. Alastair considered the angle. It wasn't perfect, but it would have to do. He sprinted toward Sebastian and leaped at the last second. He pushed off the grass wall behind Sebastian, snatched the Star Sword from the Shepherd, and launched himself at the three attackers. No way to change his tactics in midair. He was committed.

Alastair crashed into the warrior on the right, running him through as he took him to the ground. Then Alastair was up, using the body as a shield. The second attacker threw a reckless stab that, with Alastair's help, sank deep into the dead body. Alastair whirled around the dead man and lopped off the second attacker's arm. With two quick thrusts, one forward and one backward, Alastair dropped the one-armed man and the third attacker.

Alastair raced back to the Shepherd. "Sebastian, Sebastian, are you hurt?"

"No…just tired," he replied. "They must hear…they must know."

Alastair looked up. They wouldn't be safe for much longer. Wolfguard soldiers were everywhere. "Who must hear? Hear what?"

"Shepherds, Alastair," he replied. "They must hear the voices on the wind."

"Look, I don't understand."

"Put me in the grass."

"What?" Then Alastair understood. He helped Sebastian to his feet, and suddenly the tall grass directly in front of them thinned out. There was almost a path.

"Put me in there," said Sebastian. "And then...pray."

Alastair did as he was told and pushed the Shepherd inside. Sebastian fell to his knees and the grass sprang up around him, sealing him off. *At least he'll be safe in there,* Alastair thought.

The wind howled. Lightning flashed ahead. For a moment, Alastair thought he saw wings. Were the Windborne here? *Bah, if only they would fight!* Alastair sprinted away and tried to maneuver around the perimeter of the fighting. He needed room to plan and perform his tactics.

Killing Gorracks had been one thing, but now he was killing men. It made him sick to his stomach. Each of these, some of them just in their twenties, had been drawn to Morlan's cause by promises of power and riches—just as Alastair had been drawn. And now they were dying.

But Alastair would not stop. This was Morlan's doing. All the killing, all the wars, all the time wasted—it had all been Morlan's doing.

Alastair cut down one soldier, dove, and plunged his blade into the next. He glanced up through the rain and could barely see the outline of Anglinore Castle. Abbagael was there, and so was Telwyn.

What does that mean? he wondered as he continued to fight. The prophecies had said that the Halfainin was supposed to throw off the chains of the Dark King. The Dark King had to be Morlan. But how could Telwyn be of any use? Telwyn was too young. Alastair had a fleeting image of seven-year-old Telwyn standing in the midst of the battle. He shook the nightmare from his mind and sought his next opponent.

"What is happening, Mi-Ma?" Telwyn asked, standing on his toes near the wall and straining to see through the rain.

"This is war, Tel," she whispered. "There is another king who wants to take this castle as his own, wants to be king here."

"Why?" asked Telwyn. "This is just stone built up on grassland."

Abbagael had no direct answer. "All I know is that this king has a rotten heart, and he wants everything to be his."

"Mi-Da won't let him, right?" he asked. "Mi-Da and King Aravel…they'll stop the bad king, right?"

"I hope so," she replied.

There was a loud swoosh, and a Windborne soldier landed on the turret. "Have the Wolfguard come here yet?" he asked. "Have they attacked the castle? I can bring word to King Aravel. I can divert soldiers here."

"So far, no," Abbagael said. "Their fight remains on the Naïthe, but…" She looked left and right as if searching for something. In truth, she was trying to think with some measure of wisdom. Surely Aravel knew that Maren had gone to Vulmarrow. But he could not know that she had never returned. "Please," she said, "there is an urgent message for King Aravel." She told him what it was, and the Windborne soldier leaped into the air and was gone.

Alastair heard heavy grunts and the ring of metal. He raced around the bend, and there he was…after all these years. King Morlan. He was hammering away at King Ealden, and the

Wayfolk leader seemed to be tiring. Alastair wouldn't let Morlan win that fight. Just fifty paces and Alastair knew he could be on him.

"You're not first generation Wayfolk, are you, Ealden?" Morlan said, slamming the flat of his heavy axe against Ealden's weakening blocks. "A shame. So many ways you can die."

"Not at your hand, Sabrynite!" Ealden countered, slashing his glaive and missing Morlan's stomach by a foot.

"So, you know where my heart is, do you?" asked Morlan. "He is real, Ealden, unlike your silent First—"

Alastair's Star Sword flashed beneath Morlan's chin, but just missed.

Morlan struck out with a wide swipe, forcing Alastair to roll backward. On his follow through, Morlan cut a deep rend in Ealden's shoulder armor.

Alastair found himself cut off from the Prydian leader. The other way to look at it was that they had Morlan surrounded. But Alastair didn't think Morlan looked worried.

"Al-as-stair Cold-hol-low!" Morlan said. "You do live! And you still have my sword! Pity you weren't slain by Gorracks." He laughed and lunged.

His swiftness took Alastair by surprise. His axe struck the pommel of the Star Sword, breaking it from Alastair's grasp…for a moment.

Alastair snatched it out of the air and rolled away from the blow he expected from Morlan. He nearly lost his head. Morlan's axe fell just a step from where he would have been. If he hadn't caught the glimpse of metal, it would have been over.

Alastair dove away, ran up the slope of a hill, and backflipped. His sword slashing beneath him, he landed and lunged for the killing stroke. But Morlan was gone. Alastair spun left and right, but didn't see him anywhere. He heard a groan and turned just in time to see King Ealden fall backward, blood pouring down his forehead.

"*No!*" Alastair yelled. He was at the fallen Wayfolk leader in a heartbeat.

"I'll live, I'll live," Ealden said. "It was just a glancing blow."

"There's a lot of blood."

Ealden ran his forearm across his forehead. "We Wayfolk are bleeders. I'll be fine."

"Did you see where he went?"

"No, no, too much blood."

Alastair had to stifle a laugh. "Right. I'll go after him." He turned to leave.

Ealden grabbed his arm. "I am sorry."

Alastair nodded, freed his arm, and sprinted away.

The Windborne delivered the urgent message to King Aravel and waited for a response. "May I aid you in any way?"

But King Aravel did not respond. Everything had spun out of control. Queen Maren and their unborn child had gone to Vulmarrow. She had not been heard from in more than a week. What did that mean? And here was Morlan and his army. Morlan was a traitor. He couldn't think straight enough to calculate the time necessary for Morlan to march his army to Anglinore. Had he been there when Maren arrived? If not, why hadn't Maren returned?

"Can you bear me to Vulmarrow?" the king asked.

"Yes," the Windborne said. "I am strong and swift."

Aravel saw Morlan then. He was back on his dark horse, riding through the battlefield, slashing men as if harvesting wheat. "Wait," said Aravel, "wait! I must think. I cannot leave. My armies need me here. But…Maren. Why?"

"King Aravel!" Alastair sprinted up the hill to join the king. "I saw the Windborne! What is the news?"

Aravel told him everything. "But I cannot leave, you see," the king said. "These are my people, and I am their king."

"I'll go," Alastair said.

Aravel turned and said, "No, I cannot ask you to do this." But eager hope flickered in his eyes.

"You do not need to ask." Alastair took the king's shoulders. "I will bring her home or I will die trying."

"You are a good man, Alastair Coldhollow."

"By the designs of the First One only." Then, with his eyes ablaze, he exhorted the king, "Take care of Morlan. End this."

CHAPTER 53

BORN INTO FIRE

Those why pay the price of victory rarely
live long enough to see it.
The Writings of Elrain Alriand

10 CELESANDUR 2219

Once they were airborne, Alastair could barely hear or speak, but he tried anyway. "What's your name, Windborne?"

"You could not pronounce it," he called down.

"What's it start with?"

After a puzzled silence, the Windborne said, "It starts with my first name."

"No, no, no…I mean, what is the first letter of your first name, the one I can't pronounce?"

"Teth," he said. "What you call, 'T'"

"It okay if I call you 'T,' then?"

The Windborne shrugged, which yanked Alastair up and down.

"Well, okay, T," Alastair said, "you sure are strong."

T did not reply.

"You know, I wish your people would fight. This thing could be over a lot faster."

"Do you want me to drop you?" he asked. And he wasn't smiling.

"No," Alastair said. "It's just that our forces are outnumbered by Morlan's. I'm afraid of what we might find when we come back."

And he truly was afraid. If King Aravel could not stop Morlan, if the Wolfguard overcame the Wayfolk and the Anglish Guard, if they overran the castle of Anglinore...he tried to shake those thoughts from his mind. But he couldn't. Abbagael was there. Telwyn was there. Alastair felt a sudden cold chill. Morlan will kill Abbagael. He will kill Telwyn. *Anything to hurt me,* Alastair thought.

His mind turned to more perilous possibilities. If Morlan were the Dark King of prophecy, the one the Halfainin was supposed to defeat...if Telwyn was the Halfainin...what would happen if Morlan killed the fabled hero before he came into his own? What would that mean for the world itself?

Wind whistled in Alastair's ears. They were picking up speed. He could hear it in the beat of T's wings. *Wind.*

"T!" Alastair yelled, startling the Windborne.

"You do that again, I might actually drop you."

"T, listen, do you know where Shepherd's Hollow is?"

"It is directly on our way."

"Take us there as fast as you can. Anglinore will fall without the Shepherds."

Wolfguards had thrown her into a cell somewhere in the catacombs beneath Vulmarrow Keep. Queen Maren had tried to keep track of the days, but there was no window to the world. Just a torch on the far wall outside the cell. Guards had come from time to time to bring her brackish water and a strip or two of blackened meat. Given the straw on the floor and the smell, she guessed the cell had been used for animals. Maren lay now, quietly moaning on the straw. *Foolishness*, she thought, her mind drowning in grief. The baby was coming.

T spiraled down above Shepherd's Hollow. He was at first aiming for the courtyard in the inner bailey, but he saw movement outside the walls. A great deal of movement.

"There!" Alastair yelled. "Near the garden! Take us there!" Thunder rumbled overhead as T set Alastair on his feet near a huge trellis of roses.

A tall man wandered out from the group. He wore dark blue armor crisscrossed with straps for pouches of all shapes and sizes. He had flowing snowy white hair and beard and seemed to steady himself with a long gnarled staff. "You are fortunate," he said. "I might have burned you from the sky with a bolt of lightning."

"Mosteryn!" Alastair gasped. It had been a very long time since he'd seen the old Shepherd.

"Yes," Mosteryn said. "What brings you to Shepherd's Hollow in time of war and without invitation? Wait..." He stepped closer. "I know you. You were Synic Keenblade's apprentice for a time, weren't you?"

"I was...a long time ago," said Alastair, but he did not give the Shepherd his name. "I have come over many leagues and I bear dire news. King Morlan of Vulmarrow has showed his hand at last. He has assaulted King Aravel's armies just outside of Anglinore. They return victorious from the Gorracks, but depleted. Shepherd Sebastian—"

"Yes, yes," Mosteryn said impatiently. "If you will give us peace, we will leave for Anglinore this very moment!"

Alastair's mouth fell open. Indeed the host of Shepherds had gathered there in that garden. But what he had not noticed at first was that they were all girded for war. "You...you already knew?"

"Sebastian sent warning on the wind," Mosteryn said. "Word of great upheaval, tragedy, and betrayal. We did not know with certainty what was happening, but we inferred most of it. Now, if you please, step aside. When the Shepherds go forth to battle... there will be calamity."

She had tried to fight it, praying *Not here, not here!* But there was no use. The muscles in her body were contracting. She could feel the child moving down. The pain was nearly unbearable, and it had gone on for hours. She bit her lip, grabbed the cell bars, and pushed. She felt a sharp pain and almost screamed. Somehow, she was able to swallow it back. She had to stay quiet, for now.

The agony again. It felt like muscles cramping, tearing. She thought she might pass out, but she pushed through it. Then, all at once, there was relief. And a cry. Maren rose up on her elbows and saw...her son.

"Lochlan," she whispered, weeping. And she picked him up and held him. "My son...you are here...here at last." She tore off a panel of her sleeve and wrapped him in it. Then she fed him. And for a few brief moments...in the worst place she could imagine, she was at peace.

That time passed, and she knew her window of escape was closing fast. She placed young Lochlan in a bed of cloth, chain mail, and straw. "I'm going to have to be loud," she told him. "Do not be afraid. It will be over soon, and then I will take you home."

Queen Maren screamed. All the pain she had felt in labor and delivery, she let it all out now, releasing a banshee cry of agony. "Aaahhh! Guard, come quickly! Ah, aaahhhh! Something is wrong!" She wailed and wailed, writhing on the straw.

"Whazzat now?" came the breathless voice of the guard as he bounded down the stairs and ran to her cell. "You keep quiet now! Woke me up, you did. You don't want Cythraul down 'ere, do you?"

"Aaahh! Guard, guard! I have given birth to my..." She arched her back and screamed again. "My...my sons! Ah, but something is wrong. The second child won't cry! Help me! I cannot rise get to him. Help me, please!"

"You need to shut yer mought," said the guard, jangling the keys to get the cell door open. "You'll bring Cythraul, I'm warning you." He entered the cell. "Here now, what you think I can do?"

Maren writhed on the ground. "Just look! Can you see what's wrong...what's wrong with the other child?" Maren knew what he'd see. Blood, and a lot of it, from the afterbirth. "Pleeaase," she begged.

The guard glanced at the cell door and up the hall. Then he sidled over to the queen's side and looked. "Uh, oh, there's blood," he said. "I don't know what—"

"Closer," she urged. "Is he breathing? Please tell me he lives."

The guard scowled but bent over to get a better look. "I don't see—"

Maren struck. Summoning every ounce of power, she unleashed a kick beneath the guard's chin. She heard his jaw break, but even as he was toppling to the ground, she rolled, snatched out the guard's dagger, and finished him.

Working quickly, she cut Lochlan's umbilical cord and tied it off. She sliced off a piece of the man's tunic and used it to further insulate Lochlan. Then she piled straw over the guard's body and locked him in the cell. The dagger in one hand, Lochlan clutched to her chest with the other, Queen Maren fled the cell.

T set Alastair down in the same courtyard that Maren had come to. There were no guards anywhere in sight, but Alastair didn't want to take chances. "T, do you see anyone? Guards?"

"Outside the city," he replied, craning his neck to look at the towers and clefts of walls. "But not here."

"T, I know you're very strong, but I don't know what you've got left."

"If I understand you," T said, "then I can tell you I have whatever you need left."

"Good, then I want you to hover within calling distance."

"But there is no one here."

"So it appears, but I know this place. There could be a thousand soldiers within a hundred yards of us, and we would never see them until it was too late."

"No one will catch me," he said, and then he was gone.

Alastair drew the Star Sword and disappeared into Vulmarrow Keep.

Keeping Lochlan held close to her chest, Maren found herself guessing again. She'd been wandering for hours and had come to more cross tunnels than she could imagine. Too often she had come too close to a guard and had had to turn back lest she be discovered. Once again, the path split. So she guessed and went left.

After a few minutes of walking, she wondered if she'd made a poor decision. The passage inclined a bit, but there was a foul smell permeating the air. And she hadn't seen a torch for more than a hundred paces. But she continued on. Up had to be better than down.

She thought she saw a glimmer up ahead, so she picked up her pace. It turned out to be a candle. A red candle. It seemed so odd resting there on a little iron sconce. But in its light, she saw a strange gap in the floor. *Fortunate*, she thought. *I might have stepped into it and broken my ankle.* But as she stepped over the gap in the floor, the smell she'd detected earlier intensified tenfold. She choked as she crossed and hurried away up the path. There were more red candles spaced evenly along the steadily inclining path. She turned a corner and emerged in a nightmare.

Hundreds of red candles clustered in the corners of a cavernous chamber. Strange white benches lined the floor in even rows. And the framing of the room from floor to ceiling was a mixture of black and white. *Bone.* It was unmistakable. She recognized the shapes: skulls, spines, arms, and legs. Bones were everywhere, diabolically arranged into furniture and decor. And toward the front of the room was an altar where a man stood with his back turned. He seemed busy with something in front of him on the altar. But she knew who he was. She turned to run—

"Do stay," Cythraul said, and he turned around. He had a strange, curving blade in one hand and something wet in the other. "You will find the way blocked now in any case." His eyes bored into her from across the room. "You gave birth to your child," he said. "In that horrid cell. Boy or girl?"

Maren held Lochlan close, but refused to answer.

"I am going to guess...a boy. Ah, I see from your eyes that I am right. Is that not an irony? Finally, an heir to the throne of Anglinore. Or he would have been if Aravel had survived."

"What do you know about my husband?" Maren blurted out.

"I know he will die," said Cythraul. "He may already be de—"

"Hello, Cythraul," came a voice from behind. "Remember me?" A sword burst through Cythraul's chest. He gasped for breath, fell forward, and slid off of Alastair's blade.

"First One be praised!" Maren said, her knees buckling. "Belliken...how did...how did you know?"

Alastair was at her side in a thought. He helped her back to her feet. "Your son, he is beautiful. Lochlan, right?"

"Yes, Belliken," she replied. "He's—"

"You don't need to call me Belliken anymore. I am Alastair Coldhollow. And we need to get you out of here."

"Do you know the way?" she asked. "I've been lost for hours."

"No problem. I used to work here."

They emerged in the courtyard at last. Alastair had slain more than a dozen guards on the way up, but the courtyard was still empty. Alastair reared back and unleashed a powerful whistle. Then he yelled out "Teeee!!!"

In minutes, the Windborne appeared. He landed and nodded respectfully to the queen. "Your Majesty, are you ready to go home?"

"We both are," she said, and she showed him the child. She turned to Alastair. "What...what about you? How will you get back?"

"I guess I'll be walking."

"No, you will not," said T. "Just outside the eastern gate I have hitched a warhorse. She is fed and watered and will bear you much faster than your legs."

"T, I do not know what to say...Thank you, thank you, indeed."

Once Lochlan was secured in a harness made of her chainmail hauberk and leather straps, the queen was ready to depart. "Tell me, Alastair, what will I find...in Anglinore?"

"I wish I knew," he said. "When I departed, the castle stood unassailed. But now, I do not know. So much depends on the Shepherds, I think."

"Shepherds?" Maren's eyes opened wide with hope. "What of the Shepherds?"

"We went to Shepherd's Hollow just before coming here. I told them what was happening in Anglinore. They already knew. They were mustering for battle and leaving. But...I don't know what they will do. Morlan has thousands and thousands of fresh soldiers. There weren't that many Shepherds there."

"How many, Alastair?" asked the queen.

"I counted at least twenty ready to travel and fight. There may have been more, but we did not stay long enough to be sure."

Maren's face lit up. "Alastair, you fill me with great hope. Twenty Shepherds, depending on their gifts, could be worth ten thousand knights."

Alastair blinked. "Ten thousand?"

"Are you ready?" T asked.

"Yes," she said. "Bear me home. I have hope now."

Alastair was encouraged by the queen's reaction. But he didn't know. She hadn't seen the army Morlan had brought to bear on Anglinore. Alastair whispered a prayer and left those concerns with the First One. Then he sprinted out of the courtyard and made his way to the eastern gate.

A wound to the heart took so much longer to heal. Cythraul rose up off the floor at last. It was the second time he had been beaten. "Alastair Coldhollow," he breathed the name through a blood-soaked throat. He raced to Morlan's throne room to gaze once more into the Black Stone Table.

CHAPTER 54

THE TEST

Many are surprised to discover that the power
they have been seeking…has also been seeking them.
An inscription on one of the few intact stone arches
found in the ruins of Grayvalon

12 CELESANDUR 2219

The Shepherds passed the borders of the Naïthe, still leagues from
Anglinore. And yet they knew tragedy awaited them. The eastern horizon seemed to bleed black blood up into the sky. It was
smoke…dark, oily smoke.

"It is as if the vast grasslands of the eastern Naïthe are on fire,"
said Velebrimbir, Shepherd of Lyrimore, Ellador's capital city.

"Morlan will answer for this," Mosteryn said. Thunder rumbled overhead.

"What of Alfex?" asked Shepherd Galea from Brightcastle in
Amara. "Do you think he is involved?"

"It grieves me to say," Mosteryn said, "but I cannot see how
he could remain pure."

The Shepherds found the eastern Naïthe a scene of mayhem. The field was littered with tens of thousands of dead. But the battle still raged. Morlan's Wolfguard clearly had Aravel's forces outnumbered and had cut them off from the castle of Anglinore.

"Best get to work," Shepherd Surrand said to his brethren.

"Let's get their attention first," Mosteryn said. "Rein in your steeds." Mosteryn raised his arms and his hands began to shake.

The clouds that churned above the smoke began to roil like waves on an inverted ocean. Then, without warning, the sky above disgorged a blinding, white bolt of lightning. It struck in the midst of Morlan's force, near their southern flank. The thunder crack that followed jolted everyone into terrified silence. Thousands of combatants froze in place and stared.

"That ought to do it," Mosteryn said with a wink. "Take no chances, my brothers and sisters. I deem there is more to this conflict than a battle of arms."

"Agreed," Shepherd Galea said. "I feel the weight of Shadowfinger."

"Everywhere," said Shepherd Surrand. "There is much at stake."

Mosteryn exhaled a long, sad breath. "Remember, if you are struck down, get to an ally—one of us, an Anglish Knight, one of the Wayfolk. But do not take your last breath near an enemy." He looked each of the Shepherds long in the eye.

They understood.

He held up his hands again. Lightning crackled. And twenty-one Shepherds rode down into the field of battle.

Shepherd Velebrimbir was the first to the fight. He dove off of his horse just twenty yards from a massive glut of Wolfguard soldiers. Velebrimbir rolled to a crouch and looked about in the grass. He found what he needed and hurled a rock high in the air. It shattered above him, but the pieces—hundreds of pieces—hung in the air…until the Shepherd waved. The tiny shards of rock hurtled forward faster than crossbow darts and drove into the

Wolfguard, passing through anything less than full plate armor. More than a hundred Wolfguard soldiers fell in an instant.

Shepherd Galea rode north until she came to a place where the battle had created a natural culvert in the grassland. Rainwater flowed steadily, and Galea intended to use it well. Turning to the battle, she located a group of Anglish Guards who had been hemmed in by the enemy. They were maybe thirty seconds from being overrun.

She closed her eyes for a moment and water from the culvert leaped into the air. She opened her eyes and the water flew forward in fifty streams. Each stream hit one of the Wolfguard. But the blow wasn't the harm. Each stream coalesced into a kind of droplet larger than a warrior's head. Suddenly each one of the warriors struck could not breathe. Some leaped from their horses; others struck at the droplets with daggers; and still others ran frantically about. But there was nothing they could do. One by one, they drowned...in a droplet just inches larger than their own heads.

Shepherd Surrand's gift took a little more time, and he needed to be careful...at first. He shooed his horse away and stood in the open grass with his arms out, palms facing the ground. He closed his eyes and began to scream. Many of Morlan's men turned and rushed toward the seemingly helpless Shepherd. He opened his eyes, and close to a hundred warriors stopped. They'd seen his eyes. They'd seen the fire in his eyes.

Suddenly the ground began to shake and, right beneath the Shepherd's hands, the ground burst in a red hot gout of liquid fire. Shepherd Surrand's gift was molten rock. He drew it from the depths underground, and then he turned it on the enemy.

Morlan sat on his warhorse high above the fighting. In fact, he was watching from the slope just a few hundred yards from Anglinore Castle. He turned to look upon the majestic structure. He knew he could ride to the gatehouse unopposed and kill everyone inside with ease. He wondered if he would be able to kill Maren. *Yes,* he thought. *I think I could.* A flash of angry orange drew his attention back to the battlefield.

Morlan sighed. *So the Shepherds come after all,* he thought with mixed emotions.

He'd almost resigned himself to the idea that his Wolfguard would defeat Aravel's forces outright. But Sabryne had whispered, *Patience.*

As promised, Morlan's patience had paid off. He tried to count the Shepherds…certainly more than ten. There was lightning, fire, water, light, dark, stone—the ground opened up and swallowed a dozen men. Morlan knew there were other gifts… many others. *Not for me,* he thought. *Not yet.*

Morlan hadn't used his gifts at all. Not once. No, in all the days leading up to his treachery, he could not use his gifts, could not reveal what he'd learned…what he'd done. But now, at last, the time had come. Morlan spotted Aravel in the midst of the fighting. He spurred his horse.

"Time for the test of your life, brother."

Aravel's thoughts were ever on Maren and their unborn child. He did not pray, as a general rule. Not since his father had leaped from the cliff near the Seat of Kings. But now he did pray. He prayed for the safety of his family, no matter the cost to himself.

A shadow fell upon him. He dropped to a crouch, held his sword up horizontally without blocking his own field of view. Morlan's axe smashed into the sword blade.

But Aravel wasn't so foolish as to absorb the full blow. He slid out from under it and let Morlan's axe embedded itself a foot into the turf. Aravel's return stroke was swift and precise, aimed at Morlan's legs.

Morlan remembered that stroke from all those years ago in the fencing chamber. He shook his head even as he yanked his axe from the ground and evaded Aravel's attack. "Why the legs, brother? You might have had my head."

Aravel's follow-through led his sword in a short arc until he was holding it with one hand. He slashed down with the extra speed and connected with Morlan's shoulder armor. "Is that more to your liking?"

"Yes," said Morlan. "Much." Morlan roared and rushed at Aravel, throwing axe and sword strokes high and low and at odd angles.

Aravel backpedaled but always maintained control.

There were other enemies about. But whenever the two kings came near, the Wolfguard backed away. Morlan had soundly warned them. "King Aravel is mine."

Morlan continued to rain down blow after blow, both axe and sword notched dozens of times. "How does it feel, brother?" Morlan seethed. "To have everything that is yours taken away? Your throne...your castle...your kingdom!"

Aravel did not let himself get distracted. He blocked twice, then struck hard. "You will never have what is mine!"

Morlan laughed. "I will have more."

Aravel saw an opportunity. Morlan's last block had thrown him off balance on his backhand side. Aravel charged in, hammering away at Morlan's weaker side, pushing him more and more off balance.

Stroke after stroke, it became a guessing game. How many times would Aravel strike the same side before attempting the kill stroke? Even Aravel didn't know. He would feel it, when Morlan was so off balance that he would not be able to block.

But Aravel missed it. Morlan had lifted his left foot off the ground...for just a moment. But Aravel struck Morlan's weak side one more time to be sure. And by that time, Morlan had reestablished his footing and easily blocked Aravel's attempted kill.

"*Why?*" Morlan screamed at his brother. "Why do you always wait! You are too careful!"

Breaths coming hard, the two stood ten feet apart and glared at each other. Those who looked on saw a strange mirror's image. Their faces, their eyes, their posture, their stances, so similar. They were brothers, and they were twins. But they were more different than strangers continents apart.

"Too careful," said Morlan. "That has always been your problem. You deny risk and lose reward!"

"Reckless," said Aravel. "That has always been your problem. You invite risk by allowing passion to rule you."

"How long would you have waited?" Morlan asked. "The Gorracks grew stronger year after year. It was only a matter of time before they took all of Myriad. Tell me, brother, if I hadn't pushed you, how long would you have waited?"

Aravel had heard enough. Ever this man, his own flesh and blood, had gnawed at him. And whatever Morlan did turned to mischief or sorrow. It was as if Aravel were watching some hated part of himself. It had to end.

Aravel had learned a few things watching Alastair. He saw his first few strokes, saw Morlan's replies, and knew what his brother would expect. Except this time, Aravel would do something different.

Morlan met Aravel's charge, blocked twice with the flat of his axe, slashed for Aravel's arm, missed and yanked the axe back in a wild play for Aravel's gut.

Aravel countered by taking a step backward and striking a ringing blow at the backside of the axe as it went by. This added momentum to Morlan's stroke, and he couldn't afford the time it would take to stop the stroke and reverse it. Morlan let the momentum spin him round and tried to power through Aravel's block.

But Aravel did not block, not in the way Morlan expected. Aravel lunged inside Morlan's swing-arc and thrust his sword straight down into the turf. The blade went deep just as Morlan's axe came round. The wooden haft of the axe split on the sharp sword blade and the head of the axe flew harmlessly away.

In that moment Aravel used the sword to vault a kick straight into his brother's chest. Morlan flew backward, slammed to the ground, and dropped what was left of his axe.

Morlan shook away the daze and rose to one knee…and found himself staring at the point of Aravel's sword. "That was a step in the right direction!" Morlan said, coughing out the words. "Finish it! You coward! Finish me!"

Aravel's sword wavered. His arm trembled.

"Can't you do it?" Morlan chided him. "Why? Because I'm your brother? I'd have murdered you long ago, if I'd had the chance." Morlan had to push Aravel past every breaking point. He grabbed the sword blade and placed the tip on his chest. "Just one thrust! That's all it will take to be rid of me forever!"

Aravel's mind went ten thousand places in those few seconds. Morlan was right—just one push and it would be over. He thought of Maren and their unborn child. What would he tell them? He saw his father, King Brysroth…

And then he lowered his sword.

"You fool," Morlan said. "Do you need an excuse?" Quick as a snake, he drew a dagger from his boot and dove for Aravel.

Aravel heaved the suddenly heavy sword around his body and struck his brother. Morlan fell backward in a spray of blood. The dagger fell harmlessly on the ground, just a few feet from Morlan's severed hand.

Morlan cradled his bloody wrist against his chest and rocked himself against the pain. "You fool! Don't you know who I am? I won't stop unless you kill me! I won't ever stop!"

Aravel did not turn around. "I will do far worse than kill you, Morlan," he said. "I will send you across the Dark Sea."

CHAPTER 55

HOMECOMING

When those who fight lay down their arms
Enamored by deceivers' charms
The world beset by ceaseless harms
New hope will rise from field and farms
Bells will ring urgent alarms
In the day of the Halfainin
Sung by Cecil Pevins at the hearth of Grim's Table

17 CELESANDUR 2219

Aravel had been kneeling so long on the stair that he'd fallen
asleep. A dream consumed his slumbering mind. There was a dark
doorway ahead, and he walked toward it. There was a child at his
side…six, maybe seven years old. He told the child to wait and
left him there as he walked through the doorway.

Gossamer light fingertips brushed across Aravel's shoulder.
He startled awake.

There stood Maren. Colored light from the stained glass shone
down behind her. She was beautiful, more radiant than he had

ever seen her. And she held a child. "Here is your son," she said, handing him the child. "Your son."

Aravel held the child and whispered, "Lochlan." He looked up at Maren. "Tell me I'm not dreaming. Is this real?"

Maren sat beside him and traced her fingers across his cheek. "It is real, my husband. Alastair came. He slew my captor and delivered me. Come, bring your son, and let us go to our chamber."

Sebastian watched them leave Clarissant Hall and didn't utter a word. His fellow Shepherds had made it possible for the Anglish Guard and Wayfolk to utterly defeat the Wolfguard. Most were captured. A few surrendered and were now shackled with their so-called king in the dungeon holds beneath the castle. King Ealden and Queen Briawynn lay wounded in the infirmary, but both would recover.

But Alastair Coldhollow remained missing.

"There is something I would like you to read," Alastair said in the dream. He handed her a page of parchment. "Read it aloud so Tel can hear it."

Abbagael looked at the handwritten text and did not recognize the script. "I thought this was one of your letters from when—"

"Just read."

Abbagael blinked and let the letters become focused. "'Be it known to all that Alastair Coldhollow was declared guilty for crimes against the free people of Myriad. Be it known that for his part in the murders of hundreds, a blood warrant was placed upon him. And be it known, that on this day, the 23rd of Octale of the year 2219, the killer known as Alastair Coldhollow was put to death.'"

Abbagael gasped, and she looked up at him as if he might fade and disappear. But Alastair lingered and told her to read on. Reluctantly, she did so.

"'Be it known to all that the blood warrant for Alastair Cold-hollow has been paid in full. The killer he was is gone and a new man stands in his place. Alastair Coldhollow is hereby absolved of all crimes. He is hereby granted full immunity from all future prosecution. He is hereby granted the rights of a free and full citizen of Myriad. And he is hereby named Friend of Anglinore and entitled to all rights implied by that title.'"

"It is signed by King Aravel and Queen Maren!" Abbagael said. "Oh, how I wish this was not a dream."

"Abbagael, this is no dream. Look at me."

Abbagael sat bolt upright. "Alastair! By the stars! It's you!" She grabbed him and kissed him.

"Mi-Ma," said Telwyn. "Don't hurt him!"

"No, it's okay, son," Alastair said. "I am long overdue for this sort of pain."

CHAPTER 56

THE SHIP OF NO RETURN

To the man who commits evil a second time, it no longer seems a crime.
Lady Tirill Dolaran, a parishioner at Maiden Vale Sanctuary

6 MUERTANAS 2219

High King Aravel, King Ealden, and all the surviving royalty of
Myriad stood on the dais at the front of the great angular hall in
Grahlthek, the last remaining military fort in what once had been
the Gorrack Nation. Shepherd Sebastian had but one final paragraph of the war reparations treaty to read.

"And so, in light of our crimes, Anglinore and all nations who
spilled Gorrack blood do hereby pledge swift payment of all necessary reparations. The precious metals and jewels we provide will
be surpassed only by the efforts of our engineers and builders to
raise the Gorrack Nation anew. We acknowledge full responsibility for the horrors of this war, and we will make amends."

Razeen Ghash, the new Gorrack king, reclined in his immense
throne. The hall remained silent for some time. But at last the
Gorrack steadied himself on the armrests and came to his feet.

"There is guilt upon you." His accent was harsh, but he spoke the language of Anglinore better than most Gorracks. "Upon you all. Gorrack blood spilled...burned away." His voice rose to a deep roar. "Can you bring back the dead? Nay. Take your gold and stone. Most of all, take your heathen flesh from this place! We will build the Gorrack Nation to thrive again. And then you will make amends on our terms. We will take payment, only in blood!"

18 Muertanas 2219

Three tall ships departed the port of Anglinore and sailed north into the Dark Sea. Only two ships would return. It was a nineteen hour journey to the place where the currents and winds shifted wildly. There were three small islands there, like markers. Someone in ages past had inscribed a nickel-plated sign and hung it from the largest tree on the foremost island. "If beyond these islands you seek to pass, return thee not to Myriad."

Both ships anchored just south of the Barrier Islands. "The Ship of No Return" was prepared, and the prisoners were brought at last up onto the deck.

King Aravel watched as Morlan and seventeen Wolfguard soldiers were lined up in front of the main mast. King Ealden read a passage from Canticles. Queen Briawynn sang. Then King Aravel read the charges against these men.

As he listened, Alastair couldn't help feeling that perhaps this exile across the Dark Sea should also be his punishment. Who could say if any of these guilty men, save Morlan, bore any more guilt? Alastair shook away the thought. He was becoming more adept at denying such thoughts an audience. King Aravel had declared him a free man. In Anglinore, he was now considered a hero. Still, Alastair felt there was a stain lingering on his soul, something only the Halfainin could take away.

"...and for your crimes," King Aravel continued, "you are condemned to lose more than your life. You, the condemned..." Aravel lowered the parchment. He didn't need it for this part, and he wanted to see Morlan's eyes. "You, the condemned...you forfeit all of Myriad. You renounce your personhood. You no longer exist in this world." He turned to King Ealden and his handpicked guards. "Take them to their ship."

The condemned filed across the gangplank between the two ships. But before he crossed over, Morlan hesitated. "Aravel," he called. "Aravel, please."

Something in his brother's voice compelled Aravel to draw near. "I have nothing more to say to you."

Morlan glanced left and right. He seemed nervous. Then swiftly, he took his brother's hand and held it in his only good hand. Morlan stared into his brother's eyes. "I wish...I wish things could have been different between us."

Aravel drew his hand back sharply and shook his head with pity. "Even your final words are a lie." Rubbing his hand, he said to the guards, "Take him across."

"It is not a lie, brother," Morlan said as he crossed the gangplank. "I really do wish things could have been different between us." The guards locked him into his harness, and Morlan yelled. "I wish I had been born first!"

The harnesses were checked and secured. The ship's wheel was permanently braced. The guards returned across the gangplank and drew it back from the condemned ship. King Aravel went to the bow to watch the chain's release. Three guards pushed the giant tool through the rails. Its diamond-shaped head fit perfectly into the socket on the chain which held the Ship of No Return to its anchor. The guards twisted the implement once, twice, and on the third twist, the chain separated.

Morlan's ship began to float free. Morlan himself stood at the port rail and stared. Malice glistened in his yellow eyes...wolf's eyes. And in that moment, there came a sudden strange breeze.

"Did you feel that?" Alastair asked.

King Ealden nodded. "Very odd. Too cold to be a trade wind."

Nothing more was said about it, and they joined King Aravel on the bow.

The king was glad to have their company. This was a hard thing. Perhaps the hardest thing he'd ever done. It was a decision that had to be made, but he did not feel good about it. He rubbed his temples. A swift headache was coming on. In fact, Aravel realized he didn't feel well at all. He coughed twice and felt a burn in his throat. *I'll get some water,* he thought, as he watched the wind fill the sails of the other ship.

It passed the last barrier island. The currents took it, and it raced away...across the Dark Sea.

King Ealden went with King Aravel belowdecks to get some refreshment. But Alastair stayed above. Morlan's ship was already just a black speck on the horizon.

He wondered how he had so misunderstood the words of the First One. There was a sense in which Telwyn did help defeat the Dark King. Alastair thought of the strange chain of events that had led from Telwyn's arrival to this day. And yet it seemed so clear that the Halfainin had to be grown to adulthood, had to bring fire from a stone, and had to throw down the Dark King. Maybe the prophecies just weren't meant to be understood. The Dark King was gone. Myriad was free of all threat. Alastair shook his head. *Telwyn is a gift from Allhaven, yes, but he cannot be the Halfainin.*

Alastair Coldhollow found himself gazing away from the beautiful sunset and into the darkling sky on the horizon.

"Look, sir," said one of the guards, "you can see a sliver of moon there."

"I am not looking at the moon, lad," said Alastair. "I'm looking at the stars."

Queen Maren had not accompanied her husband on the voyage to exile Morlan. She had no desire to see Morlan. For her, he was already an unbeing. Utterly erased. Instead, she had left baby Lochlan in the care of wetnurses and had spent the afternoon sitting in the courtyard. She found herself staring at the well in the center.

Uncomfortable irony, she thought. *Morlan is dead to me, but here I am sitting in his favorite place in the castle.* She realized then that she still wanted to remember the Morlan of his youth. He was always troubled, but not so twisted. He had a mind then. A sense of humor. Maybe even a heart. He had loved her, this she knew. But even then, she feared his love. There was always something perilous about it.

Maren stood and walked to the well. It was cobbled stone, mostly dark stones, marbled together with untold years of mortar. It stood four feet from the flat ground and had an arched wooden roof overhead, supported by thick columns of dark wood. There was no bucket on a rope for drawing out water—not anymore. Many years earlier, the water in this well had turned foul. The buckets and spool of rope had been removed, but the well remained.

Queen Maren ran her fingers along the curling ridge of stone and stared into the dark water far below. Morlan had always come here to think. It did nothing for her. Just empty, wet blackness. When had he turned? Somewhere back in time, Morlan had gone from spiteful and sneaky to murderous and altogether wicked.

The dark water below trembled slightly. A small bubble rose to the surface and popped. Maren leaned over to see better. Another bubble surfaced with a soft pop. The wind kicked up, sending dead leaves racing and howling under the eaves of the surrounding roof. Maren watched the trees in the garden bend and waver in the strong gusts. Then she turned back to the well, looked down into the black water, and saw a skull.

Grinning up at her, the broad skull seemed to float half in and half out of the water. There were other bones connected to it and around it. Maren screamed.

At last the guards fished the rest of the skeleton out of the well. They laid it section-by-section on the grass a few yards from the well and in the direct sunlight. It had been an extremely large man. Large and broad, if the ribcage and shoulder girdle were any indication. The last piece to come up was a right arm. Its hand had curled in rigor, and there was a sparkle of gold on one of its fingers.

The guards had not been able to persuade Queen Maren to leave the courtyard, and she approached the skeleton. She knelt by its side.

"Your majesty, don't," one of the guards said. "You don't know what pestilence could be upon it."

"Thank you for your concern," she replied, "but this poor soul has been dead for too long to confer any disease to me." She lifted up its arm but had to turn the hand to see what the golden shine was. She gasped and fell back, half crawling. "No, no, no, no...it cannot be."

Anglish Guards lifted her to her feet, but still she tried to push backward, away from the skeleton.

"What is it?" one guard asked.

"It's a ring," said another guard, stooping to look.

"Not just any ring," Queen Maren said, tears streaming down from her wide eyes. "It is a signet ring."

Coming in 2011 from Living Ink Books

THE ERRANT KING

(BOOK 2 IN THE DARK SEA ANNALS SERIES)

Wayne Thomas Batson

www.SwordInTheStars.com

www.DarkSeaAnnals.net

Deep in the caves of the distant Hinterlands, an ancient menace stirs. Townsfolk shudder at violent memories of The Red Queen and even dare to whisper the name Raudrim. At the same time, word comes to Alastair that Cythraul has at last resurfaced, seeking a devastating weapon in the ruins of Grayvalon. Blood-soaked clues lead Alastair into a confrontation from which only one warrior will return alive. Meanwhile in Anglinore, young Lochlan Stormgarden, the new High King of Myriad, leaves the pomp and politics of the throne once too often. While blending in with the people of his kingdom, Loch suddenly realizes that he's put them all at risk. The fate of his new found love Arianna, his best friend Telwyn, his family, and indeed the world of Myriad all depend on the decisions of the errant king.

For purchasing information visit

www.LivingInkBooks.com

or call 800-266-4977

Coming in 2011 from Living Ink Books

THE WOLF OF TEBRON

(BOOK 1 IN THE GATES OF HEAVEN SERIES)

C. S. Lakin

ISBN-13: 978-0-89957-888-0

All Joran wanted was to live a peaceful life in his forested village of Tebron. But when his wife, Charris, is captured by the Moon in a whisk of magic, he must go on a grueling journey to the four corners of the world to rescue her. On his way, he befriends a wolf named Ruyah who becomes a trusted companion while he solves riddles and eventually battles the Moon to save his wife.

For purchasing information visit

www.LivingInkBooks.com

or call 800-266-4977

Coming in 2011 from Living Ink Books

THE MAP ACROSS TIME

(BOOK 2 IN THE GATES OF HEAVEN SERIES)

C. S. Lakin

ISBN-13: 978-0-89957-889-7

An ancient curse plagues the kingdom of Sherbourne, and unless it is stopped, all will fall to ruin. The King, obsessed with greed, cannot see the danger. But his teenage twin children, Aletha and Adin, know they must act. A hermit leads Adin to a magical map that will send him back in time to discover the origin of the curse. Once back, Adin must find the Keeper, who protects the Gates of Heaven, but all he has is a symbol as a clue to guide him. Unbeknown to Adin, Aletha follows her brother, but they both arrive in Sherbourne's past at the precipice of a great war, and there is little time to discover how to counteract the curse. An epic fairy tale with surprising twists, embracing the enduring power of love.

Coming Soon from Living Ink Books

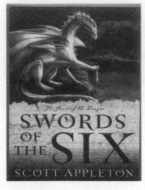

SWORDS OF THE SIX

(BOOK 1 IN THE SWORD OF THE DRAGON SERIES)

Scott Appleton

ISBN-I3: 978-0-89957-860-6

Betrayed in ancient times by his choice warriors, the dragon prophet sets a plan in motion to bring the traitors to justice. On thousand years later, he hatches human daughters from eggs and arms them with the traitors' swords. Either the traitors will repent, or justice will be served.

For purchasing information visit

www.LivingInkBooks.com

or call 800-266-4977